CICELY'S DARK HALLOWTIDE

Sandra Heath Wilson

Sandra Heath Wilson is the multi-published British author of over 80 books, many of which have been translated into seven other languages. She writes mainly historical fiction, and has a number of pseudonyms, including Sandra Heath, Sandra Wilson, Sarah Stanley and Jeannie Machin.
Plus, of course, Sandra Heath Wilson.

To Kelly Ferjutz,
for being my best friend, and for all her help
with publishing this book

First published 2018
ISBN: 9781729500811

CICELY'S DARK HALLOWTIDE

The torch brightened until the approaching horseman could be seen along the deserted Ridgeway. On reaching the remains of the pagan bonfire at the ancient stone monument, he observed something shining on the ground. Reining in, he dismounted to retrieve the object from the earth, where it had been stamped upon contemptuously. In the uncertain, flickering light he could see it was a plain golden band, engraved with a heart and his own dog emblem.

Removing his left gauntlet, he looked at the matching ring on his own finger. He and his bride had exchanged them at their wedding. With a heavy heart, he put both rings in his purse.

But then, looking at the remains of the Hallowtide bonfire, where such vile things had gone on only minutes earlier, loathing and disgust hardened his mouth and lit the vivid green of his eyes as he tugged the gauntlet on again and remounted to urge his horse away.

His wife had made a fool of him for the last time!

Cicely Plantagenet's story so far...

CICELY IS ONE of the daughters of King Edward IV of England's second marriage. The profligate Yorkist monarch had, when young, first secretly promised to marry Lady Eleanor Talbot in order to seduce her. By consummating this promise, he made the contract a legal fact, but kept it hidden.

Then he deserted Eleanor for Elizabeth Woodville, whom he married bigamously and declared to be his queen, even though Eleanor was still alive. Eleanor remained silent, and died four years later without ever having revealed the truth. Edward's second marriage was false, and all the children resulting from it were illegitimate, but he kept silent, fully intending his eldest baseborn son by Elizabeth Woodville to succeed him as King of England.

Edward died suddenly, and his clandestine first marriage was exposed. Illegitimate children could not inherit the crown, which meant that Edward's only remaining brother, Richard, Duke of Gloucester, was his lawful blood heir. Richard was invited to ascend the throne as King Richard III.

Edward had left two sons and five daughters, and Richard sent his nephews abroad secretly, to his sister—their aunt—the Duchess of Burgundy, whom he knew would care for them in safety. He and his ailing queen, Anne, took the girls under their protection and treated them very well indeed. Then Richard's only legitimate son died, followed closely by Anne. Devastated by this double tragedy, Richard needed an heir, and the obvious choice was another nephew. Jack de la Pole, Earl of Lincoln, the son of Richard's other sister, the Duchess of Suffolk, was fiercely loyal to Richard.

Then, in August 1485, traitors betrayed Richard, who was perfidiously slain at the Battle of Bosworth. They acted for a slippery Lancastrian usurper, Henry Tudor, who seized the throne as King Henry VII. Henry accused Richard of murdering the sons of Edward IV, whose whereabouts had never been revealed. But Cicely and her elder sister Bess – soon to be Henry's queen – knew the truth. The sisters are now in conflict over Richard. Gone is their former closeness.

Henry crafted many lies about Richard, and his malicious propaganda gradually gained credence. He had acquired some support at Bosworth because he vowed to unite York and Lancaster by marrying Bess. He had to do this to have any hope of keeping the throne and calming his still-turbulent realm. But a king could not marry an illegitimate woman, so reversing Richard's claim to the throne was essential. Unfortunately for Henry, legitimising the York children gave the missing boys a better claim to the throne than his own. In the meantime he continues to heap calumny on Richard III.

Cicely despises Henry for Richard's death and the endless blackening of his character. She and Richard loved as they should not, but their feelings could not be denied, and when he perished at Bosworth, he did not know she carried his son, Leo, who was born six months later on the Feast of St Valentine. She married Henry's sympathetic half-uncle, Sir Jon Welles, who pretended the baby was his, but Henry suspected all along that Richard was the real father.

At the time of Leo's birth it seemed that Henry was on the point of finding out the truth, so Cicely and Jon pretended the boy was stillborn, and sent him to be cared for and brought up by the Kymbe family, Lincolnshire gentry who were loyal to Jon. Mary Kymbe is Cicely's faithful maid, and her brother, Tom, the head of the family, has become Cicely's friend.

Soon Henry and Bess also have a son, named Arthur, who is declared to be the true embodiment of York and Lancaster, and is set to one day become the new King Arthur. But Henry is still resented, because he is harsh, and his only blood right to the throne is through his mother's baseborn line, the Beauforts, who had been forbidden the crown a century earlier.

But Henry does not love Bess. Instead he is obsessed with Cicely, and coerces her into his bed by threatening those she holds dear, including Leo, of whose survival and true identity he has become fully aware.

Cicely and Jon were content together until she fell in love with her dashing cousin, the Yorkist heir, Jack de la Pole. Countless Yorkists regarded Jack as Richard's rightful successor, and he trod a dangerous line as he remained at court, but plotted against Henry. In the summer of 1487 he rebelled and was defeated at the Battle of Stoke Field. Thought to have been killed, he escaped to his aunt in Burgundy to elude both Henry and the murderous intent of his own younger brother, the sinister, amoral Edmund de la Pole. Edmund wants Jack's position as York's heir for himself, and the only way to achieve this is by Jack's death. Edmund is not alone in seeking Jack de la Pole's demise, because Henry is also seeking him, having realized the Yorkist leader survived Stoke. In the meantime Jack remains in Burgundy, where the duchess says nothing about where she has hidden Cicely's brothers. Nor even if they are still alive. Jack slips back to England from time to time to see Cicely and confer with his Yorkist allies about the next Yorkist attempt to topple Henry.

Thus Cicely leads a hazardous triple life. She is outwardly Viscountess Welles, the queen's sister, but as Jack de la Pole's lover and supporter, she is a traitor to Henry. Finally she is Henry's unwilling mistress, because he will not let her go. She finds it surprisingly difficult to truly hate the flawed Tudor, who is prey to insecurities and a dark, unpredictable temperament, against which he struggles every day.

But Cicely is not the only one with a secret son, for Henry has one too. Roland de Vielleville was conceived after a clandestine marriage during Henry's exile in Brittany, where—as a fugitive heir of the House of Lancaster—he had been under house arrest. Roland was born and raised in Brittany, but is now at Henry's court, where no one knows anything about him. He is not aware of being Henry's son at all, let alone the king's *legitimate* firstborn, or that his mother was still alive when Henry married Bess. Like Edward IV, Henry has committed bigamy, and Prince Arthur is baseborn. Bess, like her mother before her, is no more than the king's mistress. History has repeated itself. It is something that could topple Henry from the throne and bring back the House of York.

His secret is not as closely kept as he thought, because it has come to Yorkist attention, although as yet they have been unable to *prove* anything. His enemies are intent upon exposing the truth, and work hard to gain legal proof.

Cicely knows about Roland because Henry has confided everything in her. But as things stand in the autumn of 1488, she has been forced to hold her tongue through a mutual hands-off pact with him. Provided she keeps silent about Roland, no harm will come to Leo. Always, *always,* she has to remember that Henry is more than capable of carrying out his threats to those around her.

But before continuing Cicely's story, it is necessary to go back to an obscure, apparently unrelated event that took place on the Berkshire Downs at Hallowtide, 1485, only two months after Richard's untimely death at Bosworth. . .

Prelude

All Souls' Eve, 1485

FROM THE CHALKY heights of the Berkshire Downs on a clear day, it was possible to see north over the Vale of the White Horse as far as Abingdon, where the dazzling towers of the great abbey church caught the sun. But on this chill, damp autumn twilight, everything was obscured by a thick pall of icy cloud, while low in the west an eerie red glow marked the sun's final progress into night. Henry Tudor did not reign up here, nor had any mortal king before him, not even his predecessor, Richard III, for this was believed to be the domain of the great god Woden. The Grim One. The All-Father.

Down in the vale, below the hanging swathes of Hallowtide mist, candles had begun to glimmer in cottage windows to welcome the departed Christian faithful home for the last time. Cosy fires burned in hearths, and platters of soul cakes awaited alongside jugs of mead, but at the same time there would be wild garlic bulbs over doorways to ward off evil. Before midnight, the benign spirits of the beloved dead would assemble at every crossroad, where lanterns waited to show the way to their heavenly afterlife.

The previous night—Hallowe'en—the gates of the supernatural world had opened, and a stream of diabolical beings, visible and invisible, had flooded into the temporal world. Pagans welcomed them, and tonight the rites on the escarpment would be a step toward what they hoped would be the eventual destruction of Christianity.

The old Ridgeway drove road, which traversed England

from East Anglia in the north-east to Devon in the south-west, followed the spine of the Downs, passing an isolated mound fronted by sandstone sentinels. It was known as Wayland Smith, and was said to be the forge of Woden's blacksmith god. To everyone in the surrounding area it was a perpetual reminder of the bleak past.

In front of the Smith, a hundred or so pagans stood in the darkness around a large, unlit bonfire. They were mere shapes in the clammy murk as they awaited their mysterious black-clad leader, at whose true identity they could only guess. Whoever he was, obedience to him was paramount because they believed he was sanctioned by Woden to summon a bloodthirsty host of dark elves, hobgoblins, red-eyed hounds and hideous huntsmen mounted on wolves, which coursed through the night sky. It was called the Wild Hunt, and was led by Woden himself on his eight-legged steed, Sleipnir. Anyone pursued by this dread horde, be it man, woman, child or animal, would be torn to shreds.

Someone kindled the bonfire, and the flames spread eagerly. Cloud and moisture recoiled from the sudden heat, revealing the worshippers to be wearing strange clothes and skins, with animal heads, antlers and other grotesque effects.

A woman dressed as a white nun stood next to a tethered goat. Her haughty, immodest manner was far from pious, and in one hand she held a beautifully jewelled white dagger. With the other she gripped the shoulder of a frightened boy of about five, dressed in a torn red tunic and pale leggings.

At a signal, the pagans began to move slowly, almost ponderously around the fire. Their direction was widdershins, against the path of the sun, and they hummed and droned tunelessly as they went. The primitive monotone became louder with each circuit, until silenced abruptly when a very tall, strongly-built man in a flowing black robe and gilded face mask appeared on the top of the Smith. He held aloft a golden chalice, the precious stones of which shone in the light from the bonfire, especially a large sapphire. A black tomcat sat beside him, its eyes glinting yellow in the dancing light.

In spite of the dampness and chill of the night, the nun proceeded to undress to a flimsy shift. Then, describing patterns in the air with the dagger, she performed a sensuous dance around the motionless onlookers. She was not in the first flush of youth, but still shapely, with firm breasts, a narrow waist and wide hips, and there was a wedding ring on her left hand. Was she really married? Or perhaps she was a bride of Woden, for her nun's habit was clearly a mockery of Christianity. But then she removed the ring and stamped upon it. So, not a symbol of Woden after all. Next she placed the dagger against the goat's throat. That was all, for it was not yet time to sacrifice the animal, which bleated plaintively, almost as if it knew its imminent fate. The little boy remained where he was, too young, terrified and dazed to think of escape. Perhaps some drug had been administered, for he was oddly compliant, just standing there, crying.

The leader descended toward the gathering and was admitted to the circle. After placing the chalice on the ground beside the boy, he spread his arms to command attention. His voice was loud and booming, even behind the golden mask. 'Hail mighty Woden, the All-Father!'

Everyone responded. 'All praise to great Woden, the Grim One!'

He seized the weeping child, pulled up the red tunic and then held him aloft to show his back. Clearly visible in the firelight was the black-scratched outline of another ancient landmark of the Downs, the White Horse, which was carved into the chalk not far eastward along the Ridgeway. The horse, which gave its name to the wide, fertile vale below, was originally thought to be Woden's eight-legged mount, Sleipnir, but now it possessed only four. The rest were said to have been destroyed by an early saint of Holy Church. On the boy's back it still possessed eight.

The leader addressed them all. 'Woden has bestowed his favour on this child, who will one day lead you as I do now.

But the *next* boy I bring to you—three years hence—will be of royal blood, and will rule the whole land in the name of the Grim One. Henry Tudor will no more live his allotted span than Richard, whose throne he seized. Or Edward before that. Tudor will be the last Christian monarch, because Woden's many adherents are to unite to form a vast conquering army. The All-Father will be omnipotent!'

He shouted the final sentence, and cries of joy spread around the bonfire as he lowered the sobbing boy to the ground again and then produced an apple that was tied with red cloth of the identical shade to the boy's tunic. With a loud incantation, he hurled the apple into the heart of the fire, which died for a moment before bursting into life again, this time with lurid emerald flames that shed an unearthly light over everything. Rapturous sighs and gasps spread around the pagans as the boy screamed and then fell to the ground like a little heap of rags.

At that very moment, a powerful new sound jarred the night, like the bellow of a monstrous bull. It seemed to be everywhere at once, as if emanating from the darkest past. The tomcat yowled, spat and arched its back, before bounding away into the shadows.

As the pagans' concentration was shattered, the emerald flames reverted to natural reds and golds. The spell was ruined, and the gathering was filled with dread, only able to think that Woden was displeased. But the canny leader looked in one direction only, along the Ridgeway toward the White Horse. No, perhaps a little beyond it. He knew the origin of that unnerving sound, but could not imagine who might be responsible. Especially on a night like this. It was no coincidence. Alarm and suspicion glittered in the eyes behind the golden mask. The bonfire collapsed unexpectedly in a storm of sparks and crackling, and in the ensuing confusion, he slipped away unseen, carrying the unconscious boy with him.

As the fire settled amid its ashes, everyone was transfixed

by the new sound of a horse cantering slowly toward them. Was it a herald of the Wild Hunt? Maybe even Woden himself? Then they saw the unsteady flicker of a flaming torch undulating to the motion of the horse, and at last they too found the wit to flee. Still holding the dagger, the woman in the nun's habit paused only to collect the chalice, before running after the others. The goat was abandoned.

The torch brightened until the approaching horseman was revealed. Richly clad in a knee-length beige coat, black thigh boots and a scarlet hood with a scarf, he halted his powerful roan horse so that it reared and snorted. Its saddle and bridle were costly, and its tail and mane were combed and plaited.

Manoeuvring closer, the man tossed the torch aside and bent down to cut the goat loose. 'Be off now, Billy, you are spared this time.' As the goat trotted away, disappearing beyond the arc of dwindling firelight, the man observed something shining on the ground. He dismounted to retrieve the ring the woman had stamped upon. It was a plain golden band engraved with a heart and his own running-dog emblem.

With a sad sigh, he removed his left gauntlet, and in the uncertain light looked at the matching ring on his own finger. They had been gifts he and his bride exchanged on their wedding day. His heart was heavy as he removed his ring, and then put both in his purse.

He had prayed Jane would keep her solemnly sworn oath to adhere only to the Christian faith, but he had returned from Calais to find. . .*this!* Loathing and disgust hardened his mouth and shone in the vivid green of his eyes as he tugged the gauntlet on again and remounted. His wife had made a fool of him for the last time!

Chapter One

Three years later, Abingdon, 26th July 1488

CICELY, VISCOUNTESS WELLES, sensed that the hitherto affable conversation with owlish Abbot John Sante was about to take an uncertain turn. July sunlight beamed into the small private dining room at his palace at Abingdon Abbey, brightening the carved wall panelling and the chased gold of a crucifix on the chimneypiece. The door to the high-walled garden stood open to admit both the sweet scent of roses and the sound of bees.

Legend claimed the abbey was where the Roman emperor Constantine had been educated, and Sante had amused his dinner guest by suggesting that his own aquiline nose indicated a bloodline descent. He had further enlivened the conversation with anecdotes from his long and varied career serving her father, the Yorkist King Edward IV, at whose funeral he had officiated. But those days had gone, and now Cicely knew that Sante's support went to the Lancastrian King Henry VII.

She wished the abbot would come to the point. If there was one. He probably hoped she would approach Henry on his behalf, for she was known to have the royal ear. Not so generally known was how much of the rest of Henry Tudor she had as well. It shamed her that she, a proud daughter of York and sister of his queen, was forced to be Henry's secret lover. But to refuse him would endanger lives.

Had she but known it, Sante's thoughts were no less troubled. Far from having given his loyalty to Henry, he was still a clandestine Yorkist intent upon restoring the vanquished House to the throne. Not the line of Cicely's father, Edward IV, but the succession as it *should* have descended from Edward's youngest brother, Richard III. The problem for Sante was that he wished to involve Cicely in his schemes, but could no longer be sure where her true loyalties lay.

Until some ten months ago, her staunch support for York—specifically for Richard—had never been in question, but then came whispers of a scandal at Winchester. Henry's court had assembled there for the birth and christening of the new royal heir, Cicely's nephew Prince Arthur, in whose small frame the warring Houses of York and Lancaster were supposedly united at last. The whispers connected her rather shockingly with Henry himself.

Now, right here in Abingdon, where Henry had recently stayed on his way from Windsor to Kenilworth, the abbot had discovered the rumours to be only too true. It was hard to credit that cold, suspicious Henry, with his fear of rebellion and increasingly irrational belief in alchemy and the supernatural, would indulge in such a dangerous liaison. He needed his marriage to Edward IV's senior daughter to cement his hold on the throne, so would he *really* risk everything simply to dibble his queen's alluring sister?

But oh, how alluring. She was only nineteen, yet had the air and understanding of a much older woman. Her wide grey-brown eyes were warm and unconsciously inviting, and she had Plantagenet charm aplenty. Soft wisps of dark chestnut curls were swept beneath her pearl-encrusted headdress, and her lavender silk gown was perfect for her. He did not want her to be untrustworthy, but it had to be considered.

After dismissing the young monk who had been in silent attendance, the abbot poured more of his most prized white wine into her silver goblet and then sat back. 'My dearest lady, I trust the endeavours of our kitchens were pleasing to you?'

'Very much so, Abbot John. All concerned are to be congratulated upon their skill. But I am curious. You have been an attentive host, yet I can tell you have some ulterior motive for inviting me.' The startled expression on his face amused her. 'Oh dear, how to proceed now your prey is wise to the chase?'

The abbot's desire to be subtle and circumspect vanished into a completely unguarded response. 'Good King Richard was a great loss to England, Lady Cicely.'

Startled, she lowered her goblet. 'You express such a view when *Henry* is king?'

'I think it safe enough to say such a thing to you, my lady, for you cannot help but be for York. Can you?'

'You touch upon treason, Abbot Sante.' She was cool.

His disarming smile was all bravado. 'Perhaps you will understand if I tell you I am a close friend and Yorkist associate of your cousin, the Earl of Lincoln, who remains King Richard's chosen heir, of course.'

Wariness engulfed her, for not only was he claiming to still be Yorkist, but he used the present tense about Jack. 'I do not know what this is about, Abbot John, but Lord Lincoln *was* very dear to me. Everyone knows he died at Stoke Field last summer.' She saw Jack in her mind's eye, with his tumbling almost-black curls, roguish smile, sinfully masculine body; and kisses that would melt a glacier.

'My lady, Lord Lincoln is alive and with your aunt, the Duchess of Burgundy, who delights in being a thorn in Henry's side. Your cousin is again in excellent health, and is raising yet another invading army against Henry. I trust that this time he will succeed.' Unseen, Sante crossed his fingers, because if he had misjudged this, he was consigning himself to Henry's not-so-tender mercies.

Cicely was frozen. This *must* be a trap! What had this man of God, so apparently firm for Henry, to do with such delicate Yorkist affairs? And why had Jack never mentioned him? Another thought struck coldly through her. Did the abbot know about Leo, her son by Richard? She had not heard anything of the boy for almost two months now, and was becoming very worried. He was hidden safely away on the Isle of Wight, and word had always been regular. Until now.

Sante proceeded gingerly. 'Another of my good friends and associates is Sir Humphrey Talbot, the Marshal of Calais, whom I suspect you know as Tal.'

Now a great black pit yawned. Tal was Jack's close friend and confidant, and certainly well known to her, if not liked and trusted, but Sante's name had never passed *his* lips either. Her thoughts sprang to Henry, who was quite capable of setting the abbot to test her. Henry did not trust *anyone,* even his own self. Somehow she feigned calm as she met the abbot's gaze. 'Yes, I am acquainted with Sir Humphrey, sir.'

'On the day the king arrived here from London, he permitted Sir Humphrey an audience.'

'Oh?' What was this leading to? Something, or nothing? And if Tal had been in Abingdon, why had he not called upon her? He knew she was going to be here, and at which address. 'Is Sir Humphrey still in Abingdon?'

'I. . .have no idea. He may be. He certainly is not lodging here in the abbey. But his manor of Kingston l'Isle is not far away to the south, at the foot of the Downs. Where things are not. . .entirely as they should be, I fear.' Sante cleared his throat, because Kingston was a problem to both Sir Humphrey *and* the Church. While the majority of the residents were Christian, there was also a large and strong band of pagans who worshipped the old god, Woden. Sir Humphrey had vowed to destroy them, because his estranged wife had numbered among them. It was an unhappy situation.

Cicely sought to redirect the conversation to something less dangerous. 'I wish to visit Kingston l'Isle, to take the water of the holy well.'

'Holy well?'

'Woden does not hold sway over *everything* in Kingston,' she pointed out. 'The well is dedicated to St. Margaret of Antioch, and renowned for protecting the falsely accused and for curing female barrenness.

'Ah, yes. That well. As it happens, should you choose to visit Kingston now, the timing would be excellent. Sir

Humphrey's sister, the dowager Duchess of Norfolk, is staying there at present.' He inhaled awkwardly. 'We digress, I think, for you asked about my acquaintance with the Earl of Lincoln and Sir Humphrey. Their families have large holdings here in Berkshire, so it is inevitable that I have always known them. Indeed, they have dined with me in this very room. We have discussed many a Yorkist matter.'

In a trice Cicely felt that Henry was not in Kenilworth at all, but right here in the room. The abbot's invitation was a trap after all! 'You are determined to speak treason, sir, and I will *not* be dragged into it.'

'Please hear me out, Lady Cicely. You see, it is vital to me that the House of York is restored. That the succession from *Richard* is adhered to. There, the full treason is exposed.' His tightly-crossed fingers were now quite painful. 'York is the true ruling house, and should be restored, with Lord Lincoln as king, because Richard chose him. It is my hope—belief—that you share this view.'

She knew she should leave, but something held her back. 'My cousin as king? Why not one of my brothers? After all, they may still live, with my aunt in Burgundy, and Henry has very conveniently made them trueborn again.'

'Your father committed the great sin of bigamy, so your brothers were never and could never be Richard's heirs. And he *was* the true king, which means that Lord Lincoln—being trueborn—should succeed him.'

'You are right, of course, my siblings and I are all misbegotten, but why does it not content you that York and Lancaster are now united in my nephew, Prince Arthur? Surely *he* promises a safe and peaceful future for England?'

'Arthur has no blood right at all. His father is a Beaufort usurper, and his mother is illegitimate. Such a pair on the throne of England flouts all that is right in the eyes of the Church. And the people.'

'But Henry *conquered* Richard, sir, and has been crowned and anointed, so he *is* now the legitimate king, whether you like his Beaufort antecedents or not.' Her fears that Henry was somehow in the room were completely assuaged, for he would not stand by in silence while the Abbot of Abingdon expressed such shocking opinions.

'Can I trust you, my lady?' Sante asked.

'Can *you* trust *me?* I rather think that at this moment *I* am the one needing reassurance about trust. Besides, if you really do know those you say you do, you already know where my allegiance lies.' There, she thought, interpret *that* as you will.

'I know *some* things about you, Lady Cicely, but not all.'

'I pray that is so, sir, for no woman wishes the Church to know everything about her. Heaven forbid that should be so. Priests—and abbots—do not understand women, and never will. But women understand them,' she added.

'Whatever you tell me will be safe,' Sante promised.

'Well, you would say that, would you not?' But something perverse in her *wanted* to confide in him. . .to confess to the very Church she had just derided. 'True trust and confidence can be assured in the confessional,' she said then.

'Are you a sinner, my lady?'

'Oh, yes, Abbot Sante, I am a sinner.'

'Do you repent your sins?'

'No.'

'Do you intend to sin again?'

'Yes.'

'Then there is no contrition in your soul. You do not fear to forfeit Heaven or endure the agonies of Purgatory.'

'If you will not hear me as my confessor, I will leave and no more will be said.' Her eyes challenged.

He did not want that. 'Lady Cicely, your determination to continue upon your sinful course prevents me from being your confessor, but I will hear you as a friend. . .with the avowed confidentiality of a confessor. Will that suffice? Will it help if I say that Lord Lincoln and Sir Humphrey have faith in me?'

'So you tell me.'

'It is the truth.' Sante gave a faint smile. 'I *vow* I will not repeat anything you say to me, Lady Cicely.' He pressed his pectoral cross to his lips.

She searched his face. 'Very well, 'I will trust you too, if only because you *do* fear the horrors of Purgatory.'

'Your point is made, Lady Welles. So, what is it you wish to say?'

'That given the choice again, I would not change the way I have conducted my life, except to have stolen much more time with the man I will always revere and adore above all others. My Heaven has been here, on earth, in the arms of men created by God, *His* creatures, as am I. I do not speak of the fleshly act alone, but of what is in my heart. The Almighty has granted me a great capacity to feel *everything* for the men with whom I have lain. All of them. And what men they have been.'

She lowered her eyes. She had a very sensuous nature, needing to love and be loved. When her heart was given too, the joy could be almost insupportable.

'You are still only nineteen, Lady Welles,' the abbot pointed out a little patronizingly, believing she spoke with youthful exaggeration.

'Maybe, sir, but there have already been five lovers in my life, including my husband.'

'Five?' Sante was shocked.

'I may not have been a faithful wife to Jon Welles, but I have been a good wife. He has not been faithful either, but is a good lord to me.'

She looked away. Once perhaps, he was, but not now, because even though she continued to hold him in high regard, he had changed toward her. He had been her gallant saviour from the scandal and censure of childbirth outside marriage, but six months ago, on discovering that Jack was still alive and was her lover again, Jon had taken himself north on Henry's business and there had been silence from him ever since. She could not blame him. But he would always mean a great deal to her, enough to continue protecting him by giving her body – if not her heart – to Henry Tudor.

Sante pursed his lips. 'Well, as honesty is the order between us now, Lady Cicely, perhaps you should be aware that I know you flout the Seventh Commandment with King Henry.'

Cicely's face was a mask. 'I imagine you have heard about Winchester?'

'Yes, and I was not fooled recently when the king halted here on his way to Kenilworth. He went to you, covertly, in the house across the market square. I think the same will happen when he returns tomorrow.'

Her mind raced. There was an atmosphere in that house that she only now recognized as one of being watched. Probably being eavesdropped upon too. She would make sure there were no servants there tomorrow, not even a scullion! Her thoughts tumbled on. The house belonged to the London merchant John Pasmer, who also happened to own Pasmer's Place, the mansion in the capital where she and Jon resided. She knew from Jack and Tal that Pasmer was another secret Yorkist.

So, Henry *was* the reason for today's invitation. And rightly so, she supposed, her guilt stirring. She knew secrets of Henry's that would benefit the House of York, but was afraid of his revenge if she divulged anything.

'Do you love the king, Lady Cicely?' Sante studied her closely.

She looked away. No, she did not love him. His lovemaking aroused fierce desires and there had even been times when she had cared enough to shield him from harm. Yet with him she did not know that deep, aching, *incomparable* elation that could carry her through every adversity.

'My lady?' Sante prompted.

'All you need to know is that I am true to my House.'

'But you *do* see the problem you present to York, Lady Cicely? You have been invaluable to the cause, but are now embroiled in a passionate liaison with Henry Tudor. How can your friends know you are still to be trusted?'

Chapter Two

THE ABBOT HAD gone too far, and her brief faith in him was dismantled as she leapt up. 'My *friends* know I can, sir! And pray allow me to point out that although they may have told you of me, *your* name has not crossed their lips.'

The abbot's heart sank as he too stood. 'My lady—'

'No one could be more aware than me of the damage Henry has done to York,' she interrupted, 'so I do *not* need your lecture! I cannot hate or rebuff the king whom I know so very intimately, but I *have* to lie with him, to protect others. Have you *any* idea what it is like to be trapped in such a way?'

Had his guest been a man, Sante would have known exactly how to calm the choppy sea and manoeuvre the conversation into smooth waters again, but he had foundered because his life was noticeably lacking in female influence. 'Forgive me, I *beg* of you, Lady Cicely. I did not mean to upset you. Please be seated again. *Please,* for I am ashamed of my lack of feeling. I exist in a world of men, which has made me insufficiently sensitive to the fair sex. You are right, the Church and its servants do not understand women, but I *do* accept that you are in an almost untenable situation.' He ventured an olive branch of a smile. 'His Majesty spoke with me of his excessive interest in superstition, magic, alchemy and all similar arts, which is alarming and has to be deplored, of course, but on spending time with him, I have come to realize he is not quite as people generally believe. Especially if he should smile. Which he did. Once.'

She knew she ought to have left anyway, but instead accepted the peace offering. How contrary she was being, but she could not help it. There was something about this occasion that made her capricious. Perhaps it was the wine and the heady scent of the rose garden. 'Henry *smiled* at you, Abbot Sante? A rare occurrence. Be at ease, because you are safe with me, but may I ask *why* I have never heard of your involvement?' She resumed her seat in a rustle of pale lavender silk.

Immensely relieved, he sat too. There was a moment of silence that was only disturbed by the bees droning outside. 'My lady, I imagine that the only Yorkist conspirators of any consequence you know are Lord Lincoln, Sir Humphrey. . .and perhaps Master Pasmer. Is that not so?'

'No.'

He was surprised. 'And the others are. . .?'

She did not reply. Her thoughts were of the loyal Kymbes of Friskney in Lincolnshire, and *Maître* Étienne Fryon, Henry's secretary of the French language, who was probably her aunt of Burgundy's spy as well. She had overheard him with Tal and Master Pasmer, and so knew he was involved in Jack's network.

The abbot shifted a little uncomfortably. 'You are right, of course. The fewer who know, the better to fend off betrayal.'

'So that is why I have not been told of you?' she enquired wryly.

'I can only think so.'

'Yet you have been told of me.'

He had no answer. 'I do not know why, Lady Cicely, but let me demonstrate my good faith by telling you of my role in the Yorkist network. I am a man of many resources here in Abingdon, and able to raise useful funds. My part is as paymaster to the House of York. I provided much toward Lord Lincoln's valiant struggle at Stoke Field last year.' He sighed wistfully. 'If only things had not gone against him.'

'His men fled, on wrongly believing he had been killed.' Cicely thought back. 'That aside, Jack should have rebelled in his own name, not someone called Lambert Simnel, even if that someone was actually my thirteen-year-old cousin the

Earl of Warwick.' Warwick was the attainted son and heir of her paternal uncle, George, Duke of Clarence, the brother between her father and Richard, and whom her father had executed for treason some ten years ago.

Sante sighed regretfully. 'It was a poor decision on Lord Lincoln's part, I grant you. One over which I had no influence. He chose his course, and then followed it. To defeat.'

'I will never understand his reason, because Warwick shares his father's attainder.'

'Such things can be reversed,' Sante pointed out.

'True, but why give him that ridiculous name? And why not rally men to the bear and ragged staff badge of Warwick? There are many who still remember his maternal grandfather.'

'The great Richard Neville, Maker of Kings? Ah, what a great man and warrior, even though he deserted York for his own purposes. You are right, Lord Lincoln regrets the decision.' The abbot paused. 'There is also the other Warwick, the "changeling" whom Henry holds in the Tower.'

The story of the two Warwicks was intricate. In 1478, just before Edward IV arrested, tried and condemned him as a traitor, George of Clarence so feared for his baby son's life that he substituted another boy for him. The real Warwick was despatched to safety in Burgundy, just as Richard had later sent Cicely's brothers. It was the changeling Warwick whom Henry had arrested and imprisoned in the Tower in 1485, after Bosworth. There the unfortunate boy remained to this day.

Then, last summer, at the head of a Yorkist army, Jack had brought the *real* Warwick to challenge Henry, but named him Lambert Simnel. After Jack's defeat, Henry had captured the boy whom he was convinced was fraudulent, and sent him to slave in the royal kitchens at Windsor, turning spits and cleaning floors. If the real Warwick had so wished, he could be rescued at any time, but he was a frightened boy who now shunned his heritage, and without his cooperation, there was nothing more to be done. Jack had little time for this attitude. To him, blood and duty were everything.

The abbey bell rang out, echoing over the town and down to the Thames and its meadows. As the sound died away, Sante continued. 'Lady Cicely, while we speak of Yorkist claimants, did you know there are rumours concerning a boy at present in Lisbon?'

'Yes, I have heard.' Henry had told her. It was thought to be one of her brothers, but which one? Edward, the elder, or Richard, the present Duke of York?

'Do you know who he is?' Sante asked. 'Has Lord Lincoln perhaps mentioned it?'

'I fear not. Only that he may be one of my brothers. You do not know either?'

Sante shook his head. 'When the king learned, he despatched your miscreant maternal uncle, Sir Edward Woodville, to visit the Portuguese court for information.'

Cicely was ashamed of her mother's numerous Woodville kin, who were ruthlessly ambitious and had made a strong bid for power when her father died. They would have murdered Richard in the process, but were outwitted.

'In my opinion your brothers are both dead,' Sante said then. 'I believe their ship went down in a storm in 1485. No witnesses or survivors. Which is why there has been no hint of them since the summer of 1485. It is not that the duchess is holding her tongue, more that she did not receive them and knows nothing. Her silence keeps Henry on tenterhooks.'

'The fact remains that we do not *know* what befell them.'

'I concede the point, Lady Cicely, but still feel I am right.'

'We know Richard did not order their deaths, but nor did Henry. If they were disposed of with intent, rather than perishing at sea, it was at the hands of some third party. Do not ask me for a name, because I do not have one.'

'One might suspect the King's Lady Mother,' Sante murmured.

Lady Margaret? Cicely thought for a moment. It was always possible, she supposed, given that lady's ruthless determination to see her son usurp the throne. At court she was known by the almost formal title of the King's Lady Mother, and was the foremost woman of the land, certainly pushing the queen into second place.

The abbot sighed. 'Still, at least Lord Lincoln's mistake at Stoke Field will not be repeated. Next time he will raise his own banners against Henry. The only person to whom he would concede now would be a legitimate heir of *Richard's* body. Such an heir does not exist, of course.'

She met his gaze squarely. 'You are right, Richard did not leave a legitimate heir of his body. Nor yet, it has to be said, has Lord Lincoln.'

The abbot pursed his lips. 'And should the latter die—which God forbid!—the Yorkist succession will pass to his corrupt snake of a brother, Edmund, from whom may Heaven save us all. Edmund already believes himself to be the heir, of course.'

Sante's lips twisted as he thought of the enigmatic seventeen-year-old, who was an immoral, conscienceless coxcomb, entirely devoid of integrity. Edmund was sometimes effete, sometimes cruel and sometimes smoothly gallant, and always prepared to stoop to anything in the pursuit of his own ambition. He had now tried to kill Jack twice, and the second attack had prompted Jack's latest return to Burgundy, for there was nothing to be gained by dying in a London alley when another Yorkist army needed to be raised against Henry.

'My lady,' Sante murmured, 'I think there is something disagreeably ambivalent about Edmund. He enjoys manipulating emotions. A beautiful, cruel youth, who appears to transfix members of both sexes, but is himself hollow inside. I would not even trust his pronouncement on whether to fry an egg or coddle it, because I would suspect him of intending to suck it raw all along. Dangerous jealousies would be aroused were he to become leader of York.'

'I agree wholeheartedly. He is a first cousin I would rather be without.'

The abbot regarded her. 'Would you ever support him?'

'No. My support was for Richard, and therefore Jack. Richard would *never* have chosen Edmund.'

'Your loyalty to your uncle is to be commended.'

'I will never be truly, irrevocably loyal to any other.' Should she admit the truth? The cherished but *sinful* truth? After all, Sante was still sworn to silence.

He saw the indecision on her face. 'What is it, my lady?'

'I. . .spoke earlier of my lovers.'

'Yes?'

'Well, the one man I will always adore and revere above all others. . .is my uncle, King Richard.'

The abbot thought he misunderstood. 'I am not sure I—'

'I loved him in every way, Abbot Sante. Truly loved him, and he returned that love. We lay together.'

Sante's owl eyes widened. 'Do—do you know what you are saying, Lady Welles?' he gasped, holding his pectoral cross so tightly that he almost drew blood.

Cicely smiled sadly. 'Oh, yes, I know, but my feelings for Richard were—are still—without condition and without conscience. To me he remains the finest man who ever drew breath, and nothing will *ever* change that opinion. Oh, do not look so holy and shocked, for I am sure you have happened upon far worse crimes than mine. Your little stories tonight have hinted as much, albeit mischievously, and is not breaking the Fifth Commandment infinitely more diabolical?'

'*All* sins are diabolical.'

'But how can true love ever be regarded as sinful? Richard and I were not married to others at the time, and so we hurt no one but ourselves. Do not condemn him, please. Yes, he was thirty-two to my sixteen, and he was my uncle, but he fought against what he felt for me. In the end I made it impossible for him to deny the truth. It was *such* a love. I will honour him until the day I die, and then from beyond my grave. Every beat of his heart was a beat of mine. Do you understand?'

Sante was utterly confounded. He had thought to test her mettle today; instead his own was being tested. Mightily. 'You do not repent at all?'

'Did you ever meet Richard?'

'I had that singular honour.'

'What did you think of him?'

'I liked and admired him very much. He had "charisma".'

'What does that mean?'

'It is a Greek word to be found in the Bible—Romans, I recall—and refers to a gift of grace in the spiritual sense, but I think it applies to Richard, who had an abundance of honest charm and fascination, but who was also a fair and just man of great intelligence and ability. His true friends remained his friends throughout.'

She nodded. 'Yes, that was Richard, and there was no lord in the realm who had more courage. He should still be on the throne, still guiding England. So no, I do not repent a single second spent with him.'

Sante saw the sincerity shimmering in her eyes, heard it in her voice. . .and could not understand how she could have loved Richard to such a sinful degree, yet now grace the bed of his slayer.

She read his thoughts. 'Nothing is straightforward, my lord abbot, so please do not think you understand me, for you do not. There is a great deal more that you do not know.'

'No matter how you defend your incestuous love, Lady Welles, it is—was—cursed. *Cursed.*' Trembling, Sante set sunbeams swirling in the slanting light as he hastened to close the door to the garden, even though there was no one out there and the postern in the high wall was bolted on the inside. The room became hot and still, and the sun was refracted through the window glass.

Cicely gazed at him, wondering if he would faint clean away if he knew she had borne Richard a son. Clearly Abbot John Sante was not ready to learn of Leo's existence. If he ever would be. She began to leave the room, but paused. 'Abbot Sante, you are not quite as close to Yorkist matters as you think. And do not make the mistake of thinking you now have knowledge with which to beat me, because Henry knows my uncle was my lover. So do Lord Lincoln, Sir Humphrey *and* my husband.'

Sante gaped as she walked out. Her maid, Mary Kymbe, was waiting, and fell into step behind her. Within moments Viscountess Welles had departed.

Chapter Three

ABINGDON'S OLD MARKET square was always busy, but never more so than when the king himself was expected. It was the day after Cicely supped with Abbot Sante, and the English countryside basked beneath another hot sun.

Trumpets had already heralded the royal cavalcade's approach from the north, along the Oxford road, and within minutes the clatter of hooves sounded upon the hard-packed surface of the streets, followed by shouts to clear the way. Banners floated—the arms of England and France, with Tudor roses and dragons. It was a spectacle worthy of London, but the cheers were not wholehearted, because Jack de la Pole had been liked hereabouts, and everyone thought Henry had buried him shamefully at Stoke Field with a willow stave through his heart. Or so the fame went.

John Pasmer's fine town house in the market place was a striking four-storey building, gabled and half-timbered, with large, diamond-latticed bay windows on floors that projected one above the other. Cicely was at the open casement of the first-floor parlour, waiting with guilty anticipation for sight of her royal lover. She wore an azure gown, and a headdress embroidered in rainbow colours. Later, when Henry came to her, she would leave her hair loose. As he liked it.

On the small table beside her was a large bowl of roses from Abbot Sante. She guessed he had pause for thought after her departure, and wondered if his admonishments had been too strong. Might he fear to have provoked her into going to Henry about his Yorkist activities? Well, he need not worry. His adherence to the White Rose protected him as far as she was concerned. Unless he ever posed a threat to Leo.

She glanced across at the abbey gatehouse, next to which

was the church of St Nicholas, where her attention settled. A tall, almost cadaverous man lounged against the church corner, apparently engrossed in whittling a stick. He had a sallow complexion and straggly, bright-red hair, and was dressed neither well nor shabbily, just somewhere in between. She thought of him as Romulus, because sometimes he was replaced by a swarthy, shorter, much plumper companion with a limp, who, naturally, had to be Remus.

Her new awareness of being secretly observed inside the house had cast the men's vigil in a fresh light. She had been curious about them; now she was deeply suspicious. Who might be paying them? The abbot? Henry, with his millstone of unrelenting jealousy and suspicion? Henry, whom she could never fully trust either? Her thoughts slid uneasily to Leo, and the lack of news from the Isle of Wight. He was in the care of a Kymbe cousin, who had hitherto always—*always*—sent word consistently Was Henry's hand at work there as well? Her hands curled into fists as she strove to quell the dread. She would not give in. She would be *strong!*

The cheers increased as the royal cavalcade streamed into the square. Henry Tudor, King of England and of France, Lord of Ireland, was not a handsome, appealing man, as Richard had been, but had effortless grace, even when controlling his suddenly fractious white horse. He was thirty-one, and wore a quilted brown silk doublet with ermine trimmings. Not just brown, but a rich, warm shade that enhanced the russet of the hair falling to his shoulders. Such a colour looked good on his tall, slender frame, and his black hose and thigh boots showed his long legs to be well shaped and strong.

A circlet of gold gleamed around his forehead as he raised a gauntleted hand to acknowledge the crowds. He was expressionless, for it was his policy never to reveal what he felt or thought. The winter sea was in his hooded gaze, especially his left eye, which was disinclined to act in concert with the right, thus disturbing the beholder. Cicely knew the vision of his good eye was getting weaker, already requiring him to wear spectacles for reading.

He had high cheekbones, arched eyebrows, hollow cheeks and a small but not receding chin, and was lean enough for there to be a pronounced shadow along the line of his jaw. His wide, thin-lipped mouth was almost always a straight, emotionless line, and he exuded an air of ominous mystery, of harshness and a lack of charity; of concealed truths and conjured falsehoods.

Yet he was not always the assured monarch he seemed in public. His health—physical and mental—often failed him, and he feared being no longer strong enough to defend his ill-gotten crown. So he resorted to anything or anyone he believed might assist him, including practitioners of dangerous dark arts.

Tears filled Cicely's eyes. He had not engaged her heart and had forced her to be his lover. Every time she went to him, she failed Richard, who had perished defending his realm against this usurper. Sometimes, as now, the pain of guilt was so great she could hardly bear it.

Henry knew she would be at the window, and directed a first smile across at her. It changed him. That smile—rare, warm, natural, uninhibited—revealed the private man, whom she thought of by his Welsh name, Harri Tudur.

The cavalcade passed from view beneath the abbey gatehouse and Henry was lost beyond his noisy, colourful retinue. Among the riders was a handsome, notably blond young squire by the name of Stephen Perrings, who had recently become the sweetheart of Cicely's maid. Mary called him Perry, both for his name and the particular blue of his eyes. Cicely had teased her that the periwinkle was also known as the sorcerer's violet.

Mary spoke behind her suddenly. 'My lady?'

Cicely whirled about, not having heard her enter.

'Forgive me, my lady, I did not mean to startle you.' Mary curtsied quickly. Her green gown was prettily embroidered, and her brown curls were swept up beneath a modest bonnet. She was Cicely's age, with rosy cheeks, gentle brown eyes.

Cicely relaxed. Mary Kymbe was her confidante, and had been with her for three years now. 'There is no need to apologize, Mary. You will be pleased to learn that your Perry is in the king's entourage.'

The maid blushed. 'I hope you will permit me to see him?'

Cicely lowered her voice and put a finger to her lips in a reminder that complete discretion was now needed in the house. 'If he is sincere with you, then of course. You know that. I trust you do not disclose anything to him?'

Mary's response was also very low. 'Only about myself, my lady. Perry *is* sincere.'

Cicely prayed the maid's trust was well placed. Perry was attractive, ambitious, and in Henry's household, so could he *really* be in love with a mere maid? Even if that maid's mistress was Viscountess Welles? Unless, of course, he was aware of the closeness between the viscountess and the king. By now Cicely was seeing agents, schemers and foes in every shadow.

Mary held up a letter with a broken seal. 'This has arrived from my brother Tom, my lady. It was delayed, I fear.'

Leo? Cicely's breath caught hopefully.

Mary was dismayed to have given false hope. 'Oh, no, my lady, it is not news of Master Leo. Forgive me, please. It is to tell me that my aunt has regained her health.'

The maid's elderly aunt, Mistress Kymbe, was dear to Cicely. A wisewoman and midwife, steeped in spells and herbs, her magic could be detrimental or beneficial, and she was gifted with both the "vision" and the "cunning". She had brought Leo into the world.

Mary was anxious to reassure her mistress. 'You *will* hear soon,' she said softly. 'I told Tom of your anxiety, and when he wrote this he was about to leave Friskney for the Isle of Wight. He must be there by now, and will send word directly. Master Leo is well, I am sure.'

Cicely trusted Mary's brother completely, and liked him too. She inhaled deeply to steady herself again, and then spoke in a whisper. 'I must be certain all is secure when His Majesty comes to me tonight, and as I suspect there to be agents among the servants, I intend to dismiss them all until midday tomorrow. You will be the only one to stay.'

'Yes, my lady.'

The July day was almost done, and shadows merged across the square. There was no one around, not even Romulus or Remus, and the final beams of the sun shone with dazzling gold and crimson on the abbey towers. Cicely waited again at the open window. The servants had been sent away, leaving only Mary, and it was so quiet that mice could be heard behind the panelling.

Mint freshened Cicely's breath, as it had always freshened Richard's, and her hair was brushed free. The plum brocade gown she had chosen was one that Henry particularly liked for the way it revealed her shoulders and the curve of her breasts. Her only jewels were gifts from him: an emerald ring and silver dragon pendant.

The dragon was strikingly beautiful, but cruel too, coiling around to bite its own back and claw its tail. The malevolent gleam of its diamond eyes gave it life. Henry was as tormented and imperfect, and it was all the fault of his ruthless mother.

Lady Margaret Beaufort's antipathy toward the House of York caused her to scheme and plot remorselessly to bring Richard down. His betrayal at Bosworth had come about because of her, but in spite of everything, she and Cicely had formed an unlikely friendship. That was how Cicely knew Margaret nursed a very guilty conscience for having forced her own goals upon Henry's youth and early manhood. He had spent fourteen years of exile and detention in Brittany, as a political pawn at the mercy of Brittany, France and Yorkist England. Such tuition could not be unlearned, and it had moulded him. What he might have been would never be known, but he was a tortured soul now.

A tall, cloaked figure emerged beneath the gatehouse

opposite, and she recognized Henry's lithe, easy gait. Then he coughed. That alone would have identified him, for it was a hollow sound that told of a weakness in his lungs. . .and was a herald of the future. Consumption would surely claim him one day. He would not live to be an old man.

A minute later Mary had admitted him, and his soft steps were upon the stairs. But as Cicely went out on to the landing, where what was left of the day shone through a narrow window at the rear of the house, instinct warned her that something had changed drastically since he smiled across the square. She sank to her knees, knowing better than to say or do anything else until he indicated. Before bowing her head meekly, she stole a glance at him as he reached the landing.

He paused to unfasten his cloak and then tossed it over the newel post. His long hair was tangled against the ermine trim of the same brown doublet he had worn earlier, and the rich golden collar across his shoulders was aglow with rubies, amethysts and pearls. The subtle scent of cloves always accompanied him, and was pleasing. He had a magnetic effect upon her, an almost diabolic appeal that seemed to crackle in the air, stirring her blood, but also her fears. He wore his guardedness like a suit of armour, and she knew this was not Harri Tudur, but the other, much darker Henry.

Even the shadows seemed nervous, changing and deepening as night closed in. Henry's wariness increased too, and the oddness of his left eye was pronounced as he fingered the dagger hilt at his hip. He was as taut as a bowstring, which was not surprising because *anyone* could be lurking in the pools of darkness. He was accustomed to attempts on his life. Both Edward IV and Richard had sent agents to try to kill him in Brittany; Tal had attacked him as he slept at Esher, and his own queen had poisoned his wine with a steadily accumulating dose of Russian powder, before Cicely realized and confronted her.

He spoke. 'Lady Welles, I asked your maid why the usual servants did not attend the door. She told me you have temporarily dismissed everyone. Why?' His soft-spoken voice still bore a faint trace of the Wales of his birth.

'Because I wished to be sure we are alone, Your Majesty.' She was not about to tell him the truth! Then she added, rather unwisely. 'If there is anyone else in this house, he or she will need the mantle of invisibility.'

Unamused, he made much of rubbing his left eye. 'You think such things do not exist?'

She could have bitten her tongue. His keen concern with astrology, alchemy, spells and having the future told from all manner of horrible things had become too entrenched. 'I crave your indulgence, Your Majesty, for I meant no offence.'

'Nevertheless, you *have* offended me.'

He was spoiling for an out-and-out argument, she thought. Why? Anger pricked her. Maybe something had happened to upset him, but she did not deserve to be treated this way. Did he know how unpleasantly he was behaving? Her spirit flared into life, and she rose without permission. 'You are not pleasant company, Henry Tudor. Perhaps you should not have come here.'

His strange eyes were like ice, as was his voice. 'You dare to speak to me in such a manner?'

She raised her chin. 'Oh, yes.'

'You are presumptuous, madam!'

'No, Henry, I am your concerned lover,' she said softly, manipulating him although he did not realize it.

He hesitated. 'Name my transgression,' he said then, and she heard a small note of puzzlement enter his tone.

'You have greeted me coldly, when all I want to do is welcome you and be in your arms again.' She allowed her voice to soften still more, hinting at the pleasures that would result from such an embrace. 'Oh, Henry, please tell me what has happened to distress you so.'

'I am not distressed.'

'Yes, you are,' she replied, still gently.

He closed his eyes briefly. 'I should not let you read me.'

'I will *always* read you.' *As I always read Richard. . .*

'We *are* alone in the house?' he pressed, still uneasy.

'Yes, except for Mary.' Everything was supposedly secure, every window closed and every door locked and bolted, but had something been forgotten? A secret entrance?

He cleared his throat to quell a cough, and her anxiety stirred. 'Are you feeling unwell, Henry?'

'No more than usual. Sometimes I cough, sometimes I do not' His glance wandered around the landing, as if to find some source of comfort previously overlooked. 'I. . .so wanted this to be a perfect reunion,' he said then.

'Why should it not be?' she asked.

'Because I am never allowed to rest. The vultures always seek their prey.'

His tone was affecting. 'Henry?'

'Cicely, *cariad*,' he whispered.

It was the Welsh word for sweetheart and his attraction in those seconds was quite devastating. Everything about him—*everything*—twined inexorably around her, snaring her senses and tapping secret emotions.

'Oh, Henry, let me help you. . .comfort you.' She went a little closer, drawn like a moth to a flame, but still not daring to touch him.

He hesitated, and a change entered his eyes. 'Forgive me for coming to you in such a way. You are right to be angry.'

The portcullis lifted, and she went right to him, catching his hand and raising it gently to her cheek.

His other arm moved around her waist, pulling her against him. Cloves settled over and through her as he hid his face in her hair. She put his fingertips to her lips and kissed each one lovingly, before drawing his forefinger into her mouth to caress it with her tongue. She could feel his loins pressed to her, hard now, and offering her so very, very much

He moved against her, slowly, almost imperceptibly, but the pleasure imparted to her was as great as any he gleaned for himself. It was so erotic and enticing, inviting her to steal more delight. And more. Desire flamed through her now, and she sought his lips, kissing him with such ferocity that she was lost in her chaotic senses. She wanted him. Now.

He lifted her against the wall, his passionately relentless response allowing no quarter, but demanding immediate gratification. When he entered her she could have wept for the joy of it. She so wanted to hate him, but it was impossible. Even loving Jack as she did, and above all, Richard, she still wanted this unfathomable man who was capable of great cruelty, but who was sometimes as essential to her as she was to him. This Tudor king cast a spell over her, and took her to a fleshly paradise that might have been fashioned for her by none other than Satan himself.

His breath shuddered as elation swept him along. 'Oh, those secret little muscles, *cariad*, those secret little muscles,' he whispered, his voice muffled as his lips paid homage to her throat. He would not be able to prolong it, for his emotions had been running riot since before he came to her. She was his saviour, his balm, his refuge, and he needed to surrender everything to her. He groaned as he came, and as always he made certain she shared the climax with him. He was a considerate lover; never selfish.

Cicely twined her fingers in his hair, and her lips clung to his again, with all the reward he could possibly want. Her attentions were tender and trembling. . .and as honest as she could ever be to him, because when the cold light of day dawned, and he had gone, the guilt would return. But for these moments nothing else mattered. They were alone on the dark landing.

At last he lowered her feet to the floor, permitting her gown to fall back into place, and then he took her face in his hands. 'You rescue me from myself, *cariad*,' he breathed. 'I could not bear to live if I lost you.'

'Please do not say that.' The guilt came early.

'Even though it is true? But now I wish to talk to you. Confide in you. Just you, without any chance of your trusty maid overhearing. So we should be even more private.'

Please let the house be secure! She hardly dared to acknowledge the fearful thought. 'We can go to the parlour,' she suggested. 'Or dispense with that and go straight up to the bedchamber?'

He released her and laced his spent masculinity into place again. 'The bedchamber holds great appeal, my lady, and I am sure you would prefer more comfort than a wall.'

Chapter Four

THE PRINCIPAL BEDCHAMBER was directly above the parlour, and extended over it. A double-branched candlestick, lit earlier by Mary and left on a table, cast a soft sheen over everything, and the open casements allowed in the cool of the late summer evening. The shutters were partly in place, to prevent anyone in the abbey gatehouse and other buildings around the square from seeing in.

A large, canopied bed dominated the room. It was handsomely carved with scenes of Tristan and Yseult, and the rich tapestry coverlet reflected the same romance. The hangings were crimson tartaryn, luxuriously silky and embroidered in gold with mythical creatures. Such a fine bed was almost fit for a king. Almost, but not quite.

Cicely bolted the door and leaned back against it to watch Henry move slowly around the room, drawing a long, slender finger over this and that before pausing by the bed. His mental pain was palpable.

He faced her at last. 'I am fearful of betrayal, *cariad*,' he said quietly. 'Oh, I see by your face that you think there is nothing different about *that*, after all, am I not *always* fearful of betrayal? Is not my entire reign based upon it?' He smiled wryly. 'Your beloved Richard was betrayed by those who chose to support me instead. For their own reasons, not because they thought I had the right to the throne. And so here I am, the traitors' monarch, faced with the knowledge that if those men turned upon their king once, they can as easily do so again.'

He had expressed this sentiment many times before, and she knew it was not what concerned him now. Something of much greater importance lay behind this.

'I am already beset by my enemies,' he went on. 'Well, admittedly some of them are England's enemies, not just mine. The rebellious Irish, for instance, who prefer the House of York. And then your other pest of an uncle, Sir Edward Woodville, who has taken most of the men of Wight to Brittany in defiance of me.'

She had no time for Sir Edward, or any Woodville, but pursed her lips. 'You inspire the word hypocrite, Henry Tudor.'

'Oh?' He was all innocence.

'Yes. I see your scheming in my uncle's expedition. He has gone with your hidden blessing, and if he returns victorious, all well and good. But what if he does not?'

Henry smiled. 'Then it will be entirely his fault, of course.'

'Of course.'

'By the way, a strange little footnote. The overall commander of the Breton forces is none other than the Regent, my former brother-in-law, Marshal Jean de Rieux, maternal uncle of *Écuyer* Roland de Vielleville.'

'The unacknowledged son for whom you feel nothing paternal.' She *prayed* there was no one else in the house. If word of Roland spread, Henry would believe she was guilty.

Henry paused. 'You would have me love Roland? It is Arthur I must love. *Must* love.'

'I feel sorry for Roland.'

'I know. But in you he has at least *someone* to care for him.'

She did not understand him sometimes, and this was one such moment. Perhaps he did have some affection for his innocent firstborn, who knew nothing of the circumstances of his birth. Nor even yet that the King of England was his father. She watched as Henry removed his gold collar and placed it on the table beside the lighted candlestick. Such slow grace. Such fascination.

'I have missed you so much, Cicely. Kenilworth was the arse end of the world because you were not with me.'

'Consider the scandal if you took me instead of your queen. Winchester would pale to insignificance.'

'Many a time I have been tempted to brazen it out, and let the world know I love the wrong sister.'

'It would be a grave error.'

'I know,' he replied ruefully. 'So, I have to be philosophical and make the most of my marital lot.' He glanced away momentarily. 'I do not actually know what my marital lot is at the moment. First she strives to send me to my Maker with poison, the next she is all doe-eyes and smiles.'

'*Bess*?' Cicely was startled. Bess had become so hard of late that it was hard to imagine her as Henry described.

He nodded. 'It appears I am suddenly *invited* to her bed.'

'That is surely a good thing? The less strife, the better?'

'It is unnerving, *cariad*. All I can think of is her former hatred, so I do my duty and leave her again at the first opportunity. But. . .' He glanced away again.

'Yes?'

'She now enjoys what I do when I am there.' He met her eyes for a moment. 'She too has those secret little muscles.'

Cicely was dumbfounded. When she and her sister had been friends, she had tried so hard to persuade Bess that Henry's lovemaking was well worth inviting. The very idea had repulsed his queen. What could have brought about such a transformation?

'I do not trust her, Cicely. She administered that poison in person, in front of you, and now. . .? It makes no sense, and I marvel I am able to complete the fucking!' He smiled craftily. 'I pretend she is you and cannot contain myself for the excitement.'

'I hope she never realizes *that!* Perhaps she is ready to try to improve things at last? Henry, I have never wanted to interfere in your marriage, or stand in the way of any rapprochement between you and my sister. I would be happy if you and she were content together.'

'I would much rather you were ferociously jealous of her.'

If he were Richard or Jack, she *would* be ferociously jealous. But he was neither, and would never be their equal.

'*Cariad,* I will never trust your sister, and so now carry some unicorn horn as a safeguard,' he went on, in the matter-of-fact tone of one who believed implicitly that this was an overall protection against poison.

More superstition, she thought. He had also begun to take quintessence, a secret substance provided by his astrologer, Master Rogers, who told him it was the legendary water of life. He was also told that it might be the philosophers' "stone", which drove away—among other afflictions—consumption, devils, poison and gout. Rejuvenation was promised, and if one knew the secret, it could even convert base metal into the finest gold. Oh, there was nothing this marvel could not do, or so Henry, in his increasing desperation, was prepared to conclude. Perhaps she should also believe in it, as so many did, but she could not. 'Unicorn horn as well? Henry, is Master Rogers's secret essence not protection enough against poison?'

'I resort to anything that will be of benefit to me. I want my health back, Cicely.'

'So you also turn to prophecy?'

He paused. 'Yes.' His glance encompassed her for a moment. 'I think I know what you are about to say.'

'Aha, you have developed the sight.' She smiled. 'I am going to call you two-faced for banning prophecy to your subjects while resorting to it yourself. Shame on you.'

'The noble and saintly kings of York would *never* do such a thing, I suppose,' he remarked dryly.

'Certainly not.'

The mice chose that moment to scramble around in the wall. Henry turned. 'You have an infestation, I think. I recall hearing them when I was last here.'

But was it simply mice? All things alchemic and astrological evaporated as alarm seized her instead. She managed to meet his glance without flinching. 'I believe the house cats are overwhelmed. A rat-catcher will have to be engaged, and Master Pasmer sent the charge.'

'Indeed.' He paused, rubbed his eyebrow, and stifled a yawn.

She smiled. 'I am boring you?'

He returned the smile. 'Never. I *am* tired, though.'

'I hazard that it is to do with your wretched personal accounts. You pore over them into the small hours of a night, checking every figure and putting your initials to each one. There you sit by candlelight, squinting like a mole. You are so intent upon lining your coffers that you ignore your own wellbeing.'

'If one does not guard the farthings, the shillings may not tally.'

'And then there is your horrible notebook,' she continued tartly.

'*Horrible* notebook? I must be sure to credit the right person with the right remark. Any small thing could be an indication of treachery to come.'

'I am told that a while ago your new pet monkey became so angry that it tore the notebook to pieces, much to the relief of your entire household.'

'It is true, he did, but I have forgiven him. And I now have a new notebook.' He looked away. 'Surely you understand why I keep these records? I *have* to be sure of those around me.' Now he was serious.

'Am I recorded in there too?'

'No. I always remember every word you say.'

'I will have to hope your memory never fails,' she answered.

There was fleeting amusement in his glance as he murmured, '*Oh, Cecille, la belle dame douce, mais sans charité.*'

'Like my sister?'

The amusement faded. 'No, *never* like your sister. She may be beautiful and lack all charity, but she is *not* sweet!'

Cicely returned him to the matter of his superstition. 'Henry, I cannot say whether or not unicorn horn is an effective safeguard against poison, but I am sure that the eclipse on the ninth of the month would not have made any difference to your journey from Windsor. You had no need to delay because of it.'

'But do you *know* so?' he replied.

'Well, no, of course not, but—'

'There cannot be a but, *cariad*. Eclipses are warnings, and I am not foolish enough to ignore them. Remember, there was an eclipse on the day Anne Neville departed this earth.'

It was true. An eclipse had marked the death of Richard's queen. Many people took it as a bad omen for Richard himself. 'There was one on your birthday this year as well,' she pointed out, 'but here you are, safe and sound.'

'Maybe, but I feared it portended my death and so took care not to celebrate. My temper was foul, if you recall. And there was another eclipse only days after Stoke Field,' he pointed out.

'But not *during* Stoke Field, and you emerged triumphant! It was my cousin Jack who was defeated,' she answered. 'So, if anything, the eclipse marked *his* failure, not yours. You have to abandon such superstition, Henry, for it begins to rule you.'

'I suppose you will mock my fear of Fridays too? Easy to do when you were born on a Monday.'

She was cross. 'You were born on a Friday, Henry Tudor, but have survived to be a man full grown, and King of England, too. Friday did not treat you badly, I fancy.'

'Then let me remind you of a very old verse. *He that is born on a Friday and grows to full manhood, Will be too cursed and unloved to be hailed as good. Because in his heart truth will find no haven, He can only be despised forever as craven.*'

Cicely eyed him. 'It supposedly refers to *everyone* born on a Friday. So they are *all* cursed, unloved, unjust, loathed and craven? Please, Henry, stop this.'

'But do they all fit those criteria as completely as me? Cicely, I am a cursed, unloved king, I am said to be unjust, and I have been castigated for not having fought in the forefront at Bosworth or Stoke Field.'

'You are what you have made of yourself, not what fate decided on a whim.'

'Perhaps, but I still believe there will be an eclipse on the day I die, and that it will happen on a Friday.' He met her eyes. 'You are the only person on God's earth to whom I could confide this. The only one.'

'You may be the King of England, and the enemy of my House, but as a man you mean a great deal to me.'

'Only because I have forced you,' he answered frankly. 'I fool myself by thinking otherwise.'

She was cornered for a moment, but dissembled successfully. 'You broached an important matter earlier, before deliberately changing the subject.'

Now he became the evasive one. 'I suffered greatly tonight before finally escaping Sante's suffocating hospitality. I thought I would *never* find a secret little postern through which to slip unnoticed. I needed that cloak of invisibility.' His fingertips ran comically across the table. 'If I heard of his London house once, I heard of it half a dozen times. It is called La Mote, it is in King Street in the Westminster parish of St Margaret of Antioch, and is "a goodly house, with cottages and sixty acres. It is to be lamented that the parish church is in a sorry state of dilapidation".' He mimicked the abbot's voice.

She gazed at him. 'Oh, Henry, I *want* to help you, but if you refuse to tell me how, I vow I will send you away.'

'Will you indeed?' He smiled.

Cicely nodded. 'I might even bundle you unceremoniously into the square. Imagine that, the King of England landing on his arse in the Abingdon dust.'

'Most unedifying.' He went to the window. 'I hate the endless responsibility of being king, *cariad*, and wish I had stayed away from England. All I ever wanted was my father's title and estates. Just to be Henry, Earl of Richmond. Nothing more and nothing less. Instead, here I am, occupying the throne *you* still think of as Richard's.'

'Then why *did* you invade three years ago?'

To her surprise, he ignored the question and finally came to the point. 'Here is my torment, *cariad*. A messenger arrived this evening from my mother in Westminster, with new information about the mysterious boy in Lisbon. You remember I told you of him?'

She nodded.

'Some months ago when I despatched your Woodville uncle, I also took the precaution of paying a certain bearded Scotsman twenty guineas to follow and spy upon Sir Edward.'

'How like you. A spy to catch a spy. Do you ever forget whom you have sent where?'

'Never. Well, Woodville returned to say the lad greatly resembles your father, but I still awaited the Scotsman. He has now returned as well, and reports to my mother that the boy's likeness to your father is remarkable.'

'So, you think he is one of my brothers?'

'That is the obvious conclusion. Your Burgundian harridan of an aunt has a hand in it, of course. Intuition warns me that he will be my greatest threat yet. Perhaps my fate.'

She could not say anything. The last three words—filled with superstition—were the real kernel of his mood tonight.

He changed the subject again. 'Cicely, Sir Humphrey Talbot tells me you wish to visit Kingston l'Isle?'

She was startled. 'Sir Humphrey? Why, yes. I wish to take the waters of a holy well dedicated to St Margaret of Antioch.'

'Oh, spare me that hallowed lady! Perhaps Talbot's manor is also called La Mote?' But his smile, admittedly fleeting, was not unkind.

'Sir Humphrey's sister, the dowager Duchess of Norfolk is there at the moment.'

'So I am given to understand. May I ask why you wish to go there, *cariad*?' He was not interrogating her, but was genuinely concerned.

'Because I have become barren, and the water is believed to correct the affliction. If I beseech St Margaret, she might grant my desire to present Jon with an heir.' Even as she spoke she knew it was idiotic. There was such a rift between Viscount Welles and his lady that they were at opposite ends of the realm, let alone in the same bed.

'Copulation is surely essential for this?'

'I know, but. . .' She paused. 'Well, no matter what my differences with Jon now, he deserves to have an heir. Which he can only have from me. Do you not understand that?'

'I understand *your* feelings, yes.'

She wondered why he made the distinction. 'I know that you are potent, Henry, because Bess has been with child three times now. Yet I, who have lain with you so often and with such passion, have not even known a late month. Sir Humphrey told me of the well some time ago, and when I asked if it would be acceptable for me to visit, he assured me I would be welcome at any time. And, now, the duchess's presence will make a visit perfectly acceptable to you. I would never wish you to think. . .'

'That you are on heat for my rather elderly Silver Hound?' Henry furnished the words with a laugh.

He called Tal his Silver Hound because of the Talbot family's heraldic emblem of a running dog. Well, a hound, actually. A talbot, the breed from which the family took its name. Or was it the other way around? She could not recall. However, elderly was *not* an appropriate adjective for Tal, who was a very fit, strong and agile man who seemed far younger than his age. 'Henry, I would not wish to give you cause to doubt me.'

He came close, and brushed the back of his fingers softly down her arm. '*Cariad,* I did not realize quite how heavily this weighed upon you.'

'You have your astrology, magic and alchemy; I have my beliefs and hopes as well.'

'And you have Jon Welles, God help you.'

The edge she noticed a moment since was now unmistakable. Had he and Jon fallen out?

Henry read her expression. 'Yes, sweetheart, I am somewhat disenchanted with my uncle at the moment. He is not worthy of your affection, and should be grateful for his good fortune in having you for a wife. It is far more than he deserves.'

'Henry?'

He took her hand. 'Has it not occurred to you that if you are *not* reunited with the Welles cowpat, your new fruitfulness, courtesy of St Margaret, might produce *my* child? Or do you expect me to leave you alone until he has condescended to do his husbandly duty?'

She looked away. 'I have not really considered anything fully, Henry.'

'You wish to go to Kingston as soon as possible?'

'If the duchess is there, yes.'

His fingers tightened around hers. 'Go with my blessing, but I will be disagreeable enough to pray that my uncle fails to ever visit you again. Then, maybe, fate will bring *me* the prize I have long yearned for; that you will bear my child. Oh, how I shall pray for it.' He kissed her so tenderly that his lips trembled against hers.

Then he released her, and lightened the atmosphere. 'So, *you* believe in a sacred well, yet challenge *my* belief in the occult? I see little difference.'

'If astrologers could see all they say in the stars—and your fragrant stools—do you not think *they* would be the kings?'

'I will have you know my stools are particularly regal.'

She laughed. 'I am sure they are, but I have no desire to examine them.'

He became serious again. '*Cariad*, I *need* such arts to help me. I am not sound in body, and know my recurring cough is a portent of worse to come. But I am not sound in mind either, as I have shown even tonight. There are veils within me that only you can draw aside. Please do not mock what you see as my pathetic gullibility and dependence upon magic. I must pursue *whatever* remedy I can.'

'You break my heart, Harri Tudur,' she whispered.

'I *do* understand your wish concerning the well. Truly I do.'

'I know.'

'*Cariad*. . .'

'Yes?' Her heart began to sink. He was going to tell her something he knew would upset her.

'Forgive me for this, but are you *sure* my uncle is the husband you think he is?'

Now her heart turned over.

He ventured a little further, unwillingly, but clearly feeling he had to say *something*. 'Jon Welles has never lacked female attention in the past, certainly not when he was with me in Brittany, so how can you be so sure he goes without it now? He knows about me, and about Richard. And presumably about Jack de la Pole. There he is in the north, going about *my* business, far away from you, knowing you and I are most probably sharing a bed. Maybe he feels it is time to forget faithfulness for a while.'

She met his gaze. 'You know he is doing this, do you not?'

'No, *cariad*, I merely hazard idle guesses.'

'Please do not tiptoe around this. Tell me.'

He took her hand again. 'There is a whisper. That is all.'

'Who is she?' Cicely managed to ask.

A pause. 'I have no idea.' His thumb smoothed her palm.

Yes, you do, she thought. You know *exactly* who this woman is and do not intend to say. Tears stung her eyes. 'Tell me, Henry. Please. Let me at least know her name.'

'I really do not know her name,' he repeated.

He was being as tactful as he could, which only served to make her realize that this new love of Jon's was serious.

Chapter Five

HENRY GATHERED CICELY gently into his embrace. 'Jon Welles is a halfwit not to be true to you. If I could have you for myself, openly, God knows I would do so in a trice.'

'Henry Tudor, you are as unfaithful as Jon, and as bigamous as my father.'

He released her slowly. 'We have been through all this before. Mine was a youthful indiscretion, no more.'

'For your sake I wish it had been, but it was solemnised by a priest and vows.'

'Do not remind me.' He ran his fingers through his hair and turned away. This was the secret he knew could end his reign, perhaps even his life; the secret he forced her to keep with threats and a sworn promise.

As an impetuous youth in exile he had entered a clandestine marriage with his highborn Breton guardian's youngest sister, named Tiphaine de Rieux. It was a match soon regretted and never discovered, so that when he was sent to another place of confinement, he hoped he and his bride could both forget it. Tiphaine had been forced into another marriage, and only when it was too late had Henry discovered she had borne him a son, subsequently named Roland de Vielleville. Vielleville was the French version of Coskäer, the name of the unpleasant Breton noble he believed to be his father. Henry, of course, had eventually returned to England, defeated Richard at Bosworth and then "married" Bess. He only accepted custody of Roland—never to acknowledge him—when Tiphaine had begged from her deathbed. Her brutal husband had begun to suspect the boy was not his, and she feared for Roland's safety.

Henry glanced at her. 'You still condemn me, do you not?'

'You can hardly expect me to applaud you.'

'Ah, such harsh candour. Well, I deserve it, I suppose.'

'I am hardly an innocent in this, Henry. I keep your secret in order to protect my own.'

He rested his palm gently against her cheek. Always he had to touch her. 'You see before you a traitor, a bigamist and a regicide, do you not?'

'I would not presume to say so.'

'Oh, yes, you would. My dearest darling, how hard it must be, to hate me and want me at the same time.'

'I admit it.'

He embraced her again, one hand slipping into the hair at the nape of her neck to twist it gently and draw her head back until her lips were presented to his. Then he kissed her, achingly, needfully, his mouth dragging slowly over hers, sometimes fully, sometimes sliding slightly away before claiming her again. It was a clove-rich kiss that knew the corners of her soul and drove honesty and truth out into the night.

But then the moment was shattered by a loud slithering and rattling from behind the wall. Dislodged plaster and bits of falling lath! Cicely's breath caught with alarm. It was too much noise for mice, maybe even for rats. Something two-legged perhaps? Armed and with ill intent? Such fear engulfed her that she could not speak or move.

Henry's attention was fixed upon the sounds in the wall. Tense and wary, he eased her aside gently and put a finger to his lips. Then he drew his dagger. Every sinew was taut and quivering as he weighed the hilt in his palm—a slow, compelling motion—before stepping softly toward one of the panels.

He slid the dagger comfortably into his full grip, his long fingers pale and tight around it. The tip of the blade caught the candlelight as he paused by the panels where the noises seemed most concentrated. His head was tilted, his gaze set and focused as in a split second he drove the blade between the panels. Such force was used that it passed right through, and there was a high-pitched scream from the other side.

The screech seemed human, and Cicely's blood froze in her veins. She pressed her hands to her mouth, her eyes huge. Had Henry stabbed a spy?'

He stepped back from the panelling, thinking the same, but then the cry became unmistakably animal and there followed a terrified squeaking and scrambling as what had to be rats fled in all directions at once. Henry exhaled slowly and returned to her. 'Damned vermin,' he muttered.

'I thought it was a. . .a—'

'A man? So did I.' He came to brush a reassuring kiss on her cheek. 'But it is done now. They have gone for a while, at least. You see? I am a raticide as well.'

She could not manage a smile. The incident had shaken her, and reminded her of her own falsehoods.

He stroked her hair back, and then put his forehead to hers to whisper. '*My eyes doth see thee, my sweet lady, My eyes doth see thee well. My hand doth touch thee, my sweet lady, My hand doth touch thee well. But my lips. . .my lips do kiss thee, sweetest lady, My lips do kiss thee, oh, so well.*'

Then his lips did indeed kiss her well. Her eyes closed for the eroticism of it.

'Now I will *prove* my words,' he said softly. 'Here, in the comfort of this bed. You may command me as you will, and if it is physically possible, I will pleasure you all I can.'

That same night, Cicely awoke suddenly. The candles had long since gone out, except for the night light on the mantel, and even that was guttering, close to extinction. Patterns loomed and swayed eerily over the room, and she could see Henry's dagger still between the panels. Outside, beyond the half-open shutters, it was dark, and she started as the watch officers suddenly called the hour of two below the window.

But it was not the watch that had awakened her, because as their voices died away around a corner, she heard something else—the soft tremble of the bedchamber door latch. The door was still bolted on the inside, and the sound was not that of someone trying to come in, more the result of a draught. Yet the night seemed still.

She slipped from the bed. Henry stirred a little, without awakening. How easy it would be to kill him now, and rid England of Richard's nemesis. His dagger was even to hand. But in spite of all he had done, she could not murder him. Kisses before shedding his blood? No. She was fiercely Yorkist, but could never do that.

Again the latch shook, and this time she knew it was a draught, as if an outer door were open so that the faint flow of air sucked softly through the house. Enough to move the door. The night light died, and the room became completely dark, except for the starlit sky outside. Had someone entered the property? Cicely's skin pricked as she donned her robe. The cream silk was cool, as were the floorboards beneath her bare feet as she slid the bolt and went out to the landing, leaving the door ajar.

Out here the draught was tangible, and she shivered, although not with the cold. The dark staircase led both up and down from where she stood, and it seemed silent and undisturbed, except that she had the strangest feeling someone else had been here only moments before. Please let it have been Mary.

Then she heard a muffled sound on the floor above, where the maid had her room. The closing of a door perhaps. Yes, that was it. A door. And then the low murmur of a male voice! Had there been something more than rats behind the panelling after all? And was Mary party to it? But common sense prevailed, for it was much more likely that Mary's visitor was her sweetheart, Stephen Perrings. An assignation? Was Mary Kymbe being foolish enough to entertain her swain while Henry was here?

Both incensed and incredulous, Cicely went silently up to the next floor. Mary's door faced the stairs, and beneath it was a glow of candlelight.

The maid's voice was anxious. 'How did you get in?'

A man answered. 'There is not a window through which I could not climb to be with you, my love.'

So, a window, not a door, Cicely thought angrily. And it *was* Stephen Perrings.

'My lady will be outraged if she finds you here.'

'It has been a long time since we were last together, and I must have at least one kiss to sustain me.'

'Oh, Perry. . .' Mary's voice trailed away.

Cicely opened the door without ceremony. 'Yes, Mary Kymbe, my lady is very outraged indeed.' She spoke quietly, but to very good effect.

The pair by the bed jumped apart, and a candle on a shelf cavorted for a moment, twisting the light. The maid's pretty face was frightened. She hugged herself, as if insufficiently clothed, although she was more than adequately attired in a voluminous night robe, with a bonnet keeping her brown curls at bay. 'Oh, my lady! My lady!' she cried, sinking to her knees in the utmost dismay.

'Keep your voice down!' Cicely hissed, fearful that Henry would be disturbed, even though he was a floor below. Did Perrings *know* about Henry? She tossed an enquiring look at Mary, who shook her head earnestly.

'No, my lady! No. I have not said anything! I *swear*!'

Perry recovered his aplomb and executed a hasty bow that did not lack respect. His hair was almost impossibly golden, and his eyes were a true periwinkle-blue. Of medium height and lean but strong build, he was a dashing figure in Henry's royal colours, and Cicely could understand why Mary was attracted to him. But this intrusion was unforgivable. Mary *knew* that complete secrecy was essential.

'What have you to say for yourself, Mary?'

Perry hastened to exonerate the maid. 'Mary did not know I would come here like this, my lady. The fault is all mine.'

'So, Master Perrings, you are here simply to be with her?'

He shuffled uncomfortably. 'Yes, my lady.'

'For no other purpose?' Cicely watched him carefully.

'No, my lady. I speak the truth. Seeing Mary is my sole intention.'

He sounded sincere, Cicely thought. 'Give me a good reason why I should not have you arrested and reported to the king?'

'His Majesty?' He was horrified.

The expression on his face was sufficient to tell Cicely he did not know Henry was so close by. It was reassuring, but not entirely. 'You are a squire in the royal household, are you not, Master Perrings?'

'Temporarily, yes, my lady.' He continued. 'Please, I implore you, this was no more than a lover's foolishness, a desire to be with my sweetheart. I will swear it upon any saint you name.'

Cicely gazed at him. There was something about this incident that did not rest easily with her. It was more than simply a lovers' tryst. Was Stephen Perrings *really* just Mary's swain? She held his gaze. 'Temporarily in the king's household, sir. In whose household are you usually situated?'

'I am Sir Humphrey Talbot's esquire, my lady.'

Cicely was shaken, for Tal's was the last name she expected. Why had Mary not mentioned this? The maid *knew* the link to Tal would be a matter of great interest to her mistress. 'Well, Master Perrings, you may be sure I will tell Sir Humphrey that I disapprove of your conduct. Now, please leave, but before you do, you are to help Mary to secure the window through which you were so easily able to break in.'

'Yes, my lady.'

'And if I *ever* find you like this again, Mary will be dismissed. I trust you have enough regard to spare her that.'

The maid was stricken, but Stephen was at pains to reassure her. 'I do hold you in such regard, Mary. Truly.' He looked at Cicely. 'You will never have cause to chastise me again, Lady Welles.'

'That had better be so, Master Perrings. Now go. Do not make a sound. And once you are away from here, you are not to speak of this. I have no desire for the world to learn how ill-protected this house has been.'

Stephen bowed again, and reached for his hat, which he had tossed on to a chair. It had a sprig of periwinkle tucked behind the simple brooch. Bowing again, he hurried out, and Mary followed, choking back sobs. They were very quiet as they descended to the ground floor, and then there was a long silence before the maid returned, to find her mistress waiting. 'Which window was it?' Cicely asked.

'The scullery, my lady. The catch does not look broken, but it is. Perry and I tied it firmly and then put all manner of pots and pans on the ledge. There will be a terrible clatter if it falls. I let him out through the kitchen door. And locked it securely,' she added hastily.

'Mary, I regard this very seriously. By all means see him again, but your assignations will take place elsewhere. And you are never, *never* to divulge anything you may know of my private affairs. Is that completely understood?'

'Yes, my lady, but I have not said anything. Truly. I vow on my aunt's life.'

If he was Tal's man, he might know too much anyway, Cicely thought, but such an important vow was evidence of the maid's veracity. 'Why did you not tell me he was Sir Humphrey's man?'

'I did not know, my lady. Tonight was the first time he said anything. I thought he was in His Majesty's household permanently.'

An impression given in order to appear more important in his sweetheart's eyes, Cicely guessed.

'I love him very much,' Mary went on. 'My aunt once told me that the periwinkle flower would one day mean everything to me, and that I would bear its name. I pray she is right.'

Cicely smiled. 'Well, now he has been caught in your bedchamber, *I* will see that she *is* right. He will make an honest creature of you, or rue it.'

The maid blushed again. 'I. . .do not know if he wishes to marry me.'

'He should have thought of that before he indulged in this escapade. But I think you may rest assured that he wishes to make you his wife. It is in his eyes when he looks at you, and was certainly in his voice when he leapt to your defence. I will warrant he gave you the sweetest and most loving of kisses before he departed.'

'Yes, my lady, he did.'

'Mary, would it be advisable for a wedding to take place as soon as possible?'

'I am not with child, my lady!'

'Yet. Tell me, have things reached a point where you might very well become so?'

The maid's crimson cheeks were all the answer needed.

A swift wedding *would* be prudent, Cicely decided emphatically as she returned to her bedchamber and removed her robe.

Henry awoke. *'Cariad?'* he murmured drowsily, and stretched out a hand. 'Come back to bed.'

She allowed him to draw her down into his arms. The scent of cloves was pleasing as she curled as close to him as she could, and hid her face against his shoulder. 'Hold me tight, Henry,' she whispered.

He did as she asked. 'What is it, *cariad?* I know all is not well. Why were you up?'

She had the wit to adhere as much to the truth as she could. 'There was a draught and it awakened me. I thought I heard something on the landing, and, and then I remembered the rats. What if it was *not* rats we heard earlier? I am frightened for you, Henry.' And she was, yet she herself had thought of killing him tonight! Of killing Harri Tudur, for Harri was the one she was with now.

'I am well and safe, here with you, sweetheart.' He leaned over to kiss her.

Later, the sky was luminous as sunrise began to burn away a low dawn mist that had crept up from the Thames meadows and settled in a shallow blanket over the town. Henry stood by the window. He had pushed the shutters aside to admit more cool air.

Because he was in profile, she could see his virility, soft and heavy now as it emerged silkily from the tangle of hairs at his crotch. 'You may be observed from the square, Your Majesty,' she murmured.

He glanced around. 'I doubt if I would be recognized without my regal trappings.'

'Your face is your fate, Henry Tudor. Far too memorable. Please come away from the window. Or do you *want* the world to see the royal yard swinging in the breeze?' She stretched luxuriously.

He smiled and made much of looking down at the yard in question. 'Damn you, lady. It would take more than this to make such a prodigious organ swing.' He glanced out again. 'I must leave in a few minutes, so cease your tempting writhing, for it reminds me too much of strawberries.'

Neither of them would forget a May night at Westminster. The sumptuousness of the bed, their nakedness, the crushed fruit on her breasts, her navel, and between her legs. The softness of his tongue, the iron-hardness of his loins. The laughter when they rolled over a little too far and fell to the floor, where they made love again on rare white sable furs presented to him by Master Pasmer. Oh, such sweetly erotic hours. There had been no thought at all of royal blood, of York, Lancaster, Plantagenet or Tudor, just of being lovers.

His gaze caressed her. 'That was one of the happiest nights of my entire life, *cariad*, and I will always give thanks for it.' Almost embarrassed by emotion, he cleared his throat and spoke of something else. 'Do you enjoy watching the jousts?'

'Of course. Does not everyone?' She sat up. 'Not that I have attended such an event in a long time.

'I have decided there will be jousting at Windsor this Hallowtide. In the upper ward, where Edward III decided such things should be held. And there will be disguisings, merriment and generous entertainments.'

She pretended to be shocked. 'You intend to *spend*?'

'Any more of that and you will not be invited.' He returned to the bed, from which he pulled her up into his embrace. Then he slid his hands down to her buttocks, and pressed her against his loins. 'Oh, how I want you again, *cariad,* but one thing will lead to another. . .and another.' He kissed the top of her head. 'I really must return to the abbey and pretend to have slept like a babe in Sante's miraculous bed. But first I must dress, or my prodigious organ will swing left and right all the way across the square.'

She laughed, and helped him to don his rich clothing. He placed her robe around her, and took her hands to stretch them down. Then he swayed, so slightly she might almost be dreaming it. She swayed too, as if to the sound of minstrels in an adjacent room. There was something entrancing deep within this man. It found its way past the crimes of which he was undoubtedly guilty. . .as well as those of which she feared yet to learn.

'Now then, Lady Welles,' he whispered in her ear, 'I know there is something preying upon your mind. What is it?'

'There is nothing.' But there was. She was trying not to face it, but a raw anxiety gnawed through her whenever her guard was down.

'Liar, lady. Just as you can read me, so I can read you. Let me guess. It is not your fool of a husband, because we have already spoken of him, so who else? Your son by Richard?'

Now it was said aloud, she could no longer pretend. Tears sprang to her and she could not speak.

'What concerns you about him, *cariad?*' Henry asked.

She drew back awkwardly. 'You—you *would* tell me if you were looking for him, would you not?'

At first he was nonplussed, then hurt and disappointed. 'You have so little faith in me? We have a pact, remember? We each protect the secret of the other's son. I have honoured that. So, what has happened?'

'I have not heard anything of him for two months.'

Leo was the most precious thing in her life, a living reminder of Richard, who had never known she was even with child. She had not known herself until after Bosworth. Henry was a danger to Leo, pact or not, because there was Harri Tudur. . .and there was Henry Tudor.

York flowed richly through Leo's veins, albeit from an incestuous union, but even so he might be dangerous enough in Henry's eyes to warrant being imprisoned. Or done away with completely. That was why the boy was hidden on the Isle of Wight, in the custody of trustworthy Will Kymbe, Mary and Tom's cousin, who had always sent word once a month. Now two months had passed without news, and she was growing more distraught by the day. It was reassuring to know that Tom had gone there. . .but what if he found bad news waiting? What if Leo had had an accident? What if the sweating sickness had visited the island?

Henry's face had hardened as he released her. 'Two months' silence, and you immediately wonder if I have not only found Leo, but *taken* him? Maybe even disposed of him?'

She sensed his darker self. 'No, I do not really think you have done anything. Oh, forgive me. Please. I am simply over-anxious and beginning to clutch at any possibility, no matter how unlikely. I *know* you would not do anything like this, and I would probably ask the same of the Angel Gabriel at the moment.' Her large eyes implored, and she used all the immense Plantagenet charm at her disposal.

'Gabriel? You list me alongside the archangels?' His face softened again. 'My darling, I have no idea where your son is, let alone instructed that anything be done to him. Truly, I do *not* have him. Please, trust me, as I trust you.'

Her arms slipped around his waist, and she leaned her cheek against his chest. 'I do trust you,' she lied.

To her relief he embraced her again. 'I am sure all is well with Leo.'

'When will I see you next? You are returning to Windsor today, and—'

'And will be much occupied with affairs of state for the coming weeks, maybe months. But be assured that I will send for you whenever I can. I need you as I need to breathe.' He kissed her again. A parting kiss. 'If you want my help regarding Leo, you have only to tell me. Trust me, I can have him returned to you without delay. And take note, I mean it when I say "returned to you".'

With that he retrieved his dagger from the wall and left. She watched from the window as he walked anonymously toward the gatehouse, seeming to wade through the threads of the mist, which was only waist-deep. As the vapour coiled and eddied, she heard him cough once, then he was lost from view.

Suddenly a male voice addressed her from the bedchamber doorway. 'There he goes, like Beelzebub into the belching bowels of Hell.'

Whirling about, she saw Tal standing there, tapping his black hat against his leg. Alarmed, she glanced quickly outside again, but Henry had gone and all seemed well.

Making an effort to appear calm, she closed the casements and shutters and then faced her unwelcome visitor.

Chapter Six

SIR HUMPHREY TALBOT, Marshal of Calais, was a lean, strongly built, engagingly confident man in his mid-fifties. Being the youngest son of the Earl of Shrewsbury's second marriage, no Talbot titles would ever come his way unless a host of siblings and nephews should conveniently pass away. Nor would the de l'Isle titles or lands of his mother's family come to him, because she too had been married before, with other children who benefited. It was Tal's lot to have all the connections but none of the prizes.

His shrewd eyes were a striking green, and his long sun-bleached hair was streaked with grey. Many years of sea air had tanned his complexion, and as always, he looked as if two weeks or more had passed since a razor last touched his chin.

Fashion did not figure highly in Humphrey Talbot's scheme of things, so that his black leather boots disappeared under a rather well-worn calf-length gown of olive-green leather. Beneath the gown was a white shirt, its laces dangling loose from the frilled neckline. A knightly girdle rested low on his hips, with a sword, purse and dagger, and around his neck was a heavy gold chain from which hung a jewelled crucifix and a gold pectoral of St Catherine's wheel.

He had already been on pilgrimage to Rome, and had recently approached Henry for a licence to go to St Catherine's Monastery on Mount Sinai. There was much of the crusader knight about him—maybe even the Templar. Cicely was always susceptible to scents and fragrances. Henry was cloves, Jack was thyme, Jon was rosemary and Richard had been mint and costmary. This man was cinnamon, bringing thoughts of far warmer lands than the temperate climate of his homeland in Shropshire and the Welsh marches.

He always touched a nerve in her, because of his unerring ability to irritate and stir mistrust, and there were times when she could see in his eyes that he was laughing at her. As he was now! She was furious. First the intrusion of his esquire, and now the master himself was brazen enough to come right into her *bedchamber*!

She strove for dignity. 'Why are you here, Sir Humphrey?'

'Oh, dear, so it is to be Sir Humphrey? How very chill and formal between friends.' The Welsh Marches were in his accent as he straightened from the door and came closer. 'Forgive me, Cicely, I know I should not be here. Our friendship needs a little mending, it seems.'

Her anger snapped. '*Mending*? Like *this*? You enter my house uninvited and proceed to my private chamber? I wonder you bothered to wait until Henry had left!'

'Cicely—'

'You have been spying on me *and* set others to spy on me too. Then everything is relayed to Abbot Sante! Last night you even sent your esquire to pry. Mary Kymbe loves him, and I had convinced myself he was sincere toward her, but it seems not. I detest you, Humphrey Talbot!'

His expression had become impenetrable. 'I should be accustomed to your tirades by now, but you still amaze me every time. Why is it so often like this between us, Cicely? You are another version of my wife. One look at me and you have to find every fault under the sun, although, thanks be to God, you have not yet attempted to skewer me. Or bring Woden's wrath about my unfortunate Christian ears.'

His wife, the former Jane Champernowne, was no longer quite sane. Her obsessive devotion to Woden had so loosened her mind that the only person with whom she was now able to live in some semblance of peace was Tal's sister, the Duchess of Norfolk, at Kenninghall in Norfolk.

'Cicely, Perrings came here of his own accord, and his purpose was entirely amorous. He did not know I would be here, and still has no idea. I saw him, but he did not see me.'

'That had best be the truth, sir, because if your activities cause my maid any distress—' Her thoughts broke off. Just how many people had been creeping around this house during the night? It verged on the absurd!

'It *is* the truth.'

Cicely searched his eyes in the half light. 'Well, if not Master Perrings, you have certainly set *someone* to watch whatever goes on in this house.'

Surprise lit his eyes. 'Have I indeed? Clearly I issue orders in my sleep.'

'You deny it?'

'Of course. Cicely, it may come as a surprise, but my every waking moment is *not* spent engrossed in you.'

The cutting response reddened her cheeks. 'For which I certainly give thanks,' she replied on a similar note. 'How many times have you tittle-tattled to Sante about this house?'

'Never.'

'What about the spies across the market place?'

'What spies across the market place?' he responded exasperatedly.

She told him about Romulus and Remus, and he spread his hands. 'They are nothing to do with me. Maybe with Sante, or maybe even with Henry, but not me. Nor will they have seen me here. How impossibly mistrustful you are.'

'You have given me ample reason to be so, Humphrey Talbot, after all, I once overheard you say you would take Leo away from me.'

He groaned. 'For which I have grovelled ever since. Well, I am not about to grovel again. If Sante is involved in something at the moment, he has not included me.'

Her thoughts turned to all manner of other reasons for his presence. 'Surely you do not have more thoughts of killing Henry?'

'Because killing kings is my forte?' He was scathing.

'Oh, adopt that tone if you must, but the fact remains that you *have* been quite active in that pursuit.' He had indeed, having attempted to stab Henry at Esher, and before that, along with Jon Welles, he had poisoned her father. Both men had family grudges to avenge.

'Use your common sense, lady, provided you still have any. Last night I had several opportunities to put an end to Tudor, but chose not to because it would have meant him expiring in *your* bed. Which, on reflection, is probably no more than you deserve.'

Heat stained her cheeks.

Tal spoke with deep-seated bitterness. 'I make no excuse for disposing of your cursed father. He broke my sister Eleanor's heart and she loved him too much to expose him for the viper he was. She was his rightful queen, but he left her for your mother. When Richard came to the throne, he did the right and honourable thing by my sister, declaring her marriage to have been true, which is why I still support his cause to this day. And his line,' he added deliberately, bringing Leo into the room. 'And now we have your precious Tudor, destroying her again for his own dynastic ambitions. I wish to God my attack on him at Esher had been successful. That day was her birthday, if you recall.'

'And you were in drink.' But remorse crept through Cicely. 'Tal, I do know how you feel. Truly. But when will you learn that trespassing in the houses of others is too dangerous? It was what very nearly brought about Jack's death at Knole last Christmas.' Tal and Jack had secretly observed on the night Henry first met his inconveniently legitimate son, Roland de Vielleville, who had been newly brought over from Brittany. The Yorkist intruders had barely escaped.

Tal was irritated. 'Your precious husband threw the dagger, but if Jack had died, it would have been privately, at the hands of your royal lover!'

'Henry says he was trying to *save* Jack, but was knocked unconscious from behind by an unseen assailant.'

'And you, my beautiful Plantagenet gull, want to believe him.' Tal laughed cynically 'The fact is that if I had not gone back for Jack, Tudor would have tortured him to death. *I* was the one who saved Jack, whom I love as a son, and I thoroughly enjoyed kicking Tudor in the balls. It was a pity he was senseless on the floor at the time!'

'The only person who could say whether it is Henry or you telling the truth is Jack, and he cannot remember.'

'How flattering of you to be so impartial,' Tal observed acidly. 'Tudor robbed the world of Richard, but *you,* Richard's niece and lover, choose to believe *him* over me.'

'That is not fair', she replied stiffly.

'Oh, yes it is.'

There was a stony silence, during which his glance moved to where the dagger had been in the panels.

She saw. 'So, *you* were in the wall?'

'I do not deny it. You clearly do not intend to divulge much of what Tudor says, so when I saw a chance to eavesdrop upon you, I took it.'

'Would you tell *me* every detail of *your* sweet whispers with your mistress?'

'I have no mistress, but if I did, I doubt that she would be of the same immense significance as Henry Tudor. Cicely, if you choose to tell him I have come here like this, I will be trussed in a sack with my dick in my mouth, then dumped in the Thames before the Lord's Prayer can be said over my sad remains.'

'I am hardly likely to tell Henry you have been in my bedchamber.'

'I suppose not. Your royal *inamorato* almost gutted me, by the way. And before you set about me for watching your passionate frolics with him, let me assure you that I did not *see* a thing. Wood is rather inclined to be opaque. It also muffles conversation, so that I hardly heard anything either. It was most disappointing. Lady, if you are under scrutiny, *I* am not the scrutiniser. My guess would be that Henry himself is behind any spying. He may love you, but he does not trust *anyone.* Oh, Cicely, you are becoming perilously attached to the fellow.'

She could not answer.

'I know it started because of his threats, but now part of you is more than willing. He is the enemy of all you hold dear, including Richard, Jack, the Kymbes and your son, but *still* you enjoy squirming beneath him. He can be so appealing—like a sad little puppy—that he melts your palpitating Yorkist heart. And he knows it! He preys upon your riven soul, and the erotic reward he gains from your sympathy and surrender is so great that I wonder he can walk afterwards!'

'Please leave.'

'I have a message from Jack.'

Hope leapt. 'You have seen him?'

'Yes. Briefly. One night, out in the marshes near Calais during my recent fleeting visit. I am to tell you he cannot bear being away from you, and intends to return in the autumn, albeit for a short time only. He will let me know when and where.'

'I miss him so,' she whispered, tears stinging her eyes.

'I am sure Tudor's prick compensates.'

'Are you jealous perchance? After all, your prick does not have a great deal to do.'

He smiled.

She felt guilty for the taunt. 'Thank you for telling me.'

'Oh, the sound of teeth being drawn.'

She hesitated. 'What do you know of Abbot Sante?'

'I am a neighbour and know him well. He is a good man.'

'Why have you and Jack never mentioned him?'

'No need arose.'

'Yet you told him about me.'

'No, Master Pasmer told him about you. Pasmer believed

the abbot should know because you would be here, in this house. Our merchant friend will be chastised, you may be sure of that, but not too much, for he is very useful to our cause.'

'Tal, were you really unaware about Stephen Perrings?'

'I have told you so, have I not?'

'Well, you certainly know now, and I believe it warrants him marrying my maid.'

'She has been compromised?'

She gave him a look. 'Of *course* she has. He was in her bedchamber in the middle of the night.'

Tal raised an eyebrow. 'Has he got her with child?'

'No, but only by luck, is my guess. As his master, I expect you to attend to whatever responsibilities you have in these matters. He is going to do the correct thing by Mary, and you, sir, are going to see that he can afford to keep her well. Do I make myself clear?'

'Oh, abundantly. You are apportioning my money for me.' But he smiled and held up his hands in a gesture of surrender. 'Yes, yes, I will do it all.'

'See that you do.' She breathed out slowly, needing to speak of something else. 'Tal, who is this new Yorkist claimant of whom both Henry and Abbot Sante have spoken? I am told he greatly resembles my father.'

'Then he may well be one of your brothers. Cicely, whatever is going on, Jack has not conveyed anything to me. I do not think he knows.' He went to the window to peer through a small slit in the closed shutters. 'One thing I *did* hear Tudor say to you was a monstrous untruth.'

'What?' Her heart began to sink.

'That if you want his help regarding Leo, you have only to tell him, and he, virtuous St Harri, will have him returned to you without delay.'

'He meant it. Every word.' But her fingers were crossed in the folds of her robe.

'Then you are fooled again. Firstly, there is a fairly mundane reason why you have not heard of your son for so long. I received word from Master Pasmer—who has contacts on Wight and is aware of Leo's presence on the island—that the Kymbe cousin who has care of your boy, has been unwell and has not paid the messenger who usually brings word to you. The messenger refuses to act again until that payment is made. I went to Wight immediately, and encountered Tom Kymbe, who had also gone there concerning Leo. We found Wight crawling with Henry's men. Cicely, he is having every corner of the island scoured for a boy answering Leo's description.'

Cicely stared at him, stricken. No, Henry would not have lied about this. He *could* not!

'Tom and I stole Leo, and took him to Kingston, where my sister fusses over him like a bejewelled hen with but one chick, and Tom keeps watch. Cicely, I do not for a moment imagine Henry's purpose is to give Leo fond hugs and kisses.

She felt numb. 'How can you be so sure they were Henry's agents?'

'Royal livery *is* rather telltale.' Tal replied a little trenchantly. 'They were likely to happen upon the Kymbe house in Fishbourne at any moment, so Tom and I took your son before he could fall into their hands. Tudor lied to you, here, not half an hour since. If your boy had fallen into his clutches, what do you think your dear Harri Tudur would do? Mm? Return him to his mother's loving Yorkist arms? I think not. You may be sure that Richard's son would soon be no more, even though the murder of children is regarded as one of the most shocking and detestable killings of all. Which is why Tudor accuses Richard of that very crime. Sweet Harri will then be convincing about what he tells you, because his bed would be very cold and empty without you, and he would not want *that*.'

Cicely's heart felt as if it were being wrung.

'You have to accept it, my lady.' Tal pushed the shutters

open again, and the pale new day lightened her face. 'Oh, and by the way, do you actually wish to know if Leo is well?' The tone was acerbic.

She struggled for the spirit to respond in kind. 'Well, I hardly imagine you would have come here if he had fallen ill in your custody. Better to hold your tongue and I might never learn the truth.'

He inclined his head. 'How well you think you know me. Be that as it may, my wish now is to take you to him today, unless. . .maybe you have so little faith in me that you would rather not come to Kingston after all? Perhaps I will do away with you as well? Now there's a thought.'

'How ungallant you are to taunt me. Is it the best you can manage?' Her eyes were bright with unshed tears, which she would rather he could not see, but knew he did.

He relented. 'Leo is well and happy, overjoyed to see Tom again and asking for Mistress Kymbe. My sister expects me to return with you, so I hope you will do so. You already have Henry's consent.'

'If the duchess knows I am Leo's mother, does she also know who his father is?'

Tal shifted uncomfortably. 'Yes. But you may trust her completely.'

Silence fell, and he went to pour some wine. She shook her head at his enquiring look. He put the jug down, and then returned to her. 'I have already sent word to Jon at Sheriff Hutton, and pray he will come as quickly as possible.'

'I cannot say that he will.'

'Why? What is wrong?'

'Did you not overhear? Perhaps you dozed a few moments, for to be sure Henry knows and spoke of it during the night. He tells me that Jon has a new love in the north. A serious matter of the heart, I believe. Henry claims not to know her identity, but I think he does.'

'Henry is quite capable of inventing such a thing in order

to drive a wedge between you and Jon,' Tal observed shrewdly.

'Not this time. I can tell. Henry is not always impassive, and last night I knew he really had heard something. I am such a fool, Tal. It did not even occur to me that Jon would have a new mistress.'

'You can hardly blame him.'

'I know.' She needed no reminding of her own failings.

'Cicely, you make no secret of feeling a great deal for Jon Welles, so you may count upon it that Henry is jealous. He covets you, and it would be just like him to drip with arsenic. Or puff out his vulture's wings, talons at the ready. *Anything* to shatter your marriage.'

'He has no need to shatter it, Jon is doing that quite well by himself.' She told him of the distance and coolness that now ruled in the Welles match. 'It is no brief parting, Tal, so I doubt very much if he will respond to your summons.'

He heard the slight tremor in her voice. 'Oh, Cicely, *cariad,* I am sorry about this. Truly.'

It was always strange to hear him use the same Welsh endearment as Henry, even though he had grown up with the language, but this time it almost proved her undoing. Her lips trembled and she struggled not to give in to tears. She would not cry, she would *not!* 'Why apologize? It is my fault, not yours, that Jon seeks his pleasures elsewhere.'

'It is my fault that you view me with suspicion regarding Leo.' Tal deliberately steered away from Jon Welles. 'Please believe that I would never harm your boy, and certainly would not take him without your consent. . .unless it was for his safety. Which is the case now.'

'I know,' she conceded reluctantly, 'it is just that I really do not want to believe Henry has been lying to me. But I *do* understand your motives in opposing him in secret, because I know how much Eleanor meant to you.'

'Good. It is settled then,' he said with typical male

bluntness. 'The weather has been good recently, so the roads are firm and dry. We can be in Kingston this afternoon and you will see that Leo is in perfect health and complete safety.'

'I wish I *could* leave so immediately, Tal, but I dare not.'

He frowned. 'Why? Tudor is not coming back, and leaves for Windsor this morning.'

'Exactly. I must wait until he has departed. He will emerge beneath the gatehouse, and look toward this house to see me. I *must* be at the window.'

'Oh, the rosy world of lovebirds. But I acknowledge the point you make. We wait.'

'*We* do not wait, Tal, *I* do. I want you to quit this house now. And there must not be any chance at all of your being seen, so you are *not* to leave by the front entrance. You must creep out the back way, just as you no doubt crept in. Somehow. Please come to the main entrance when Henry has gone beyond the town. All will appear acceptable, should Henry have set a spy on me.' *Someone* had set Romulus and Remus to their task, and she was obliged to suspect Henry. If he lied about Leo, then he was capable of lying about everything else. Excepting that he loved her.

'As you wish.'

She searched his face. 'Is there any more word from Brittany? I know you and Jack are awaiting fresh documents to prove Henry's marriage to a woman named Tiphaine de Rieux. And that Roland is the result of that union,' she added.

'You even know her name?' Tal smiled. 'My, my, how Henry does trust you. No, there's no word yet.' His lips tightened with frustration and he struck a fist against a bedpost. 'We had all the proof we needed! If that damned cat had not caused the fire in in St Andrew-by-the-Wardrobe! If it *was* a cat, of course.'

'You think there is an Iscariot in our midst?'

'It has to be feared. If I had to suspect anyone, it would be Henry's scribe, Fryon. That damned Frenchman serves too many masters. As to the lost documents, fortunately there are still people in Brittany who know what happened when Tudor was held there. The old priest is prepared to confess it anew if the price is right. Through Sante, I will pay them handsomely, and this time any papers' whereabouts will not be divulged to anyone. *À bientôt*, Lady Welles.'

Turning abruptly on his heel, he left her. His steps descended the stairs and then she heard nothing more. He did not leave the house by the front entrance.

Chapter Seven

THE MIST HAD long gone as trumpets, church bells and shouts heralded the royal procession's departure from the abbey. Henry rode alone at the head of his glittering entourage. The sun was bright, gleaming on his circlet and collar. He wore blue cloth-of-gold, and was every inch the sovereign as the cavalcade passed through the crowds that had gathered again.

There were two processions, because Abbot Sante was accompanying the king as far the bridge over the Thames. The abbot was dressed in the finest black silk with a dazzling mitre, but although he displayed jewels, he was careful not to rival the king. He rode on a handsome mule that had a gilded bridle and rich saddle, and behind him was a line of monks.

Henry looked across the thronged square to the window, smiled and raised his gauntleted hand to the woman who meant so much to him. She had sent word to him that she was leaving shortly for Kingston l'Isle, and she felt his silent support for her visit to the holy well.

Her heart was heavy as she returned the wave. How she hoped she appeared as natural as the previous day, but was it possible now that Tal had told her about events on the Isle of Wight? She wished she could trust Henry more. Her conscience pricked. Being untrustworthy was not his sole preserve, for she trod a deceitful path of her own.

The double cavalcade moved on down the street toward the Thames. Just before passing out of sight, the King of England turned in the saddle to look back yet one more time.

A little later it was plump Remus who watched from across the square as Cicely and Mary emerged to accompany Tal and his retinue to Kingston l'Isle. The shabby spy toyed with the strap end of his belt, and twirled an ear of wheat between his teeth as the small band clattered away from John Pasmer's house. The mounted men-at-arms wore Talbot green and the silver hound badge, and Perry numbered among them. There was one exception to the green, a burly, blond German dressed in the immaculate blue-and-yellow striped leather of a Landsknecht mercenary.

Cicely was relieved when a corner took them from Remus's view. What would he and Romulus do now? Follow? If so, might they see Leo and know he was the child Henry sought? She faced ahead nervously as her party crossed the bridge over the small River Ock, which flowed into the Thames. A glance back showed only the empty road as they left Abingdon and went south across the Vale of the White Horse toward the distant shimmering haze of the Downs. It was a landscape of rich, flat farmland, with soil that became increasingly streaked with chalk, until it was white in places. The sky was blue, the sun was bright and birdsong was shrill across pastures where wild flowers bloomed. Lying close to the foot of the escarpment, about seven miles ahead as the crow flew, was King Alfred the Great's birthplace, the town of Wantage.

Narrow strips of dense woodland flanked the road as the riders approached a shallow ford, but before reaching it, Mary sensed something behind them. 'We are being followed, my lady.'

They both reined in to look back, but there was only a farm boy they had just passed as he drove hogs toward Abingdon. Whoever it was must be taking care to keep out of sight, Cicely thought in dismay.

Tal had heard and joined them. 'I see no one,' he said.

'I cannot *see* him, Sir Humphrey,' Mary responded, 'but he is there.'

Tal knew the maid's intuition should be heeded, and beckoned the raw-boned Landsknecht, whose name was

Friedrich, and who Cicely now knew had been among the two thousand such German pikemen and foot soldiers who had fought valiantly for Jack at Stoke Field. Friedrich was in his forties, with a very precise, smooth beard and wide-set grey eyes. His fair hair formed a noticeable peak on his forehead, and his jaw had a very firm set. The silver hound badge was pinned proudly on his breast.

'Sir Humphrey?' He had a heavy German accent, and rolled the "r" of Tal's name.

'Friedrich, ride back through the trees. Keep out of sight, and if you see *anyone,* I want to know. But be wary and do nothing. Is that clear? Just report to me.'

'*Ja,* Sir Humphrey.'

'Take Perrings too. He should have some true business to attend to. Idle weeks around the king have softened him. He needs sharpening up if he is to attend to his forthcoming marital duties.' Tal winked at Mary, who went very pink.

As the two riders disappeared into the trees, where the soft, mossy ground deadened their hoofbeats, Cicely looked anxiously at Tal. 'If we are followed, we will lead someone to Leo.'

'We will not lead anyone anywhere, Cicely. Trust me.'

'But—'

'Trust me,' he repeated quietly. '*Cariad,* you should know by now that my cherubic exterior is very deceptive.' Then he turned his horse to continue to the ford, where they all paused to refresh the horses.

Some time passed before Friedrich and Perry returned. 'A single rider, Sir Humphrey,' the Landsknecht said, 'but he sensed us and rode off. Perrings is sure he has seen him before. By ze abbey gateway in Abingdon.'

Perry nodded 'Yes, Sir Humphrey, I am sure it was the same man. I could not see him in great detail, but he was tall in the saddle and very thin, with hair the colour of polished copper, although much dirtier, I would guess.'

Romulus, Cicely thought, her heart plummeting.

'His horse is chestnut with four long white stockings,' Perry continued. 'I would know both again.'

Friedrich nodded too.

Tal looked enquiringly at Cicely.

'It fits Romulus,' she answered.

He smiled faintly. 'Do not fear for Leo. He will be safe. You have my word.'

They rode on to Wantage, where they halted at the busy White Hart in the market place. Tal received a hearty welcome from the balding, pot-bellied landlord, with whom he was clearly very well acquainted. Drawing the man aside, he indicated a particularly large white horse in an adjacent paddock.

Cicely imagined Tal was buying it, because money changed hands and both men seemed well pleased, but when he returned to her he did not explain.

'You and the landlord seem friendly,' she observed, for something to say, his silence seeming rather pointed.

'Yes. Bassington was a longbowman and served me at Calais, but he broke his shoulder badly, and became unable to draw his bow. Because he was a good man, and once saved my life with a particularly timely arrow, I considered myself to be in his debt, so I saw that he had a suitable pension, and gave him the White Hart, which had always been his ambition.'

'That was very kind of you.'

'It was no more than I owed and he deserved. Come, we need to eat.'

Bassington could not have done more to ensure the new arrivals' comfort, ushering them to the best trestle board by an unglazed window that would be shuttered every night or in bad weather, and that faced the thronged square. Cicely sat with her back to the scene outside, opposite Tal, and they were served with plain but wholesome fare—bread, cheese, ham, ale and wine. The men-at-arms stayed outside beneath a shady, wide-spreading tree.

Mary, seated inside with Perry and Friedrich, noticed something in the square, and nudged Perry to make him look. His face changed, and after exchanging an urgent glance with Friedrich, hurried over to Tal. 'By your leave, Sir Humphrey, if you look outside at that man by the horse trough. I am *certain* he was the one who followed us earlier. Friedrich agrees.'

Cicely's heart sank anew as she twisted around on the bench. Yes, it was Romulus, with a wide-brimmed hat to give shade to his eyes, and perhaps conceal his face. He had tucked his conspicuous red hair out of sight, but one straggling, rather greasy lock had escaped to brush the shoulders of his brown coat. A worn boot rested on the trough, and he swung his horse's reins in one hand while drinking a mug of ale from the other. How foolish he was to risk standing there in full view, she thought as she nodded at Tal. 'It is the one I call Romulus.'

Tal frowned. 'This fellow begins to irritate me. Does he think I am a simpleton? He must be dealt with.'

'Be careful, Tal,' Cicely said quickly. 'If he *is* Henry's man, it will be dangerous to do anything to him.'

'It will be even more dangerous not to. Romulus is going to disappear, and it will be some time before it is realized. By then some secure plans will have been made for Leo's further protection and fresh concealment.'

'What if Remus is somewhere here as well?'

'I will root him out as a pig does a truffle.'

Friedrich was summoned, and Tal indicated Romulus. 'Dispose of him. *Verstehen Sie*?'

Friedrich grinned. 'Oh, *ja, wirklich*, Sir Humphrey.'

Cicely watched how quickly he unpinned his livery badge. It was not the first time such a task had been required of him.

Tal looked at Perry. 'You go with him. It is time to be fully initiated in my little ways. Be aware of the possibility of a second man. He is – ?' He raised an eyebrow at Cicely.

'Shorter, very plump, dark, with a limp. About the same age,' she responded.

Tal leaned across to take her summer mantle, which Mary had placed earlier on the edge of the table, and pressed it upon Perry. She did not hear what was said next, because Tal rose to speak confidentially. Perry looked embarrassed, but followed Friedrich out into the yard.

Tal resumed his seat, and refilled Cicely's cup of wine.

'I am still to trust you?' she enquired.

He smiled. 'Always.'

A few minutes later there was a clatter and commotion as a small, swift party of riders, apparently including Cicely, dashed out into the square. "Cicely" was Perry, enveloped in her mantle and riding her palfrey. Romulus was caught off guard, but then flung his mug away and mounted to give pursuit.

Tal sat back with a satisfied smile. 'That, my friend, was the worst decision of your life,' he said softly.

The rest of the party left Wantage shortly afterwards. Cicely now rode Mary's pony, while the maid had a small mare, hired at the White Hart. They travelled west along the ancient Icknield Way, which breasted the lower slopes of the Downs. Another such track, the Ridgeway, ran parallel along the top of the escarpment. No one knew the age of these roads, only that they were believed to have been created by magic. Perhaps by Merlin himself.

The Downs loomed in an almost inviting way, Cicely thought. Up there the summer air would be fresh with wild thyme, and one would find ancient monuments, such as Wayland Smith and the White Horse. This part of England felt mysterious and almost enchanted, she mused, as if every myth and legend in the world had started here. The very daylight seemed to tingle, and occasionally there was such a silence that she could even sense the beating of the earth's heart. She stole a surreptitious glance at Tal. His pendants proclaimed his unshakably Christian beliefs, so it must have been a sickening shock to learn the truth about his wife's worship of the god Woden. It was something Cicely knew all about, and for which she sympathized with him.

By late afternoon they at last approached the final crossroad of their journey, but Tal reined in just before reaching it, his attention turning to a little-used path that disappeared northward into dense adjacent woodland. A lean black tomcat crouched there, yellow-eyed and almost menacing, and Tal glanced at it before looking skyward as two large, raucous crows swooped and fluttered around the treetops.

Cicely was curious. 'Are we going to use that path?'

'No.' Then he changed the subject by pointing the other way, to the summit of the Downs. 'There is a peculiar old sarsen stone up there, all dimpled with holes that worm right through it. If a man knows how, he can blow into it and make a booming noise that can be heard over six miles away. Bassington's brother is master of the art. The stone is said to have belonged to King Alfred. When he needed to assemble his Saxon armies against the Danes at the Battle of Ashdown, the stone was used to alert his men of the enemy's approach.'

'Is it true, do you think?' Cicely asked.

'I have no idea. I was not there at the time. Old I may be, but not that old.' Tal smiled, tightening his grip as his horse danced around. 'The stone is called the Blowing Stone, and the hill—very unoriginally—is named after it. The legend is supposed to have given rise to the manor's name, King's-stone. The l'Isle part came later, when my mother's family, the de l'Isles, became lords here. I merely lease it from them.'

'Well, that has successfully diverted me from the matter of the path, has it not?' she murmured.

His green eyes were eloquent, but he said nothing.

Hoofbeats descended the hill. It was Friedrich and his companions, and Perry was now relieved of the embarrassingly ladylike mantle, which instead was flung over his pommel. There was dust and clatter as they reined in.

'Well? Did you dispose of him?' Tal asked the German.

'Oh, *ja*, Sir Humphrey. No vun vill find him now.'

'You are sure of that?'

'I know how to be rid of problems.'

'You did well. I will see you are rewarded. All of you.'

'*Danke, danke,* Sir Humphrey.' The German beamed, clearly knowing his master was a man of his word.

'Friedrich, I will miss you when you finally take your German hide home to. . .where is it? Augsberg?'

'*Ja*, Augsberg.'

Tal turned to Cicely and pointed to a column of smoke that rose perhaps a quarter of a mile to the northeast, beyond the woods. 'Do you see that smoke? It is a bonfire near the manor house. The same spot is always used, so do not fear it is the house itself.' He laughed. 'Come. We are almost there now.' He moved his horse north off the Icknield Way, on to the branch of the crossroad that led down into the vale again.

Cicely soon saw Kingston l'Isle, which was one of a number of settlements along the spring-line at the foot of the Downs. The first building they encountered was the three-hundred-year-old church of St John the Baptist, a small, sturdy structure built of a mixture of chalk and a soft limestone known as clunch. The little building had no tower or spire, only a bellcote, and seemed to grow out of the earth, as if its foundations had a tap root that reached into the bedrock. She would learn that it had supposedly been founded to protect the village against pagan worship on nearby White Horse Hill and at Wayland Smith.

A young priest emerged from the porch, blinking in the sunshine. Sandy-haired, with a receding chin, ruddy complexion and angelic expression, he seemed almost saintly, and Cicely wondered if he had mislaid his halo.

'Welcome home, again, Sir Humphrey!'

'I have not been away long enough to warrant such enthusiasm.' Tal reined in. 'How are you, Gregory Melton?'

'In excellent spirit, Sir Humphrey.'

'Which is just as well, because I am sure the local damsels will be flocking around you, eager for your hearth, so take care.' Tal led his party on toward the fortified manor house, which rose directly behind the church.

Chapter Eight

THE MANOR HOUSE was built of the same materials as the church, and stood atop a long slope that led down to a tree-choked valley containing three large, irregular fish ponds. Cicely could see Blowing Stone Hill to the south, as well as the woods beside the Icknield Way.

Tal's residence was set protectively around an inner court, with an impressive gatehouse and a dry moat, and its prosperity was evident immediately in all the activity around it. Boys drove cows into a barn, and a small herd of goats complained from the pen that kept them away from the plums and apples beginning to ripen on some trees. There were ducks and geese around a shallow pond, and hens scratched everywhere. Women draped fresh washing over bushes, and men were busy with numerous tasks, but everyone stopped respectfully as Sir Humphrey Talbot returned. Men at the roadside snatched off their bonnets, and Cicely could feel their curiosity following her.

Crossing the moat by a wooden bridge, the riders entered the shadows beneath the gatehouse, and emerged in the wide courtyard that was noisy with horses, waggons, carts and men. To the left and right were two-storey lodgings for visitors and the more important servants. The main house was directly opposite, with the tall arched windows of the great hall to one side of a three-storeyed porch, against which honeysuckle and white roses flourished. The kitchens were to the other side of the porch, and behind them rose a tower that formed the highest point of the house.

Two men emerged from the porch entrance, Tom Kymbe and Tal's balding, thickset steward, Martin Deakin. A middle-aged countrywoman dressed in dull blue came out as well, but lingered behind the men. Her hair was tugged up beneath a crisply starched cap that was tied under her chin, and she had an amiable face. . .except when she glanced at the steward, whom she did not appear to like. Cicely decided she was probably in charge of the female and lower male servants.

A pack of small, pale, lop-eared hounds bounded excitably from an archway which Cicely imagined to lead to the stables. Talbots, she thought, recognizing them from Tal's badge. They leapt delightedly around his legs as he dismounted.

The steward assisted Cicely, and Tom gave her a quick smile before helping his sister, who was so delighted to see him again that she almost fell from her horse into his arms to hug him tightly. And then, blushing prettily, she introduced Perry as the man she wished to marry. Tom's steady hazel gaze raked the squire from head to toe. Stephen Perrings was *not* going to be accepted at face value alone.

Mary's weather-tanned brother was good-looking, with curling nut-brown hair. He was a tall, strong man in his mid-thirties, who had never taken a wife because the love of his life had been married to a cruel husband from whom she had fled. Her child by Tom, a baby boy, had died not long after birth, taking his mother with him, and leaving Tom heartbroken. It was in the guise of this lost baby that Leo had been presented to the Kymbes, who substituted him as if Tom's son had lived.

Tal came to Cicely. 'Welcome to Kingston l'Isle, Lady Welles. Leo *is* safe and I *did* bring him here for the right reason. I trust you will soon believe me.'

'I do believe you, Tal, but wish I did not.'

'Tudor will always let you down, *cariad,*' he said gently, and then changed the subject, lowering his voice. 'Cicely, although my sister knows about Leo's father, she does *not* know of my, er, regicidal tendencies.'

'I will hold my clacking tongue, sir.'

He smiled and offered her his elbow. 'Come, I know Elizabeth is anxious to meet you. . .and that you are anxious to see your boy.'

'I am. Very.'

The woman in blue stepped aside and curtsied as they reached her. 'Welcome home, Sir Humphrey.'

'Thank you, Gwen. Lady Welles, allow me to present Mistress Woodall, who is a veritable lynchpin here.'

Gwen curtseyed again. 'My lady.'

'Mistress Woodall.' Cicely inclined her head.

Tal looked at the woman. 'I trust all is well with you?' He was clearly referring to something in particular.

'Yes, sir.' But there seemed to be a hint of reservation in the woman's voice, and she glanced uneasily behind into the screen passage, where the same black tomcat from the woodland path sat on a table against the panelling. Cicely usually found cats to her liking. But not this one.

Tal scowled at the animal. 'Meet Tybalt, our premier mouser.'

Cicely noticed Gwen shudder when the creature's name was mentioned.

Mary stepped past suddenly to whisper to the animal. Its ears flattened immediately, and it growled as it leapt down again to slip into the great hall when some maids opened the door.

Cicely was puzzled. 'What did you say, Mary?'

'Old words that it understood, my lady,' was the reply. 'It is not a good cat. Never try to stroke it or win its favour.'

Gwen nodded at the maid. 'You are right, my dear. It is evil and your words are well chosen.'

Mary smiled, and Cicely knew that an immediate bond of trust had been established.

But Tal chuckled. 'Anyone who tries to stroke Tybalt will be well and truly clawed. Rodents are his business.'

With the door left open, Cicely could now see into the great hall. Trestles and benches were being set out for the next meal. There was an arched doorway in a far corner, and—

directly opposite the screens passage—an immense fireplace behind a dais. The dark roof timbers overhead were supported by brightly painted angels, each one presenting the de l'Isle arms.

Tal conducted Cicely along the screens passage and up a winding stone staircase toward the private apartments. She wanted to hurry up ahead of him, but contained herself. A king's daughter did not run! There was a small landing on the first floor. To the left was the solar, where Leo's laughter could be heard, but on the right hung a curtain that seemed to conceal a doorway.

Tal saw her look at it, and explained quickly. 'When we arrived, did you notice a tall tower? It was originally a watch tower, because it gives an unparalleled view over the vale, but it is now in a ruinous state and has been abandoned completely since a stonemason fell to his death on the worn staircase. The tower can be reached from this door, but it has been locked for years, and I doubt if anyone even knows where the key is now.'

But Cicely had already lost interest, because she heard her son's laughter turn to delighted squeals.

Tal conducted her quickly into the solar, and she halted in the doorway of the well-appointed chamber, watching Richard's son. He had changed even in the few months since she had last seen him. Taller and steadier on his feet, he reminded her so much of his father that she could only gaze at him. That smile of his would one day break hearts, she thought, as Richard's had vanquished hers.

Leo Plantagenet, known as Leo Kymbe, was now aged two years and five months. Dressed in a little knee-length green kirtle and brown leggings, he was playing amid a litter of silvery talbot puppies, watched over by their placid dam. His dark chestnut hair was cut short, and the Isle of Wight air had clearly agreed with him, for his cheeks were pink and his grey eyes shone. He giggled delightedly as the puppies gambolled around him, tails wagging.

Tal spoke in her ear. 'You see? He has come to no harm.'

Leo fell into fresh gales of laughter as he rolled on the floor and the puppies smothered his face with wet licks. His laughter stopped as he saw Cicely in the doorway, then his face brightened still more and he scrambled up, the puppies forgotten.

'Cissy! Cissy!' he cried and ran to her.

She swung him up to hug tightly. 'Oh, Leo! My lovely, lovely boy!' she breathed, closing her eyes as his arms went around her neck and he hid his face against her shoulder. She could have wept for sheer joy. Richard should be here now, and at this moment the longing for her lost love was so intense that she was almost overcome.

Figures moved by the large arched window, which had a trefoil of rich stained glass. Half a dozen ladies were there, all but one seated on the floor in front of the window. Those on the floor were ladies-in-waiting in pale, rainbow-hued gowns, but the woman on the cushioned window seat was clad in costly midnight-blue brocade embroidered with black beads and river pearls. Her hair was completely hidden by a headdress that was draped with a filmy black gauze scarf that hung down her back. An enamelled pendant against her breast was formed like a borage-blue flower, which was Elizabeth Talbot's chosen emblem. The dowager Duchess of Norfolk, was perhaps ten years younger than her brother, and of legendary beauty, with big blue eyes and a slender figure.

The duchess rose and dismissed her ladies. As they hurried out, eyes lowered, Cicely was dismayed that they had witnessed her only too maternal reunion with Leo. The list was lengthening of people who knew or might suspect. She gave him to Tal in order to sink into a respectful curtsey to Elizabeth, who accorded her the same courtesy.

'Welcome to Kingston l'Isle, Lady Welles. I am here because my brother will not come to me. He hates it when I stay too long, which I think I may well be doing.' Her voice was soft and mellifluous. She came closer, over the reflections cast by the stained glass on the rush-matted floor, and glanced fondly at Leo. 'How very like his father, he is.'

Cicely smiled, but did not otherwise respond. She had yet to gauge Tal's sister, who may not be at all pleased about receiving the daughter of Edward IV. At that moment, Lady Eleanor Talbot's shade drifted among the sunbeams.

Elizabeth was kindly. 'Your resolve to protect your son is admirable, my lady. I will be direct, and tell you I share my brother's regard for King Richard, and—forgive my forwardness—can understand your attachment to him. We cannot choose with whom we fall in love, and he was admirable as a man, duke and king. Henry Tudor, on the other hand, I will *never* like or respect.'

Tal had clearly *not* told his sister that Henry was Lady Welles' lover.

Leo was anxious to return to the puppies, and on being lowered to the floor again, rushed to pick up his favourite of the litter. 'Puppy. My puppy,' he declared.

Tal smiled. 'Does he have a name?'

'Puppy.'

'I see. But he will grow up into a hound. What will you call him then?'

'Houn'.'

Tal laughed, for the logic was simple.

Elizabeth smiled as well. 'He is charming, Lady Welles.'

'Thank you. I think so too.'

The duchess indicated the cushioned window seat. 'Come, my dear, let us be comfortable. There will be a good supper a little later, but in the meantime I have anticipated your arrival.' She indicated a table upon which stood a dish of green ginger, some honeyed titbits and a jug of quince wine.

'You are very considerate, Your Grace,' Cicely observed.

'If you address me thus, I will be obliged to be formal as well. May I venture to suggest first names? Tal has told me so much that I feel very well-acquainted with you already. Be assured, all that he said was complimentary, and will remain in confidence. Please do not fear a less than sincere welcome from me, for you are not to blame for the past.'

The oblique reference to Eleanor gave Cicely some reassurance as she cast a wry glance at Tal. Complimentary? *Everything?*

He responded with a smile of wide-eyed innocence.

Elizabeth continued, 'Your visit is to be a very enjoyable experience for you, my dear Cicely, as is the hospitality of the Talbot family. Tell me, how many ladies do you have in attendance?'

'Only one, a maid named Mary Kymbe.'

Elizabeth was taken aback. 'A king's daughter with only a single maid?'

It was such an echo of Henry and his mother to the same point that Cicely smiled. 'I am more than content with this particular maid. She is Master Kymbe's sister.'

'Ah. He is a good man of whom I approve.' Elizabeth fixed her brother with a stern look. 'Do you not have duties to attend to, sir? I am sure you wish to confer with the stalwart Master Kymbe, or that scoundrel of a steward.'

'Martin Deakin is *not* a scoundrel,' Tal growled.

'One only has to look at him not to trust him.'

'He serves me well and has *never* behaved questionably.' As Tal left, his face reflected volumes of hoping his sister would soon return to pleasantly distant Kenninghall.

Elizabeth and Cicely adjourned to the window seat, and Elizabeth smiled sadly. 'I believe this is a moment to express a regret, my dear.'

'Regret?'

'Concerning our family connection that no longer exists. No, not Eleanor. I refer to the marriage of my departed daughter, Annette, to your younger brother, the little Duke of York, whom I believe you called Dickon?'

'Yes, we did. Still do, after all, he may yet be alive.' The marriage Elizabeth referred to had been between small children. Anne Mowbray had inherited her father's great fortune and was Duchess of Norfolk in her own right. When she died suddenly, her inheritance went to Dickon, and Edward IV made sure it all stayed in royal hands. He had coldly and calculatingly robbed the Mowbrays of everything. Elizabeth had no reason at all to think fondly of the dead king who, one way or another, had done such harm to her family.

'I have lost my husband and daughter, Cicely, and I loved them both so much. I cannot pretend to possess any kind thoughts of your father, but I do not include you or King Richard in that dislike. Believe me, it has been a joy to look after your little boy for these few days. I have pretended to be a mother again. In a manner of speaking.'

Leo lost interest in the puppies for the moment and came to the window seat, wanting to sit between them and enjoy a honey cake, which he held in both hands to eat. His fingers and mouth were soon sticky, and crumbs went everywhere, but he enjoyed it. Then he licked his hands and held them up to show that they were clean again. That they were still sticky was immaterial to him.

Elizabeth's thoughts lingered on her lost husband and daughter. 'My husband was thirty-two when he died, as was Richard, but there was no battle. If anything, his was the crueller, more pointless death, for Richard died to a purpose, defending all he held dear. My John simply. . .died. One night he was hale and hearty, the next morning he was no more.'

'What happened?'

The duchess paused for a long moment. 'I believe it to have been my fault. You see, I told him the truth about Eleanor and your father, and I fear he must have let the story slip to the wrong ears. His death was not natural, and every day I wish I had never confided in him. If I had not, perhaps he would still be with me. Perhaps we would even have had another child. I still miss him.'

'You think my *father* might have had the duke killed?' Cicely was startled.

Elizabeth was belatedly tactful. 'Oh, I do not know what I think, my dear. It was all so distressing. Please do not take offence.'

Cicely put a hand on her sleeve. 'I do not take offence. My father was very wrong to treat Lady Eleanor as he did, and to retain your daughter's inheritance to your complete exclusion. And when he died, the Woodvilles had no right to set themselves against Richard.'

'Just remember that I do not hold *you* guilty of anything, my dear. Or Richard. Mind you, the latter did nothing to alleviate the matter of my daughter's inheritance, but I comfort myself that he would have, if there had been time. Something would have been returned. He was a just man who died too soon, and now I fear I can be certain beyond *all* doubt that Tudor will not put anything right!' Elizabeth drew herself up and smiled brightly. 'Some refreshment, my dear? Perhaps this delicious quince wine? And another honey cake for Leo.'

The little boy understood and clapped his hands.

Chapter Nine

SUPPER THAT NIGHT was in Tal's private parlour, which opened off the solar, and was a smaller, more intimate chamber that he always preferred. Gwen alone had served the cosy meal, and her comfortable manner set an agreeable atmosphere from the outset. Now she had withdrawn, and the three at the table served themselves.

Mary had earlier mentioned Gwen to Cicely. 'Mistress Woodall is a good woman, my lady. You may trust her.'

'You know that from one brief meeting, Mary?'

'She is a good wisewoman, my lady. Good as distinct from dark or evil. We recognized the same in each other.'

'One glance, and everything is revealed?' Cicely smiled.

'Yes, my lady,' Mary answered seriously.

'She does not like the steward, I think.'

'Very few here like him, my lady,' Mary said as she put the finishing touch to tucking Cicely's hair beneath her headdress, and then teased a few select strands of curl into view again, just as Cicely liked.

That had been before supper, and the maid was now in the servants' hall with Perry and Tom. Cicely had yet to speak to the latter, but felt he would give his approval. He loved his sister dearly, and would want her happiness. She guessed that agreeing on the terms and dowry, and then planning the wedding itself, would be uppermost in their conversation.

Leo was in his nursery, being prepared for sleep, but his nurse would bring him to the parlour to say goodnight. His mother looked forward to giving him another hug and kiss.

The unshuttered window arches admitted the twilight

scent of honeysuckle, candles cast pools of light and moths fluttered softly around the flames. Sounds from the great hall carried through a small peep hole that afforded a direct view over the scene below. There was a similar hole in the solar, so that Tal could be in his private apartments yet always know was happening. Occasionally the steward's raised voice was heard as some minor misconduct came to his notice, but mostly there was only chatter and the pleasant playing of Tal's minstrels. He preferred his music to be at a distance.

The duchess nibbled upon her favourite shellfish, which were brought fresh twice a week from the sea at the Solent. Then she sipped some wine. 'Well, my dear, what happens now?' she said to Cicely. 'My brother has rescued Leo from Tudor's dirty paws, but the child clearly cannot stay here. Henry knows where you are, and his spies have spies. His mother—St George save us—has even more.'

'The boy *can* stay here if necessary,' Tal said, even though he knew she was right. He was irritated, as often seemed to be the case where his sister was concerned. Elizabeth was inclined to correct and advise him all the time, and was fast outstaying her welcome. As was probably *always* the case.

'You, my brother, will be mostly in Calais—at least, you *should* be, but have not been much of late—and in the meantime you have no lady capable of overseeing the child's proper upbringing and education. Leo is Richard's son, a prince of York, no matter from which side of the blanket, and must *never* be at a disadvantage among his peers. Surely you understand that?'

'Elizabeth, I am fully aware of what *should* be provided for this child. When he reaches seven, he needs to go to a magnate's household to be taught the arts of knighthood and chivalry, to read, to write, to speak languages, and all the other things expected of a noble. I may not be a magnate, exactly, but I am more than literate and also trained in manly accomplishments. Thus I am *perfectly* equipped to see to Leo's upbringing. Until the opportune moment arrives, he can quite easily be passed off as my bastard son.'

He avoided Cicely's eyes as he spoke, but knew she was not unaware of the significance he placed on Leo's lineage. If he could one day promote the boy as Richard's son, he would try to do so. And if he could somehow prove Leo to be *trueborn*, so much the better.

Elizabeth flushed. '*Your* son? Do that and it will be tantamount to announcing that you have broken your marriage vows.'

'Oh, for pity's sake, Elizabeth! Jane has long since ceased to be my wife.'

'Not in law or the eyes of the Church.'

'Enough! I have done the right thing by her, and she is *not* going to dictate my life evermore.'

'Is the king not about to grant you *and* Jane ownership of that new house in Pickering Street in Calais? And other property there?'

Humphrey looked blankly at her. 'What has *that* to do with it?'

'Simply that you still need her, Tal. She remains your wife and is thus included in documents concerning joint property.'

'I am *burdened* with her, and so are you. If she now says her prayers like the rest of us, all well and good, but I cannot forgive the pagan worship.' He reached for the wheel of St Catherine against his chest. A nerve flickered at his temple, and his whole manner had stiffened.

'Even so, it is our duty to forgive, Tal.'

Now he was really incensed. '*Forgive*? How can you say that? Three years ago, my dear wife participated in the abduction and mutilation of an orphaned village boy. *She* was the one who kept him imprisoned until he was required for their filthy rites.'

Cicely was appalled, and Elizabeth too stunned to speak.

Tal moderated his tone. 'Perhaps mutilation is too strong a word for marking his back permanently, and no, they did not sacrifice him. That fate was reserved for a goat, which was saved by my timely intervention. The child was returned to his frantic grandmother two days later. He was left at St Margaret's Well, and was unharmed except for the likeness of the White Horse scratched on his back. It had the eight legs of Woden's stallion, Sleipnir. Those crude scratchings will be with him for the rest of his life. He had been a normal boy until then, but is now much changed. He seldom smiles, does not play with other children, and has become difficult and morose.'

'And *Jane* participated in this?' Elizabeth's face was pale and shocked.

'Yes. There is no mistake of that. I was close enough to see her, barely dressed, holding a white dagger to the goat's throat. She fled when I appeared—they all did—and the dagger was found later in her chamber here, together with the chalice, which had been taken from the church. The chalice is back there again now, but mightily chained! I dare say Gregory Melton, being naïve, has no idea of its true nature. The chalice is of no use to Woden without the dagger, which I have hidden in a place of which only I know.'

Elizabeth's lips parted, but Tal shook his head. 'No, I will not say where. As far as the world is concerned, it has simply disappeared.' He managed a grimace of a smile. 'If you need corroboration of what I have said, please ask Mistress Woodall, for it was her grandson who was taken three years ago.'

Cicely closed her eyes, not wanting to even imagine how she would feel if such things were to happen to Leo.

Tal continued. 'There is a leader of the coven, or whatever it is one calls a collection of pagans. In numbers they are a coven ten times over. This fellow is such a giant that I am led to suspect Cheney. However, I could not with justice implicate him that night, so maybe he is innocent after all.'

'You refer to *Sir John* Cheney?' Elizabeth asked.

'The same, but even he cannot be in two places at once. On

the night in question he was unwell, here, in this house, and I left him abed when I rode to Wayland Smith. There was no way he could have overtaken me, yet a man greatly resembling him for height, voice and general build was there at the bonfire. Cheney was still here on my return, and Deakin vouched that he had not stirred from his bed.'

Cicely knew Sir John Cheney, a huge man, six feet and eight inches tall, who had been her father's Master of the Horse. His wife was not only ten years older than him, but half his height, which made them a very odd sight together. Perhaps aware of this, Cheney made sure he was with her as little as possible.

In 1483, when Richard ascended the throne, Cheney refused to believe Edward IV's marriage had been bigamous and changed his allegiance to Henry Tudor, solely because of Henry's vow to marry Bess. He had been Henry's personal bodyguard at Bosworth, where Richard, so slight a man in comparison, had unhorsed him with a single blow from a broken lance. It was a humiliation Cheney preferred to forget, of course, but which Richard's niece preferred to remind him whenever she could.

Now Cheney was high in Henry's favour, and in March had been granted the constableship of Barnard Castle far in the north of England, but Cicely did not know if he had gone there yet. Or even if he would. He possessed a number of Kent manors, and some in Berkshire, including Compton Beauchamp, adjacent to Kingston.

Tal leaned back in his chair. 'Tybalt was there that night as well. At the bonfire,' he observed.

Cicely was curious. 'The *cat*?'

'Yes. If ever there was a witch's familiar, it is that evil tommer, but I am told there is not a rodent that is safe from him.' Tal sighed. 'Anyway, this whole disgusting Wayland Smith episode is what finally prompted me to send Jane to Kenninghall.'

'Carefully omitting all mention of little boys and sacrificial goats,' Elizabeth said reproachfully.

'I thought you would be better able to deal with her without knowing. Besides, you now tell me she is as Christian as Our Saviour.'

Elizabeth's chin was raised crossly. 'Humphrey Talbot, there are times when I could wring your arrogant male neck!' Her glance fled to Cicely, and she became apologetic. 'Forgive us, my dear Cicely. First we discuss family matters as if you are not here, then we speak of the unspeakable, and finally I threaten to throttle my brother. I promised you a memorable stay here, but this was not quite what I had in mind.'

'Do not apologize, for I am sure – '

But the duchess continued. 'Nor should we forget that the king is now your brother-in-law.'

'That is *his* honour, not mine,' Cicely replied.

Tal snorted. 'Oh, I would *revel* in him hearing you say that! But, to return to the matter of Leo's safety, there is something you should know, Elizabeth.' He told her of Romulus.

His sister accepted his cool explanation without surprise or disapproval. 'You did what was right. But it is now *imperative* that Leo disappears. The question is, where to? What of Lord Welles' remoter manors? One he *never* visits?'

Cicely shook her head. 'That is out of the question.'

'Why? Welles has many, so surely *one* can be found?'

'I do not wish to ask my husband for anything, Elizabeth,' Cicely answered quietly.

Tal diverted his sister from the Welles marriage. 'Where would *you* suggest, Elizabeth?'

'With me, at Kenninghall,' was the prompt reply.

'No.' He was adamant. 'My insane wife is there. For pity's sake, you now know all about her and her collusion in the harming of Gwen's grandson. You also know that she attacks me with a knife at every opportunity! Yet here you are, recommending that Leo is placed beneath the same roof!'

Elizabeth was outraged. 'It is our duty to forgive, Tal! Christ preached so! Jane is not beyond all redemption, as she has proved during the time she has been with me. She believes I am in London, not here with you, so all she needs to be informed is that I am caring for Leo for a dear friend who is in difficulties. She will not press for more details. She is no longer a devil.'

Cicely spoke up. 'With all due respect, Elizabeth, I do not want my child to be anywhere near Lady Talbot.'

Tal nodded. 'Be fair, Elizabeth, Jane is an obstacle. Knowing her, I suspect she is pulling the wool over your trusting eyes. You cannot expect Cicely to agree to what you suggest.'

Elizabeth's lips parted to argue, but Tal prevented her. 'Your *real* reason for suggesting Kenninghall is that you want Leo with you all the time. You have enjoyed him so much that you wish he was your own.'

The duchess glanced guiltily at Cicely, before lowering her eyes and nodding. 'But that is not to say I lie about Jane. I really do think he would be safe at Kenninghall, and I urge you to consider it. If I thought for a moment that Jane would pose a threat to him, I would *never* suggest it.'

Tal gazed at her, and then poured more wine for them all before venturing a smile at Cicely. 'Now I too must apologize for our arguing in front of you.'

She returned the smile. 'You have both been very kind to me, in spite of my father's callous behaviour. I am ashamed of him, and often wish I was not his daughter. Your family has good reason to dislike mine.'

Elizabeth was pensive. 'Eleanor loved your father and bore him no grudge, although she eventually had second thoughts. Too late, of course. She always wished she had never met him, but was prepared to remain silent.'

Tal studied her. 'There is much more for you and I to address, is there not, Elizabeth?'

Cicely felt a sudden charge in the atmosphere.

'More? Such as?' Elizabeth's voice was light, almost bland.

'I do not know, but there has always been something *you* know about Eleanor that I do not, and it casts a shadow over everything.'

There was suppressed animosity in every word; a palpable conviction that his remaining sister did not trust him with something of huge importance.

Elizabeth toyed with the dish of nuts on the table before her, and the way she did it held Cicely's attention. Tal was right.

The moment was shattered by the sound of shouts and horses in the courtyard. Then the hounds set up a clamour, disturbing other dogs and animals. The minstrels stopped playing in the hall and Deakin issued swift commands. Benches scraped as servants rose to perform their required tasks.

'What in God's own name—?' Tal got up quickly to look out over the courtyard from a narrow window, and observed with dismay that the newly arriving horsemen bore familiar black and white colours. 'Talk of the devil. Cheney! What the fuck brings *him* here at this hour?'

Chapter Ten

ELIZABETH WAS TOO dismayed to reprimand Tal for swearing. 'Cheney? Oh, no! I pray he does not remain for long. He can be so coarse and ungallant. Please do not bring him up here.'

Tal turned from the window. 'I will have to welcome him, *and* invite him to join us. Behave yourself, Elizabeth. We must do our Christian duty, must we not?' This last was said with cutting sarcasm.

Elizabeth flushed, but said nothing more.

He looked urgently at Cicely. 'Remove your ring, *cariad*. Cheney will recognize it and is capable of telling Henry, who in turn will wonder why you wear the ruby but not his own emerald.'

She slipped Richard's ring into her purse, which contained other mementos. Gifts from those she truly loved.

Tal strode out, and Elizabeth leaned closer immediately. 'You have Henry Tudor's emerald?' Countless questions were buried in the simple enquiry.

'Yes. He gave it to me on the occasion of my second wedding vows with my husband, who is his half-uncle, if you recall. We were deemed not to have been be truly married at the first ceremony, and so the king insisted upon a second.'

The giving of such a costly emerald had caused embarrassment at the time, and had raised many eyebrows in the royal chapel at Westminster. Henry had done it deliberately, and only smiled when she upbraided him afterward.

They fell silent as the peephole admitted the sound of Tal greeting his unexpected guest. Or rather, admitted Cheney's booming voice all the way from the screens passage.

Elizabeth sighed. 'I fear he will be virulently critical of Richard, my dear.'

'He will receive as good as he gives, I assure you. I do not fear him, because Henry already knows everything.'

'Everything? Surely not!'

Cicely did not respond, for they heard Cheney stomping up the stairs with Tal, and halting on the landing. 'Will you *ever* repair the tower, Talbot?'

'No, nor do I intend to. The whole structure needs taking down and rebuilding. I am merely the tenant. If my de l'Iisle kin wish to do it, then I am agreeable, but not from my own purse.'

Cheney had to bend beneath the parlour's stone lintel. He was of an age with Tal, and brought with him the unmistakable odour of stale sweat and horses. He was clad in a fairly old, padded grey doublet and faded, dusty hose that disappeared into well-worn thigh boots. The handsome collar across his shoulders bore a pendant of his coat-of-arms – black fleur-de-lys on a white ground, with a black diagonal line and three golden martlets.

Long brown hair fell beyond his shoulders, and his weatherworn face was lined, his cheeks folding in toward his long, straight nose, causing pronounced vertical shadows. He knew Elizabeth and greeted her politely with a bow, but then his deep-set eyes lighted upon Cicely. 'Why, Lady Welles, what a very agreeable surprise.'

She inclined her head.

His lips twitched as he bowed belatedly, and then addressed Tal. 'Forgive my intrusion, but I was passing from Wantage and thought to take the opportunity to consult with you about some estate matters. I did not realize you had company.'

Elizabeth's lizard smile would have done credit to Henry. 'Please join us, Sir John.' She might have been inviting him to hurl himself from a great height.

He sat, and Tal cordially requested him to eat as he chose, pointing out the blue-streaked goats'-milk cheese, to which he knew his visitor was particularly partial. To his surprise, Cheney declined, albeit with great reluctance.

'Much as I would like to devour it all, I fear that now it always disagrees with me. No, not indigestion, but the most hell-sent headaches you can imagine. I first succumbed three years ago, at Hallowtide. Here, as I am sure you recall. Such afflictions are termed migraines, and are incapacitating. I puke, am in agony, and even see lights and flashes, whether my eyes are open or closed. Doctors tell me they are caused by vapours rising in the brain and that it is due to too much plethora and sharpness of the stomach, but *I* know it is blue cheese!'

Elizabeth sliced a large portion of the offending cheese, and proceeded to eat it with deliberate enjoyment. Tal frowned at her as he poured his guest a large measure of wine. Cheney guzzled without pause for breath, wiped his mouth on his sleeve, and then belched. 'How very pleasant and sociable this is, to be sure,' he remarked, looking longingly at the cheese, but settling for a chicken leg, which he tore apart with his teeth.

Elizabeth's refined nose wrinkled as the fat oozed over his hands.

Tybalt had slipped into the room with the two men, and to Cicely's amazement proceeded to rub almost lovingly around Cheney's ankles. The tomcat even licked the greasy hand held down for him.

The giant grinned at Tal. 'I believe I could entice your prized mouser to Compton.' His eyes flickered to Cicely, specifically her breasts, to which he directed a question. 'Is Lord Welles here with you, my lady?'

'The king's business keeps him in the north.'

'Indeed.'

He knew about Jon's mistress! 'When do you go to your duties at Barnard Castle?' If only it had been last week.

'After Hallowtide,' he replied shortly.

Just then Leo was brought in by his nurse. Cicely stood quickly to kiss his cheek without taking him, for it was best he was removed again as quickly as possible, but Cheney's curiosity was raised in an instant.

'Who is this?' he demanded, his voice very loud in the otherwise quiet chamber.

Leo flinched, looked at the giant and began to howl.

Tal gestured at the nurse to take the child away. The woman bobbed a hasty curtsey and scuttled out with Leo still yelling. His din could be heard long after the door had closed behind him.

As Cicely resumed her seat, she wondered if, by getting up at all, she had given herself away. It had been instinctive.

Sir John suddenly roared with laughter. 'I have a fine effect upon tomcats but not upon children, eh?' He became serious again. 'But who *is* he to be brought in to say goodnight? Clearly not a servant's offspring. He bawls like royalty.' He looked at Cicely.

Tal answered. 'He is mine.'

'Yours?' The giant was startled, but then recovered. 'So, you have broken loose at last, eh? You old dog. I am amazed you endured the marital chains for so long, all things considered. Who is his mother?' His eyes returned to Cicely.

'My son is not for discussion,' Tal answered.

'Eh? Oh, well, yes. I did not mean to cause embarrassment.' But Cheney had not yet done with his questions. 'What brings *you* to Kingston, Lady Welles?'

She was prepared. 'Friendship, Sir John. My late cousin, Lord Lincoln, introduced me to Sir Humphrey, and now I have the honour to call the duchess my friend too. Lord Lincoln is a great loss, I am sure you will agree.'

'He suffered for his misplaced loyalty,' Cheney replied shortly, glowering at her. 'And before you ask, I do *not* know, nor wish to know, his prancing tick of a brother.'

What an odd remark, she thought. Why mention Edmund? But she smiled as she reached for a nut, and proceeded to crack it noisily and deliberately with the little silver hammer provided. The allusion was intentional, and she enjoyed Cheney's flinch.

'Well, since we have had one boy tonight,' he responded, mumbling because his mouth was full of more chicken, 'let me mention another. What are we to make of Roland de Vielleville, mm? Who in damnation is he?'

Elizabeth was puzzled. 'I have not heard of him.'

Cheney grunted. 'You should come to court more often, Duchess. He is an esquire – a mere *écuyer* from Brittany! – but enjoys such a very comfortable life of ease that I think he must be the king's by-blow.'

Elizabeth's laugh tinkled. '*Henry's*? I hardly think so.'

The giant shrugged. 'De Vielleville's advent is not popular in all quarters, I can assure you. Henry has appointed two companions for him, Edmund de la Pole and Thomas Howard, and I am told they resent it, regarding themselves as too highborn for such a nonentity. Which they are, of course, even for a king's bastard.'

Cicely said nothing. All three youths were linked to a certain troublesome creature – her younger sister Ann, known as Annie. The youths were all around the same age, with Edmund just the oldest at seventeen. Foolish Annie was betrothed to the unlovely Thomas Howard, but flirted secretly with the other two. Thomas was the grandson of John Howard, for whom Richard had created the new dukedom of Norfolk, the previous title having become extinct on the death of Elizabeth's little daughter. The new Duke of Norfolk had died alongside Richard at Bosworth, and Henry had stripped the Howards of the title and lands. Precocious Annie, who would only be thirteen on 2 November, All Souls' Day, had ambitious hopes of the title being restored, so that one day she would become Duchess of Norfolk. In fact, she was *determined* upon it.

Cicely found Thomas Howard repellent, and did not think even a little madam like Annie deserved such a husband. Word had it that he had a penchant for beating buxom laundry girls. Maybe it was the smell of starch that aroused him to such an abominable pleasure, but Annie should be saved from such a savage degenerate, who might at any time find something about *her* worth beating too.

She should also be very wary indeed of toying with Edmund de la Pole, because heaven alone knew what excited *him!* Of the three, only Roland seemed likely to be normal, and he had been compromised by Annie in front of Henry. This had deterred poor Roland, who now did all he could to avoid her. But she would not let him.

Tal cleared his throat. 'The king does nothing without reason, Cheney, and if he wishes to treat de Vielleville well, it is not our concern.'

'Oh, I concede the point, but it is intriguing, for all that. I thought Lady Welles might be able to shed some light on the matter. After all, she and Lord Welles are the lad's guardians, so to speak.' Cheney discarded the chicken and reached for some roast duck breast instead. The ensuing sucking and chewing noises disgusted everyone else unfortunate enough to be at the table.

Cicely responded to his remarks about Roland. '*Écuyer* de Vielleville is mostly in my husband's care, Sir John, I have very little to do with it. And no, I am not aware of any more information.' She watched the swift devouring of the duck, and recalled how different Richard had been when eating. Grease had not dribbled from *his* mouth, nor had he held the meat so tightly that his hands ran with juice and fat. He had eaten cleanly, resorting to a napkin, and then washed his hands afterwards. *Never* would he have been guilty of such a display as this. Nor would Henry, she conceded, wondering if Sir John Cheney sank to such table manners in front of his new king. As the devouring came to an end, she anticipated the use of his sleeve. She was right.

Tal could not endure it, and tossed his own napkin across the table. 'I see I have neglected my duties as host. Here, please use my napkin.'

'Mm? Oh, yes.' The napkin was employed to wipe hands *and* for a noisy blast of the nose. Then Cheney belched again and sat back. To Cicely's relief, he did not treat them all to a fart as well.

He regarded Tal. 'You must be relieved your lady is now well removed from the pagan filth hereabouts.'

Tal's smile was thin.

'By the way,' Cheney continued, 'about that bonfire. I understand that both the chalice and the white dagger were recovered. The chalice is once again chained up in the church, of course, but where is the dagger?'

Tal shrugged. 'I have no idea.'

'Really? But it is a very valuable item. Your wife took it. Forgive me, I will reword that. I was under the *impression* that she took it.'

'Cheney, if she had it, she would have plunged the blade in me to the hilt. I do not give a damn where the dagger is, provided it does not fall into pagan hands again. As I understand it, the chalice is of no significance without the dagger. Is that right?'

'You are asking *me*? Good God, Talbot, how the f—? Er, how the hell should I know? I always hoped that after that last bonfire, such profanities would die away, but it seems not. It has a grip hereabouts.' Cheney belched again, and Cicely could not help leaning as far away from him as possible.

'Do you know who the leader is?' Tal asked lightly, avoiding the women's eyes.

'No. I would see the evil bastard burn if I did.' Cheney chuckled then. 'He is my image, I am told. A lost twin, eh?'

Cicely watched the moths fluttering around the candles, and tried to imagine Cheney was elsewhere. Night air drifted into the parlour, and she breathed the honeysuckle.

Tal held his unwanted guest's gaze. 'Cheney, I will sweep Berkshire clean of Woden. Christianity is my faith, and I will not have such depravity and paganism on or near my land. Anyone involved in it will be punished severely.'

Cheney grunted. 'You will have many to punish.'

'I am told there are more on *your* land than mine.'

'Really? Well, it is the first I have heard of it. I will, of course, render whatever assistance you require.' There was another grunt. 'You had best watch over your son, Talbot. They took just such a little boy last time. Maybe they will this time.'

'This time?' Tal's eyes sharpened.

'Yes. Did you not know? I believe Woden has been promised another boy at this year's bonfire.

In the stillness that followed this announcement, Cicely thought she could hear those moths. All she could think of was Leo, and she struggled not to show it. Her heartbeats had quickened unpleasantly as she fiddled with the folds of her gown on her lap.

Elizabeth was upset too, but managed to sound unconcerned as she changed the subject. 'Sir John, please satisfy my curiosity. Are you related to another John Cheney, who is the tenant of my manor at Oare, in Wiltshire? It is several miles south of Marlborough.'

Cicely saw Tal's face change, his expression suddenly tense and filled with incredulity.

Sir John belched. 'No. Never heard of him.'

'It just occurred to me that the names were the same.' Elizabeth nibbled daintily on another walnut, and studiously avoided Tal's gaze, of which she could not help but be aware.

Cheney stayed another hour, during which, to the relief of the ladies, he was closeted elsewhere with Tal. The summer evening had closed into night when he departed to ride the mile or so to his own manor, and when Tal returned, he almost slammed the door to confront his sister.

'Oare was Eleanor's manor, Elizabeth. How is it now yours?'

The duchess shifted on her seat. 'There is nothing mysterious about it, Tal. She wished to be sure her manors did not go where they should not, and so she gifted them to me before she died.'

Tal's face was frosty. 'Go where they should not?' he repeated softly. 'And what, pray, does *that* mean? That they should not go to me?'

Elizabeth was dismayed. 'Oh, no, Tal, please do not think that! No insult or mistrust was intended to you.'

'What else am I to think?' The hurt almost glittered around him. 'Oare is barely fourteen miles from here. So, at the time of Eleanor's death, when I imagined it all went to the Crown and Edward, who gave the manors to her in the first place, in fact *you* held her estate. Nothing would have surprised me where Edward was concerned. But *you* had them, and have seen me countless times since then without bothering to mention it!'

'Tal—'

'Damn you, Elizabeth! And damn Eleanor for thinking so little of me!' He thumped his fist down upon the table and then straightened. 'I have something to attend to. Ladies.' Inclining his head to them both, he left.

Elizabeth stared down at the table, her lips quivering, her eyes shining with tears she tried not to show.

Cicely did not know what to say. Even less what to do.

The duchess looked at her at last. 'Forgive us, Cicely. Family squabbles are seldom edifying.'

It had not been a squabble, Cicely thought, more a case of Tal being desperately hurt to find himself excluded from something to which he should definitely have been party. It *did* smack of a lack of trust in him, perhaps even his sisters' shared fear that *he*, not Edward IV, would snatch the property.

Elizabeth sighed heavily. 'Oh, how stupid of me to mention Oare,' she breathed, not to Cicely, but herself.

Feeling very awkward, Cicely placed her napkin on the table. 'I think I will retire now, Elizabeth. It has been a long day.'

Elizabeth nodded.

As Cicely returned to her allotted chamber, she passed an open doorway through which candlelight shone on a green-and-white tiled floor. She paused, for it had been closed earlier. Curiosity drew her. It was a simple private chapel, with a small altar and cross. Behind the altar there was another arched trefoil window with stained glass that was colourless now the daylight had gone.

Tal was leaning back against a wall, arms folded, head bowed. His distress was still palpable, but she could not go to him. He wished to be private and she had no right. She stepped away again, intending to continue to her room, but he spoke.

'Cicely?'

She turned. 'Forgive me, I did not mean to intrude.'

'You do not. I would welcome your opinion. Do you think I am wrong to find this business both insulting and wounding?'

'No, of course not. I would feel as you do. But I am sure the duchess and your late sister did not mean to hurt you. They would have had a reason, yes, but it would not be distrust.' She advanced reluctantly, and saw that in his right hand he held the book of poetry he often kept close. The book was bound with red silk, and embroidered in silver with a running talbot hound. It was a beautiful thing, a comfort resorted to at times of stress, perhaps. As now.

'Then why did they do it? Why not inform me? I would not have said or done anything to prevent their actions, but *they* did not trust me.'

'I do not think it had anything to do with a lack of trust.'

'Then what? Elizabeth has come here many times, and we

have spent long hours talking into the night, remembering our youth and everything that happened to Eleanor, but there was not one word uttered about those manors.' He straightened from the wall. 'There is much more to this. I know it. I have sensed it ever since Eleanor died.'

'Do not let it fester, Tal. You are already weighed with anger about Eleanor. Do not quarrel with your other sister because of something that is over and done with. Something that Eleanor herself chose to do. I feel for you, truly I do, because I know what she meant to you.'

'Maybe I have been wasting my emotions on her. Maybe I should forget her altogether.'

'You do not mean that.'

He met her gaze. 'I think I do. But for now, forgive me.' He placed the book of poetry in a little niche, and then looked at her. 'I will escort you to the well in the morning. We will take Leo with us.' He bowed over her hand and left the chapel, passing Tybalt, who was seated in the doorway.

Chapter Eleven

EARLY NEXT MORNING, Perry and two of Tal's strongest men-at-arms waited at the porch with three saddled horses, ready for Cicely's visit to St Margaret's Well. The irrepressible talbots were ready as well, and milled around expectantly, but Elizabeth would not be going, because matters were still frosty with Tal.

It was a beautiful day, with skylarks tumbling overhead in the light breeze. Workers pretended to be at their tasks around the courtyard, but were surreptitiously watching the activity by the porch. There were even people in the doorways of the lodgings, or peering from the windows, so great was the curiosity about Viscountess Welles, whom they had learned was King Edward's daughter and the sister-in-law of King Henry.

Mary and Perry were already mounted. Both wore blue—and besotted smiles—as they gazed at each other, and Mary carried a posy of honeysuckle and white roses from the porch, for Cicely to place before St Margaret's image at the well.

Tal came out of the house, and when he was on his horse an excited Leo was carried out by Tom Kymbe, who swung the little boy up to Tal's waiting arms. Leo clapped his hands excitedly, for he loved it when he was taken out riding like this. The hounds delighted the boy even more, and as he giggled and squirmed to look down at them, Tal's arm tightened accordingly.

Tom bowed as Cicely emerged. 'My lady.'

He was dressed as he had been the day before, and the breeze stirred his nut-brown hair as he lifted her on to her palfrey. She felt the brush of his hand as he gave her the reins.

His smile was warm, as were his eyes, and she was reminded that when he was present, nothing seemed quite as difficult or upsetting. Yet his amiable exterior concealed great strength—and a capacity for violent but controlled response that made him an invaluable protector.

'It is good to see you again, Tom,' she said. 'I am so glad Mistress Kymbe is fully recovered.'

'Indeed she is. Death will eventually have a real battle on his hands.'

Cicely laughed. 'I think you are right. Tom, I am very grateful that you and Sir Humphrey rescued Leo. What would I do without you?'

'I will *always* be here for you, Lady Cicely. Never doubt it.'

Deakin came out, and glowered at Tom, whom he saw as usurping the steward's duties. He addressed Tal. 'Do you have further instructions, Sir Humphrey?'

'No, just be vigilant. I am to be told immediately of anyone, *anyone*, who does not belong here. And *no one* is to be admitted to the house in my absence, is that clear? No one at all. You are even to keep the king himself outside the gate. These instructions are permanent until further notice. Do you understand?'

'Yes, Sir Humphrey.'

But as Cicely prepared to leave, she pondered the purpose of visiting the well at all. She had lain awake at dawn, watching the changing colours of the new day, knowing that her marriage had almost certainly been lost forever. Her husband was in love with someone else, and even if his wife became as fertile as a rabbit, there could only be a child if he lay with her. Henry was right. If St Margaret granted her plea, she was more likely to bear *his* child.

The riders moved away from the porch, and Leo squealed with joy as the talbots streamed alongside excitedly. The Silver Hound rides forth with his silver hounds, Cicely thought.

Leo demanded Tal's full attention. 'Whassa?' A chubby

finger was pointed. 'Whassa?' His curiosity was insatiable.

They rode out past the church to the road, then across to strike west up a long, low incline of chalky farmland that was rich with crops and dotted with trees. The summer air was fragrant, and the Downs shimmered in the morning haze, their mysterious atmosphere seeming to beckon. Once again Cicely sensed the legends that dwelt up there. The very air seemed haunted by the far distant past. Or was she simply being influenced by what she knew went on at Wayland Smith?

The ground was hard beneath the hooves. Insects whirred, and butterflies were disturbed from the wild flowers and waving grasses beside the dusty track that led to the crest of the slope. Beyond the crest, the land swung down quite sharply toward the hollow where the holy well was sheltered by a clump of mature willows. Two crows—Cicely felt they were the same two as yesterday—hovered over the willows, cawing aggressively at something on the ground, and as the horses drew nearer, she saw Tybalt. She wondered how the cat ever had time to catch mice. All three creatures had the air of being a witch's familiars, she thought. As she watched, the crows wheeled away toward the west, and disappeared over a low hill beyond the well and the trees.

A man, woman and boy were coming from the well toward the riders. Cicely recognized the priest, Gregory Melton, and Gwen Woodall, who held the hand of a dark-haired boy of eight or thereabouts. The grandson who had been disfigured in the name of Woden?

The boy was sullen, as Tal had said. He had a flat, square face, his lower lip jutted almost truculently and his pale eyes were narrow and secretive as he glanced at something Melton was concealing behind his back. Cicely was surprised to find herself taking as immediate a dislike to him as she had to Tybalt.

'What brings you here, priest?' Tal asked, reining in.

'Pagan offerings, I fear, Sir Humphrey. Two effigies of a disgusting nature. The well receives unchristian attention.'

'Burn them.'

'I will, Sir Humphrey.'

Tal then looked kindly at Gwen. 'You always have my support.'

'We are grateful, Sir Humphrey.' She curtsied, and the boy bowed, albeit after a moment's hesitation.

Tal nodded that they could all go on their way, and then called after the priest. 'Remain wary of those intrusions before your hearth!' Then he chuckled.

Cicely smiled, but chided him. 'Shame on you, Tal. You know priests are not supposed to consort with the fair sex.'

'Nevertheless they do, and I am merely letting friend Melton know that I will not carry tales to the Bishop of Norwich!' Tal chuckled again.

'Is Luke the boy who – ?'

'Yes. Gwen wishes him to enter the Church. She sees that as the only way to shield him from the evil that has been done to him. It seems Luke is resisting such a notion. He is disobedient. She has pampered him because of his ordeal, and now reaps the consequence.'

'But would the Church accept him? Marked as he is?'

'I have no idea. The Church is a law unto itself. It has a strict set of rules for us, and an entirely different and more relaxed set for itself.'

Cicely watched them. 'What happened to Luke's parents?'

'Ah, well, that is a little delicate. His mother was Gwen's daughter, Agnes Woodall, who was unmarried. The village talked of little else for a while, because she refused to name the father. So the boy is known only as Luke Woodall.'

They rode the final yards to the well. Willow fronds swayed in the breeze, and the talbots scattered amid the bushes and tall grasses, investigating everything. Leo's interest was boundless as he twisted hither and thither in Tal's hold, trying to see what the hounds were doing.

The men-at-arms took charge of the horses and led them to the edge of the trees, leaving Tal and his lady guest seated on a grassy bank that was dappled with shadows. The talbots flopped in the shade as well, and prepared for a doze. Mary and Perry sat nearby watching as Leo, seemingly tireless, continued to dash around.

Cicely watched him too, and then glanced at the well. It was about four feet wide and seven feet long, and protected on three sides by a low stone wall, beyond which a rivulet emerged from a tiny fold in the ground and trickled north into the Vale, its course marked by a line of trees and bushes. A short but steep flight of steps descended invitingly toward the well from the open end. She should be feeling a tingle of hope, of trust that St Margaret would favour her, but she felt nothing at all. At this moment, if she brought Jon to mind, he was a featureless figure. She could remember the piercing blue of his eyes, but not his smile. Or his voice. Or his lovemaking. He had moved to the periphery of everything.

Leo broke into her thoughts as he ran from Mary to Tal and then to his mother, flinging himself into each pair of arms in turn and screeching with laughter. The game pleased him so much that he kept on and on until at last he was quite exhausted and went to sit with Mary, who persuaded him to lie down on a little blanket. His eyes soon closed.

Tal breathed a sigh of relief. 'St George be praised.'

'Are you feeling your age, Sir Humphrey?' Cicely asked, smiling.

'It would seem so.'

She looked at the well, and then down at the posy of roses and honeysuckle Mary had placed beside her. 'Is not St Margaret also the patron saint of those who have been falsely accused?'

'Yes. Why?'

'Then she is Richard's saint.'

Tal plucked a blade of grass and twirled it between fingers

and thumb. 'St Margaret was also supposed to have escaped a dragon by making the Sign of the Cross,' he said then. 'Just imagine it, the Sign of the Cross and away the Tudor is whisked, into Perdition forever more. What a pleasant thought.' He hesitated. 'You think I should make my peace with Elizabeth?'

'She is your only full sister. But who am *I* to advise you? Bess and I cannot abide the sight of each other now, but we were once as close as sisters could be. I wish we still were.' Cicely knew it was unlikely there would ever be the same intimacy between them again. Not when she, Cicely, had won the hearts of both Richard and Henry. To say nothing of Jack de la Pole. Bess had wanted Richard, and made no secret of it during his life. But his love had gone to Cicely.

Relations were no better with Annie, who preferred to cling to the queen rather than mere Lady Welles. Katherine and Bridget, the remaining daughters of Edward IV, were still very young and had yet to come to court.

Tal spoke. 'I find it hard to accept that my sister believes me capable of taking Eleanor's manors. Or that Eleanor herself would think it.'

'I do not imagine that was the point of it, Tal. Please, you have to ask Elizabeth to explain fully. We only have one life here on earth, and I would hate to think yours was spoiled forever by something that you may well be able to resolve now, simply by hearing what your sister has to say.'

'You care?'

'Of course. You annoy me, very much sometimes, but that does not mean I am indifferent to your happiness. If Jack were here now, his advice would be exactly the same as mine, as you well know.'

'Yes, but it is inevitable that Elizabeth and I will fight.'

'*You* are likely to be the one doing that. You have climbed up on to that high horse of yours without really knowing what went on when Eleanor died. If you do not discuss this now, the rift may become far worse. She will leave for Kenninghall, you will stay here or go to Calais, and who knows how long it will be before you see each other again? Then again, fate might step in. We are not immortal.'

'A comforting thought.'

'But true, nevertheless.' She was thinking of Richard. If the last words she exchanged with him had been sharp, how would she have felt after Bosworth? How would she *still* feel? But their last words had been loving; their last contact a kiss.

He took her hand suddenly. There was no incorrectness in the gesture, only friendship. 'You are a remarkable woman, Viscountess Welles.'

'I merely manage to get into frequent predicaments.'

'You are here now in a bid to resolve at least one such predicament, and I have brought you something that will please St Margaret, as I pray it will please you.' He reached into his purse, and pressed into her palm a little pewter pilgrim brooch of St. Margaret of Antioch.

'Oh, Tal—'

'It was my grandmother's token, and served her truly when she too sought the saint's help. She laid it on the altar of a church dedicated to St Margaret, and then—miraculously—discovered it in her purse again. Well, I believe my grandfather rescued it, but she never knew. Anyway, not long afterward, she found she was with child. That too was my grandfather's doing, of course.' He smiled and closed her fingers over the brooch.

'You cannot give it to me, Tal.'

'Yes, I can. Elizabeth no longer has any use for it, but you do, that is, if you *will* insist on wanting to please the unpleasable Jon Welles. *Are* you still determined?'

Time seemed to pause. The trees whispered, and she saw Tybalt slinking through the grass nearby. The moment of decision was upon her. *Was* there anything to be gained by proceeding?

Tal did not perceive the direction of her thoughts. 'You

only have to say what you will to the saint, and then drop the token into the well. No doubt it will join hundreds of other such offerings, because before Christianity this was a place of veneration for the Celts, the Romans and the Anglo-Saxons. Hence its continued importance to the wretched pagans hereabouts. No matter what *they* may think, St Margaret watches over it now, not Woden. Your plea will fall on friendly ears.'

'My plea? That I bear a child to a husband who will no longer lie with me? I think St Margaret may be insulted.'

'No. She is a woman, and will understand your quandary.' He began to perceive the depth of her doubts.

She glanced at him quickly. 'I do not think I should beseech her on account of my marriage.' The admission came almost before she realized it.

'Jon Welles will never cease to love you, Cicely.'

'He has already ceased.' Her voice was stronger, her purpose decided. 'But I can still appeal to St Margaret for Richard's soul. He is so falsely accused.'

He smiled and put his hand over hers again. 'Then pray to her for him, *cariad*. Do not waste your visit.'

She rose to go to some earthenware jars and jugs that lay in the grass behind the well, where the rivulet emerged from the ground. They were for the floral offerings, some of which were already in place on the parapet around the well. Soon the roses and honeysuckle had joined them. Except for one rose, which she kept as she stood at the top of the steps.

At the bottom there was a place to stand in front of a low archway that protected the unseen water. Above the arch, in a niche in the stonework, was a little statuette of St Margaret, wearing a delicately twined and fretted coronet, her long hair plaited and coiled around her ears. Around the saint's feet twisted a dragon. Just like St George, or Henry's St Armel, Cicely thought as she descended slowly.

At the bottom she turned to look back. Tybalt was sitting

there at the top of the steps, the tip of his tail flicking. The cat's stare suggested it could read her mind, and she turned swiftly to the front again, to look instead at the saint's serene face. The breeze fell away suddenly. Not even the willows moved, and the well's atmosphere seemed to wrap around her like a mantle. Her attention was now solely on St Margaret and she did not hear Tal come to shove Tybalt away with his boot. Nor did she realize that he stayed to watch her in some concern.

Those seconds of intense concentration were astonishing, focusing and yet blurring her thoughts so that suddenly she could imagine Richard was there with her. The conviction was so strong that she whispered to the saint.

'Protect my dear lord Richard's soul, I pray you. Shield his good name and honour from those who would destroy both.' Her voice shook with the force of her feelings.

She wanted the sculpted face to smile, or the carved robes to stir, but St Margaret of Antioch was made of stone. Still, the plea *had* been heard, she knew it had! She trembled. Everything was so strange here.

Tal came down toward her. '*Cariad*?'

She did not hear, but went to the little archway and leaned in to drop the rose and the token into the water. The offerings disturbed the surface, setting ripples in motion, and then there was silence again. *Such* a silence. The air seemed heavy, weighing upon her, and there was no substance to anything. Her senses began to spin and she could only hear the pounding of her heart. She was breathless, and then her legs gave slowly beneath her.

Tal caught her as she lost consciousness. Swinging her up into his arms, he carried her out of the well to the sunny bank. Leo still slept, and Mary came running anxiously. 'My lady? Oh, my lady!'

Tal placed Cicely gently on the cool grass of the shady bank, and as Mary removed her headdress, Perry went to dip his kerchief in the well. Tal accepted the wet cloth and then nodded at them both to return to Leo. Mary was reluctant, but

Perry ushered her away.

Cicely stirred a little, and Tal sat on the grass beside her to dab her hot face gently with a corner of the wet kerchief. 'There, does that feel better, *cariad*? You are safe now.'

She looked up at him, uncertain for a moment, but then her memory cleared.

He smiled as she glanced uncertainly at the well. 'All is well at the well,' he joked lightly, but then became serious as he helped her to sit up. 'What happened down there?'

'I do not really know.' She described what she remembered, starting with Tybalt, and including her conviction that Richard had been with her.

Tal nodded. 'I hope he was, because it would make your plea all the more meaningful. As for that mangy tomcat, pay no attention to him. He was sent on his way at the end of my boot. Sometimes I wish he *would* take himself off to Cheney's fond embrace.'

The hounds suddenly scrambled to their feet, whining and yelping as they gazed up at the incline to the west, away from the house and village. Tal's eyes sharpened as a horseman reined in against the skyline, clearly intent upon the hollow.

Cicely saw too. 'Who is it?'

'You definitely do not know him?'

She looked again. The rider was just a man, without anything to set him apart, especially when outlined against such a bright sky. But he was not plump. 'It is not Remus,' she said, her glance moving anxiously to Leo.

Tal concentrated on the rider. 'The fellow knows he has been sighted. There, he is leaving. Guilty flight, I think.' He turned swiftly to his men and jerked a thumb after the horseman. They mounted and gave chase, Perry with them.

Cicely glanced at Tal. 'The man is to be another unexplained disappearance?'

'Yes. My men know what to do. When I protect, I protect, sweetheart. Never forget it. Cheney is suspicious about Leo, and I imagine he has sent a scout to find out what he can.' Tal smiled. 'Cheney is dangerous and will take anything and everything to Henry. Elizabeth is right, the sooner Leo disappears from Kingston, the better.'

Her hand crept to her throat. 'Kenninghall? You think he should go there in spite of your wife?'

'I am reluctant to trust Elizabeth's judgment, but if she really thinks Jane will be harmless to the boy, then perhaps it *is* the wisest course.' He shrugged.

'But Cheney has already seen Leo. How will you explain his disappearance?'

'Why, that I have sent him way to be brought up by his mother's family. Aristocratic, of course, and not to be identified in order to protect his mother's identity.'

'You sound very convincing.'

He grinned. 'Not from great experience of hiding my shocking private life, I assure you. Now, have you recovered enough to return to the house?'

She would learn later that the rider eluded Tal's men. He had not gone as far as Compton Beauchamp, but up into an ancient woodland that spread over the lower face of the Downs, below the famous White Horse. There they had lost his tracks.

Chapter Twelve

TAL CHOSE NOT to approach Elizabeth about Eleanor for the time being, with the result that for the rest of the day the ominous atmosphere between brother and sister continued to simmer. It was not until evening, in the parlour, that it all became too much for Cicely. She wanted to shout at them, knock their heads together; do *something* to make them reasonable again.

'This really will not do,' she declared, standing. 'I think my presence is actually hampering you from talking—quarrelling, snarling or whatever it is you both need to do—so I will retire. But *please,* settle your differences and make peace again.'

Elizabeth shook her head. 'Please sit down again, my dear, for we do not wish you to go.' Then she faced Tal, as angry with him as he was with her. 'Nothing more needs to be said. Eleanor gifted her manors to me. That is the end of it.

'No! *Not* the end of it!' Tal sat forward, bristling visibly. 'Why keep it secret, Elizabeth?'

'I did not, I—'

'Do not keep *lying*!' he cried, leaping up and going to the smoke-blackened fireplace, where he leaned a hand on the stone mantel and bowed his head. 'You *both* excluded me, quite deliberately, so neither of you trusted me.'

Elizabeth gestured crossly to Cicely, who had remained standing, to be seated again. 'Please do not draw conclusions that are not there,' she said as she went to the window, where the draught was cool. To be as far from her brother as possible? Perhaps. She spoke, not looking back into the room. 'There was no mistrust of you, Tal, truly, just a desire not to burden you more than you already were.'

'*Burden* me?' He turned. 'Eleanor was alive then, because she *gifted* the manors to you, so how could *I* be burdened? For pity's sake, Elizabeth, do not say anything unless it is honest. We were three full-blood siblings, and had always been close. What was done to her has affected me in ways you cannot imagine, because *you* have never mourned her as I have.'

Cicely expected Elizabeth to be outraged by such an accusation, but she only came back from the window, the dark silk of her gown shining as a nearby candle guttered.

'You are right, Tal, but we must continue our lives.'

'Oh, how very sensible,' he responded acidly. 'Well, *I* did not find it so simple, and I have been avenged, believe me.'

Elizabeth went closer. 'What do you mean?'

Cicely gazed at him. Was he going to confess his part in her father's death?

He deliberated, then, having come this far, chose to continue. 'I was responsible for the somewhat painful and premature demise of King Edward IV, to whom I administered poison.' There was no mention of Jon Welles' part in the murder.

'You, you *what?*' Elizabeth was so aghast that she had to feel her way to her seat.

'I was clear enough.' Tal then proceeded to describe his involvement in Yorkist plotting, and finally, his attempt on Henry's life at Esher. Jon's name did not figure at all.

Elizabeth might have been sculpted from marble. 'You have done such things because of *Eleanor*? If I had known. . .'

'Then what?' Tal prompted sourly, his bitterness unpurged by confession.

'Please, Tal,' she whispered. 'You are my dear, most beloved brother. Eleanor and I would not have hurt you so for all the world.'

'Then for God's own sake, tell me.'

Elizabeth's eyes were filled with tears, and she pressed her lips together in an effort not break down. 'There is a very good reason why I have not grieved for Eleanor. It. . .it is that she is still alive.'

Cicely's heart seemed to halt within her.

'*Alive*?' Tal was almost dazed.

'Yes, and living at Oare.'

It was too much for him. Fists clenched, he strode from the parlour.

Elizabeth almost went after him, but then halted and looked at Cicely, who was rooted, shocked. 'Bring him back, Cicely, for I must tell him everything now I have begun. He will come if you ask him.'

'Elizabeth—'

'Try. Please.'

Cicely went to the chapel again. Tal was not there, but the book of poems had gone. Catching up her skirts, she went down to the great hall, where there was still music and dancing. Deakin hurried over when beckoned.

'My lady?'

'Have you seen Sir Humphrey? The duchess wishes to speak urgently with him.'

'Indeed I have seen him, my lady. He said he was going down to the fish pools.'

'Tell me how to get there.'

'My lady, he does not wish to be disturbed.'

'This is too important. The blame will be mine, not yours. Which way will I find him?'

Tom Kymbe had heard and joined them. 'You cannot go alone, my lady, for the paths are confusing and it is dark now. I have been down there, so please, allow me to escort you.'

Deakin scowled, clearly hard put not to lay hands upon the presumptuous newcomer, but he bowed and moved away.

Tom indicated the door to the screens passage. 'If you will come this way, my lady. . .?'

The summer night was warm as they followed a path that wound down toward the trees in the valley where the ponds were to be found. An owl hooted, and a vixen screamed. Far above, the moonlit sky was filled with myriad stars, and the Downs rose barely a mile away. On such a night, their influence seemed stronger than ever.

Tom and Cicely emerged from the trees on the valley floor, at an area of flat grass where butts had been set up along the shore of a long, deep and wide pond, one of the string of three she had observed on arriving from Wantage. The ponds were separated by causeways and sluices, and on the opposite side the valley slope rose again, cloaked with the woodland Tal had almost decided to ride through the previous day.

He was leaning against the gnarled trunk of an old oak that spread its branches low over the water, and held the book of poetry. His posture was exactly as Henry's had been on the day the pact was made, when he too had leaned against a tree, watching a stream that flowed past his feet.

She turned to Tom. 'Perhaps it is best if you return to the house. Sir Humphrey will escort me back.'

Tal straightened irritably on hearing her.

'If you are sure, my lady?' Tom observed Tal's reaction and did not want to leave her.

'Yes, I am sure.'

'As you wish, Lady Cicely.' He bowed and walked back along the path. She knew he would stop when he was out of sight.

Tal addressed her. 'Go with him, *cariad*.'

Undeterred, she approached the oak.

'You should not have come here, Cicely. I will be having words with Deakin.'

'I overruled him, and accepted Tom's protection.'

'I need to be on my own. Can you not understand that?'

'All I understand is that you *must* return to Elizabeth. She wants to tell you everything, Tal.'

'A little late, do you not think?'

'Oh, Tal, a hair shirt does not suit you. Return with me.'

He ran a hand distractedly through his hair. 'She is alive, Cicely. *Alive*! And I have been fooled for all these years.'

'Maybe for a very good reason. How will you know if you refuse to hear Elizabeth now? Please, Tal.'

Finally he nodded. 'Very well.'

As he pushed the book into his purse, she had to ask about it. 'Why does that book mean so much to you?'

'It was my father's, and out of all his children, he left it to me. I know he took it everywhere with him, and so it makes me feel close to him again.' He smiled. 'A maudlin tale, I think.'

'No, for it shows the love of a man for his youngest son. And of that son for his father.'

The duchess was pacing up and down restlessly, and halted apprehensively on seeing them.

Tal confronted her. 'I will hear you out, Elizabeth, although I do not know what you can say that will make your actions acceptable to me.'

Once again Elizabeth prevented Cicely from leaving. '*Please* stay, my dear. Your presence will be beneficial.'

Cicely sat as far away as she could, and Tal stationed himself rather imperiously with his back to the fireplace.

Elizabeth resumed her seat at the table, and toyed nervously with the dish of nuts. 'Tal, Eleanor and I decided to exclude you because King Edward was showing you favour and seemed likely to advance you. His conscience maybe, but we wanted it to be to your benefit. We thought it unfair that you would not inherit a title or lands within the family.'

'So, Edward advanced me out of guilt? Heaven forfend that he might have thought I had ability.' Tal's green eyes were cold.

'Oh, I think he discovered you were a more than competent soldier and sailor, Tal, but maybe you would not have come to his attention so prominently in the first place if it were not for Eleanor.'

'Prominently? I am Marshal of Calais. That is all.'

His sister eyed him. 'Perhaps because you proved to be less than warmly disposed toward him. You failed to play your cards cleverly. That was not my fault, or Eleanor's.'

Tal did not respond.

She continued. 'The decisions Eleanor and I made, including her apparent demise, were agreed prior to you and I escorting Cicely's aunt to Bruges to marry the Duke of Burgundy, and did not concern belittling or mistrusting you. The king knew nothing. We deceived him too.' She hesitated. 'Tal, maybe I did seem less shocked and distressed than you, but it is hard to ape those things when you know the death has been fabricated. No one else would have noticed the small ways in which I betrayed myself, but you did.'

'Why make the decisions at all?'

Elizabeth swallowed. 'She had become increasingly fearful of the Woodvilles. Forgive me, Cicely, but it is the truth.'

There was more to it, Cicely thought, remembering Elizabeth's words the previous day, over the quince wine.

'You see,' Elizabeth continued, 'I am sure that my husband was poisoned, and—'

'What?' Tal exclaimed. 'I thought it was no more than a sudden stopping of his heart. A *natural* death.'

'My instincts tell me otherwise,' Elizabeth replied. 'He was a healthy man, with a strong heart.' Tears shone in her eyes.

'Why would anyone want him gone?'

The duchess lowered her eyes. 'Because of me, he found out about Eleanor and the king and confided in someone he trusted, I do not know who. That person took the tale to the Woodvilles.' Another apologetic glance was directed at Cicely. 'A week later, my lord was dead. It was no coincidence. I believe the poison was in a jug of mead. Eleanor and I were meant to take it as well, but it was removed by chance, and my John alone had drunk from it.'

Elizabeth's voice trembled as she remembered. 'Cicely, it so happened that not long afterward I had occasion to be alone with your mother. I made sure of being all that a loyal and loving lady should be, and I think I soothed her suspicions. Eleanor was a different matter, however, still being the king's legal queen. There would have been another jug of mead, or whatever new method they chose for her extinction. She was terrified, as you may imagine, and so we devised a plan for her to "die" while you and I were in Bruges, Tal. Instead she went secretly to Oare, where she is protected by a few loyal servants. Her name now is Dame Wigmore, and she lives in retreat.'

Cicely remembered that Wigmore in Herefordshire had been one of her father's castles, inherited from the great Mortimer Earls of March, whose title he had also inherited.

Tal's resentment burst suddenly, and he kicked furiously at the nearest andiron in the hearth. 'Oare! So close to here that I could have seen her on so many occasions! It would have been *such* a comfort, which *you* have denied me, Elizabeth!' He glared at her, a nerve twitching at his temple. 'Who was buried in her stead, mm? I take it there *was* someone? Not merely some sacks of Norfolk soil?'

'A Kenninghall serving girl who had no family, and who happened to die at the same time. No, we did not dispose of her, she died of an ague. We—my ladies and a few trusted menservants—decided to use her body instead of weighting the coffin. She had a very honourable funeral, I assure you.'

'Did Edward ever express his true feelings about Eleanor?' Tal demanded then. 'If he was ever capable of true feelings, of course.'

Elizabeth lowered her eyes. 'Yes. He wished he had never behaved as he did. He loved her, and regretted what he had done. Tal, there is something I have yet to tell you.'

Tal stiffened. 'Sweet Satan, there is more?'

Elizabeth glanced uncomfortably at Cicely. 'My dear, after his acknowledgement of your mother as his queen, your father did not abandon Eleanor, but continued to visit her in secret. For four years, until he was told that she was dead.'

Cicely was shocked, but Tal was furious. 'You are saying the royal *shit* continued to fuck Eleanor even though he was parading Cicely's mother as his legitimate queen?' he cried.

'Do not use such language, Tal, and keep your voice down.'

'To hell with keeping my voice down!'

'You are *shouting*, sir!' she replied sharply. 'Do you *want* the entire household to hear?'

Their eyes met, and then he turned away, lowering his tone. 'And while all this went on, *I* knew nothing. May I hope you have now finished with your revelations?'

'Not quite. Tal, it is important that you know Eleanor always welcomed his visits. They were both so very happy when he came secretly to Kenninghall. But then there was the poisoned mead, and after that. . .'

'Yes?' Tal prompted.

Elizabeth drew a long breath. 'What finally made up her mind to pretend to die was finding herself with child. A boy, as it happened, who died very young.'

Tal's lips parted. 'A *child?*' he repeated slowly, as if learning Eleanor had borne a litter of unicorns.

'The king never knew.'

Cicely was now quite dumbfounded. Both her father *and* Henry had secret firstborn sons! *Legitimate* sons. If Eleanor's boy had lived, the true succession to the throne of England would be in even more hidden chaos! Richard would never have ascended the throne himself, but would have supported Eleanor's son.

Elizabeth glanced at Cicely. 'Did you know your mother was aware quite early on that she was not really the queen?'

'Yes. When we were in sanctuary at Westminster and learned of Richard's reasons for ascending the throne, she confessed the truth to me and the present queen. She said she used her knowledge to coerce my father into advancing her family. For which I cannot entirely blame her. She had been deceived as well.'

Elizabeth nodded. 'Your allegiance to King Richard sets you against your maternal kin, does it not?'

'My allegiance to Richard takes precedence over everything.' Cicely looked at Tal. 'When he found out about Eleanor, he felt exactly as you do now.'

'I fail to see how.'

'Because he had been left out too, and felt bitterly betrayed when he learned. He had always served so loyally – my father could not have done without him – but if the truth had not come out, my baseborn brother would have been crowned King of England, an honour to which he had no right at all. As things stood, my father knew that Richard was his heir, but said nothing. It destroyed the devotion Richard had always given to him so selflessly. My father was guilty, Tal, but your sisters did not mean to hurt you. So forgive them, go to Oare, be reunited with Eleanor, and then be your own man again.'

Elizabeth was immeasurably glad of the support. 'Listen to her, Tal. We can *all* go, even little Leo, and – '

'No!' Cicely said quickly. 'This is Talbot family business and has nothing whatsoever to do with me. Eleanor will not wish to meet the daughter of the woman who supplanted her. I will stay here and be with Leo.'

'My dear – '

'No.'

Tal looked at his sister. 'Leave it, Elizabeth. Cicely is right. It should just be you and me.'

Tal and Elizabeth stayed two nights with Eleanor, in what had proved to be a truly joyful reunion. Far from being dismayed to see her brother, Eleanor had hastened into his arms, and they had both wept with relief that the great secret was in the open at last. There had been such talking, so many things to say that they had been up well into the night. Tal's bitterness was assuaged, and he was able to return with a much lighter heart.

Cicely in turn enjoyed time with Leo. It was so good to be with him all day, every day, playing with him, teaching him little things, and watching him with the puppies he loved so much. They rode out together, Tom carrying Leo as Tal had. They were good rides. Leo was happy, and Cicely and Tom were at ease in each other's company. The great disparity in their ranks made no difference at all.

There were often tears in her eyes as she thought of Richard. The time had gone when in her grief she had been able to summon him in her imagination. On those occasions he had seemed so real again, a living, breathing man, but she had to accept that he was *not* real. He was all in her mind.

The morning after the return from Oare, Tal invited Cicely to ride up the escarpment to view the White Horse. He offered to take her to Wayland Smith as well, but she declined. That place had too many unpleasant connotations, whereas the Horse seemed different.

The skies were overcast as they ascended Blowing Stone Hill to the Ridgeway, which was wide and open to the elements. It was formed of different tracks and paths that wandered within yards of each other, sometimes crossing. The recent good weather had hardened the ground, so that merchants, packhorses, peddlers and an occasional ox-wagon were passing to and fro upon their business. There were flocks of sheep and herds of cattle being driven east, most of them destined for London markets. Drovers whistled to their working dogs, and there was a tinkle of bells and much bleating as a tribe of about thirty goats passed by.

The promise of rain made the air particularly clear, so that Cicely was *sure* she could see the towers of Abingdon Abbey, pale for a moment as a sunny beam managed to find a way through the canopy of cloud. She gazed around at the sweeping chalk rises and falls of the famous Downs. There were some copses and drifts of bracken, and the scent of wild herbs pervaded everything. Patches of yellow vetch were alive with blue butterflies, and tangles of eglantine threaded through wayside bushes. Insects hummed and throbbed, birds sang, and there was such a sense of freedom that she felt she could breathe more deeply. But something else breathed up here, and she was very aware of it.

She could not see the White Horse at first, for it could only be viewed in its entirety from a distance down in the vale. As she and Tal dismounted to walk the final yards over the crest of the escarpment, she knew nothing of how close the Horse was until she suddenly trod on a narrow strip of hard, flattened chalk.

Taking his dagger, Tal crouched to scratch the point over the compacted chalk. 'We stand on the head of the Horse. This is what the whole image looks like.'

She watched the picture he scraped. 'Is that *really* what is here?'

'Yes. Why?' He straightened to sheathe the dagger again.

'Well, it does not look at all like a horse, but a running hound. A talbot hound. Your badge.'

'Well, the Talbots are an old family, but I doubt if they were around when *this* was created. And our roots are in Shropshire and the Marches, not here.' He smiled.

'Nevertheless, it looks more a hound than a horse.'

'It is said that sometimes at Hallowtide a horn sounds from the Smith, and the Horse ups from here to canter to be reshod. Its hooves are said to shine brightly the next day.'

She looked at the crisp edges of the chalk, and the lack of weeds or shrubs. 'Who looks after the site? It is obviously well cared for.'

'Cheney. Once a year, at his own expense. Yet another

reason for my suspicions about him. At the very least I would expect him to demand I share the responsibility, but he seems almost possessive of his rights. Many villagers from Kingston go to assist. It is quite a festive occasion.'

'All of them pagans, do you think?'

Tal pursed his lips. 'Probably, but it is quite a festive summer occasion, and *everyone* likes such diversions. Also, it takes place in daylight, so there are no overt nods toward Woden, Wayland or any other god. It is impossible to prove who is what, unless they are caught at the rites at the Smith.' He gave a dry laugh. 'They *all* attend church, of course. No doubt with their unholy fingers crossed behind their backs.'

He paused. 'Cicely, there are two things I think you should know. Things Eleanor said. Firstly, and the lesser matter, is that the turquoise ring your father gave to you, and that you have since given to Jon, was in fact originally given to your father by Eleanor. I just thought you would prefer to know where it came from. And no, she does *not* expect its return. It is yours to do with as you please.'

Cicely lowered her eyes. Yes, she had given it to Jon, but it was very doubtful indeed that he still wore such a token of affection from the wife he no longer wanted. It rightly belonged to Eleanor.

'The second matter, and by far the more significant, concerns how Richard was informed of your father's bigamy. It's something Elizabeth did not know either.'

He had her full attention. 'Go on.'

'It happened when Eleanor learned of your father's sudden death, and knew that his son, your brother, was going to ascend the throne. Obviously, she also knew that the boy was baseborn. Had your father lived a few more years, and your brother been of age. . .well, who knows? As it was, Eleanor felt she could see to it that the truth was told. So she made sure Richard was shown something that proved her marriage to your father.'

Cicely gasped. '*Eleanor* was responsible for that?'

'Yes. A document signed by two witnesses to the ceremony was given very privately to Robert Stillington, the Bishop of Bath and Wells. He did not know whence it had come, of course, but he realized the document was authentic. He took it with all haste to Richard, still Duke of Gloucester and named Lord Protector by your father. Your brother's coronation was immediately postponed. Richard went himself to speak to the witnesses, and when he was satisfied that it was all true, he presented the evidence to Parliament. The facts were verified and Richard was urged to accept the throne, because he alone had the legitimate right.' Tal smiled. 'There, a great mystery solved.'

A strand of his long fair hair blew across his face, and the breeze seemed to sigh, as if the dragon slept within the hill. It was one of those odd moments that would be kept in her memory forever. Like a painting. Sir Humphrey Talbot as she would always wish to recall him. Up here, in the free summer air, on the White Horse.

When they returned to the manor, Deakin hurried out with an urgent message from Sir John Cheney. Tal told Cicely to go on inside, and five minutes later he came up to the parlour, where she was seated with Elizabeth, enjoying a sip of quince wine.

'It seems a decisive battle has taken place in Brittany,' he said without preamble. 'At a place called St Aubin du Cormier. The French invaded and crushed the Bretons. Sir Edward Woodville was slain, as was his entire force. The Isle of Wight has lost a huge number of its menfolk. Cheney has informed me because he knows I will have to go to the king as soon as possible.'

Cicely could imagine Henry's reaction. The hoped-for outcome had not materialized because Brittany had not held out against French aggression. But clever Henry, who had made his acrimony toward Sir Edward so public, could not be accused of entering the lists against France. The French would be suspicious, but would not blame him outright. Cicely was saddened by Brittany's downfall and the loss of so many Englishmen, but not by the death of her uncle, who had been another traitor to Richard.

'It will mean my return to Calais,' Tal went on. 'Henry's lily-white hands will be held up for all to see, and the world will pretend not to see the dirt under his fingernails.' He sighed. 'But that is beside the point, because I will have to seek an immediate audience with him at Windsor. Cicely, you can remain here for as long as you wish, or I can escort you back to Pasmer's Place, provided you prepare to leave quickly.'

With Elizabeth already having arranged to take Leo to Kenninghall in a day or so, there was nothing to keep Cicely at Kingston. 'I will go to Pasmer's Place,' she replied.

Chapter Thirteen

A MONTH HAD passed, and in late September London was a place of dust, dirt, crowds and too many unpleasant smells. Cicely found it stifling and unpleasant after the wide, fresh air of Berkshire and the Downs. Henry and the court were still away in pleasant Windsor, but Viscountess Welles had to remain in Pasmer's Place, waiting to be summoned.

Of the three mansions in St Sithe's Lane, Pasmer's Place was the smallest, but also the most elegant and well-appointed, with a sheltered, enclosed garden to the rear, where summer flowers continued to bloom well into autumn.

The house was in the heart of the city, yet Cicely sometimes felt entombed in silence, even when London's noise drifted through an open casement. But she was *not* alone, because the Kymbes were with her, Mary, Tom and Mistress Kymbe, who had come to London for the wedding. Mary and Perry had been married only yesterday at nearby St Anthony's church, on the corner of St Sithe's Lane and Budge Row. The bridal pair now occupied a pleasantly secluded room at the back of the building, Tal having left Perry in Cicely's household to enjoy the first few weeks of married life. A return to the service of the Marshal of Calais would come all too soon.

Cicely stood at the parlour window, looking over the courtyard and high wall to the lane, which ran between Budge Row and Pancras Lane in Cordwainer ward. The old city sprawled from the Thames up to St. Paul's atop Ludgate Hill, and glancing up, she could see the great cathedral's immense steeple sailing against the sky. But looking down again, she noticed a black cat padding along the courtyard wall, before jumping down into the lane. A chill shivered through her, because she could not help thinking of Tybalt. Ridiculous, she decided, because Tybalt was far away in Kingston. A black cat in London was just a black cat in London.

But unease was her constant companion now that she knew Henry had lied about Leo. There had been so many lies and odd events. She had been able to forget them for a while at Kingston, but now, here, they seemed to crowd upon her. Above all, she had to accept that it would be harder than ever before to face Henry. Previous meetings had always proved easier than seemed possible, but this time it did not help that he had been seeking Leo on the Isle of Wight, and had denied it to her. And *he* had to be the one who set Romulus and Remus to spy upon her.

He had insisted on the pact—and now it was clear his only concern was keeping her silent about Roland, while he, Henry, went about whatever he chose to do regarding Leo. All she could do now was bear in mind at all times that the safety and wellbeing of others, especially Richard's child, depended upon her continued influence on Henry Tudor's desires. Leo, Jon, Tal, the Kymbes—and Jack, of course, were Henry to realize he still lived. They would suffer whatever punishment appealed to Henry's perverse mind at the time. He was devoured from within by his dark self, and the terrible punishment he had inflicted on Richard's other son, John of Gloucester, must never be forgotten.

What had he intended to do if Leo had been secured on Wight? Would he have disposed of him? It was the obvious course for an insecure king who dreaded being usurped as he had done to Richard. Leo was a royal child of the House of York, and his illegitimacy did not really make him any less of a threat. If he lived to manhood, he would *be* the House of York, for there could not be another who more represented that blood line.

How she wished the meeting with Henry were over and done with. He was *bound* to know she was here, because Tal would have told him, but he had too much else on his mind.

The news from Brittany continued to be bad, and he was blaming Sir Edward Woodville, as well as the ineptitude of his former brother-in-law, Jean IV de Rieux, commander of the crushed Breton forces. And there was the mystery of Lisbon to consider, as well as the countless general duties and ceremonies expected of a King of England. Before Bosworth, Henry Tudor had no idea at all what was entailed in becoming king; no idea at all about the endless responsibilities that Richard had taken in his stride. It was a lesson Henry still found exhausting to learn.

There was no word from Jon, nor had she expected any. He had someone else now, and wanted no more of his troublesome Plantagenet wife. It was a sad end to a match that had once been so fond and close.

Tal was in Calais, and had also been silent. Had he seen Jack, whom she prayed would still come to her at Hallowtide? A profound new thought had begun to take root. It was to ask Jack to take Leo with him when he returned to Burgundy. She would stay in England, and with luck Henry would be some time discovering the boy's exile. Maybe years.

A rider arrived outside, his horse clattering on the courtyard cobbles. He wore the queen's colours, and had come with a sealed message that he handed over when Tom went out to greet him.

The following morning, in bright autumn sunshine, Cicely took passage upstream on the Thames to Windsor, in a barge with eight oarsmen. She was accompanied by Mary, Tom and her personal men-at-arms in the Welles colours. Beneath a light mantle she wore demure pale-blue silk over a white undergown, and her hair was completely concealed by a headdress. Bess had summoned her, and Cicely, while wondering about her sister's purpose, did not intend to be provocative in any way, least of all in her choice of clothes.

The barge flew Jon's banner, a prancing black lion on a vivid yellow ground, which was recognized on the quay as the vessel rocked toward a mooring in the shadow of Windsor Castle. The great fortress rose along its chalk cliff, some hundred feet above the river, with the town clustering in its lee. Some properties even clung against the foot of the curtain wall.

In her summons, Bess had made clear her undiminished loathing by instructing Lady Welles not to approach the royal apartments through the privileged private entrance in the octagonal Rose Tower. Instead the queen's sister was to suffer the ignominy of the more circuitous and lowly route through the Spicerie Gate. It was typically sour and petty, and showed how very far away the queen was from the Bess to whom Cicely had once been so close.

Men hastened to attend as the barge nudged the quay. Suitable horses were immediately provided, and the men-at-arms fell in behind as the party from Pasmer's Place progressed slowly along the wharf and then up the hill from the river, passing around the great walls of the imposing castle that had been first built by the Conqueror.

A fair was in progress in the town, and as the court was in residence, Windsor bustled with people and noise. The wealthy jostled with beggars, hawkers, thieves, pickpockets, market wives, animals and farmers from the surrounding lands. A column of nuns scurried downhill, and a swift detachment of mounted archers overtook Cicely's slower party on the ascent. Jon's colours continued to be recognized, and her men-at-arms had to clear the way through a crowd intent upon gawping at one of the highest ladies of the land.

The castle was laid out like a figure-of-eight, with a huge mound or motte at the centre of the eight. On top of the motte stood a remarkable round tower, wide, with a great striking clock installed in the reign of King Edward III. The tower overlooked the two main wards or baileys, the upper of which was where the private apartments were to be found, while the lower was dominated by the as-yet-incomplete restoration of St George's Chapel, where Cicely's father was interred.

The crowds that followed her party included importunate beggars, clacking and rattling their bowls loudly. Cicely's palfrey rolled its eyes and capered anxiously as one man managed to come too close, brandishing his bowl like a weapon. Tom intervened, using his own mount to force the man away. Then, as Cicely struggled to keep the palfrey moving, she became unpleasantly conscious of someone's close scrutiny. Turning swiftly in the saddle, she scanned the crowds, but did not see who it might have been. Her palfrey was increasingly fractious because of the crush, and she had to plead with Tom. 'We *must* move on. I am not a very good rider and may be unseated!'

Seizing the bridle, he led her on toward the upper gatehouse, where Jon's banner was all the identification needed to gain admission. Once inside the ward, with the crowds excluded, the palfrey became calm again. Cicely closed her eyes and took a deep breath. The watching eyes had been imagination, she told herself. But the unease remained.

The royal apartments occupied the north-east corner of the upper ward, enjoying fine views from the cliff toward the river and the rich rolling landscape beyond. The magnificent first-floor windows of St George's Hall caught the sunlight, as did the stained glass of Henry's new private chapel above the Spicerie Gate, where the humiliation of Lady Welles was to commence. Alongside the gate, directly beneath the hall, was the vaulted undercroft where the servants rested and took their meals. It was where the royal Earl of Warwick—under the name Lambert Simnel—could often be found, when he was not turning a spit in the kitchens. She would like to see him again, but it was inadvisable. If Henry learned, his suspicions might be aroused, and anyway, the boy wished to forget his bloodline.

It was only when grooms hurried to attend the horses, and two men in royal livery crossed the ward toward her, that Cicely realized they were all wearing black arm-ribbons. Mourning? For whom? Looking around, she saw others, yet there were no marks of mourning amid the many flags and banners fluttering from the towers and battlements. She felt disagreeably conspicuous—and disrespectful—in her pretty blue gown, without so much as a single black pendant.

On alighting, she was conducted alone toward the Spicerie Gate. Apprehension gripped cruelly, and then sank its claws in still further as she entered the lobby, where everyone wore mourning of one sort or another. The riotous colours of the painted walls were comforting as she was ushered toward the public stairs that led up to the state and royal private apartments, but she halted abruptly on seeing three youths at the foot of the steps. They all wore black bands or ribbons, one clearly tied in haste, and were conversing with Abbot Sante, whose retinue of Benedictine monks from Abingdon waited nearby, heads bowed, hands clasped neatly before them.

Bess's servants had to halt as well, and exchanged frowning glances as Cicely watched the group by the staircase. The identity of the youths commanded her attention, for they were Edmund de la Pole, Thomas Howard and Roland de Vielleville. Roland's presence startled her, because he was supposed to be in the north with Jon. Did this mean her husband had returned?

Annie's fifteen-year-old betrothed, the dour and lantern-jawed Thomas Howard, resembled a gloomy old nag, and Cicely could only think of his sexually deviant tastes.

Jack's corrupt younger brother, Edmund, was seventeen, with an air of cool, dangerous, almost supernatural fascination. He was tall and inordinately handsome, with fine features and the sort of pale complexion that should have had a thousand freckles, yet had not one. Light chestnut curls tumbled sensuously over his shoulders, and soft brown eyes shone beneath dark eyebrows and lashes. They were clever, expressive eyes, and he knew how to use them. Everything about Jack's younger brother was seductive. What had Abbot Sante said? That Edmund was a beautiful, cruel youth, who appeared to transfix members of both sexes, but was himself hollow inside? How true that was.

Edmund was dressed in gold and pine-green parti-colours that emphasized his short, tightly laced doublet and even tighter hose. The brightness of his clothes told that he too had been caught out by the royal mourning, as did the untidy black silk bow around his arm, which she guessed was a last-minute acquisition.

Cicely's gaze moved to Henry's secret son, the blond-haired Roland de Vielleville, who stood slightly behind his companions, and who carried himself regally, even though he believed himself to be only Breton nobility. His fifteenth birthday had been on 16 June, the day dedicated to his legendary namesake, Roland of Roncevaux, hero of French romance and chivalry.

Roland's clothes were dark blue, and his left shoulder boasted the prancing red lion badge of Briand de Coskäer, the cruel man he believed to be his father. The boy's straight hair formed a perfect roll of under-curl that was at present no lower than his ears, but six months ago it had rested on his shoulders. He had a full, sulky mouth and a haughty expression that not even Henry could have bettered. But it was all bravado, because behind it all he was shy and unhappy. Cicely had achieved a friendly relationship with him, which he appreciated. He was terrified of Henry, who was formidable, it was true, but what on earth could have happened to arouse such absolute dread in his son? It must have been something truly appalling.

One of the waiting royal escorts coughed meaningfully, but Cicely had no intention of proceeding. Bess could wait. Summoning a serene smile, she approached the group at the foot of the staircase, intending to address the abbot, who turned when the three young men reacted to seeing her.

Sante hesitated, because their previous meeting had ended awkwardly, but then he smiled and extended a hand for her to kiss the gold ring of his office. 'Lady Welles, how very agreeable to encounter you. Our supping together at Abingdon seems an inordinately long time ago.'

'Indeed it does, Abbot John,' she replied, curtseying low.

He turned to the three young men, who immediately executed elegant bows. Well, elegant enough. Thomas Howard was respectful, but she noticed a smirk on his lips. Edmund pretended to be all that was gallant. Of the three, only Roland's greeting smile was honest.

She inclined her head to Thomas and Roland, but upon Edmund de la Pole she bestowed only a frosty look. It was his sworn purpose to be rid of his inconveniently resurrected older brother. And probably of me too, she thought.

The intense dislike between the two first cousins was mutual, for his eyes were no less frosty.

Abbot Sante drew her aside, leaving the others to whisper together. 'I do trust I am no longer in your bad books, Lady Cicely?'

'Of course not, Abbot Sante. I appreciated the roses.'

'I am glad. Do you not think that Brother Geoffrey's exquisite singing and readings seem too long ago?'

Her mind was blank. Who could he be talking about? The only brother she knew from Abingdon had been the young monk who waited upon their table, and he was neither a Geoffrey *nor* possessed of a melodious voice.

Sante's eyes danced mischievously. 'I think perhaps he can be persuaded to reward us again, for he has accompanied me from Abingdon.'

'Indeed?' What on *earth* did all this mean?

He glanced at her blue gown. 'I see you have not been made aware that the queen has commanded there to be mourning for Sir Edward Woodville.'

'So *he* is the dear departed?' Bess had never given him a thought in life. This was spite, pure and simple, using Sir Edward's demise to humiliate Lady Welles.

'Indeed,' the abbot agreed. 'However, the order was only issued this morning, immediately after Henry's departure.'

'The king is not here?'

Sante shook his head. 'He has gone on some urgent private visit or other, and will not return for at least a week.'

'Where has he gone?' Was it relief or disappointment that swept over her?

'Only his close advisors know, and they are not saying.'

She smiled. 'The queen's actions do not surprise me, I fear, Abbot Sante.'

'Maybe not, but she *has* changed of late.'

'What do you mean?'

'It has something to do with the king, but no one seems to know what. She has even been seen to smile at him, which he finds visibly discomforting.'

Cicely remembered Henry's description of the transformation in the royal marriage bed.

The abbot edged the conversation on. 'Did you know that Lord Welles is in Windsor?'

'I thought so, because *Écuyer* de Vielleville is here. I take it my husband is not alone?'

He was surprised. 'You know of the, er, woman?'

'Yes. It is of no consequence.' *Liar! It is of great consequence!*

Sante sighed. 'It is common knowledge at court, although the woman's identity is not. She stays behind the closed doors of the house Lord Welles has taken in Windsor town. However, I do have word of Lord Lincoln. He will be with you again soon.'

'Oh, I pray so.' She paused. 'I am surprised you pass on a message from an adulterer to his adulterous love.'

He smiled. 'Lady Cicely, some marriages become lost causes. Your husband has deserted you, and Lord Lincoln's wife wants nothing to do with him. This being so, I do not think you will ever take yourself off to a nunnery, or he to a monastery.' He cleared his throat. 'Perhaps we should speak of something else? Did you enjoy your brief sojourn in Kingston l'Isle?'

'Yes.' She did not explain further.

When they returned to the youths, Edmund observed her as if he knew everything there was to know, and the disagreeable smirk still graced Thomas Howard's lips, suggesting to Cicely that Annie had told him exceedingly colourful tales of Lady Welles. Heaven alone knew what outrageous embellishments there might have been, but Annie was capable of anything. How long would his sneer endure if he were to be told of dear little Annie's dalliances with both Roland and Edmund?

Abbot Sante set about the two. 'I trust, sirs, that your gloating, unpleasant expressions are nothing more than indigestion?'

Thomas's face became a mask, but Edmund was not fazed. 'Forgive me, my lord abbot, I did not intend to appear gloating or unpleasant.'

'Indeed? Nevertheless, that is what you have succeeded in doing. It must cease forthwith. If it does not, I am well able to make your life at court very uncomfortable. Do you understand?'

'I understand fully, Abbot Sante.' But Edmund's beautifully sculptured lips were thin and angry. He did not take kindly to being criticized. Or threatened. But a mitred abbot was not to be treated lightly.

Sante turned his attention to Thomas. 'Well, sir? You should know that your noble and entirely admirable grandfather would most certainly deal harshly with you were he still here. Before Bosworth, he charged me to make sure you never wander from the path of righteousness. Certain sordid tales have been reaching me. You, sir, had best mend your ways, or it will be the worst for you.'

Thomas's eyes widened, before being lowered.

Roland spoke up suddenly. 'My lord, is it known when the king will return?' He seemed to hold his breath as he awaited an answer.

'I fear not, *écuyer*.'

Roland plainly would not mind if Henry *never* returned. Cicely caught his glance, and for a moment it seemed that he had a whole volume of secrets to hide, but then he looked swiftly away.

Abbot Sante ended the meeting. 'Agreeable as it is to converse with you again, my lady, I must take these three angels to St. George's Chapel, where they—and a gathering of their peers—must endure my excessively long sermon.' He paused. 'I trust you and I will sup together again soon?'

'You are assured of an invitation to Pasmer's Place, Abbot Sante.'

He smiled and leaned closer to whisper. 'The old Duke of Norfolk did not really ask me to watch over his grandson, but it will not harm the loathsome young pup to think he did.'

She watched as he made his way toward the entrance, followed by his charges and the column of patient monks. Thomas and Edmund accorded her the minimum farewell that was acceptable, but Roland ventured a smile, which she returned.

But as they disappeared from view into the upper ward, the tall figure of Sir John Cheney entered. Cicely turned away quickly, not wanting to speak to him. When she glanced back, he had gone.

The royal servants still waited, now venturing to display their impatience, and she girded herself for what lay ahead. She soon heard sombre music from the queen's apartments on the first floor. Bess was playing the grief-stricken niece to the full. Richard would not have taken any nonsense from her. That being so, nor would Lady Welles.

Be with me now, Richard, Cicely thought as she was shown into Bess's presence.

Chapter Fourteen

THE QUEEN'S APARTMENTS were magnificent, with walls and chamfered rafters that dazzled with colour. Yellow ochre was particularly prevalent. There was a magnificent stone fireplace sculpted with Tudor roses set amid the sun's rays, and arched windows with painted glass that admitted a riot of tints upon rich furnishings, wall hangings and brilliant floor tiles. So much gold leaf shone that it was dazzling.

Bess was seated on an ornate chair that was almost a throne. The Queen of England was twenty-two, and regal as only she could be, wearing charcoal robes, with a black headdress that hid the warm-gold hair of which she was so justifiably proud, and which was shaved back to create a fashionably high forehead. Strikingly lovely—albeit more buxom than even a year ago—she had a perfect oval face, full lips and bright blue eyes, and had been their father's favourite. Coming first was something she had always expected, so it had come as such a very rude shock to realize that Cicely was much more to the liking of both Richard *and* Henry. Bess's pride and vanity had been severely tried.

Annie was among the ladies on the floor around Bess. The Lady Ann Plantagenet was always in attendance upon Bess now, and had certainly been the only sister at the great St George's Feast celebrations in April. The glint in her almond-shaped slate-blue eyes warned that she, like Bess, intended to take mean pleasure at Cicely's expense.

The third surviving daughter of Edward IV seemed older than her almost-thirteen years. Her hair was long, straight and silver-fair, and her face was pale and sweetly formed. However, she was certainly *not* the gentle angel-in-the-making she seemed, being more a fully-formed Circe. Slender and willowy, she had dainty breasts and a narrow waist, and her dark-grey gown should have appeared demure, yet somehow did not. The fault of the wearer, Cicely thought acerbically, imagining a match between Annie and Edmund de la Pole.

Cicely sank to her knees, as if before Henry himself. The funereal dirge of the minstrels continued as Bess subjected her to a long, disapproving gaze that was tinged with utter loathing. 'How very remiss of you, madam, not to observe mourning for our dear uncle, Sir Edward Woodville.' Her voice was rimmed with frost.

'I crave forgiveness, Your Grace.' Cicely wondered how long the late Sir Edward been *dear*.

'You shall not have my forgiveness.'

Cicely's ire stirred. She always found it next to impossible to submit to Bess's goading—to *anyone's* goading, including Henry's—but today she had steeled herself with Richard's strength. So she found a reasonable response. 'I believed Sir Edward had offended His Majesty, Your Grace, and did not wish to cause additional offence. If I have transgressed, I pray you will find it in your heart to overlook my error. I will not be guilty of such dereliction of blood duty again.'

Mentioning Henry spirited the man himself into the room, just as Cicely intended, and all three sisters knew whose case he would uphold. At least, Cicely hoped he would, for his recent silence rather brought that into doubt.

Bess's eyes were like flint as she dismissed her ladies and the minstrels. The music came to a confused halt as the latter scrambled with their instruments and hastened to follow the sombrely clad ladies from the royal presence. Annie hesitated, but then remained where she was. Bess saw, but did not send her packing. The sign of favour prompted the little miss to wriggle closer to the royal chair, and go so far as to rest her head against the arm in a rather proprietorial manner.

At last Bess indicated to Cicely to stand, but not to be seated. 'So, Lady Welles, I trust your sojourn in Abingdon was a comfort to you? I believe you sought Abbot Sante's counsel?'

'Your Grace is very well informed.'

'Indeed.'

'Abingdon was most agreeable, Your Grace.' Cicely's eyes met the queen's. *And while I was there I rolled your liege lord between the sheets until he could barely breathe of the ecstasy, or walk afterward.* Oh, how gratifying to utter it aloud!

'One can only imagine your reason for such a visit.' Bess dripped with pure vitriol.

'I sought spiritual guidance,' Cicely replied.

'And for that had to go all the way to Abingdon? Have you no confessor of your own?'

'I had heard good things of Abbot Sante, and wished to consult him. He was most kind, and his words were very wise. I left Abingdon much comforted.'

'To go to Kingston l'Isle. With Sir Humphrey Talbot.'

Bess was *remarkably* knowledgeable, Cicely thought. 'Indeed so, Your Grace,' she answered. 'I went for two reasons. Firstly, to make the acquaintance of his sister, the Duchess of Norfolk, who was staying with him at the time. And secondly to—'

'The duchess was there?' Bess's chagrin was palpable.

Cicely relaxed, because if Bess did not know of Elizabeth's presence, then she could not know of Leo's either. 'Indeed so, Your Grace,' she said, 'and a more pleasing and charming lady I could not hope to meet. I am invited to visit her at Kenninghall whenever it pleases me.'

'Really.' Bess was reptilian. 'And the second reason?'

'St Margaret's Well.'

Bess frowned. 'What?'

'A holy well, Your Grace. The waters are beneficial for fertility.'

Bess was amused. 'So, you still hope to become with child by. . .um, *your* husband? One can never be sure whose lord it might be.'

Annie sniggered, and Cicely glanced coldly at her. 'I am surprised to find you here, madam, for I understood His Majesty had banished you to our mother at Bermondsey.' It was a bleak reminder of the circumstances under which Henry had issued such an order. There had been a banquet at Pasmer's Place when he and Cicely herself had caught Annie in Roland de Vielleville's bedchamber.

Annie's sneer subsided abruptly. 'I am not at Bermondsey because the queen sent for me. And you misled the king about me,' she added, for Bess's benefit. Clearly the misdemeanours at Pasmer's Place had not been fully disclosed.

'Misled?' Cicely evinced amusement. 'I hardly think so. He had the evidence of his own eyes.'

Bess glanced at Annie. 'If you have not been entirely truthful with me, miss, you will soon rue it.'

'I have told all, Bess, truly.' Annie cast a diabolical look at Cicely.

The queen's attention also returned to Cicely. 'One presumes that by now you understand the futility of wishing to provide Lord Welles with a child. Only divine intervention could bring that miracle about. You do know he is here in Windsor with his doxy?'

'Yes, I know.'

Bess was disappointed, having hoped to pierce Cicely. 'Well, this woman appears to be his true love. His Plantagenet princess is no longer of consequence.'

'Perhaps he is no longer in my heart either.' Once again the words brought Henry into the room.

'You think the king loves you?' Bess laughed, but oddly. 'He uses you, my dear. He relieves himself into you, and that is all. You are a safely fruitless vessel for the royal seed. And maybe he is not going to bother with you again. You have not crossed his mind since you returned.'

Annie's amused snort made Cicely's eyes flash. 'Well, Annie, would it be equally amusing if Thomas found out about you and *Écuyer* de Vielleville?' She kept Edmund de la Pole for another time.

Bess's lips twitched, for this was the first she had heard of Roland and Annie.

But the girl's airy response was not as expected. 'Oh, I am not concerned with Thomas *or* Roland. Not now.'

Bess pounced. 'And what does *that* mean?'

'That I am content to wait for whatever husband you and the dear king choose for me,' was the sweetly glib response.

Too glib by far. For a moment Bess and Cicely looked at each other. A fleeting second, and they were sisters again, as in the past, but then a lady-in-waiting ventured timidly into the chamber with a pretty silver dish laden with fresh, very unseasonal, strawberries.

'Craving your pardon, Your Grace, but the King's Lady Mother has sent these. They are from Collyweston.'

Margaret had an almost magically green-fingered gardener at her favourite country estate. He was able to coax early-summer fruit right through until autumn in a heated, large-windowed building with a sunny southern aspect. Or so Cicely seemed to recall Margaret saying.

Bess looked at the strawberries, and her cheeks reddened, not with anger but with something else. Embarrassment? Cicely could not imagine what the emotion was, but certainly Bess was pleased and more than willing to accept the gift. That in itself was odd, because there was no love lost between Henry's queen and his mother.

'Please send my warm thanks to the King's Lady Mother.'

Warm thanks? Cicely kept her eyes lowered. Bess had never been all that fond of strawberries, believing they brought her out in red spots, yet now it seemed not.

The lady bobbed a curtsey, placed the strawberries on a table and then withdrew. Silence fell as Bess gazed at the dish.

Cicely could not prevent her thoughts from winging back to the strawberries of that famous May night with Henry. It had been a night when what she felt for him had briefly tipped over into love itself, only for his shades and jealousy to ruin everything the next morning. But that was Henry. He could not help himself.

Suddenly she felt Bess's gaze upon her. And what a gaze it was, overflowing with jealousy and guilt. But why? Then Bess looked at the strawberries again. The sisters had once been so close, that Cicely knew intuitively that they were *both* thinking of the same night! Bess had been at Westminster at the time, perhaps able to witness what had happened. Maybe she too knew of the secret passage and the door behind the tapestry.

Had seeing what Henry could really be like aroused her physical desire? That night, Harri Tudur had been an exquisite lover, humorous, gentle, knowing and considerate. In short, he had been the man from whom Cicely herself found it difficult to turn away.

Bess's instinct was as sharp as Cicely's, and she knew she had given herself away. Her voice was oddly controlled as she spoke to Cicely, keeping her voice inaudible to Annie. 'Henry is mine, and mine alone, Lady Welles. *I* am the one he must come to for heirs, and he now enjoys me far more than you would wish to know.'

'I have always wanted you to be happy with him, Bess.'

'How noble.'

How the exchange might have continued would never be known, because there was another interruption, this time by a nurse bringing Prince Arthur to see his mother. 'Your Grace, I have brought the prince, as you instructed.'

For a moment Bess regarded her as if the Devil Incarnate had been announced, but then recovered a little, and sat down again. 'Very well.'

Arthur Tudor, to be Henry's Prince of Wales, was a month short of his second birthday. A quiet, reserved child, he looked as if he seldom romped enough to become dirty. His eyes were the same wintry seascape as his father's, but without Henry's unfortunate cast. Nevertheless, they were hooded eyes and he had Henry's high cheekbones. He was a Beaufort, not a Plantagenet.

His clothes were rich and beautiful, and like Leo, he was intrigued to see a new face. Suddenly he stretched out his arms and almost hurled himself from the nurse's grasp toward Cicely, who had to move hastily to catch him. This delighted him, because it was a game, but his laughter was not boisterous like Leo's. It had nothing to do with being oppressed or badly treated, because he was quite clearly in the best of health and enjoyed his little game. It was simply that his nature was his father's.

Cicely smiled at him. 'We meet again, my lord prince. I have not held you like this since your christening.'

Bess did not like it, and snapped her fingers for the nurse to retrieve the child and take him away. Suddenly she wanted everyone gone, including Annie.

'Get out! I will be alone!'

Annie scowled, but Cicely was relieved to escape.

The return down the hill to the river was even more difficult than the ascent, because an overturned wagon of logs had now partially blocked the way. At the bottom of the slope a row of small shops clung limpet-like against the base of the castle wall. Cicely had not paid attention to them on arriving, but now noticed a bootmaker's shop, its sign a pair of battered, black-painted thigh boots. It opened directly on to the roadway, and a plump man with a limp emerged. Remus! Maybe he sensed something, for he looked directly at her. His face changed as he realized she recognized him, and he took to his heels into the crowds, soon disappearing.

Cicely stared after him. Had his been the eyes she had perceived earlier? She was so preoccupied that when the crowd surged around again, and her palfrey reared, she was ill prepared. She screamed, and the crowd was shocked into silence as she was hurled to the ground. Agonising pain lanced through her, and she lost consciousness.

Tom and Mary jumped down to attend to her, while Perry led her still-upset palfrey aside. Mary looked urgently at her brother. 'We must take her back into the castle, but not to the queen. The King's Lady Mother must be alerted. Perry and I will ride back immediately. You bring my lady.' She knew that Margaret regarded herself as Cicely's friend.

The chastened crowd parted in silence as Mary and Perry rode away swiftly. Tom lifted Cicely carefully from the ground to give her to one of the men-at-arms, to hold while he himself remounted. Then he bent to gather her close again, his arm around her protectively as he urged his horse after the maid and her husband.

Lady Margaret Beaufort, Countess of Derby, had been thirteen when she gave birth to Henry. The travails had been arduous because she was both small and young, and her little body had been left so damaged she had never had another child. It might be thought she would loathe Henry's twenty-five-year-old father, Edmund Tudor, Earl of Richmond, the elder of King Henry VI's half-brothers, for consummating their marriage when she was still only twelve, but she would not hear a word against him. She had loved him then, and loved him still. He had been kind and gentle with her, and her heart had broken when he died of plague while a prisoner of the Yorkists. Henry had been born posthumously. At the end of her life she wished to lie alongside him in Grey Friars, Carmarthen.

She was now forty-five, and her distinctive Beaufort looks had been passed on to Henry. She and Cicely had formed an unlikely friendship because of Henry and Jon, the two men—her son and half-brother—who meant most in the world to Margaret.

Tom carried Cicely up to the royal apartments, from where Margaret had already sent an urgent message to Henry's physician and astrologer, Master Rogers. Cicely was laid gently against a pile of rich pillows on a bed in a guest chamber that overlooked an inner garden court.

Margaret ushered everyone away, including her cluster of ladies, but instructed Tom to remain with her. She knew of him, and was curious, especially now she had seen his strong but quiet mien. And good looks. 'So, you are Master Thomas Kymbe?'

'My lady.' Tom executed a very respectful bow.

He knew how to conduct himself with the highest in the land, she thought, inclining her head in response. 'You clearly have great concern for Lady Welles' comfort and wellbeing.'

'Indeed so, my lady.'

'And you are an adherent of my brother, Lord Welles?'

'Yes, my lady, I have that honour.'

'Yet you did not go north with him?'

'I would have accompanied him gladly, but he did not request my presence, my lady.'

Margaret nodded. Her spies had told her of the Kymbes of Friskney, and how they had taken care of Leo. She also knew that Henry was jealously convinced that this man was in love with Cicely. Henry's mother was now inclined to agree, because everything about Tom suggested a deep, enduring devotion to Cicely. 'Thank you for taking care of Lady Welles. I will see that you are rewarded.'

'I desire no reward for protecting her, my lady.'

'That is your prerogative, sir. Very well, you may go now. Oh, where are you lodging?'

He paused. 'My duties are at Pasmer's Place, my lady.'

'I see.' Margaret nodded his dismissal, and watched him as he withdrew. This was a situation that would have to be watched, she decided, sitting at Cicely's bedside to await Master Rogers. She had dismissed Mary, whose skills she persisted in regarding as uncomfortably close to witchcraft. Better to wait for Master Rogers and his astrology.

She took Cicely's hand. 'Come back to us, my dear,' she

said quietly. 'I could not face my son if I had to give him bad news of you.' There was no response.

It was not long before Master Rogers arrived, for he had only been in the town. Elderly, clad in black, with a long white beard and a skull cap, he was an impressive figure. Astrology, spells and charms were his forte, and it was mostly from him that Henry's reliance on superstition, omens and such things had stemmed.

He examined Cicely and after consulting his charts, announced that she would recover soon. When he had dressed her forehead with a wet, lavender-scented cloth, he selected some medicaments—yellow salve, a pink potion and a little box of black pills—from his large casket. After issuing instructions, he departed with a promise to return later. Margaret knew that as soon as Cicely came to, she would dispense with his instructions in favour of whatever her maid provided. Some of that noxious green cure-all salve, no doubt. Margaret's lips pressed together disapprovingly.

It was evening before Cicely regained consciousness. She was bruised and aching, and to shift even a little on the pillows was a painful exercise. Her head thudded so much that she found it difficult to open her eyes.

Margaret brought a little honeyed wine in a goblet. 'Take a sip of this, my dear, and swallow these two black pills. Master Rogers assured me they would help your headache. Something about making them from boiling the juice of willow bark. At least, I *think* that is what he said. And the wine will warm you from within, of course. Always a good thing when one has suffered a shock.'

Cicely tried to smile. 'Thank you so much, but can my maid be sent for? Please?'

Margaret sighed. 'Oh, very well, but you know I cannot favour her unchristian ways.' She clapped her hands and a lady came running. Moments later a message was on its way to Mary Perry.

Margaret's sour glance fell upon a corner of the coverlet,

which bore the unmistakable evidence of monkey teeth. 'I do wish Henry had taken that wretched ape with him.'

Henry had chosen the name Crumplin for his new pet, because it referred to someone with a crooked back. It was therefore a jibe at Richard.

Margaret was bristling. 'The vile creature follows me everywhere, and relieves itself upon my kerchiefs. Now I find *this*!'

In spite of her situation, Cicely had to overcome an urge to laugh, because it would be painful. But the thought of the tiny brown miscreant's antics lightened her spirits.

'The horrible beast's only redeeming feature is that it loves Henry.' Margaret paused as something more immediate struck her. 'Did you know Jon is here in Windsor?'

'Yes.'

'Has he approached you?'

'No.'

Margaret searched her face. 'Do you wish him to?'

'Only if he intends to be civil.'

'I have some very *uncivil* words waiting for him, you may be sure of that,' Margaret declared. 'How can he possibly think it is acceptable to toss aside a princess in favour of a—a—*trollop*?'

At that moment Crumplin bounded tail-high into the room and onto the bed, where he sat chattering. His eyes were as sparrow-bright as Mistress Kymbe's and he was about one foot tall, with a smooth coat and very long tail. Seeing Margaret, he bared his teeth in what might have been a smile or a grimace, Cicely could not tell.

Margaret watched with distaste as Crumplin ventured onto the pillows. Unable to bear it, she rose to brush the creature away to the foot of the bed, which only resulted in a torrent of furious gibbering and screeching.

Cicely addressed it quietly. 'Crumplin?'

The monkey stopped and looked intently at her.

'Do you miss your master?'

The gentle voice brought the little monkey closer, making soft, sad noises.

'Henry will be back soon.' Cicely reached out tentatively, half expecting a bite for her trouble, but the monkey edged closer until he was in the crook of her arm as if he had known her forever.

Margaret stared. 'No one else can *stand* the little wretch. The only accolades came when it destroyed Henry's hated notebook. For a while the noxious animal was adored by everyone who feared being featured in its pages. They all knew they were included, because Henry would insist on writing in it in front of them. He still does, in a new book.' She sighed, and changed the subject. 'My dear, I see by your gown that you were lured into the mourning trap today. Henry will not be pleased with your sister when he finds out, but she will never forgive you for your kings.'

Cicely smiled and sipped the wine. Together with the cool lavender cloth and black pills, it was already having a soothing effect upon her headache. As was Crumplin, who cuddled up to her as he clearly cuddled up to Henry.

'How is Leo?' Margaret asked suddenly. 'Safe, one imagines? The question was uttered after a noticeable pause.

'I sincerely trust so.' Where was this leading?

Margaret rubbed her eyelid, a mannerism shared with her son. 'Perhaps you should know that Henry did *not* send men to the Isle of Wight.'

Cicely was startled. 'You know about that?'

'Yes. One of my best fellows learned there were men in royal livery seeking your boy. I know you think it was Henry's doing, but it was not.'

'How do you know I thought it was?'

Margaret smiled. 'You were *bound* to think it, my dear. I would in your place. All I know now is that the men scoured the island, but found nothing. Except a cousin of the Kymbes, which in itself tells to me that your Leo had indeed been there.'

Cicely avoided her eyes.

Margaret smiled again. 'My dear, in this at least, Henry has not been false with you. Think now, a man like my son would have been infinitely more circumspect, and *not* sent men who tramped openly all over the island in his livery. He is far too subtle.'

Cicely gazed at her. It was true, Henry *was* too subtle. Why had she not considered that? The thought led on that if Tal was wrong and Henry was innocent, who *had* sent them?

'And before you wonder if *I* am the guilty party,' Margaret continued, 'let me vow here and now that I am not. My agents are tasked to watch and report, but that is all.'

Cicely's eyes were intent. 'Did you send two men to Abingdon?'

'No. I did not send anyone to Abingdon, my dear.'

The question was written large in Cicely's eyes, and Margaret provided an answer.

'My dear, we have not long since been speaking of your sister.'

Cicely closed her eyes with fresh pain, but there was no gainsaying that Bess *did* seem to know a lot about Viscountess Welles' whereabouts.

Margaret was sympathetic. 'I am sorry, my dear, but who else would be able to send men to the island in royal colours? Two spies to Abingdon would be even easier.'

Chapter Fifteen

Cicely slept as the night closed in. Crumplin was still curled up with her, and the sounds of the castle drifted over the room. But then sleep was driven away by the arrival of Margaret and two holy men, Abbot Sante and a hooded monk. They had come to pray for the invalid's swift recovery.

The monk was introduced as the mysterious Brother Geoffrey. His hood was pulled so far forward that not even his nose could be seen, and he was utterly silent.

Margaret was curious. 'Why do you not say anything, Brother Geoffrey?'

It was Sante who answered. 'My lady, he has taken a vow of eternal penitence due to a childhood sin, and has also undertaken to never speak or let his face be seen.'

Silence? Cicely looked askance at the abbot. So much for the good brother's wonderful voice.

Margaret was still puzzled, but accepted the explanation.

Abbot Sante clearly hoped to be alone with Cicely, but Margaret elected to pray with them. So he and Brother Geoffrey knelt on either side of the bed, each placing their hands over one of Cicely's. The abbot began to murmur the Lord's Prayer. '*Pater noster qui es en caelis sanctificetur nomen …*'

Unseen by Margaret, who stood behind him, Brother Geoffrey slipped something into Cicely's palm, then closed her fingers over it.

She had the wit not to react. What was happening here? All she could tell was that she now held a sprig that had small spiky leaves.

There had been no opportunity to inspect it by the time the men departed again. Margaret would have lingered, but

Cicely pleaded a need to sleep. Only when she was alone could she look at what was in her hand. It was a sprig of thyme. Her heart almost stopped. Jack! Brother Geoffrey was Jack de la Pole!

Suddenly almost ridiculously happy, she curled up with Crumplin, as much as her bruises would allow. Jack had held her hand again, and soon he would hold all of her.

Four days later, on 2 October, Cicely stood at the window of her fire-warmed room in Margaret's apartments. The chill of autumn was in the evening air outside, and she shivered a little. Crumplin was sitting on her shoulder, admiring his broken reflection in a little looking glass.

Her bruises were much improved, thanks mainly to Mary's green salve, although Master Rogers's black pills had definitely soothed the headache immediately after the accident. In the morning Tom would come with some men-at-arms to conduct her safely back downriver to Pasmer's Place. Her thoughts were of Richard, for today would have been his thirty-sixth birthday. Many Yorkists would be remembering, especially Jack, who was somewhere nearby, here in Windsor. There had been no further word of him, but it was enough to know he was so close. She was sure of seeing him once she had returned to Pasmer's Place.

He was not the only one from whom she had not heard, for there was still a resounding silence from Jon and Henry. And from Bess and Annie, who had to have learned of her fall by now.

She looked down into the king's garden courtyard, where torches would soon illuminate the close-clipped lawn. The private apartments were grouped around the court. Two more courtyards extended north-east, but she could not see them. The first was the cloister court, where Henry sometimes walked. The other was the kitchen court, across which her cousin Warwick would have to go to the servants' hall from his toil in the kitchens.

Mary arrived to attend her, having been to Pasmer's Place to see that preparations were made for her mistress's return. 'Tom sends a message, my lady.'

'He does?'

'Brother Geoffrey will await you in the kitchen court tonight at eight. He will be near the well.'

Cicely's lips had parted. An assignation? *Here*? Jack had already taken a great chance by accompanying Abbot Sante. Surely a true assignation would be an audacity too far!

'My lady, Tom urges caution. If you should be caught doing this *anywhere*, let alone right here in Windsor Castle, it will be treason.'

Pragmatic Tom was right, and Cicely knew the danger, but resisting Jack de la Pole was impossible. She so longed to be in his embrace again that caution was impossible. 'Please thank Tom when next you see him, but I will meet Brother Geoffrey as requested.'

Mary smiled ruefully. 'I would too.'

'Surely you are too happily married to be making sheep's eyes at the Earl of Lincoln?' Cicely teased. 'If Mistress Kymbe knew, oh, what trouble you would be in. She has become *very* fond of Perry.'

The maid blushed. She loved Perry, but Jack de la Pole could devastate her with a glance. 'My lady, I— Well, I have been thinking about your meeting tonight. You should wear my clothes when you go, and perhaps I should tell everyone that you are indisposed. I know the King's Lady Mother is to be with the queen this evening, because I heard her grumbling about it, but if she should return earlier than expected, I will tell her that you have another headache and do not wish to be disturbed, under any circumstances. I will extend your sincere apologies to her, of course.'

'How thorough you are.'

Mary was unexpectedly impish. 'Well, I wish to protect Lord Lincoln.'

Cicely laughed. 'You get above yourself, Mistress Perrings.'

They laughed together.

It was dark and moonless at eight, but wall lanterns provided sufficient light in the kitchen court. Well, almost sufficient, because various small buildings and stores cluttered the quadrangle, providing inky shadows.

Workers hurried to and from the kitchen entrance to the unremarkable servants' hall, on top of which rose the grandeur of St George's Hall. Against the servants' hall was the larderie vault, where fresh meat was kept, and which provided a particularly favoured spot for clandestine meetings.

The smell of baking bread from the kitchens would have been appetizing, had not Cicely been so nervous as she waited between two stores, only a few yards from the domed roof over the castle well. She was hooded and cloaked in Mary's clothes, and no one paid any heed to her.

A man and woman emerged from the larderie. They were straightening their clothes, so it was clear what they had been doing, but as the pair were momentarily visible in the light from one of the lanterns, Cicely recognized the man. Remus again. She was almost resigned to seeing him, and watched as the pair exchanged a few more kisses before making their way into the servants' hall. The fellow was totally oblivious to the fact that, right under his nose, Lady Welles was keeping an assignation with the Earl of Lincoln. What Bess would not give for such information with which to destroy her hated sister? Come to that, what would Henry himself not give to know that the supposedly dead Yorkist was actually in the castle?

Two hands came suddenly from behind to clamp over her mouth and waist, and pull her further back into the shadows. She was frightened, and her hood fell back as she began to struggle, but then Jack whispered against her ear. 'How could I not come to you on Richard's birthday, my love?'

She stared up at him. He was cowled and wearing the same habit as before, but she did not need to see his face. Swift tears stung her eyes. 'Hold me, Jack. Hold me tight.'

He pulled her into his arms, almost crushing her, and his lips found hers in a long kiss that was filled with yearning. She clung to him, cherishing every heartbeat. At last, she was enveloped in thyme again. The pressure of his body, the sweetness of his breath, and the passion of his kiss, all combined to transport her away from worldly Windsor Castle to somewhere she believed must be Heaven itself. Nothing else mattered now, only the joy of reunion with the only man alive who could command her heart and soul so completely. If anything could put her feelings for Henry into perspective, it was the kiss of this Yorkist prince. He brought the wonderful past to life again. And with it such beloved ghosts.

Not a word was spoken. Nor needed to be. They were in each other's arms, where they belonged, and she was sure that hers were not the only tears, but at last they drew apart to look at each other in the virtual darkness.

Twenty-six-year-old Jack de la Pole turned his cowl back, revealing untrammelled black curls that fell around his shoulders, and long-lashed dark eyes that were at once flirtatious, teasing and serious. He was handsome and seductive, with a smile that could persuade Satan himself to convert to Christianity. There had been many female tears when he was believed to have died at Stoke Field.

Her devoted gaze amused him. 'Have you studied me enough, sweetheart? I assure you I *am* me.'

They kissed again, their blood warming more with each second, until he drew away reluctantly. 'My darling, welcome as this is, perhaps I should tell you that I have brought someone with me.'

She released him immediately. 'Who?'

He turned a little and a few feet behind him, where the faint borrowed lantern light barely reached, she saw the outline of a sturdy youth of medium height.

Jack beckoned. 'Come, sir, it is some time since you last saw your cousin, Lady Welles.'

As the boy came closer and his face was revealed, she recognized the Earl of Warwick. He was thirteen and the image of his father, the ill-fated Duke of Clarence, but royal blood or not, the hand he extended to her was rough and calloused.

He raised her fingers to his lips. Well, almost. Not quite. His uneasiness was palpable in his shaking hand, and he released her as soon as he could. 'My lady.'

'I think the last time we spoke we were Cicely and Edward,' she reminded him.

'That was another life.'

'Yes.' Her thoughts returned to the camp at Staythorpe on the eve of the Battle of Stoke Field, sitting around a fire with Jack, this boy cousin, and Richard's staunch friend Francis Lovell. They had toasted victory on the morrow. A vain hope.

Edward was anxious. 'My lady—Cicely—I am sorry to have failed you so, but the king has not harmed me, and while I do everything required of me, I will be safe.'

'I understand, Edward. Truly.' But was he really safe in Henry's hands? Richard's illegitimate son, John of Gloucester, once briefly betrothed to her, had been tortured until he was witless, and was now incarcerated in the Tower. He was a shell, unseeing, unfeeling and incapable of speech. Henry was capable of shocking cruelty.

She recalled Jack at thirteen. He had been a young man already, not a boy, and showing every sign of becoming a great warrior. She had worshipped him even then, and she only a little girl of six.

Edward looked at Jack. 'I am not brave, and I know you think badly of me for it.'

Jack shuffled a little. 'Because I do not understand. I could *never* turn my back on my heritage.'

'You have courage, I do not.' Was the simple response.

'That is not why I have brought you here. Repeat what you heard Francis Lovell say at Staythorpe, after Cicely left.'

The boy shifted uncomfortably, glancing fearfully over his shoulder before addressing Cicely. 'That our uncle, King Richard, told him he wished with all his heart that circumstances had not prevented him from marrying you. He wished you could be his wife, because you would have made him complete. No king would have more loved his queen.'

The words almost stopped Cicely's heart. It had to be true, because Richard had used almost exactly the same phrases to her in Nottingham Castle. He had told Francis as well?

Someone called angrily in the kitchens, and it sounded as if the services of Lambert Simnel were required, *immediately!* If not sooner. Edward flinched, clearly afraid of crossing anyone. 'I— I must return.'

Cicely reached up to kiss his cheek. 'Be safe, Edward Plantagenet.'

'And you, my lady. My lord.'

The Earl of Warwick, once crowned King Edward VI in Dublin Cathedral, slipped away past the well, and was visible for a moment at the kitchen entrance, before disappearing inside to resume his duties as a kitchen drudge.

Alone at last, Jack made Cicely look at him. 'You know Richard said it, do you not?'

She nodded. 'I have admitted it before, but—'

'There cannot be buts, sweetheart. Richard wanted marriage, and he consummated the desire by taking you to his bed.'

Fresh tears stung her eyes. 'Please stop twisting it all, Jack, for I hear Tal in your words.' Tal had convinced himself that Leo was legitimate, in the same way that Eleanor's marriage to Edward IV was legitimate. 'It was *not* how it happened,' she went on. 'Both things are true, yes, but they did not occur in that order. I lay with him more than willingly, and was not coaxed by a promise of marriage. Our situation was nothing at all like that of Lady Eleanor Talbot and my father. So please cease this, because pursuing it will endanger Leo.'

'Cicely—'

'*You* are the hope of York, Jack de la Pole, not my little boy, who is baseborn and always will be. *You* are Richard's heir. So be warned—and you may advise Tal as well—that you will need my assistance in this, and you will not have it. Have I made myself clear?'

He gazed at her, his dark eyes shining. 'Then it must also be clear that I will not give up. I know what is right, and in this instance, you, my sweet lady, are wrong.' He smiled engagingly. 'But no quarrelling, mm? There are far better things to do.'

His smile demolished her, as it always did. 'Plague take you, Jack. Birds would flutter down from the trees for you.'

He gave a low laugh. 'I do trust so.'

She had to smile as well. 'However, first *this* fluttering bird wishes to know about Lisbon.'

'I am not in the charmed circle, sweetheart, and can only hazard the same guesses as you.'

It was not an acceptable answer. 'Oh, come now, Jack. Not in the charmed circle? You are *bound* to be consulted by our aunt. What you really mean is that it has yet to be decided which of my brothers he will claim to be.'

'Sweetheart, only our aunt knows everything, and she has *not* divulged anything, even to me. Or indeed to any other Yorkist in Bruges. All I know is what you know, that the boy looks very like your father. But then, Edward IV was never one to keep his dick to himself. God alone knows how many by-blows he may have sired. He was careful never to acknowledge any after he claimed your mother as his queen, but he certainly did not remain faithful to her. Now, *please* can we return to the business of pretty birds?' He put fingers to her chin and tilted her face toward his. 'I need to make love to you again, Cicely Plantagenet, before I burst of it. Have you any idea how noble and restrained I have been while we have been apart?'

'Oh, you liar, Lord Lincoln. There will have been so much temptation in your path that you are bound to have rolled by the wayside.'

'Do you judge me by yourself?' he asked softly, moving against her and brushing his lips gently over hers. 'Now, my love, I am sure the House of York can rise to your occasion far more impressively than that paltry Tudor fellow. And to better effect.'

Jack pulled her clothes up gently and tucked her skirts into her girdle, before unlacing the front of his hose. He smiled at her. 'Oh, I have been saving it all for you, believe me. I fear this cannot be a lengthy display of my carnal prowess. Next time, however, it will be in a bed and I will show no mercy.'

His kisses wrote poetry through her senses, and the gentle brush of his tongue against hers was a voluptuous, enticing ode that melted through her so warmly that she felt weak. His hands slipped inside her cloak to cup her buttocks and draw her on to the erection that now strained his loins. Still kissing her, he moved her upon his arousal, and she knew such rewards that her whole body undulated.

Her will was forfeit. She was his, and only sought to be joined with him, flesh within flesh. This man was sin itself, and she, Cicely Plantagenet, was too much given to her own carnal weakness to ever resist him. Sensations and emotions first encountered with Richard were repeated now with his nephew. For these dangerous minutes, she could surrender to the physical joys that had always meant so much to her. Such men. Such pleasure.

'Nor will I, sir. Nor will I,' she whispered.

He lifted her against the wall of the store among the shadows, and his lips found hers again as he pushed luxuriously inside her. His movements were slow and rich, long, easy strokes that indulged and gratified. Their desire heightened, and their breathing was heavy when at last they both came together. Their bodies shuddered, their very consciousness seemed in question, but the joy and pleasure ruled supreme.

They remained where they were when it was over. Their bodies were still joined, softly now, and their hearts beat in such union that there was no difference between them. A wonderful warmth spread through them both, and how they wished they were in a bed now, able to fall asleep in each other's arms. But they were not.

Jack pulled away, lowering her to the ground and then freeing her clothes so they fell back into place. Then he straightened himself, and retied the laces, before smiling.

'That will have to do for the time being, mm?' he remarked roguishly.

'I trust you can do better next time,' she replied in the same vein.

He grinned. 'You may be sure of it. I will have you whimpering of pleasure.'

'I whimper already, in anticipation.' She glanced up as a scattering of raindrops fell. 'Jack, I should go back now. I want to be in my room when Margaret returns from Bess. Where are you staying? Flemyng Court?'

'Yes.'

Flemyng Court was where Tal's town house was to be found. It was on the western boundary of the old city, not far from the Royal Wardrobe.

'And speaking of Bess,' she went on, 'there is something Tal cannot have told you, because he does not yet know himself. Henry was not responsible for the men who searched for Leo on Wight, it was almost certainly Bess.' She explained about the conversation with Margaret.

He was astonished. 'Tal was *certain* it was Henry's doing. Well, you know I have never liked your sister.'

Cicely nodded. 'You were the only one—then—who seemed to see her true colours.'

He put his hand to her cheek again. 'Have a care, Cicely. Not only where she is concerned, but elsewhere. Henry may be innocent this time, but never trust him. Or his mother, whose interests will *always* be biased toward him. I take enough foolish chances for both of us, so please stay safe. I will see you again as soon as possible. You return to Pasmer's Place tomorrow, I think?'

She nodded.

'I will send word to you as soon as I can.' His thumb caressed her. 'I need to lie in a feather bed with you, my lady, to adore you until you can bear it no more.'

'Or *you* cannot,' she replied.

'Such a time will never come,' he whispered, and kissed her a last time.

Chapter Sixteen

THERE WAS GREAT pomp and clatter the next morning as trumpets heralded Henry's return. Then came the noise of the king's entourage proceeding up toward the upper ward gateway.

Cicely was preparing to leave for Pasmer's Place, and Tom already waited with Mary in the upper ward with mounts and men-at-arms, to take her to the barge waiting on the Thames. This time Jon's cognizance was not on display, because Cicely did not want to draw attention to who she was. Not now her husband and his mistress were ensconced here in Windsor.

At first Margaret wished Cicely to accompany her to greet Henry, but when it became clear that Bess and her ladies were sallying forth for the same purpose, Margaret changed her mind. Her stated reason was simple, and maternal. She did not wish to force Henry into a public choice between her and his queen. If both were present, it would be noted and transmitted which of the two he acknowledged first. To Cicely it was the first indication that Margaret was alert to the new Bess; alert to, and wary of.

So Cicely stood at an upper window, in the much-tidied blue gown she had worn to come to the castle, watching the furore in the upper ward. Servants, men-at-arms and all manner of courtiers and gentlemen scurried to be in advantageous positions when the royal cavalcade appeared beneath the gateway. Such a lot of commotion, she thought, and yet no one knew where he had been. Not for certain. There were various rumours, but somehow he had evaded everyone. He certainly had not been accompanied by such a company while he was away, or the world and its wife would have known every mile he travelled.

She held her breath as the heralds rode ostentatiously into

the castle. Then, just behind them, came Henry, mounted on a splendid cream horse. He was always pale, but today seemed paler because his face was strained. There were shadows beneath his downcast eyes and a tense set to his jaw. An invisible wall seemed to surround him, and he did not acknowledge anyone. His outer shell was there, but the man within was not. Was he ill? Was *that* why he had left without explanation? Almost immediately she discarded the notion, because he would at least have sent word to Margaret. Would he not?

She watched him closely for any sign of his usual ailment of the chest. But there was no cough, even suppressed. He halted his horse and waited for a hurrying groom to take the reins. Then he swung his leg over the pommel in that way he had, but this time there was nothing agile or graceful about the action, and when his feet were on the ground, he held the saddle for a moment, head bowed again. He was dressed in fine clothes; purple and grey doublet and hose, with a sleeveless coat over, and much ermine to set him above and apart. A shining brooch with drop pearls was fixed to the black velvet hat he snatched off and tossed at the nearest servant. His gauntlets followed, and then he strode out of Cicely's view toward the Rose Tower, where his queen waited at the entrance.

Within moments Margaret's familiar hurrying footsteps approached. 'Oh, Cicely, I fear something is very wrong. Did you see him arriving?' she cried agitatedly, entering and closing the door swiftly behind her. 'Is he ill?'

'I— I do not know. There was no cough, and he seemed strong and swift enough as he entered the tower. But I agree, *something* is wrong.'

Margaret gripped her wrist. 'We must go to him directly.'

Cicely recoiled. 'You go, by all means, but I do not think he will wish to see me. I have always been instructed to wait to be summoned. And besides, I am about to depart for—'

'No! No, you must leave later. My dear, *you* are the one he will want to see most.'

'But Bess may be with him!'

'No, he acknowledged her graciously enough, but then proceeded alone to his inner apartments. He is there now, and no one is with him.' There was a hint of gloating over Bess.

Cicely saw no reasonable way to continue resisting. 'Then, of course I will accompany you, but I will wait in the audience chamber until I know he wishes to see me. If he does not, I will leave immediately.'

As they approached Henry's apartments a little later, Cicely was still not at all sure this was a good idea. He had sought solitude as soon as possible, and now his forceful mother was about to descend upon him, hauling Lady Welles along too. If only she had left an hour earlier.

She waited close to the door from the oddly deserted audience chamber, while Margaret proceeded busily into the next room. The door remained ajar as Henry made known his annoyance. 'My dear Lady Mother, much as I love and respect you, I wish to be left alone for the time being.'

'What is wrong, Henry?'

'Nothing is *wrong*, I merely wish to be on my own.' His voice was level, but testy.

Margaret did not take the hint. 'But Henry, how can you say there is nothing wrong, when that is plainly untrue? I have only to look at you to know it. I also know the signs of guilt. What have you done?'

He was silent for a moment. 'I cannot tell you. You, almost least of all.'

'Me?' Margaret was puzzled. 'Why? And if I am *almost* least of all, who is least of all? Cicely, one presumes?'

'I have done something that cannot be undone, and I wish to God it were otherwise. She has made a poisonous serpent of me.'

'I do not understand.'

'You are not meant to. And now I have learned there is far

more to it all; things happened upon by accident.' He paused, and there was pain in his voice when he continued. 'It is too late for me, and if Cicely should ever learn what I have done, she will never be able to forgive me. Nor, I suspect, will she wish to.'

His mother leapt to conclusions. 'You have not done something to harm her child?'

'No! Jesu, lady! How flattering to know my own mother believes *that* of me.'

'A martyr's halo does not suit you, Henry. You have done wicked things in the past, and your feelings for Cicely make you capable of more.'

'It has nothing to do with him, or with anyone's death. More the death of *something*.'

Margaret was frustrated. 'What do you mean? Must we have riddles?'

It was Henry's last straw. 'Questions, questions, questions! For the love of God, woman, leave me alone!'

Crumplin's presence was announced with screeching and chattering, and Margaret was infuriated. 'That atrocious creature! I wish you would get rid of him!'

'Go if he annoys you, madam, but *he* stays.'

Cicely had never heard him address his mother so coldly before.

Margaret was shocked. 'Henry!'

'For this once, my lady, please take yourself away.'

'Henry—'

'I will have you removed!'

Margaret did nothing for a heartbeat or so, evidently too shaken to move, but then she swept back into the audience chamber, pausing before hurrying away.

Cicely caught up her skirts to follow, but Henry realized someone else was there, and strode out angrily to see who it was. She could only sink to her knees, waiting for his wrath to descend upon her.

His eyes were steady, and unfathomable as he halted in the doorway. 'Lady Welles, I do not recall requesting your presence.'

'Forgive me, Your Majesty,' she answered quickly, not looking up.

'I suppose your little Yorkist ears have been alert and attentive?'

She met his eyes for a moment, and then bowed her head again. How did she feel to be with him again? She did not know. Her feelings and trust had lurched from hurt disappointment and anger, to relief that regarding Leo he seemed to be innocent after all.

He drew a long breath. 'My mother dragged you here, I suppose? For to be sure, you would not have come otherwise.'

'You are right, I would not. You have told me not to approach you unless requested. And now, well, I do not even know if you wish to see me at all.'

'What is *that* supposed to mean?' he demanded.

'That I have been at Pasmer's Place for over a month, and have not heard anything from you.'

'And during that month you thought only ill of me,' he countered reproachfully.

'Forgive me, I beg you.'

The apology seemed to affect him. His eyes became troubled, and he indicated that she should follow him into the adjoining room, and he closed the door firmly upon them both. The room looked over the Thames, and was as sumptuously fitted as every chamber in the royal apartments. Perhaps even more so. Crumplin was seated on a table by the window, helping himself to a bowl of sweet red apples.

Henry moved before the fireplace. 'So, you overheard?'

'I cannot deny it. What is it that makes you so anxious, Henry? If it concerns me, maybe I—'

'Maybe you can put it right?' He gave a rather mirthless laugh. 'No, *cariad,* you cannot change anything.'

'Me least of all?' she said quietly.

His wintry eyes were uneven suddenly, and he rubbed an eyebrow to conceal it. 'But how are *you* now, Cicely? I am told you had a bad fall from your mount.'

'Yes, I am well and will leave for Pasmer's Place directly.'

'I trust not because I have returned?' He spoke lightly, amusingly, and went to the window to stroke Crumplin. 'Have you seen my uncle yet?'

'No, not yet. Perhaps I will not at all.'

'Would that distress you?'

She searched his face. 'I do not know.'

'Perhaps you no longer care?'

He was all but crossing his fingers, she thought. 'I pray so, for the sake of my pride,' she replied. 'It is one thing to think what I will from afar, quite another to be face to face with him.' *As it is with you.*

He echoed her thoughts. 'As it is with me?'

'Yes, with Henry Tudor. But Harri Tudur is a different matter.' She smiled.

He smiled too. 'So, the visit to Kingston l'Isle was, after all, a waste of time?'

'It would seem so.' *Oh, what do you know, Henry? Anything? Maybe nothing at all.*

'My Silver Hound serves me here in England for the time being, although I imagine you already know.'

'I have not seen him. I thought he had gone to Calais.'

Henry moved from the window, making such a restless circuit of the room that she had to keep turning in order to face him. 'Cicely, why have you never asked to see your cousin?'

'Cousin?' Her blood cooled.

'Warwick, in the Tower, or even the pretender Simnel in my kitchens here. You asked to see John of Gloucester.'

She steeled herself. 'And look what happened. You and I quarrelled most bitterly. I do not want that, and Warwick means nothing to me. The boy Simnel even less.'

'Do not look so fearful, sweetheart, for my dark self is not about to leap to the fore.' He smiled.

It was a warm smile, and she relaxed again. 'I will see whomever you wish, Henry, you have only to say.'

'I have no wishes of that sort, sweetheart, I merely wondered. As I do about your other cousin, Edmund de la Pole.'

'I would never ask to see *him*,' she replied with feeling. 'Actually, I last encountered him on the day I arrived here at the queen's command.'

'Ah, yes. The court mourning for your Woodville uncle. I will be having words with her, you may be sure of that. I can guess *why* she did it—to punish you—but I am not pleased. And now, heaven forfend, I can be avenged by withholding my, er, favours. There, is that not a novelty?' He chuckled.

'Beware if she offers you strawberries,' Cicely replied. 'I would imagine you are not always careful enough to lock the secret door at Westminster.'

He gazed at her. 'Really?'

'The change in her almost certainly occurred after that night.'

He thought, and nodded. 'You may well be right. So, her basest desires were ignited because she spied on us?'

'We *were* rather. . .energetic. And you, Henry, were truly wonderful that night.'

'One of my better performances?' He smiled. 'So, you saw Edmund de la Pole?'

'Yes. He was with Abbot Sante, as were Thomas Howard and Roland.' She was very precise, because warm smile or not, it was likely he already knew everything and was testing her. After all, his closest advisers, Richard Empson and Edmund Dudley, had been here at Windsor during his absence, and would have kept him abreast of every small thing. That is, if he had confided his destination in them. He was wont to slip away unannounced, leaving his entire court in confusion, advisers and all.

'Do you think de la Pole wants the throne?' Henry asked lightly.

'If he does, he would not confide in me. I imagine he is as loyal to you as he appears.'

'He revels in being the new heir of the House of York. At least, in imagining he is.'

'What do you mean?' Her heart paused. Did he know Jack was still alive?

'I mean that he is only heir to the dukedom of Suffolk. My son Arthur is the heir of the House of York, *and* of the throne.' He spoke quietly. Testingly.

She was piqued, as he intended, but she hid it well. 'You are right, of course. Edmund should be satisfied with his father's titles.'

'Oh, my determined little Yorkist, how beautifully you chose and qualified that response.' He was quietly amused, then serious. 'Yes, I too should have been satisfied with my father's title, but now that I have England, I will fight to the last drop of my blood to keep what I have taken.'

'Henry, you will have *others* fight until the last drop of *their* blood.' She was taking a liberty with his sense of humour, but knew that such signs of spirit were part of her appeal to him. And she *had* to appeal to him.

He laughed. 'Only you, sweetheart, only you. But yes, the blood of others. I am not a fool. Protection of the royal person is always uppermost in my mind.' Seriousness returned. 'If Richard had shown the same wisdom, he would still be alive. Still be king, no doubt.'

'It would not have entered his head not to fight.'

'Sometimes the craven curs emerge victorious. Or the wily foxes. However, we wander from the point. It was of de la Pole we were speaking. I have never encountered anyone quite like him before. God help me, I preferred his elder brother.'

So do I, she thought.

He stroked a forefinger against the side of his nose, gaining a little time. 'Am I a fool to keep trusting you, *cariad*?'

'No more than I am for trusting you,' she countered.

'Ah, there you have me.' He caught her hand, suddenly, to pull her into his embrace.

It was a moment that at any other time would have led to lovemaking, but not today. He became awkward suddenly, and moved away again. Whatever plagued his conscience had rushed back over him. 'I have much to do after my absence, so will let you go now.'

The dismissal worried her. 'Henry? Is this my *congé*?'

His eyes changed. 'No. Please do not think it. I am unsettled. Or maybe I am a little unwell after all.'

The tide was in favour of the oarsmen when Tom was at last able to take Cicely away from Windsor. Seated beneath the barge's canopy, she gazed over the river with mixed expressions.

Tom watched her. 'May I say something to you, my lady?'

When she inclined her head, he moved closer to exclude the oarsmen. Resting his arm along the back of her seat, he whispered so that only Cicely and Mary would hear. 'You are thinking of Viscount Welles, my lady, and I know why, but I am sure the rift will be mended. You have too much warmth and regard for each other for that not to happen.'

She smiled sadly. 'Not this time.'

He hesitated, and then put his hand gently over hers. 'Do not give up, my lady, for you and he are meant to be together.'

And that was when a royal barge swept past toward Windsor. Cicely glanced up, and found herself gazing into her husband's piercing blue eyes.

Jon, Viscount Welles was in his late thirties, a lean, fine-looking man of bearing and presence. His livery collar glittered in the bright sunlight and he stood at the prow, a booted foot upon the gunnel. The hair at his temples was close to white, whereas the rest was still brown, and he had a noble face, with good cheek bones and a firm chin that was at present concealed by a short beard. His doublet was the colour of bluebells, and over it he had a grey sleeveless coat, sparingly trimmed with matching fur. Dark hose disappeared into thigh boots.

Unsmiling, he looked down at his wife. Tom realized in a moment how it must look, he with his arm behind Cicely and his other hand resting on hers, and moved away as if scalded, but it was too late. The impression had been given.

Jon straightened and moved out of sight. No smile, no hint of recognition. Nothing.

As the royal barge slid on upstream, Cicely took a huge breath to collect herself. 'There, I believe, sails the remnants of my marriage,' she murmured, as if it did not matter. But it did.

The barge docked at Three Cranes, which was the most convenient landing for Pasmer's Place. Here cargoes of wine were brought ashore, and the quay had gained its name from the three wooden cranes that hoisted the casks on and off the vessels that crowded the busy riverside. Tal's cog, the *Elizabeth* was often to be found here, for she plied between London and Calais, and he had a licence to import wine.

Three Cranes held a special memory for Cicely, because she had once encountered Jack at the top of the steps. He was being importuned by an attractive young whore, who, it had been subsequently learned, was also one of Henry's spies. The woman had been displeased when Lady Welles claimed Jack's attention, because he himself had more exciting appeal than Henry's orders.

A hooded man waited at the top of the steps this time too. His cloak flapped in a sudden stir of crisp autumn wind from the estuary, and stray curls of his long dark hair fluttered. She knew that hair, knew everything about him, as lovers always do. It was Jack again, and this time he was quite alone. How she loved him. How she longed to be with him for all time. The hurt and regret over Jon Welles melted away.

Tom helped her disembark, and Jack came down the stairs to meet her. The desire to embrace and kiss was intolerably hard to resist, but it was too public a place.

She smiled at him. 'This time you have a Yorkist whore pestering you, Lord Lincoln.'

'No whore, but my sweetest love.'

She held her hood in place as she looked back at the crowded river. There were vessels of all sorts, including countless skiffs, any one of which could be carrying Henry's agent. Or Bess's. Or even Margaret's. All were possible.

Jack tossed his cloak back from one shoulder and drew her hand over his sleeve to lead her up to the quay. 'Cicely, Tal intends to visit you this evening.'

'I *may* receive him. After all, I have not heard a word from him since he brought me back from Kingston.'

'Henry has him pinned here.'

Cicely looked at him. 'Yes, but why? Surely he should be in Calais when there is another French war in the air.'

'He is charged to keep a very close eye on my sweet brother Edmund.'

'Henry questioned me about Edmund this morning.'

'So, the prodigal sovereign has returned?' he noted.

'Yes, and is distressed about something he has done.'

Jack was intrigued. 'Do you have any idea what it is?'

'No.'

'A pity, for I would love to make it worse!' He became serious. 'Jon stayed at Pasmer's Place last night. Alone.'

She explained what had happened on the Thames. 'So, he now suspects me of bedding Tom Kymbe,' she finished.

'Let him think it.' Jack had once held Jon Welles in high regard, but no longer.

'At least this time he did not entertain his leman in what I regard as *my* bed. Do you know anything about her?'

'Only her first name, Alice, and that she was originally from Cornwall. Her existence is common enough knowledge in Windsor taverns. There is much lascivious chatter.'

She glanced away. 'Is anything being said of me?'

'Only a tentative whisper linking you with Henry, but it is mostly rejected. Henry is not thought capable.'

'If only they knew.'

'Indeed.'

Something occurred to her. 'How is it you are here?'

He grinned. 'Not for you, alas. I have another purpose, and would have left the wharf, but then I recognized you in Welles's barge. My original reason for being here is to meet Tal at the Mermaid. He wishes to take me somewhere important, I do not know where.' He glanced past her at Tom and Mary, who waited discreetly several steps down. 'Ah, the stalwart Kymbes. But no, one Kymbe and a Perrings, I believe.' He smiled at Mary.

New wife or not, the maid was promptly put at sixes and sevens, and went deep pink.

Jack grinned. 'Oh, pretty Mistress Perrings, you always do my vanity such immeasurable good.'

Mary looked fit to faint.

He offered Cicely his arm. 'Come, your route takes you past the Mermaid. Perhaps you can see Tal for a moment.'

They set off, with Tom and Mary behind, and the men-at-arms at the rear. The tavern was in Gough's Alley, uphill from the Thames. The alley was narrow and only about twenty-five yards long, with the bustling, noisy Mermaid closing the far end. It was to here, on a dark and stormy night, that Cicely had followed the spy-whore.

As they arrived at the entrance to the alley, Tal's hooded figure approached from the opposite direction. He was startled to see Cicely. 'We meet here again, my lady, but at least the weather is clement this time.'

Cicely smiled. 'Indeed so.' This was where she had first met him, on the same night she followed the whore.

He took her hand and raised it to his lips. It was a gentle gesture, that of a close friend, but looking back afterwards, Cicely would realize that it could be interpreted as far more. In fact, that was exactly how it *was* to be taken.

She shivered suddenly, and not only because the sun had slipped behind a burgeoning cloud. Something was wrong.

Mary whispered to Tom, who turned immediately to look further up the hill. He watched for a moment and then touched Jack's arm 'Sir Humphrey has been followed, my lord.'

Tal whirled about.

Tom pointed. 'A Minoress. She has just drawn back into that doorway, but she halted when you did, and is intent upon what is happening here.' Without further ado he sprinted uphill toward the doorway.

A nun in a brown habit and black veil stepped out from a doorway, and on seeing Tom, fled away toward nearby Thames Street, one of the busiest thoroughfares in the capital. In a few moments she had disappeared into the throng of people, vehicles and animals, and Tom had to halt at the corner, unable to see which way she had gone. He retraced his steps to the alley.

Jack glanced at Tal. 'Do you know who she could be?'

'The short answer is no. She might only have been intent upon my purse, although I think not, somehow.'

Cicely thought his answer was a little odd. 'What are you not telling us, Tal?' she asked.

He shifted uncomfortably. 'I would rather not say just yet. If I am wrong, it is better never mentioned.'

There had been a time when she would have pressed him, suspicious of such reticence, but no longer. If he thought it was best not to explain, then she accepted his decision.

Shortly afterwards, Jack escorted Cicely back to St Sithe's Lane, where they parted without stealing a single kiss, he to return to Tal in Gough's Alley.

Chapter Seventeen

OVER THE FOLLOWING days Cicely and Jack met on a number of occasions, and slept together in secret at the nearby Red Lion, renewing their passionate love. Cicely was happy. Everything else paled beside the joy of being with Jack again.

Just under a week later, when the evening came early because clouds covered the skies over London, and the wind announced the first real hint of winter to come, Cicely sat with Mary and Mistress Kymbe by the fire in the parlour at Pasmer's Place. They sipped mead while the old lady regaled them with stories of her mother, who had been far more witch than wisewoman.

The chill of the evening got into Mistress Kymbe's bones, and Mary brought some furs to tuck around her. 'There, is that better, Aunt?' she asked dutifully.

'It will do. Oh, London is such a damp, godforsaken place.' The old lady huddled in her chair.

Mary was put out. 'Even though you came to see me married, Aunt Kymbe?'

The bright little eyes were upon her. 'The sun shone that day, my dear. But your wedding was not the only reason I came. My skills as a midwife will be needed here soon.'

'Needed?' Cicely sat forward. 'The last time you said that was when you came early to Wyberton because you knew I would go into my travails before my time. You were right, and helped me through a terrible birth.'

'One that damaged your body too much for there to be more children.'

Cicely went to the window. 'Which excludes me. So who?' She turned to Mary, eyebrows raised.

'No, my lady, it is not me, for I commenced my monthly bleeding yesterday.'

Mistress Kymbe looked at them both. 'I do not yet know who it is, but I *will* be needed. I am seldom wrong.'

Later, as the church bells sounded midnight, Mary came to awaken her mistress urgently. Alarmed, Cicely sat up. 'What is it?'

'Lord Lincoln is here, my lady. Tom admitted him secretly, and he waits alone in the great hall.'

Jack had come *here?* That was one thing they had been careful to avoid, because of the servants. Something must be very wrong!

'His lordship wishes you to dress to go with him. He said to tell you it is not a tryst, but something very private and imperative. And to reassure you that it does *not* concern Master Leo.'

Cicely flung the bedclothes aside as Mary hastened to bring her clothes. It was not until she was almost ready that Cicely realized the maid was still in her nightrobe. 'Mary, should you not—?'

'I am not to come, my lady. Lord Lincoln was specific. He said it is a *very* delicate matter. He and Sir Humphrey will provide all the protection needed. Tom and Perry are not to go either.'

Protection? Cicely began to feel nervous. What on earth could it be? She turned for Mary to place a cloak around her shoulders, and then hurried down to the great hall, where Jack, still hooded, waited by the huge fireplace. He leaned with one hand on the mantel, and kicked at a fresh log, sending sparks in all directions.

'Jack?' She ran to him.

He caught her in his arms. 'Forgive me for alarming you, sweetheart.'

'What it is about?'

He glanced around the shadowy hall, and the firelight showed the tense look on his face. She knew he had to tell her something she would not like.

'It concerns Edmund, and. . .'

'And?'

'And his intimate physical involvement with your sister, Annie.'

Cicely stared at him. '*Intimate* physical involvement?' she repeated faintly, feeling sick. Oh, silly, silly Annie, who thought herself so clever and adult. But she was not yet thirteen, and had tangled with a conscienceless creature like Edmund de la Pole!

Jack took her hand and squeezed it lovingly. 'I am sorry to be the bearer of such unwelcome news, sweetheart.'

She found herself thinking of Henry's reaction should he find out. Annie was a princess of York, his sister-in-law, and had already crossed him several times. The notion of uniting her with another highborn Yorkist like Edmund de la Pole would not be tolerated for a moment. There would be no temporary banishment for her this time, but something permanent, with whatever husband Henry thought fit, and it would *not* be a man of consequence. As for Edmund. . .well, heaven alone knew what Henry might think was appropriate punishment for *him*.

Jack raised her fingertips to his lips. 'Sweetheart, she may be very young, but her emotions are fierce. She appears to believe herself truly in love with Edmund, and has been keeping secret trysts with him. Tal discovered it because he has to follow wherever my dear brother goes. Two nights ago he learned that for the past week Annie has been feigning illness to absent herself from her royal duties.'

'How long has it been going on?'

'Tal does not know. Too long, I fear. Fortunately, it seems Bess still has no inkling of it. Last night, Tal learned that Annie had been night and day with Edmund at his lodgings close to the Red Lion. Yes, *our* Red Lion. We might have encountered either of them at any time. This is what Tal had wind of that day at Gough's Alley, and did not want to mention. He had heard a whisper, and hoped it was wrong. Over the last few days he heard more, and then could not ignore it any longer. Tonight he took me to Red Lion Court to witness for myself. Not an hour since, we saw Edmund leave, and Annie watched from his window above a bakery There was no mistaking her, for she was foolish enough to hold a lighted candle.'

Cicely's heart had begun to sink, but of one thing she was certain. Tal's reticence by Gough's Alley was not entirely due to Annie. It was also to do with the mysterious Minoress.

'Sweetheart, Annie is still in Edmund's rooms right now,' Jack said gently. 'Tal has remained outside, keeping watch. We have to get her away from there before my brother returns. There is something else that makes this a matter of great urgency. Tal is one of *two* men Henry has apparently appointed to the task of watching Edmund. The other is Willoughby, who happens to be married to Tal's sister-in-law, Blanche Champernowne, and who would not miss any opportunity to besmirch the House of York.'

Cicely closed her eyes. Sir Robert Willoughby was also related to Jon, and had accompanied him north to Sheriff Hutton after Bosworth. He was a hard, disrespectful man whom Jon had been obliged to restrain physically on several occasions. Willoughby hated the House of York, and if he thought one of Edward IV's daughters was guilty of such misconduct, Henry would be the first to be told.

'Annie is bound to be discovered unless we take her away,' Jack continued. 'She has to be returned to the queen before Willoughby gets there at dawn. We need you, for propriety, you understand. She is not to be trusted, and is likely to scream rape! And—somehow—I will have to keep my identity from her, because she will tell of *that* too. Neither of your sisters is to be trusted, I fear. I marvel that you spring from the same union.'

'Do you think Annie wishes to marry Edmund?' Cicely asked. It was all she could think of. Her thoughts were running in all directions at once. Oh, Annie. *Annie*!

'I have no idea who wants what, Cicely. For all I know, Edmund may see such a match as a clarion call to supporters of the House of York. Which it could indeed be, I suppose. Ambition rules his every move, but if that *is* his plan, then he is taking an enormous risk. Henry's eye is already upon him.'

She nodded. 'Jack, have you considered that Annie may *want* to be caught? She certainly wanted to be caught with Roland when she thought, wrongly, he was destined for some great future with Henry. So she may not thank anyone for "rescuing" her.'

'I do not give a damn whether she wants it or not. She has to be removed from there and you have to tell Bess.'

Cicely's dismay plummeted to the deepest fathom of the deepest ocean.

The Red Lion tavern was not far from St Sithe's Lane, in a court of shops off Budge Row. It was a thriving establishment, named for the large, red-painted wooden lion that stood before it. In a fire-warmed room on the first floor, Cicely had lain with Jack on the eve of his first flight from England. Then, they had made sweet love together in the firelight, while beyond the window the city was cloaked in winter. It was in this same room that they had been renewing their love in more recent days.

Now the autumn wind blustered through the streets, and she and Jack drew their hoods and cloaks close. The late hour made no difference to the numbers frequenting the Red Lion, and the few women present were certainly not demure or ladylike. The tavern was well lit, but the other buildings in the court were mostly in darkness, except for a bakery, which was hard at work in readiness for the early morning trade. A window on the floor above it was candlelit.

The smell of warm bread was pleasing as Jack ushered

Cicely to the narrow alley between the bakery and the adjacent butcher's shop. They could hear a cow and several sheep behind the high wall.

Tal should have been waiting in the alley, but there was no sign of him. Jack was immediately concerned. 'Tal? Where the hell are you?'

A groan answered from further along the alley, and they hurried toward it, to find Tal slumped against the wall. There was not much light, but they could see that he was holding his forehead.

Jack crouched swiftly. 'What's happened?'

'Three of them appeared from nowhere. I was struck with something hard, and do not remember anything more. Now my head aches fit to explode, and needless to say, my purse has gone.'

Jack was wary. 'Your purse?'

Tal shook his head. 'Nothing incriminating in it, my friend. I always make sure of that. They have not escaped with a fortune either.' He glanced at Cicely, whose purse contained very incriminating things indeed. 'Perhaps this should warn you to be more circumspect, my lady,' he said, and then struggled to get up, but his head swam unpleasantly, and he sank back again. 'I will not be of any help in this, Jack, more of a hindrance.'

Jack put a sympathetic hand on his shoulder. 'Then you must stay here. Cicely and I will do what's required.

'Be quick. Your damned brother may return at any moment.'

Jack straightened and held out his hand to her. 'Come sweetheart, let us get it over and done with.'

'This will make it much more difficult for you to keep your identity from Annie,' she pointed out. 'Perhaps I should go up on my own?'

'No. I will be there as well.'

He led her back to the doors that faced each other across

the alley. The one that opened to the stairs to Edmund's rooms was not locked, and they reached the narrow landing above without event. Voices and activity carried from the bakery below, but all seemed quiet up here.

The building was poorly constructed, with cobwebs in corners, and signs of rot in the wood of the north-facing landing window that looked over the long, narrow garden and low buildings to the rear. It was Cicely's guess that only the heat of the ovens kept serious damp at bay.

There was a momentary lull in the bakery, and she heard something. A sob? It was coming from beyond a door beneath which a light could be seen. Jack heard as well, and opened the door stealthily. The room inside was reasonably furnished, because Edmund was not a lord to live too roughly. It was illuminated by candlelight from the open doorway of the adjoining bedchamber.

Annie was seated on the edge of the crumpled but otherwise deserted bed. She wore the same gown that Cicely had seen in the queen's apartments, and her hair was loose, but in need of a comb. Her face was tear-stained, and she was the very picture of wretchedness. On seeing them enter, she leapt to her feet in alarm, although she strove to hold herself mutinously. 'What do *you* want, Lady Welles?' she demanded haughtily, but even her voice was tear-stained. She did not recognize Jack, whose hood was raised.

'We have come to take you to safety, Annie,' Cicely said.

'I am not in danger!' Oh, the tilt of the chin, the stiffness of the body, the sheer Plantagenet pride and defiance! But so sadly misplaced now.

'You imagine that is what the king will say when he learns?' Jack said, disguising his voice in case she should remember it.

Annie's gaze swung to him. 'Who are you?'

'My identity is of no consequence,' Jack replied.

Cicely distracted her. 'These are *your* lodgings, Annie?'

'You know they are not.'

Jack looked at her warningly. 'Be careful with your lip, my lady, for we have come to rescue you *before* the king learns of it. But we will tell him if we must.'

Annie's eyes widened.

Cicely went to her. 'Why have you done this, Annie?' she asked gently, seeing that her sister had been weeping for some time. 'Has Edmund hurt you, sweeting?'

The endearment was too much for Annie, who burst into tears again, and they were such honest, heartbroken tears that Cicely had to gather her close. 'Sweet Jesu, Annie, tell me what is wrong? I know we have not been friendly of late, but we are still sisters.'

'Edmund d-does not love m-me,' Annie sobbed.

Cicely glanced over the silver-fair head at Jack, whose face told of a dear wish to tear his brother limb from limb.

'He is afraid, b-because of the b-baby,' Annie continued.

Jack stifled an expletive, and Cicely's heart turned over. Baby? Her thoughts leapt back to Mistress Kymbe, who might well be needed after all.

Annie pulled away, trying to collect herself. 'If he truly loved me, as he said he did, he would marry me!'

Cicely knew it was not that simple. Clearly Edmund knew as well, and yet he had done this. Why? What possible benefit could there be in it for him? Mere gratification? Surely not.

'I l-love him! I love him so m-much.' Even more tears sprang to Annie's slate-blue eyes. She swayed, and would have fallen had Jack not caught her and placed her gently on the far-from-neat bed.

At that moment heavy male steps sounded on the stairs, and Jack moved swiftly behind the door, a hand on his dagger hilt. Cicely sat on the bed to embrace Annie protectively.

Edmund entered. He wore fine rust-coloured clothes and the fascination he held for someone like Annie could not be denied. He was devastatingly beautiful, although his expression became a little foolish as he saw Cicely.

'Cousin?' he said at last, unaware that Jack was standing behind him.

'I believe you have a little explaining to do,' Cicely replied.

His gaze flew to Annie's tear-reddened face, and something passed through his light-brown eyes. What was it?

'You are despicable, Edmund de la Pole,' Cicely continued coldly. 'How could you defile a child?'

He did not respond, but his gaze remained upon Annie.

Jack spoke. 'And now you have got the child with child, brother.'

At that Edmund whirled about, and staggered backward to see his older brother. 'Sweet God! *Jack!*' he breathed, but then was dealt a savage upper cut to the jaw. He hung there for a split second, his eyes glazing, then his knees sagged and he thudded to the floor.

Annie's sobs had stopped abruptly, and she stared. 'Jack? *Cousin* Jack? Of Lincoln?' she gasped.

Chapter Eighteen

JACK FLUNG HIS hood back reluctantly. 'Yes, Annie, it is me.'

She rose shakily, steadying herself on a rickety table 'I thought you were dead. We *all* thought you were dead.'

'And that is how it must remain. For now.'

She nodded, still gazing at him. 'It is so *very* good to see you again. You make me think of Uncle Richard's court, and how happy we all were then.' On mentioning Richard, she glanced fleetingly at Cicely. It was unclear of exactly how much she was aware, but she certainly knew something.

Then she hid her face in her hands. 'This is m-my fault,' she whispered. 'All m-my fault.'

'No, sweeting,' Cicely replied, going to put an arm around the trembling shoulders. 'It is Edmund's fault. He is old enough to know what he does.'

'He was so gentle. Making love with him was perfect.'

Cicely recalled the first time she had lain with Richard. No man could have introduced her more lovingly and exquisitely to the pleasures of the flesh. But it was hard to credit that his scheming nephew Edmund was capable of the same tender care.

Jack saw a jug of wine on a table, and took great pleasure in tossing the contents over his brother, who was stirring.

Coughing and spluttering, Edmund struggled to sit up. His hair, no longer glorious, clung around his head, revealing that he had very large ears that resembled jug handles. No wonder he wore such fluffy, cascading curls! He had a flaw! Thank goodness, Cicely thought, for it made him more human.

He managed to stand. 'So, you are in London again, Jack,'

he said, trying to appear composed but failing miserably.

'How observant. And how timely my visit is, for you have been caught in a shameful liaison that stains our family honour.'

'You think I care about family?'

Jack nodded. 'Oh, yes, because it is *family* that provides you with whatever ambition you have. Except that you will not inherit anything, mm? I am still alive, still the heir of York and still the next Duke of Suffolk. You will be nothing more than the loathsome knave who deflowered a child.'

'It was not like that, Jack.'

'No?'

'No!' Edmund looked at Annie. 'You know it was not like that,' he said to her.

'But you do not want me now,' she replied. 'You said horrible things and then walked away.'

'To *think!* I did not walk away forever. I am here again now, am I not?'

Jack jerked his brother to face him again. 'Why did you do this?' he demanded bluntly. 'What possible reason could you have?'

Edmund's cheeks were red and his lips pressed sullenly together. The smooth, sophisticated, scheming Edmund de la Pole was nowhere to be seen, and in his place was a boy who had made a monumental mistake.

Jack shook him. 'Give me a reason, Edmund, or so help me I will extract your hair by its roots.'

'My reason shames me.'

'Oh? So you know shame? I am astounded,' Jack replied acidly.

'I began it out of spite. To make a fool of Thomas Howard and to teach Roland a lesson.'

Annie's little face crumpled again.

Edmund stretched a hand out, but then let it fall again.

'Roland bragged that Annie was interested in him, and as for Thomas, Jack, you *know* how bitter it has become between the Howards and us. Thomas was smirking, and I wanted to punish him *and* Roland.'

'So you punished a *girl* instead?'

'Annie is not so much the child as you seem to think, Jack. She is my equal.'

Annie's sobs redoubled.

Edmund drew a heavy breath. 'But once I had commenced, it soon changed. You may not think it, but my feelings have become involved.'

Jack's eyebrow twitched. 'Feelings? Your balls itched, perchance?'

'My *affections* became involved,' Edmund corrected.

Annie snivelled, her startled gaze upon her lover.

Cicely stared, not knowing whether to believe him or not. The Edmund she had known hitherto had been so sly, dangerous and hostile that it simply did not seem possible that this boy was the same person.

Jack thought so too. 'You think to play me like an idiot fish on a toy hook?'

'No, it is the truth. But when she told me tonight that she is with my child, I panicked. I suddenly realized the extent of my idiocy. I had been deluding myself. Thomas Howard and Roland de Vielleville do not matter, but Annie does. I implore you to offer what help you can. To Annie, if not to me. I have no excuse to offer. Neither of you has reason to assist me.'

Jack looked at Cicely, clearly unsure of what to do next.

She turned to Edmund. 'You have tried to kill Jack, and you wrote that venomous note about me to Henry.'

'I do not deny it.'

'You are the most pathetic creature I have ever known,' she breathed.

He spread his hands in submission, but did he do it too

easily? Suspicion lurked within her.

Jack came to a sudden decision. 'I do not care what befalls you, Edmund, but Annie is another matter. She must be taken to safety, away from all danger of scandal.'

'How will you prevent scandal?' Edmund asked. 'When her belly—'

Jack did not allow him to continue. 'Are you prepared to be the man and own up to your guilt? Will you marry her gladly?'

'Yes, except that the king will *never* allow it. You know that! It would be *such* a Yorkist union.' Edmund's almost liquid brown eyes—swung to Cicely. 'Unless *you* can persuade him, of course.'

'To do that will be to help you rise high in the new royal family, and I would not wish that,' she replied.

'How honest.'

Ah, a trace of the old Edmund.

Jack intervened. 'I suggest that when we have gone, you busy yourself making sure there is no sign of Annie in these rooms. Do so before dawn.'

Edmund became alert. 'Why?'

'Oh, I will leave you to find out.'

'I will do as you say. But Jack, where do we go from here?'

'*We* go nowhere! Just be careful from now on, because if there is so much as a *whiff* of trouble from you, you will go to sleep one night and never awaken again. Do you understand? I have many friends, every one of whom would be eager to do the deed, while I twiddle lilywhite thumbs in Bruges.' Jack's eyes were like flint. 'I should dispose of you anyway for what you have done to this child. You are not worth the air you breathe.'

Cicely was alarmed. 'Nor is he worth the sin of fratricide on your conscience.'

Edmund swallowed, but stood his ground by diverting

Jack. 'Do you mean to invade at the head of another army?'

'Would I have your support? The question was sardonic.

Edmund smiled. 'No, I would not support you because there is another who has a far great claim than you. Or me. Come on, Jack, you must know it. You have been in Bruges, close to our aunt's court. You cannot *not* know about Lisbon.'

Jack was very still. 'And how have you come upon this?'

Edmund's eyes cleared. 'So you *are* aware!'

Jack did not respond, having no intention of revealing his lack of information about the mystery in Portugal.

Edmund smiled. 'You support him too. I know you, Jack, for it is in your eyes. We will be on the same side after all.'

'Richard was the last true king to rule over England, and I am *his* heir.'

'You intend to adhere to that?' Edmund was clearly shaken.

Jack did not respond, but spoke to Cicely instead. 'We must get Annie to safety for the time being.'

Annie's tears still flowed, but silently now. 'I am s-so sorry, Cissy. For everything I have s-said and done to you.' She looked at Edmund. 'You only wanted to hurt Thomas and Roland?'

His expression was a mass of conflicting emotions. 'Forgive me,' he whispered.

'I will *never* forgive you,' she replied, and walked unsteadily past him, having to hold her arms out to Jack, who scooped her up. She clung to him, her face hidden in his hair and the crook of his neck. Her voice was muffled. 'I am glad you are still alive, Jack. So glad.'

Edmund's face was a mask as he watched Jack carry her out. Cicely was undeceived. Annie mattered to him very much, and he knew he had lost her.

Jack carried Annie carefully down the stairs. At the bottom, Cicely hurried to Tal, who was standing, but weakly.

'Put your arm around my shoulder, Tal. I will help you. Jack has Annie.'

'She is unharmed?'

Cicely looked at him. 'In a manner of speaking.'

They returned to the others. Annie was standing, having recovered some poise. Jack looked intently at Cicely. 'I pray you know what to do about this, because as God is my witness, I do not.'

'You think *I* do?' she replied, because as God was *her* witness, she did not know how to help Annie, except to offer comfort, support and the love of a concerned sister. As for telling Bess, oh, it did not bear thinking about.

Tal did not ask anything as they all hurried away from the bakery, but he wondered greatly. A few minutes later they were in Pasmer's Place, where Tom, Perry and Mary waited anxiously. Lady Ann Plantagenet was safe again.

As quietly as possible, so that the other servants would not be disturbed, Cicely left Mary to tend to Tal, and herself took Annie up to the main bedchamber. When the frightened girl was safely in bed, Cicely returned to the great hall, and despatched Mary to the bedchamber.

The men waited with goblets of wine, and Tal had been apprised of Annie's situation. 'So, Cicely, we were too late after all, mm? Your little sister is in dire straits.'

Jack grunted. 'Unless she finds another Jon Welles to rescue her, for it cannot be my feckless brother. Tudor would rather hack off his own testicle than permit such a dangerously Yorkist match.'

Tal leaned his head back and sighed. 'If only I had been observant a little sooner—'

'You could not have done more,' Cicely said comfortingly.

Jack banged his fist against the mantel. 'I would like to throttle Edmund! What is the matter with him? Something went very wrong when he was conceived.'

'Most hens lay one bad egg,' Cicely said, and went to him.

He smiled. 'Edmund Egg would certainly float.'

'Jack, he did not lie about his feelings for Annie. I saw it on his face as you took her away.'

'Well, I will reserve judgment on that. He was always a good actor,' Jack replied unforgivingly.

'Do you believe anything he said?'

'Not really. Edmund de la Pole has never been truly honest in his life.'

'Well, at least he is now very unlikely indeed to go to Henry about you.'

Jack nodded. '*And* he knows I will not hesitate to order his death. He may have wanted to end my life, but until now there had not been a similar threat from me. That has changed forever.' He ran his fingers through his hair. 'Oh, what a mess. Annie will hold her tongue to protect herself for as long as she can, but there will come a time when that will no longer be possible. Merlin's wand would be useful now, eh? To undo the damage.'

Tal rose gingerly, and glanced around to test his balance. 'I must hie me back to my royal duties.' He hesitated before going. 'There is something else about Edmund that perhaps you should both know. I have observed him in the company of a stranger, a young man, fair-haired and very good looking. His name is Nicolas Stalyn and he is from Tournai. He and Edmund appear to be friends.'

Jack compressed his lips thoughtfully. 'I know of Stalyn. He is connected with a Portuguese adventurer, Duarte Brandão, who is close to our aunt, the Duchess of Burgundy. Brandão now calls himself Sir Edward Brampton, but has maintained strong connections with Lisbon, where he is believed to have taken the boy we are all so interested in. He also has dealings with Étienne Fryon.' He smiled. 'Henry should pay his secretaries on time. Duplicity is encouraged by a purse rarely filled since Bosworth.'

Cicely had been thinking, and now turned her thoughts

into words. 'Perhaps the boy in Lisbon is my brother, Richard of York, who did indeed promise to resemble my father, which I understand from Henry can be said of the mysterious boy. My other brother did not look like my father, and I can only imagine something has happened to him. Abbot Sante thinks there was a shipwreck. Perhaps Dickon survived.' She looked at Jack. 'Edmund thought you would support my brother, and was taken aback when it was clear you would not.'

Jack met her gaze. 'No. I erred before, supporting the wrong banner, and will not make that mistake again. My allegiance is to Richard, not to your father's illegitimate line. A century or so ago, Henry IV, when faced with his legitimized Beaufort half-siblings, made certain to exclude them from the succession. Legitimized or not, the precedent for excluding the *originally* baseborn has been set.'

'But Henry, a Beaufort, now sits the throne.'

'You know my opinion of *that*. Henry himself knows it too, which is why he has claimed the crown by right of conquest.'

'It does not matter what Henry IV did or did not do. Thanks to the present Henry, by the law of England my brothers *are* legitimate and therefore my father's heirs,' she pointed out. 'But I do not accept that the baseborn can be made trueborn after the event. If I did, I would accept that Leo is Richard's heir. But I *do* accept that Richard was the rightful king, and that he intended *you*, Jack, to be his successor. To me, you and no other should be King of England.'

Jack shifted uncomfortably. 'Yes. Maybe.'

'Definitely.'

He smiled. 'But, we are still guessing about the boy in Lisbon. When I return to Bruges after Hallowtide, I will delve more into whatever is going on in Portugal.'

Hallowtide. It was less than a month away now. So little time to spend with him. She wanted to blurt that she would send Leo to Bruges with him, but something held her back, and then the moment had gone.

Jack did not notice. 'I will seek a private audience with our aunt and confront her with what we have learned. I suppose the survival of Richard of York would indeed explain her not confiding in me. She may fear that after the debacle of Stoke Field, my own ambitions make me somewhat inconvenient.'

Tal looked at him. 'Her support should go to you, regardless, Jack. She accepted Richard as the true king, so there is no question.'

'A tricky matter, eh?'

'Not tricky at all,' Cicely replied firmly. To her the matter was very simple indeed. Jack should be king.

Tal had to go. 'I really must return to Edmund's rooms. Willoughby expects me to be there at dawn.'

Jack was concerned. 'Are you in any state to – ?'

'Yes. I will tell him the truth. I was attacked and robbed.'

'Take care. My brother is never to be trusted,' Jack warned.

Tal's smile was grim. 'I am more than a match for that adolescent pustule.' He came to kiss Cicely's cheek. 'Look after the Lady Ann. She needs you.'

Snatching up his cloak and swinging it around his shoulders, he turned to beckon Perry. 'Accompany me, sir.'

'My lord.'

As they left, Cicely was anxious. 'Is he really well enough now, Jack?'

'Oh, yes. He would not say so otherwise. Trust him. I almost hope my brother does spoil for a fight. Willoughby is, as you know, a man to use fists first and ask questions later. If at all.'

She smiled suddenly. 'When I saw Edmund's ears, I realized why he wears his hair so long and curled.'

'He was always self-conscious about them.'

He came to embrace her, stroking the nape of her neck as his lips played seductively with hers. He tasted of wine, and there was that wonderful scent of thyme on his clothes. She pressed to him, just for the sensation of his body against hers. He felt so good.

Then he cupped her face in his hands and kissed her again, gently this time. 'I must go too, sweetheart. The longer I stay, the more the chance of a servant loyal to Jon recognizing me and sending word to him.'

'Tom must accompany you.'

'I am instructed?' He smiled.

She nodded, but was still anxious. 'Please do not stay at Flemyng Court, Jack. Edmund knows that was where you hid before, and he will think of it again now.'

'I know, my love, and will go elsewhere.' He put a finger to her lips. 'Go up to comfort Annie. I will soon let you know where I am, so that you can come to me. We will share another night, and awaken with the dawn, mm?'

Tears stung her eyes as she nodded. 'Be safe, Jack de la Pole.'

He gave her a fiercely loving kiss, and then strode away across the hall, calling to Tom as he went. They left together.

Returning to the main bedchamber, Cicely found Mary with Annie, who looked lost in the large bed. Her anxiety could almost be touched.

Cicely sat on the edge of the bed. 'I will look after you, sweeting. And I am sure Bess will too.'

'No, please! I do not want Bess to know!'

'But she has to, Annie. You are in her household, her lady-in-waiting. Her *sister*!'

'Please, Cissy,' Annie whispered. 'Promise me you will not tell Bess.'

'Annie, I cannot *not* tell her. She will be appalled, yes, but ultimately I am sure she will help you.'

'No. The shame I will bring upon our family will be too great. She will not support me because she now loves the king, and *he* will want me punished as much as possible.' Annie's lips quivered and her eyes shimmered. 'Oh, Cissy, I know the horrible things I said of you, and how cruel I was about your marriage to Lord Welles. I am *so* sorry. I understand now.' She paused, trying to speak levelly, but failing. 'I cannot have this baby, Cissy, I just cannot. I want it to be gone! You must know how I feel.'

Cicely thought back. No, she did not *know* how Annie felt, for it had never crossed her mind for a moment that she could be rid of Richard's child. Never. Leo had been conceived in love, created within her by the man she adored. But she *did* know the shame that was heaped upon women who gave birth out of wedlock. And she *did* know the terrible lengths such women could go to in order to be free of their burden.

Annie turned to Mary. 'Is your aunt here? Does she know of such things?' she asked hopefully, having heard from Bess that the old lady had delivered Cicely's child.

Mary was dismayed. 'Yes, she is here, my lady, but—'

Annie's frightened little face was streaked with tears. 'Bring her, please! She *must* help me! Please! I beg of you!' Her hands were clenched into defiant fists and she was so overwrought that her whole body shook.

The maid was distressed for her. 'Lady Ann, I know she will not do what you wish. She will *never* destroy the result of willing lovemaking. And you *were* willing, were you not?'

Annie felt all doors closing in her face. 'No!' she cried desperately. 'Edmund *made* me do as he wished!'

Cicely took one of her sister's hands. 'That is not true, sweeting, and you know it. You may hate him now, but you went to him willingly enough, and stayed with him. You were very foolish, but he did not force you into anything. The best we can hope for is that Henry will consent to a marriage between you. I will do what I can to persuade him, truly I will.'

'No,' Annie whispered. 'No, the king will *never* agree! I will be married off to a low ogre and sent away to some distant county, never to be at court again. That is what he said before, and he will do it, I know he will. Or he will send me into a convent, never to leave again!'

'Annie—' Cicely tried to soothe her, but Annie's voice rose hysterically.

'Well, I will not let that happen! I will *not*! *Never, ever*!'

She was suddenly so overcome and hysterical that she clambered out of the bed.

Cicely tried to prevent her. 'You must rest, Annie!'

'I will *not* have this baby, Cissy!' the girl cried, and before Cicely or Mary knew it, she had run out toward the stairs.

Then came a truly terrible sound, like the furious yowling and spitting of an angry cat. Annie screamed. Next they heard her tumbling headlong down the stairs.

They were in time to glimpse a black tomcat slinking away into the shadows on the landing. It was not just any cat, but Tybalt! Cicely was sure of it. But there was no time to think. Annie's screams had awakened the household, and there was uproar as servants hastened from their beds.

Illuminated by a night lamp, Annie lay crumpled at the foot of the stairs. Her eyes were closed, her face ashen, and she was utterly motionless.

Chapter Nineteen

CICELY DASHED DOWN to kneel anxiously beside Annie. Mary brought the night lamp and joined her.

'Sweetheart?' Cicely chafed her sister's hand as the servants who had been awakened came to press around. Candles waved and smoked, and there were astonished whispers. No one knew who the unconscious girl could be, until Mary's quick wits offered a plausible explanation.

'My cousin, Ann,' she told them. 'She arrived unexpectedly an hour ago, all the way from Lincolnshire, and having not eaten all day, she fainted at the top of the stairs.'

Annie did not respond to Cicely's coaxing. She might even have been dead, had not the slight flutter of her eyelids shown otherwise. Might she have broken any bones? It seemed so likely after such a violent fall.

Mary had begun to examine the girl when the peremptory rap of a walking stick against a bannister drew attention to the landing above. Mistress Kymbe stood there, clad in a voluminous nightgown, her grey hair plaited beneath a night bonnet that was tied under her chin. A black shape padded out of the shadows to sit beside her. Tybalt! It *had* to be him, even to the way his yellow eyes gleamed as he licked his paw.

Mistress Kymbe realized the cat was there and swiped at him with her walking stick, at the same time uttering some very strange, unintelligible words, very like those Mary had used at Kingston. Spitting viciously, Tybalt fled.

Mary hastened to help her aunt down the stairs and then Mistress Kymbe waved her stick at the servants. 'Away with you all, for I must see what is wrong!' she cried, but detained two of the sturdier men. 'Wait in the hall. You will be needed to carry the little mite back upstairs.'

Helped by Mary, the old lady managed to kneel beside Annie to inspect her. Mary leaned close to whisper. 'She is Lady Cicely's younger sister, Lady Anne, but to everyone here she is Cousin Ann Kymbe.'

'Indeed? No doubt you have good reason for such a pretence,' was the reply as Mistress Kymbe commenced to examine Annie. There was nothing old and uncertain about her dexterity as she ran her hands over the unconscious girl, before sitting back on her heels. 'Be easy, Lady Cicely, for she has not been greatly harmed. She has knocked her head, no more than that.' She raised one of Annie's eyelids and looked closely, before turning to Cicely. 'I now know why I had to come here and of whom I must take care. The eyes tell much, even when their owner is not conscious.'

Cicely nodded. 'You are right, Mistress Kymbe.'

'Why is the cat here? Whose eyes and ears is it?'

Cicely explained in as few words as possible.

The old lady nodded. 'It will not return now. My words will keep it away.'

The two menservants carried Annie carefully up to the bedchamber. They thought nothing of another Kymbe being shown such respect, for they were accustomed to that family's high standing with Lord and Lady Welles. As Annie was placed gently back against the plump pillows, her silvery hair spilled in all directions. She looked so delicate and lost; so very much in need of protection.

The moment the men had gone, the maid closed the door, and the old lady looked at Cicely. 'Such a bad fall may well lead to the losing of the child. The next few hours will tell.'

'Were she able, she would tell you she does not want to carry to full term. Please, Mistress Kymbe, do not judge her harshly.'

'She should not have permitted the dibbling of her little body. She *did* permit the act of love? Because if not, and she does not lose the child from the fall, I have the herbs and potions that will achieve the desired result without any risk.'

Cicely could not lie to the old lady. 'She was not forced. It was the foolishness of two young people.'

'She is too young by far, and such a fall might not only cause the loss of the child, but barrenness thereafter. Of course, falls can also render the barren fruitful again. That is the way of it. But my instinct tells me that this baby, should it live, may well be its mother's only one.'

Mary gasped suddenly. 'My lady!'

They turned to find Annie's slate-blue eyes wide open. She had heard everything.

'I— I will be barren?' she whispered.

Mistress Kymbe went closer, her walking stick tapping on the oak floor. 'You *may* become so, child. You were very foolish to do what you did.'

'You are Mistress Kymbe?'

'I am.'

'I cannot have this child, Mistress. If Edmund loved me, it would be different, but he does not. He used me to spite someone else. I am so unhappy.'

Mary's aunt leaned over to put a comforting hand on her wrist. 'I will do all I can for you, child. I know everything there is to know about these things, and although I may be old now, my hands are the safest and surest in which you can possibly be. And Mary is my pupil. We will take care of you, but we will *not* rid you of the child.'

Annie's lips trembled and as tears rolled down her cheeks, Cicely knew that her little sister was learning a very harsh lesson. The need to offer comfort was too strong. 'I think Edmund does feel for you, Annie. Truly I do.'

'Well, I feel nothing for him. I hate him.' Then Annie's face changed and she gasped as a vicious stab of pain overwhelmed her. Whimpering, she clutched her abdomen tightly.

Mistress Kymbe eyes sharpened. 'The child is to leave her. Mary, steep some lavender in wine. And boil pennyroyal, for the afterbirth.'

Mary hastened away to her tasks, and less than an hour later, nature began to take its sad course for Annie, who doubled up with successive pains, and cried out pitifully as she lost Edmund de la Pole's child.

Mistress Kymbe's skills were such that she could disguise the fact that the queen's little sister had ever been with child. 'I am able to restore virginity, little lady. I have herbs and salves that will tighten what has been loosened. Be thankful, for you have truly thrown your good name to the vagaries of fortune. Just dwell upon your escape, and accept that the awful threat—which was of your own making—has been removed. Now, this room must be kept dark and warm, even in sunlight, and you are only permitted to eat what is gentle. Do you understand?'

Annie nodded, but the look on her face suggested she would never eat again. By dawn she had sobbed herself into a sleep that was induced by one of Mistress Kymbe's sedative mixtures. The weeping was for herself, the lost baby...and for Edmund, whose name she whispered now and then.

Tal returned two hours after sunrise, and Cicely, who had not slept at all, received him in the parlour, where he accepted wine. 'How is the Lady Ann?' he asked.

'She is Ann Kymbe while staying here, Tal,' Cicely warned, before telling him what had happened.

He lowered his eyes sadly. 'So, she has the opportunity to start anew. Let us hope she keeps away from de la Pole.' He looked at her. 'There is something else on your mind?'

'Tal, Tybalt caused the accident. He tripped Annie at the top of the staircase.'

'Oh, come now, that damned tommer is in Kingston!'

'You think I do not know that is where he is supposed to be? Yet I have already seen him here in London, on the wall against the lane. Mary recognized him too. Mistress Kymbe says he is evil, "someone's eyes and ears".'

'Cheney's? Is that what you mean?'

Cicely glanced away. 'I do not know, but that man was in Windsor, and has a town house here in London.

'Do not let your imagination run off with you, *cariad*. You chide Henry for his superstition, yet here you are, indulging in it yourself.'

She changed the subject. 'What happened at Edmund's rooms?'

'Willoughby and his men were already there. Edmund was subdued, and *very* reticent about with whom he had been sharing his crumpled bed. Anyway, whether found or put there deliberately, Willoughby produced a badge of Richard's boar from beneath the pillow.'

Cicely's lips parted in astonishment.

'Edmund claimed never to have seen it before, and I believed him. His shocked denials were genuine. If Henry desires a justifiable excuse to clamp down on Edmund, Willoughby is just the man to provide the "evidence". Edmund's balls will be severed and a knot tied in his dick if Henry finds out everything else. Anyway, I must be off now, and you, lady should sleep.' He bowed over her hand.

'Thank you for all you have done for Annie,' she said.

'I did it as much for you, Cicely.'

The discovery of the boar badge did not result in Edmund's incarceration, merely in his being detained at court, where he was denied all the knightly sports and pastimes that meant so much to him. He was told that enjoyment was not to be his lot until he had proved himself to be loyal. It was harsh punishment for one who took such pursuits so seriously, and was made worse by having to endure the goading of Roland and Thomas Howard as they flaunted their freedom to do everything he could not.

But he knew he had been warned. Henry's close attention was now in the open, and only the foolish would fail to take the matter seriously.

Annie soon recovered sufficiently to return to Bess's household. The queen, who had been informed that she had suffered an ague, sent a brief message to Pasmer's Place, trusting that Annie would soon be well and in her service again, but it was hardly gushing with concern. Annoyance that Pasmer's Place was the scene of this indisposition was evident in every terse word.

But whatever Bess's attitude, Annie's desperate situation was at an end, with no one of consequence any the wiser. Now it would be up to her to conduct herself safely in future, and eventually marry the awful Thomas Howard, unless Henry could be persuaded to find another husband of a kinder, less aberrant disposition. Cicely decided to approach Margaret.

The morning came for Cicely, Tom Kymbe and two of Jon's men-at-arms to escort Annie back to Windsor, where Bess received them in her customary grand manner. She presided from the same exquisite chair-throne, and was splendid in cream cloth-of-gold, with a headdress the colour of spring violets. She was surrounded by her ladies, who were dismissed the moment her sisters were announced.

'Are you sure you are well again, Annie? You look decidedly pale.'

'I am well again, for which I thank Cissy's kind care.' Annie gave Cicely a quick smile.

Bess observed their manner together, and did not like what she saw. A reconciliation between her sisters was not at all what she wanted. She preferred Annie under her complete control and Cicely to be excluded. 'That will be all, Lady Welles. You may go.'

Annie was dismayed. 'Please, Bess, can we not all sit together a while? I would love it to be as it used to be, when Father and our uncle Richard were—'

'Enough, miss. I have dismissed Lady Welles and it is not for *you* to argue with me. Do you wish to remain at court?'

Annie's lips parted, and she lowered her eyes. 'Yes.'

'Then always do as I say.' Bess's nostrils flared a little as she returned her attention to Cicely, who had not moved. 'Get out.'

But Cicely held her ground. 'Bess, if this is a signal that you are about to be unpleasant to Annie because of me, let me warn you that I will not have it.'

'*You* will not have it?' Shaking with rage, Bess rose in a spilling rustle of costly cream and gold. 'This is *my* domain, madam, and you are nothing more than my subject. A lowly being, even if you *are* my sister.'

'The king will learn if you mistreat Annie,' Cicely said quietly.

'Ah, of course, you like to rut with him.'

'Yes, I like it very much. He is excellent at rutting, as you have begun to find out for yourself. They do say better late than never.'

Annie's jaw dropped as Bess's speechless fury was signalled by arctic eyes.

Cicely endeavoured to mend matters. 'Bess, can we not *try* to be true sisters?'

'No.'

Cicely was resigned. 'Very well, then I have to warn you that if I suspect you of anything, anything at all, I will use my influence with the king. He may not have been impressed by Annie's conduct up to now, but he will not be pleased that you are cruel to such a young girl simply out of jealousy of me.' There, it was stated in bald terms, and Cicely did not wish a word of it unsaid.

She and Bess gazed at each other with utter loathing, and then, not for the first time, Cicely turned her back on the Queen of England, and walked away.

Chapter Twenty

ON THE EVENING of 24 October, exactly a week before All Hallows Eve, Jon Welles finally came to see his wife. He gave no warning, and could not have been further from Cicely's mind as she sat at a candlelit parlour table. She paused in the middle of writing to Elizabeth at Kenninghall.

She and the duchess corresponded regularly, and that was how details of Leo's progress reached his anxious mother. Jane Champernowne was never mentioned, for which Cicely was grateful. She did not wish to know if Tal's pagan wife had so much as *looked* at Richard's son. Kenninghall and Norfolk seemed so far away, almost as far as Wight, and Cicely longed to cuddle her boy again, hear his laughter, and see him tumbling around with excited talbot puppies.

She put down her quill as her thoughts moved on. A message had arrived earlier from Margaret, summoning her to Windsor the following day "on a very private matter". A small royal barge would await her at Three Cranes. The private matter might concern almost anything, Cicely thought cynically, for there was a plentiful choice.

Jack had sent word that he was safe, but did not say where he was. Nothing had been heard from Tal, whom she imagined to still be keeping watch on Edmund.

She was about to resume her letter when Mary rushed into the parlour. 'My lady! My lady, Lord Welles is here!'

Cicely looked blankly at her, for there had been no horses in the courtyard, no voices or sign that someone had arrived.

'My lady, he walked up from Three Cranes with Master Roland, and wishes to speak privately with you.'

Cicely was sorely tempted to treat him as he treated her –

by completely ignoring him—but that would be petty. He was still her husband, and so she would hear what he had to say. She suspected he was going to tell her their marriage needed to be ended officially, although how he expected to achieve that was anyone's guess. Nonconsummation? Not even the Pope would believe *that,* nor would His Holiness want to favour one member of the English royal family over another. Unless, of course, one side had Henry's support. 'Is he in the great hall?'

'Yes, my lady.'

'Then he can stay there. I will not receive him in private. Please inform him that I will come down directly.'

'Yes, my lady. My lady? He has sent Master Roland to wait in a side room.'

'Indeed?' How curious. 'Very well. Relay my message to his lordship, and then come back to me quickly, because I wish to wear the heather velvet. With the king's dragon pendant, and all my rings.' She would *flaunt* her royal lovers!

'Yes, my lady.'

Jon waited rather exasperatedly by the fireplace in the great hall, which had been cleared of servants. Being kept waiting in what he still regarded as his own house was *not* to his liking.

He was still bearded, although it had been trimmed, Cicely noticed as she paused in the entrance from the stair hall to observe him. Someone had put his cloak, hood and hat on a chair, and she could not help but notice the absence of the turquoise ring. His brown hair was tousled and the premature white at his temples was flushed apricot in the firelight. He wore dark green, and his long legs were encased in the same tall thigh boots that he had worn when— No, she would not think of how Lord and Lady Welles had made love on a table while he wore those boots, which came so perilously high toward his loins. He had just returned from a lengthy absence, and she had not wanted to wait for him to bathe. He had been all that a virile husband should be.

Taking a steadying breath, she entered the hall. He heard the rustle of her gown and turned, the lean contours of his face taking up shadows. The vivid blue of his eyes deepened to violet as they swept her from head to toe, lingering on the dragon pendant as she approached.

They gazed at each other in the firelight. Her Jon was absent from the man who stood before her now. In his place was a hollow, emotionless double. A sense of deep regret and hurt cut into her, but she strove to appear indifferent.

'My lady.' He inclined his head.

'My lord. You wish to speak with me?'

'Yes.'

'To speak of separating formally? Of divorce, perhaps?'

She thought she saw a moment of surprise in his eyes, but then something settled over him and he nodded. 'There seems little point in pretending anymore.'

'You have not pretended at all,' she reminded him. 'You are now someone else's protector. Although, from all accounts, she has precious little left to protect.'

'Please, do not sink to verbal abuse, Cicely.'

'Why not? You, after all, have sunk to publicly ignoring me. What is that if not abuse of a kind?'

'I am sure Henry will be glad to see us part, which I trust you will tell him is your wish.'

She was pricked. 'And make it easier for you? Certainly not! You can tell him. I am not going to lift a finger to assist you. You left me to go north, found yourself a trollop, and decided you prefer her to me. If that is what you want, you can do your own pleading with him.'

'Perhaps it was simply that *I* had enough of *your* lovers, madam.' He was pricked as well.

'They had never replaced you in my heart, Jon Welles, and you know it. Your mistress, on the other hand, appears to be the only woman in yours. Fair enough, I will not put up any arguments or obstacles. If you wish us to be permanently apart, then I agree, but I am certainly not expressing such views to Henry or to your sister.'

He was silent for a moment, eyes downcast, but then looked up at her again. 'Very well, although I trust you will not blacken me too much with either of them.'

'I do not need to, you have done that perfectly well yourself. You and your mistress are common talk, in case you had not realized.'

'I could hardly fail to be unaware.'

'And do not look at me as the likely source of the chatter, because I have not said anything.'

'Even to Henry?'

'*He* told me, not the other way around.'

'Ah. I should have known.' Again he glanced at the dragon, and then at the rings she made no attempt to conceal.

She confronted him. 'You certainly should have known that *I* would not spread word about my husband's protracted infidelity with some common woman or other that he tumbled while in the north. I value my pride too much for that.'

He was amused. 'Your *pride?* Dear me, I thought that overweening entity had long since given up the ghost.'

'Clearly you prefer to overlook the original reason for my infidelity with Henry, when I protected your life.'

'And Jack de la Pole's, although protecting *him* required rolling in his bed. And in who else's bed have you lain? Tal's, perchance? Oh, no, I was forgetting, it is Tom Kymbe now, for it seems the obvious interpretation of that cosy scene I witnessed on the Thames.'

'You witnessed Tom comforting me because of *you*. He was concerned and expressed a belief that you and I would be together again. Now, if you choose to put a sordid complexion on that, it says more of you than me. Or him.' She held his gaze. 'And I would have thought that by now you knew Tom Kymbe's character well enough to be sure he would *never* do as you appear to think. Shame on you, Jon Welles.'

A nerve flickered at his temple, but he did not reply.

'But should you suspect me of desiring him in my bed tonight, my lord, let me assure you that it would be a physical impossibility, because at this moment he and Mistress Kymbe are somewhere between London and Friskney, perhaps even at journey's end. No doubt they spent one night at Huntingdon, because that would be shockingly appropriate in your warped opinion, would it not? The inn where Lady Welles gave herself to the king, and was beaten for her pains, now gives overnight shelter to her Lincolnshire squire, maybe in the same capacious bower.'

He shifted a little. 'Then it seems I will have to content myself with believing Tal to be a more likely candidate.'

'Well, he has never been my lover. Even if he had, since *you* are always in your concubine's bed, it cannot matter one whit who is in mine.'

'That is true.'

'Unless you are a truly selfish worm in my otherwise perfect apple? Yes, you probably are.' Her eyes flickered.

'Much good it would do me where you are concerned. You would cut me out and stamp on me.'

'Indeed I would. Three times, for good measure. Well, we presumably have nothing more to say to each other, so I will bid you good night.' Inclining her head, she caught up her skirts to walk away.

'Do not turn your back on me, madam! This is *my* house!'

She turned. 'It belongs to Master Pasmer, not to you, and I have no intention of removing myself from the premises for you to yet again install one of your many lemans. Let me see, this would be the third one since I have known you. Heaven alone can say how many more of whom I never learned. And *you* have the nerve to carp about *my* infidelities. So, Viscount Welles, as we speak, your leman is no doubt lying legs stretched wide in readiness for you. Please go to her. I am safe in the knowledge that she can *never* be to you as I once was.

She is no match for me between the sheets, is she?' She ended on a soft, seductive note, and then laughed, to turn the softness into an insult.

'I do not deny it, but I now have *love*, which you never provided, no matter how you dressed the language. You gave true love to Richard and to Jack, and maybe there was none left for me. So, I fully intend to go to her, because she makes me feel as if I am the only man who matters in the world to her. Did you ever do that? She is also to give me a child.'

Cicely was stricken. She tried to hide how her lips trembled, and to quell the sting of salt in her eyes, but knew she did not succeed. Of all the things that would hurt her, this was the worst.

He gazed at her, whether regretting his words or not, she could not tell. 'You may stay here as long as you wish, Cicely, for it *is* your home and I acknowledge that. My earlier remark about it being my house was merely to point out that the lease is in my name.'

She had to look away, because every cold word was slicing through her like a knife. He was to be a father, and not with her. She had failed him, and now another woman would present him with the child he longed for. A perverse smile curved her lips. 'When I think of how hard it was to convince Henry that you and I had to marry. What a complete and utter waste of time it all was, do you not agree?'

'It was meant to save Leo from the stain of bastardy, which was *not* a complete and utter waste of time to me.'

The rebuke was well aimed. Their eyes met, and the ensuing seconds seemed to be devoid of air. 'We no longer know each other at all, do we, Jon? I wish it were not so. It would be so good to have the happiness again.'

'That is not to be.'

'I know. Especially now, when she is to give you what I cannot.' She summoned a smile.

'She is not a whore, and has a name, Alice. And she is now in the queen's household.'

'How predictable of Bess. Tell me about this woman, Jon. You owe me that.'

'I owe you nothing, Cicely. I was unhappy with you and met her at a time when I was at my unhappiest. We fell in love, and now I wish to be with her.'

She absorbed the words, as much as they hurt, and then looked away. 'I can honestly say that I never, *ever* felt I wished to be parted from you, Jon. Until now, of course, when I will be glad if I never see you again. I told you once, an age ago it seems now, that there would come a day when you might regret your gallantry in offering me marriage. That day is clearly here, so perhaps we have indeed said all we have to.'

'No. Not all. I did not come here to talk about our marriage, but to see that you are told something that is very important to you. You must hear what *Écuyer* de Vielleville has to say, because it concerns your kingly lover and Jack de la Pole. And Tal too, which is why I have requested him to join us. Ah, how timely.' He glanced toward the hall entrance as they heard horses arriving in the courtyard.

Knole, she thought. Roland, Jon and Tal had all been there, as had Jack, of course. And Henry. If only Jack could remember, they would know by now of what Henry had or had not been guilty that night.

'Cicely, Roland awaits in that room.' Jon nodded at a small arched door. 'Perhaps most of all, Jack should be present as well, of course, but I imagine he is lurking across the water in the safety of Bruges.' His tone was scornful, suggestive of cowardice.

'You and Henry lurked in Brittany, and oh, how the latter lurked at Bosworth. And Stoke Field,' she replied in exactly the same tone. 'You were not at Stoke Field either, as I recall.'

There were voices, and then a servant came hastily to announce Tal, who marched into the hall, still removing his riding gauntlets. He wore a dark cloak and hood. 'You had better have a sound reason for this, Jon, because I am supposed to be wading in a certain lordling's muddy wake!'

Jon glowered at the servant. 'Be gone!'

The man took to his heels, almost slamming the door behind him.

Jon addressed Tal. 'It is a *very* sound reason. No, do not take off your hood and cloak. I do not doubt that you wear your holy pendants, which alone might identify you, let alone seeing your face.'

'Why bother about my identity?' Tal enquired, advancing to the fireplace.

'Trust my judgment in this.'

Tal's eyebrow twitched. 'Your judgment has not been particularly admirable of late, Jon.'

'No doubt.'

Tal smiled at Cicely, bowing over her hand. '*Is* my hood necessary?' he asked her.

Jon flushed at the obvious questioning of his word.

Cicely nodded. 'Yes, Tal, unless you wish to risk Roland de Vielleville realizing somehow that you were one of the intruders at Knole. Pull your hood well forward.'

Jon indicated the anteroom. 'We waste time.'

They followed him into the room where Roland waited. A recently kindled fire crackled and spat, and uncertain shadows, some monstrous, swung over the oak-clad walls; and over Henry's son, who rose nervously from the upright chair by the hearth, his immaculate under-curl shining. He wore light-brown velvet, and bowed low.

'My lady. My lords.' His nervous glance rested on Tal for a moment as he wondered whose face he was not being permitted to see.

Tal was about to hand Cicely to the chair so recently vacated, but Jon pre-empted him, playing the courteous and attentive husband. It was an empty gesture that she would rather he had not made.

Tal stood behind her, and Jon moved closer to the fire,

before gesturing to Roland. 'Very well, Master de Vielleville, you have the necessary audience, pray begin.'

'I— I do not know what to say first, my lord.'

'Last Christmas you were brought from Brittany to Knole,' Jon prompted.

The boy's eyes registered a memory he wished did not exist. 'Yes, my lord. *Maître* Guillaume de Boulvriag, my tutor, brought me because the King of England wished to honour his given word. I was glad to come here, to escape from my father, who is cruel.'

Cicely lowered her eyes. From the frying pan into the fire, for Henry was hardly a kindly alternative.

Roland swallowed. 'I had been accompanied from Brittany by an escort of armed men, who waited in the courtyard at Knole, while *Maître* de Boulvriag took me inside to the great hall, where the king awaited with you and an elderly secretary. I do not remember his name. I do not think it was mentioned.'

'Go on,' Jon urged.

'It was supposed to be a very secret meeting, although I do not know why. Then men with a mastiff came in. It caught the scent of two strangers who had been eavesdropping.'

Jon turned swiftly to Tal. 'Are we agreed on this so far?'

'It happened as the boy says.'

Roland looked at Tal again, and Cicely wondered if he had realized the hooded man was the second intruder.

At another nod from Jon, the boy continued. 'The intruders, who were well muffled, made a dash to escape, and the mastiff dragged its handlers after them. You, Sir Jon, hurled your long-bladed dagger, and it pierced one man between his shoulder blades, but both managed to disappear into a passageway and wedge the door behind them.'

Jon halted him. 'You are sure of this? *Both* men were able to enter the passage and secure the door behind them?'

'Oh, yes, my lord. You and the handlers had to batter the

door open, with the help of some of the Bretons from the courtyard. You eventually broke through to give chase.'

'And you, the king, the secretary and *Maître* de Boulvriag remained in the great hall?'

Roland's tongue passed uneasily over his full lips. 'Well, yes. At first.'

'Meaning what, exactly?'

'That the king took a candle and left the great hall the same way.'

Cicely held her breath as her heart began to pound. What was she about to hear?

Jon prompted Roland. 'What do you know of the time the king was absent?'

'Please, my lord—'

'You *must* repeat what you told me, sir. It is very important.'

'I—I followed him, my lord. He went through the door that had been forced, and into the passage. He noticed something on the wall by the doorway into the room where the wounded man was hiding. I learned afterward that the man was the Earl of Lincoln. By the manner in which the king touched the wall and then inspected his fingers, I believed it was a bloodstain he had seen. I could see him clearly by the light of the candle he carried. He smiled and then went into the room, leaving the door only partly closed behind him. I think he meant it to close fully.'

Tal's hand moved to rest comfortingly on Cicely's shoulder. She instinctively put her fingers over his. There was a pounding in her ears, and her breast, as if her heart were not simply beating more swiftly, but lurching as it did so.

'Some of the men in the courtyard witnessed, too,' Roland went on. 'One of them could see through the opening of the door, and saw Lord Lincoln leaning back against a table to face the king. His Majesty put the candlestick down very slowly, but then moved like lightning to seize a chair and hurl it at the earl. I heard this, but could not see. Lord Lincoln was too wounded to get out of the way. His Majesty leapt upon him and pulled him forward by his hair until he was face down on the floor and completely defenceless.'

Cicely closed her eyes.

'Are you *sure* of this, Roland?' Jon demanded.

'Yes, my lord. I heard it all, and there was an eye-witness in the courtyard. Like me, he was too afraid to say a word. We pretended not to know anything. Everyone did.' Tears wended down Roland's cheek. 'I wanted to go back to the hall, but could not. My legs would not obey me.'

'Continue.' Jon spoke to the boy, but was watching Cicely's face, which had slowly drained of all colour. He took a hesitant step toward her, but then thought better of it.

Roland trembled as he tried to clear his throat. 'The man in the courtyard saw the king drive your dagger further into Lord Lincoln's back, smiling as he did so. It was slow and deliberate, to cause as much pain as possible.'

Cicely could not bear it, and rose from her chair to go to the small window that looked out over the garden at the rear of the house. Was this what plagued Henry now? Had Knole finally caught up with him? Certainly it would fit what he had said about not wanting her to find out. But Roland was continuing, so she turned back to the room.

'The king then wrenched Lord Lincoln's arm, so fiercely that his shoulder was dislocated. It was too much for the earl, who screamed once and then lost consciousness. The king enjoyed every moment. His face shone with it.' The boy shuddered. 'He terrifies me, my lord, more than any man alive. I fear that he knows my thoughts, and that at any moment I will be taken away to suffer as Lord Lincoln did.'

'And all this is what Jack does not remember,' Tal murmured. 'Perhaps the lack of knowledge has been a kindness.' He loathed Henry Tudor so much in those moments that his stomach curdled at the very thought of him.

Cicely was silently distraught. *Oh, Jack, my dearest love.* If she had known this at Abingdon, she *would* have murdered Henry as he slept!

'What happened next?' Jon prompted.

'I heard a sound from the far end of the passage. It was very soft, but I knew someone was coming. My legs obeyed me at last. I had no time to get away, but there was a curtain hanging against the next door along. I hid behind it. The second intruder had returned.' Roland looked at Tal. 'It was you, sir, was it not?'

'Yes.' But Tal still kept his face hidden.

'Well, I watched you look into the room and see what His Majesty was doing. He had his back to you, and you seized the candlestick he had brought and hit him on the back of the head. He fell like a stone. You had pushed the door open and I came out of my hiding place to see.'

Tal drew a long breath. 'I *knew* someone was watching. I could *feel* it.'

'I saw you manipulate Lord Lincoln's shoulder back into its place, and cut up the king's clothes to make dressings. And—and I saw you kick him between the legs.'

'Very satisfying it was too, but I would rather have killed him.'

'I only slipped into hiding again when you pulled Lord Lincoln to his feet,' Roland went on. 'I followed you along the corridor to the room at the far end, and saw you both escape through the window. Then I ran back to the great hall. The king was found, of course, and told a very different story.'

Jon looked at Cicely. 'So there you have it. Henry Tudor in his true hideousness. Just as he was when he tortured John of Gloucester in 1485.'

She met his gaze and then looked at Roland again. 'Do you think the king believed Lord Lincoln was truly dead?'

'I do not know, my lady. He said so afterward, and a body *was* brought back from the park.'

Tal spoke urgently. 'A *human* body? Or that of a dead mastiff?' He had witnessed a dead mastiff slung over a horse, being taken back to Knole.

'The body was well wrapped, sir, and later, in the middle of the night, it was buried secretly by some willow trees. Before it was covered over, a willow stake was driven into it. I was told that this was because Lord Lincoln was supposed to have been buried that way after the Battle of Stoke. Other than that, it was as if nothing had happened. No one present that night would have dared to say anything.'

Jon smiled. 'Except you, *écuyer*. You have courage.'

But Roland looked as if he wished he had held his tongue.

'So, it was as I thought,' Tal said. 'Henry buried the mastiff, and prayed that Jack's wounds were sufficient to kill him anyway. He reckoned without Jack's Yorkist stamina.'

Roland was anxious. 'I have told you all that I know, Lord Welles. *Please* do not betray me to the king! I would rather die by my own hand than have to face him. *Please*.' The final word was a terrified whisper.

Jon reassured him. 'Not a word will be said to him. Upon my honour—upon *all* our honours—your name will *never* be uttered in connection with this information. Rest easy. Now, wait in the hall, by the fireplace.'

Roland escaped gladly.

Jon glanced at Cicely and Tal. 'I think the case against Henry is proven, do you not agree?'

Tal was dry. 'Does this mean you will come over to York again, my lord?'

'It means I intend to keep my nose out of it. There is danger in knowing *any* of my royal nephew's secrets.'

Cicely felt suddenly and utterly drained. How many times had she wondered what really happened at Knole? How many times had Henry denied wrongdoing? And with such an air of wounded innocence, of hurt and disappointment? Of reproach.

She looked at Jon. 'I do not think I wish to hear more. You were right to see that I was informed, and I accept that all the evidence points to Henry's guilt, although I really do wish it did not, because I will have to face him again. Please, Jon, I wish you would go now.'

If he resented his dismissal, he gave no indication, merely inclining his head to her, and then, more briefly, to Tal, upon whom he bestowed a look that was less than amiable. 'No doubt you two doves wish to be alone together,' he said then.

Cicely was caught on the raw. 'And you go to your whore, Jon Welles. So do not *dare* to look down your nose at me, just be thankful you are still alive, because if it were not for my whoring, you would be dead and buried at the hands of your own dear nephew. So take yourself away, sir, and do not approach me again, for we have nothing left to talk about. My debt to you has been paid in full, with my body. I asked nothing of you in return.'

Jon's blue eyes flashed with anger, and words blistered on his lips, but he turned on his heel and strode out, shouting at Roland to follow. The boy scurried after him obediently. Then there was silence.

Cicely hid her face in her hands, her whole body shaking as she wept, and Tal closed the door before pulling her into his embrace. 'Oh, *cariad*.'

'This time I know for *certain* that Henry has lied so very much,' she whispered, hiding against him. 'There will be no last-minute revelation of innocence. Nothing. Just his terrible lies and guilt.'

Tal smiled, and leaned back a little to look into her shimmering eyes. 'What? Henry Tudor lie? Never. He does not know how to. But have *you* not told *him* some very devious little fiblings?'

Her lips wobbled into a smile of sorts. 'Do not tease me.'

'I merely try to make your pain a little less, sweetheart,' he said gently. 'Henry is all deception, and you *must* remember that. Oh, I know how Harri Tudur affects you, but there is no

Harri Tudur, not really. It is far better that you know and accept the truth about him, rather than continue to pretend to yourself that there is something sweet in his hard heart that deserves your deepest affection and sympathy. Do you understand what I am saying to you?'

Yes, she understood, but even so the pain was savage. 'Where is Jack now?'

'Safe, *cariad*. On Elizabeth's barge in the boatyard across the river.'

'I want to be with him. I need him, Tal. And he needs me.'

'I will take you there tonight.'

Her eyes lit, but then she remembered. 'I cannot, for I must go to Margaret in the morning. She is sending a royal barge for me. I have to be at Three Cranes, not across the river in the Duchess of Norfolk's boathouse.'

'Then tomorrow night, or whenever you are able to go to Jack.' He paused. 'He will be in Windsor tomorrow. Secretly, of course. I will see that a way is found for you to be with him. I promise. Since learning what Roland had to say, he is as desperate to be with you, believe me.'

'Thank you, Tal.' She smiled bravely.

'Shield your heart from Tudor, *cariad*. And remember that the time will come when he will want to rid himself of the threat that is Leo.'

'No!'

'Sweet Jesu, lady, of *course* he will! He has to eradicate the House of York, except as it descends through his marriage to Bess. You have already realized this, but have not followed the thought to its obvious conclusion. Face it! Be the Plantagenet princess, *always*, not just when you wish to put me in my place.'

He smiled again, a sad little smile that took the sting from his words. 'Please, Cicely, pay full attention to me now. Be strong, wear invisible armour, call upon Richard's shade to advise you, do whatever is necessary to keep yourself and Leo safe, strong and *alive*. My advice is that you send him to Bruges with Jack.'

'I have been thinking of doing just that.'

Chapter Twenty-One

THE WEATHER WAS cold and clear as Cicely was conveyed upstream to Windsor in response to Margaret's summons. She was accompanied by Mary and some men-at-arms. Seagulls swooped and soared, and the Thames wavelets winked and flashed in the wintry sunlight. It was an appropriately crisp St Crispin's Day, and also the anniversary of Agincourt.

As the oars swung rhythmically past the Palace of Westminster, she noticed much activity there, and that Henry's standard was raised. He was not at Windsor, but here, so at least she would not have to see him today. The chill did not really touch her as she sat under the barge's canopy, wearing a green, fur-lined cloak over a simple rose velvet gown. Every dip of the oars took her closer to Windsor, a place she would now much prefer to avoid.

On reaching the castle's upper ward, they found a scene of great bustle as the stands and lists for the Hallowtide tournament were built. A similar noise emanated from St George's Hall, where the Hallowe'en feasts and disguisings would soon take place. Such important festivities required a great deal of preparation, with pageants and more stands, and Henry was not sparing his pennies. It was, after all, an ideal opportunity to display his majesty.

The men-at-arms waited as Cicely proceeded alone with Mary. Hardly had they walked six paces when they encountered Edmund, Roland and Thomas Howard. At least, Edmund followed Roland and Thomas, who were together, laughing and chattering as they carried their jousting helms, having evidently been enjoying a tilt in the Thames meadows. They were deep in laughter and conversation and did not notice her. Their cheeks were flushed and their hair windswept from riding, and she could tell that their amusement was at Edmund's expense. Roland appeared to have recovered completely from his ordeal at Pasmer's Place, she thought. Perhaps it was simply that Henry was no longer here, but in Westminster.

Edmund, sullen and silent, had no jousting helm or other such accoutrements. He was nevertheless dressed as elegantly as ever, still turning heads with his extraordinary looks. That Cicely was close by was not realized, until she addressed him.

'How now, Cousin?'

Mary immediately moved discreetly away.

He started out of his thoughts, and remembered to bow. 'Cousin?' Then he stiffened. 'Have you come to gloat over my humiliation?'

'No, I have come at the behest of the King's Lady Mother. You did not cross my mind until I saw you a moment since.'

His light brown eyes searched her face. 'Did Jack hide that boar badge in my rooms?'

She was cross. 'Jack? No. He would not abuse Richard's emblem in such a way. Do not judge others by your own low standards. If anyone hid it, I would suspect Sir Robert Willoughby, probably at the king's command. Or, of course, I would suspect you of having it all along, to proclaim your right to be at the head of the House of York.'

He flushed. 'I am not *that* foolish, my lady. I know nothing of the badge, only that someone is trying to incriminate me.'

'Well, you would know *all* about that sort of thing.'

His response was a glance from beneath lowered lashes.

She changed the subject. 'How are you?'

'I think you see well how I am,' he replied, gazing after Thomas and Roland.

'Indeed. But what do *they* matter?'

'The jousting matters, my lady. It matters so much. See?' He waved an arm at the preparations all around. 'There are to be celebrations at Hallowtide, with disguisings and other revels in the evenings, and a great tournament during the day, but *I* am to be completely excluded, while that pair of imbeciles indulge in everything!'

Cicely almost felt for him. Henry's carefully selected form of punishment was biting deep into Edmund de la Pole. 'I understand you have a new friend now?' She watched him closely.

'New friend?'

'So I am told. A young man from Tournai?'

There was a barely perceptible pause. 'How well informed you are. Well, do not imagine he is my new love. Folly bells may figure in *his* philosophy, but not in mine. He is only in my household because he is handy with horses. That is all.'

Folly bells were said to be worn by those who found members of their own gender more attractive than the opposite sex. She changed the subject. 'Have you seen Annie?'

'No.' He was defensive. 'She seems to be contenting herself with Thomas and no one else.'

'What do—did—you really feel for her, Edmund?'

Ambivalence lurked as he answered. 'It no longer matters. We are all saved from a predicament in which I never again wish to find myself. And I am sure she wishes the same.'

'I advise you to stay away from young girls, Edmund. At least, from girls who are quite that young.'

'Do *you* see Annie as the age she really is?' he challenged.

'Possibly not, but that is no excuse.'

'I am aware of that, Cousin, and have no excuse at all for what I did, except—' He stopped.

'Except?'

'Where is my brother?' he asked as a deliberate diversion.

What a sharply twisting conversation this was, she thought. 'Jack is safe.'

'From me, you mean?'

'There are others more dangerous than you, Edmund, but yes. However, are *you* safe from him?'

'Oh, yes,' he replied. 'Jack is too honourable to kill his own brother.'

Cicely studied him. 'I would not count upon it now, not after Annie. But you, sir, have never been too honourable to kill *him*, have you?'

Ghosts played in his gaze. 'I have no honour, is that not your opinion? Good day, Lady Welles.' He sketched her a deep bow, and walked on.

She watched him. Edmund de la Pole was still clever and ambitious; and therefore still dangerous, but there was something about Annie that had found its way deep inside him. Was there also more than met the eye in his dealings with Nicolas Stalyn? It seemed no coincidence that Stalyn had a connection with the boy in Lisbon.

She was not excluded from the Rose Tower this time, but permitted the privilege to which her birthright entitled her, and Mary stayed in an outer room as her mistress was shown further into Margaret's familiar apartments. But someone else was already with Henry's mother, in the grand parlour that faced past the Round Tower, to the rising grandeur of St George's Chapel. The door was ajar. Margaret must have forgotten Viscountess Welles, or she would not have risked being overheard with this particular person.

Her ladies clustered in a far corner of the large anteroom, and departed on hearing Margaret's angrily raised voice.

'How *dare* you whimper of innocence!'

Cicely halted. Should she leave too?

Margaret became more controlled. 'I care *nothing* for your feelings, Mistress Penworthy. I simply expect you to desist from this shameful pretence!'

'There is no pretence, my lady, truly there is not!' The second voice was whining and tearful; the voice of someone of lower rank.

'Oh, spare me the piping, madam, for it will not wash. You seduced my brother for despicable reasons, and now that I have found you out, I expect you to stop, or pay dearly.'

Cicely gazed at the door. Brother? It could only be Jon. The unknown woman was his mistress!

'Well? What have you to say?' Margaret demanded icily.

'I admit going to him under false pretences, my lady. But I obeyed the king's command.'

Cicely's lips parted.

'And now you will desist at *my* command,' Margaret replied.

'I dare not, my lady. His Majesty expressly commanded me to earn Lord Welles' love, and that is what I did. Please, I beg of you, do not condemn me.' Genuine fear was in the plea.

Cicely's heart twisted within. Would the King of England's deceit and cruelty never end? *This* was what weighed upon him, not Knole, although God knows, Knole was enough! Now he regretted what he had done, but it was too late. And his great fear had just been realized. Lady Welles *had* learned of his role in it, and despised him accordingly.

'Oh, I condemn you, lady,' Margaret replied, 'and if you mention to anyone that the king is your paymaster, I will tear your black heart out with my bare hands. The king has nothing to do with anything, is that clear?'

'Yes, my lady.'

'My brother is very dear to me, and so is his happiness.'

'But I *do* make him happy!' the other protested.

'You, madam, are a whore, and you do what whores do. You have taken the king's money to seduce my brother and destroy his marriage. Well, you will leave now. Leave my brother, leave Windsor, leave the realm for all I care.'

'But, I love my lord Jon.'

'Do not speak of him familiarly, wench! He is Lord Welles to you, and do not forget it. You may be accustomed to giving yourself to all and sundry in order to weed out information that will be to royal advantage, but the moment you encroached upon my dearest and only brother, you crossed me. If you have not understood *that* yet, then you are as unintelligent as you are immoral.'

'My lady, I am with child.'

There was silence, and Cicely's eyes filled with tears.

Margaret was hard and unsympathetic. 'Then that is indeed your misfortune, madam. You parted your legs willingly, and now you pay the price.'

'But Lord Welles knows of the child and acknowledges it.'

'Until he learns that you have lied to him, and the child is by a lusty cooper who rolled you one afternoon in York, or wherever you were at the time.'

'That is not true!' Alice cried.

'I think you will find that it is, my dear.' Margaret's voice was oh, so smooth and precise.

There was a sob. 'But where will I go? What can I do? The queen will turn me out when she knows I am with child' There was desperation in the words.

'I will provide you with sufficient money to simply disappear. And bear in mind, should I so wish, I can ensure that you, too, vanish into eternity.'

'But, my lord will not let me leave him.'

'Do not be so naïve, lady! My *lord* will not know until you have gone! He is at the Tower on his duties and will not return to Windsor until tomorrow dawn!' Margaret snapped furiously. 'You are a common prostitute who has managed to make herself useful as a spy, and that is *all* you are. Now, I have every intention of informing my brother of your true history, so I suggest you get to your lodgings, pack your things and leave. Today.'

'I am in the queen's household,' Alice reminded her.

'You think *that* carries weight with me?' Margaret gave a mirthless laugh. 'Dear God, you *are* green, are you not? You can forget your lofty contacts, madam, especially my brother, who will want nothing to do with you when he hears what I have to say about your sordid history, including the cooper in York. You have been plucked, gutted and trussed, lady, and had better accept it.'

'You underestimate my lord's love for me,' Alice said quietly. 'If I choose to deny it all, he will believe me.'

'Then the vilest depths of Thames mud await you,' Margaret responded coldly.

'My child will be your nephew or niece.'

'*If* it is my brother's, which I doubt, it will be baseborn, with a whore for a mother. You think that will sway me? Now, remove yourself.'

'I have duties with the queen until she retires tonight, my lady. Please do not ask me to defy her. I promise to leave the moment my duties are at an end. I will be gone before my lord returns. I vow it.'

'See that you are.'

Cicely shivered, because Henry's mother was certainly capable of doing away with anyone who obstructed her.

'Yes, Lady Margaret. You promised money?'

Margaret made a disparaging sound, and Cicely heard the chink of coins as a purse was tossed upon a table. 'And do not think of fooling me, wench, because I will *not* be fooled. If I learn of you again, I *will* eliminate you. Now get out of my sight!'

Light steps hastened to the door, and Cicely drew hastily into a window embrasure as Jon's mistress emerged. The moment she did so, Cicely recognized her as the whore who had accosted Jack on the steps at Three Cranes, and who had followed him to Gough's Alley. Now the same paid predator had hunted Jon as well. With much more success!

Alice Penworthy was in her twenties, with honey-hued hair, a heart-shaped face and, large, unexpectedly dark eyes. Her peach-coloured gown had voluminous sleeves that hid her hands until one was momentarily exposed, revealing the turquoise ring!

Jon had given such a treasured memento to his whore? 'Do I matter so little to you now, Jon Welles?' Cicely whispered bitterly, as Mistress Alice Penworthy hurried away. Except for the child, the giving away of the ring was perhaps the most hurtful thing of all. Well, it would not be on the whore's finger when she left Windsor, even if Lady Welles had to slice off the entire digit!

After taking some moments to gather composure, she announced herself to Margaret, who immediately perceived her distress. 'Oh, my dear. You heard?'

'Yes.'

'I am so sorry, Cicely.' Margaret ushered her to the chair just vacated, and remained standing herself. 'She did not come immediately when I sent for her, and you, I think, are early. I wanted her gone before you arrived. I am so angry with Henry that when next I see him I fear we will have another argument.'

'Please do not, and please do not tell him that I know.'

Margaret looked at her curiously. 'If that is your wish.'

'It is. I will find it easier if he does not know.' Cicely drew a long breath. 'I recognized the woman.'

'Oh?'

Cicely explained. It was safe enough to do so, because at the time of the incidents at Three Cranes and Gough's Alley, Jack had not yet fled into exile. He had still been a free man, outwardly loyal, not a hounded traitor.

Margaret nodded. 'She has been Henry's creature for some time, it seems. And now the queen is actively abetting by taking her in.'

Cicely looked away.

'Henry is at Westminster,' Margaret added.

'Yes. I saw as I passed.'

'I imagine you may receive a summons to go to him there.' Margaret turned to a table upon which stood goblets and a bottle of sweet bramble wine. Her conscience was troubled, for she accused Bess of aiding and abetting in the matter of Alice Penworthy, yet was she herself not condoning the doubly adulterous liaison between Henry and his sister-in-law? She knew Cicely was essential to him, but it was all badly at odds with her own religious scruples.

Pressing a goblet upon Cicely, she took a seat. 'As soon as the whore has disappeared, I will inform Jon of the truth.'

'Not all of it, please.' Cicely surprised herself, because it would serve Jon right if he learned every detail about Alice Penworthy, especially now that he had given the whore the turquoise ring, but the thought of his deep and honest pain was not something his wife relished. 'Better Jon simply thinks she has deserted him.'

Margaret searched her face. 'You still have warm feelings for my brother, my dear?'

'I will *always* have warm feelings for Jon Welles.'

'I am glad of that.'

Cicely smiled wryly. 'But he does not have similar feelings about me. I have never given him a child.'

'That did not colour his love for you, my dear. Whatever the reason for his infatuation with this trollop, it is not that he wants a child. Besides, I do not believe the child *is* his. I would not trust that whore's word for anything. There may not have been a cooper in York, but I will warrant there was a bootmaker in Pontefract, a coal-heaver in Scarborough, or some similar fellow. Once a whore, always a whore. But, for you, I will not tell Jon everything, only that she has left him. And I will see that Henry says nothing either, not that I imagine he will wish to own up to his disgraceful interference.'

'The ironic thing is that there was no need for Henry to have done anything,' Cicely murmured dryly, turning the goblet by its stem. 'My marriage to Jon was at an end anyway, in all but name.' She forbore to mention that the last straw for him had been learning of Jack's second survival. But even then he had helped Jack and Tal to escape Henry at Esher.

'You have no idea how much this all grieves me, Cicely. When you and my brother were happy together, I was happy too.'

'May I still regard you as my friend?'

Margaret was startled. 'Of course you may! My dear, there was a time when my friendship with you depended upon how things were between you and Jon, or you and Henry, but that time has gone. I like you immensely. You have become very dear to me, and you are, after all, the only person with whom I may speak honestly and intimately of Henry.'

Cicely smiled. 'That is true.' She sipped the wine. 'Did you see the turquoise ring?'

'Yes. You gave it to him.' Margaret's eyes were sad.

Nothing more was said of Henry, Jon or the harlot, and an hour later Henry's page delivered a two-word note to Cicely from the king. *'Midnight. Westminster.'*

Chapter Twenty-Two

Early that evening, long before the midnight assignation in Westminster, Tal and Perry escorted Cicely and Mary toward the arched entrance of the cobbled Windsor court where Jon resided with his mistress. They were responding to Jack's urgent message that Alice Penworthy had returned from her duties with Bess, and appeared to be preparing to leave. Cicely needed to confront the woman. It was something she *had* to do, if only to retrieve the ring.

It was dark, Jon was still at the Tower, and they knew Jack waited in the court, but as they drew near, they saw a cloaked figure trying to stay out of sight on the other side of the street, almost opposite the arched entrance to the court.

Tal halted, his hand on his sword hilt. 'Identify yourself!' he cried.

The figure dashed away around a nearby corner. Tal considered giving chase, but then changed his mind and led the others on toward the archway. Dark shadows concealed them as they looked into the court beyond, where two elegant houses faced each other across cobbles. The upper floors were so close that if people leaned from the topmost windows, they could surely have shaken hands. Neither house was exactly modest, or large and elaborate, but their proximity to the castle would make them expensive and sought after. One was in darkness, its shutters closed, indicating it to be unoccupied for the moment, but there was candlelight in the windows of the other, which had to be the one Jon shared with Alice Penworthy.

The light autumn breeze played with newly lit torches, twisting the smoke into strange shapes that came and went. It was possible to imagine ghosts, writhing and winding, before disappearing again. Jon's banner flew from a post, its ropes slapping, and overhead the clouds of night had closed in. Like slate-grey harbingers of ill fate, Cicely thought, and then chided herself for letting the approach of Hallowtide affect her common sense.

Jack waited discreetly out of the way in a corner that escaped the torchlight, and Cicely hurried to him, to be held close for a brief moment. She could only whisper, her voice muffled because she buried her face against him. 'Has Tal told you what Henry did at Knole?'

'Yes, he has. Hush, sweetheart. No tears. I survived, and your eyes have finally been opened about Tudor. Mind you, I did not for a moment imagine I would have Roland de Vielleville to thank for exposing the truth.' He kissed the top of her head.

'I have been summoned to Henry tonight,' she said quietly, moving from his arms.

He smiled. 'I know you do not wish to. Not now.'

'But I must.'

'I know that, too.' He held her gaze. 'Do not think of confronting this woman now. I would rather you wait here with Mary and Perry, while Tal and I go inside. We can relieve her of the turquoise.'

'And have her recognize you both? Especially you. You *do* know who she is?'

He nodded. 'Yes. From Three Cranes steps.'

'Then you know you cannot let her see you. She would seek favour with Henry by telling him you have been here in Windsor. He may already suspect you are alive, but she could *prove* it for him. And no, I do not want Tal or Perry to go in either, or Mary. I want to see her, face to face, do you understand? I want to watch her remove the ring from her finger and then return it to me.' She turned to Tal, who had joined them. 'It belongs to Eleanor, and if it is the last thing I do, I will see it returned to her.'

Tal disapproved. '*Cariad*, Eleanor would not wish you to return it. She gave it to your father and *he* gave it to you. That will be all that matters in her eyes. Take it back, by all means, but only to keep it.'

They all drew even further into the shadows as slow hooves sounded from the stables that served the court. A young man with hair almost as blond as Perry's came into sight, leading three saddle horses and a fully laden packhorse. He dismounted in front of Jon's house, and seemed prepared to wait.

He was well-dressed, and the horses were good quality too. A lantern above the house door shone over him, and Cicely saw his face in sharp relief. He was very good-looking, and very nervous, as if he would take flight at the slightest thing.

'Who is he, do you think?' she whispered.

Tal answered. 'It is Nicolas Stalyn, the young man from Tournai whom I have seen in company with Edmund. Why he should be *here*, I do not know. Edmund is not, for I left him sleeping off a surfeit of strong Gascon wine.' He looked at Jack. 'The ripples of all this seem to be spreading further and further.'

'Ever wider.'

Cicely gazed at the young man. 'Edmund told me he has taken Stalyn into his household because he is "handy" with horses.' Suddenly she could wait no more, and before anyone could hold her back, she walked into the court torchlight.

Nicolas Stalyn stiffened visibly, and then blocked her path. 'Who are you?' he demanded in a noticeable Flemish accent.

She paused, and was regally Plantagenet. 'I am Lady Welles, the queen's sister.' she answered coolly. 'Who are *you*?'

He gave his name willingly enough.

'Why are you here?' she asked then.

Now he was not so willing.

'Why are you here?' she repeated coldly.

Jack stepped into the nearest torchlight, still hooded but with a warning hand on his sword hilt. Stalyn took the hint. 'I am to attend Mistress Penworthy, who lives here.'

Her interest quickened. 'Are you not in Lord Edmund de la Pole's household?'

There was a noticeable hesitation. 'No. I left his service tonight. Now I am to assist Mistress Penworthy when she leaves.'

'Who instructed you? Lord Edmund?'

He did not answer.

'What is Mistress Penworthy to Lord Edmund?'

'Nothing, my lady. Truly.' His discomfort was tangible.

'You have come here from Lisbon, have you not?' she asked then.

He was startled, and suddenly even more uneasy. 'Yes, my lady. How did you know?'

'Lord Edmund told me,' she replied untruthfully. 'And you went there with Sir Edward Brampton and another youth from your country?'

'We travelled with Lady Brampton.'

'Who is this other youth?'

It was a question too many. Stalyn was suddenly alarmed. 'I do not know, lady.'

'I am sure you do.'

'I value my life. Please, do not ask me more. I am afraid,' he said then.

'Of whom?' But his lips had clamped closed. Oh, how she wanted to *shake* the truth from him! Frustrated, she tried something else. 'Who is in the house now?'

'Mistress Penworthy, her maid and some servants.'

'Where are you to take her?'

'I do not know yet, my lady. She is to tell me. That is all I know. Please.'

There was nothing more to be gained right now, she decided, and he made no move to stop her as she made her way toward the front door, which opened with ease. Inside she found a vestibule where the polished oak floor was scattered with rush mats. Panelling covered the lower walls, with bright paintings on the whitewashed walls above, and there were carved chairs and an old iron-banded chest on which lay a pair of Jon's gauntlets. Gleaming sconces with lighted candles cast a welcoming glow, and the smell of smoke came from a fireplace, where fresh coals had just been added. Two packed valises waited just inside the door.

A brawny manservant had heard the door close behind her, and came running. He was in his forties, with a shock of prematurely white hair, a snub nose and red cheeks, and was clearly capable of single-handedly turning anyone out.

'You cannot come in here, whoever you are!' he growled.

'You think not? I am Lady Welles, daughter of King Edward IV and sister-in-law of King Henry VII,' she replied in the same cool tone with which she had addressed Stalyn.

Observing belatedly how finely dressed she was, the man drew back guardedly and then bowed low, not being prepared to risk crossing a princess.

'Is Mistress Penworthy alone?' Cicely demanded.

'Yes, my lady, except for her maid.' He glanced up.

She put a finger to her lips. 'Silence now, or it will be the worst for you.'

Without another word, he retreated whence he had come.

As Cicely ascended, she heard Alice issuing angry orders from an upper storey. Suddenly a tearful middle-aged maid rushed down, halting with a gasp on seeing Cicely. Afraid, the woman pressed back against the wall, and edged her way past, then almost scrambled down to the hall, from where her footsteps pattered toward the rear of the house.

Cicely continued the ascent. She felt icily calm, and relished the coming minutes, during which she would be avenged on the woman who had stolen Jon's heart under such cruelly false pretences. Reaching the landing, she could see into the candlelit great bedroom at the front of the house. There was a large canopied bed hung with rich blue velvet, on the coverlet of which were the scattered belongings Alice Penworthy intended to take with her. Jon had made love to the creature on that bed, Cicely thought, with so much loathing she wanted to put her hands around the whore's throat.

She crossed the landing to stand in the doorway. Alice wore the same gown as earlier, but had abandoned her headdress so that her thick curls fell past her shoulders. Her forehead was very highly shaved, which Jon would not like. She did not realize Cicely was there because she was too concerned with thrusting things of value into a large valise. These included a number of Jon's rings and hat brooches, two of his jewelled collars, and Welles family silverware. Not content with deceiving him so cruelly, the whore was stealing from him as well!

Cicely announced her presence at last. 'Those jewels belong to my husband, madam, and you will *not* take them.'

The other straightened with a gasp.

'You know me, I think,' Cicely said, advancing into the room. She glanced at the turquoise on the woman's finger. What a very beautiful and choice stone it was. Fit for a king. And his queen. Not for a common prostitute!

Alice's oddly dark eyes were as black as coal in the candlelight. 'If my Lord Jon were here now, he would order you from the house,' she declared, chin raised.

'He is not *your* Lord Jon, nor is he here, and *you* are the one who is leaving.' Cicely held Alice's gaze and decided to probe for information about things other than Jon Welles. 'What is my cousin Edmund de la Pole to you?'

'He was my lover,' was the instant reply.

'Really? I think not.' But who knew with Edmund? Anything was possible.

'I know the de la Pole brothers intimately, my fine lady, and have more than sampled them both.'

Cicely chuckled. 'Both? Oh, how easily the lies slip from your painted lips.'

Alice's gaze was withering. 'What *do* men see in you?'

'Oh, I can well believe you do not know, for you have not the wit to understand men, only to lie beneath them.'

'I still managed to win your husband's heart, my fine lady, and to secure his seed to bear him a child.'

'For the first, I pity him. For the second, I have grave doubts.'

Alice dark eyes flickered. 'Lord Jon is potent, but could never impregnate *your* sad womb. You are barren, and have failed him, as he has often said.'

'Ah, but did you quicken by *him*? Now there's a puzzling little concept.'

At that moment there came the clatter of hooves in the court, and then Cicely heard Tal shout. Clearly Stalyn's nerve had snapped and he had ridden off. Or so she imagined.

Alice glanced toward the window, her face paler than before. 'What do you want of me, Lady Welles?'

'That you get out, *now*, but without anything that belongs to Lord Welles. I note you have his rings and brooches assembled, and that silver candlestick that I gave him. What else have you already packed?'

'See for yourself.' Alice indicated the valise and stood aside.

And be attacked? Cicely was not a fool. 'No, my dear, you tip everything out on to the bed.' When the other did not move, she continued. 'Very well, you will leave without it. I have not come here alone, so you had best believe that if you try to take that valise, it will be forcibly removed from you.'

'You cannot remove the most precious treasure I have from my Lord Jon.'

Cicely ignored the barb. 'And do not think of returning to insinuate yourself in his life again. You have hurt him enough and I will not suffer you to hurt him more. I still feel much for him, do you understand? He is a noble, honourable and chivalrous man. I may have quarrelled with him, and we may both have behaved badly, but my feelings for him have not lessened. There will *always* be a place for him in my heart. Always. You have no heart in which to treasure him, Mistress Penworthy, and you were warned off earlier today by the King's Lady Mother. Must I remind you that you would be very unwise indeed to ignore her?'

'The king commanded and I obeyed.'

'The king also paid you well, no doubt,' Cicely observed.

'It was money easily earned. Your husband was so very ripe for plucking. Oh, how ripe! He often told me you were faithless.'

'I am flattered to be so frequently on his mind,' Cicely answered.

'He only spoke with contempt. I am the one Jon loves now.'

Cicely stiffened at the familiarity. 'Do not—'

'Speak of him with intimacy? He bade me call him Jon, and I never go against his wishes.'

'How sweet, but then, whores are paid to be obliging. They accommodate and relieve, and then take payment.' Cicely indicated the rings and brooches. 'Winning his love is clearly not enough.'

'And jealousy greens your eyes,' Alice responded softly.

'Oh, I do not seek to be in his matrimonial bed again, nor he in mine. A reconciliation no longer holds any attraction for either of us, but I still think very highly of him. A word from me, and you will receive very unwelcome royal attention from the King's Lady Mother. Do you understand? So leave. Now. And do not forget your yellow hood. You are bound to have one somewhere.'

Prostitutes wore such hoods, and Alice's eyes hardened at the suggestion. 'You are clearly famous for your humour, Lady Welles, as well as your parted legs.'

'For which pose I do not take payment. That is the difference, is it not? Now, before we both forget, give me the ring you wear.'

'It was a gift.'

'I do not care if it is now sewn to your crooked digit. My father gave it to me and I gave it to Lord Welles. He may no longer want it, but I do.' Cicely held out a demanding hand.

'It is mine!' Alice clenched her fist and held it behind her back, clearly prepared to resist. Her voice shook. 'If you place rough hands upon me, you will be attacking a woman who is with child. May your conscience weigh heavily if you commit such a dreadful sin!'

'Give me the turquoise,' Cicely repeated quietly, advancing a step. Child or not, she was going to see that ring removed from the creature's grasp.

A male voice suddenly spoke from the doorway. 'Return the ring to Lady Welles.' Jon entered. His face was pale and strained, and Cicely wondered how long he had been listening on the landing. Stalyn had not departed after all, it had been Jon's early return she had heard. Perhaps Tal called out in an attempt to warn her? If so, it had failed, and now Jon must have heard things that sliced into him.

Alice stared at him as if at a ghost. 'Jon! She was about to attack me!'

She started to run to him, but he held up his hand. 'Give the ring to my wife,' he repeated quietly.

'But—'

'Do it!'

She removed the turquoise and glanced at the fire, clearly thinking of tossing it into the heat.

Cicely took another step forward. 'Do that and I will kill you, child or not!' she breathed.

Jon moved swiftly past her and caught Alice's wrist, which he held tightly as he forcibly unwrapped her fingers and took the ring from her palm. Then he handed it to Cicely. 'You have the ring. Now please go.'

Their eyes met, and she saw the pain he tried to hide.

'Jon—'

'Please go, sweetheart. *Please.*'

'I am so sorry,' she whispered.

He did not answer, and as she left, he closed the door softly behind her.

Sweetheart. How that word gladdened her heart. Tears leapt to her eyes as she slipped the ring on her finger and hurried downstairs. Victory? Yes, there was no denying it. Her rival had been vanquished. Jon would have no more to do with the creature now, his wife knew him well enough to be sure of that, but she was sad for him. He now knew he had been betrayed by his mistress *and* had probably been there long enough to know about Henry's part in it. A belated thought struck her. Rival? Was *that* how she regarded the whore?

Nicolas Stalyn was still in the court with the horses—at least, with the saddle horses. The pack horse had gone. The snorts of other horses that had been ridden at speed came from the stables behind the house. Jack explained. 'Jon's mount, and his two escorts. He recognized Tal and me.'

She held up her hand, to show the turquoise, which now graced her finger. 'She had stolen it, and Jon made her surrender it to me.

'I am glad, sweetheart.' He kissed her cheek.

'She was taking Jon's jewellery and other valuables. He saw. I feel sad for him.'

'He deserves all he gets.' Jack had no sympathy.

At that moment the door of the house opened again, and Alice emerged, followed by the maid carrying the two bags that had been in the vestibule. It seemed Jon had wasted no time at all about ejecting his former mistress. Alice dropped something, and paused in great haste to pick it up again. It was Jon's purse, and Cicely knew that he – like Margaret – had paid her amply for the child that might not be his. Or might not even exist.

Clutching the purse, Alice spoke to Stalyn. 'Where is the pack horse?'

Jack replied for him. 'Returned to the stables, together with its packs. And you can forget taking those valises, because heaven knows what you have stolen.' He addressed the maid, who dropped the bags as if they had caught fire. She seized the reins of the nearest horse, pulled herself inelegantly onto the saddle from a mounting block, and rode off, leaving her astounded mistress staring after her.

Alice had not recognized Jack's voice, nor could she see his face because he kept in shadow. Instead she cast a look of vitriolic hatred at Cicely. 'I will remember this, Lady Welles.'

'So will I. My memory, however, will be one of pleasure.'

'Never feel safe again, lady, for I will be waiting.'

Tal stepped forward to lift her roughly up on to another horse. 'That's enough from you, trollop. One more threatening word, and I will throw you in that horse trough. I will also tell the king a few choice lies about things you said of him. You do not want to be the object of *his* wrath, do you?' Then he slapped the horse's rump.

Stalyn had to leap on the remaining animal to follow as she was carried out of the court at a gallop.

The force of the woman's hatred seemed to linger in the air after she had gone, but Cicely's first thought was of Jon, whose world had surely been turned on its end. She gazed at the house, and then at the turquoise on her finger.

Tal read her thoughts. 'Eleanor would understand if you would rather give it back to your idiot spouse.' He smiled.

Jack said nothing, for he did not know Eleanor; nor did he understand why Cicely would wish to return the ring to the man who had treated her so badly. But he would not interfere. Whatever Cicely wished, he would abide by.

'You begin to know me too well, sir,' she replied to Tal, and then smiled at Jack. 'Thank you.'

He spread his hands. 'Thank me? Why?'

'For not saying what you think.'

Jack smiled and drew her close. 'I love you, my darling. You are everything.' His lips brushed hers tenderly, and then he turned her toward the house. 'Take it to him.' She almost heard the addendum. *I trust the bastard appreciates the gesture!*

The white-haired manservant was waiting. Clearly Jon anticipated her, she thought.

The man was embarrassed. 'Begging your grace and pardon, Lady Welles, but his lordship said that no matter what you said, he does not wish to see you. I must obey my master's instructions.'

'I understand. At least assure me you will give this back to him.' She extended the ring.

'Of course, my lady.' Relieved not to have an argument, the man accepted it.

Within moments she had emerged into the cold night air again. But now she would have to obey Henry's summons, and it made her feel sick to think of it.

Chapter Twenty-Three

MIDNIGHT HAD JUST sounded as Cicely held a candle to make her way along the narrow, unlit secret passage at Westminster Palace. The palace was crowded, but no one knew she was here. Hoods were ever useful, and it was simple to slip unseen into the passage. As she had done before, and Bess must have done that May night.

She reached the concealed door to the royal bedchamber, where she knew Henry would be waiting alone. There she hesitated. Visions of what Jack had suffered at Knole seemed to hover, mothlike, in the shadows, and Alice Penworthy's hatred was drifting along the passage behind her. Even further behind, she sensed the sad spirit of John of Gloucester. All were the doing of the man to whom she was about to surrender herself. Mastering her nerve as best she could, she knocked upon the door with a shaking hand.

Henry admitted her in person, setting the candle flame spiralling and smoking, and bringing with him a faint swirl of cloves. He wore a loose robe, cloth of gold, loosely tied, so that she could still see he was otherwise naked. This was how Richard had been at Nottingham, when she had given her maidenhead to him so very gladly. There had not been any other man she thought so worthy. Or who had her heart so completely. But she felt no such gladness now, only a fiercely controlled air of unnatural calm.

He took the candle, before bolting the door and allowing the concealing tapestry to fall back into place. It had not been bolted in May, and Bess must have had held the tapestry aside to watch her husband cavorting with her sister.

But it was not of Bess that Cicely thought in those moments. Instead it was of Richard. There was no costmary and mint this time, no treasured uncle. No dark chestnut hair and warm grey eyes. No love so sublime and radiant that it broke her heart to think it had gone forever. Driving the memories away, she turned brightly to face Henry, unfastened her cloak and allowed it to fall to the floor.

He looked at the rich folds of the velvet gown, and then smiled into her eyes. 'Not the plum brocade? Am I in disfavour?'

She wanted to tell him just how much disfavour.

He placed the candle on a table. 'The gown you wear pleases me, as indeed do all the gowns you wear. Of course, it delights me even more when you wear no gown at all.' He paused, alive to everything about her. 'What is it, *cariad?* What is wrong?'

'Nothing is wrong.'

He tapped his lips with a forefinger, before smiling. 'It is my dear uncle, is it not? Does he want a reconciliation? I know he has been to see you at Pasmer's Place, as has my Marshal of Calais. And now the troublesome whore has departed, the way back to you is clear. Or at least, so he must hope.'

'You know the woman has gone?'

'My mother told me of paying her to leave.'

Cicely wished she knew exactly what Margaret had said. Certainly it could not have been anything that implicated him.

'Now, about your husband. . .' he pressed gently.

'There is not to be a reconciliation, Henry,' she replied. 'Jon came to the house on his way to his duties at the Tower. He had a ledger to inspect for irregularities, and requested Sir Humphrey to come so they could discuss some business matter or other.' How the lies flowed. Did she sound convincingly indifferent?

'Then why was Roland present?' he asked, concentrating on the candle reflections in her eyes.

'Because Jon has charge of him, or had you forgotten? I did not ask and Jon did not say. I found it all very disagreeable, and was glad when they left.' Her concealed anger and resentment increased. So Henry's spies knew all about the meeting at Pasmer's Place. Well, they knew who was present if not what was said. How tired she was of being watched all the time. It seemed that every minute of every day, there were secret eyes upon her.

Henry went to a table where stood a little silver bowl of Margaret's precious Collyweston strawberries. Taking one, he brought it to her. He was so sensuous. The only man she could detest and desire at the same time. But he had also twisted Jack's shoulder out of its socket. She must not forget.

He slipped the fruit between her lips. 'Eat, *cariad*, as a prelude, mm?'

It was impossible to disobey. The fruit was good. Too good.

He moved behind her to unlace the gown, and as her clothes slid to the floor she had to conquer an unexpected need to shield her breasts.

If he noticed, he did not say, but caught her up to carry her to the bed. The coverlets had already been folded back. 'That is where you belong, my sweet Cicely,' he said softly, and then turned away.

The way he did it made her hold her breath with trepidation.

'I imagine Sir Humphrey was in London to see his wife safely on her way back to Kenninghall this morning,' he said.

Her surprise was genuine, her relief hidden. 'Lady Talbot has been in London?' Why had Tal not said anything?

'Did you not know? She lodged with the community of ladies at the Minoresses without Aldgate. You are aware of the establishment, I imagine?' He took off his robe, and the soft light illuminated his body. His masculinity was soft, but long and thick, on the point of arousal. He was anticipating her.

'Yes, I know. The Minoresses are at the Franciscan Convent, between Gracechurch Street and Whitechapel, and many noble widows retreat there. I am not acquainted with Lady Talbot,' she added, wanting to look away from the rich promise of his loins, but at the same time unwilling to break this new spell.

'From all accounts she is best avoided.' Henry's eyes, uneven for the moment, rested almost thoughtfully on her, taking in the pale curves of her naked body. 'You have seen the royal yard before, methinks. Is it so splendid tonight that it commands your full attention?'

She managed to look at his face.

'What is the matter, *cariad?'*

Oh, the caress in that final word. Or was it the signal of a viper slowly uncoiling to strike? She had to answer, and surprised herself with a ready explanation. 'You are still having me watched, Henry Tudor. How else do you know who was and was not at Pasmer's Place?'

She was confounded by his answering smile. 'Well, shame on you for your mistrust, lady. It so happens that I know because my Marshal of Calais told me. He had to present himself to me this morning, and volunteered the information.'

She felt foolish.

'Cease this tiptoeing around, sweetheart. This is not Abingdon, and it is not me avoiding the issue, it is you. So I must guess, and it seems to me that the one thing that is bound to cause you the most pain of all, is that your vanquished foe is carrying Jon Welles' baby. Is that not so? And your poor little heart is breaking over it.' He spoke kindly.

She stared at him, for there was so much understanding in his voice, so much sympathy and feeling that helpless tears filled her eyes, stinging for a moment before they had their way. Yes, her heart *was* breaking! She drew her knees up, turned away and hid her face in her hands as wretchedness deadened other senses. It all sank beneath the anguish caused by that unborn child. She could tell herself that it was not Jon's, but in her heart she was convinced it was.

Henry sat beside her, pulled her up into his arms and held her tightly, as if he shared her pain. He stroked her and kissed her forehead and cheeks, but not her lips. He was the embodiment of love and concern. Seduction was not in his mind now, only the need to soothe her, and caress her pain until it subsided.

Once again she was caught in a maelstrom of guilt. She wanted his comfort, *needed* it. His part in her misery was suddenly driven underground because sometimes, as now, he was the only one who understood completely.

He tilted her face in order to look at her. 'Oh, my dear love, I did not mean to bring you to this. I only wanted you to tell me what is troubling you. Just as you wanted to help me at Abingdon. You do understand that, do you not?'

I understand that she was all *your* fault, she thought, but she nodded. 'It does hurt that she is carrying Jon's child. It makes me feel so incomplete.'

'Incomplete? *You?* Sweet Jesu, my darling, there is no woman who is more *complete.* But when the Almighty created you, He decided not to let even you have absolutely everything, and so denied you one thing. A second child. Look at me, Cicely Plantagenet. Never, *ever* think you are lacking. To me you are perfect, but there is something lacking in *my* life—you beside me in a marriage bed.'

She gazed at him through her tears. *I should be hating you now, despising you, loathing you. Instead I cling to the solace you offer.*

He bent his head to brush his lips to hers. 'You must have faith in yourself, *cariad,* your king commands it.' Then, after a moment of hesitation, he kissed her properly, and this time desire inflamed the moment.

It was such beguilement, as if she had taken laudanum. Her guard was lowered, and her exposed senses lured her inexorably into the fatal enchantment he always wielded over her. No man could have been *more* tender and loving toward her than Henry Tudor had been a moment since. She drifted into his lovemaking, lying back so that he could move beside her. . .and then on her. She moved her hands over him, before sliding them down to his buttocks to press his erection between her parted thighs. There was nothing she could do to prevent herself from being spellbound by him. He seemed capable of overruling her willpower; of influencing her so that she had no strength or will to resist.

But as he sank richly into her, something shattered the spell that enveloped her. It was as if invisible sea defences had been breached, and without warning the beguilement fled into the night, driven before a tidal wave of unstoppable self-loathing. Everything this man had ever done to hurt her was flung against her like jagged wreckage. It was overwhelming, and yet kindled such a need that she could almost have devoured him.

She wrapped her legs around his hips, and a storm of gratification swept her on an unseen, incredibly compelling current of sensuality. Her kisses were wildly demanding, and her fingernails clawed at his back. She did not know what she did; nor did she care. The satisfying of this impossibly powerful urge was all that drove her now.

Her intense, almost unparalleled fervour aroused new needs within him, and he submitted to his own urges, driving in and out of her as if death itself would claim him if he did not.

The raw pleasure heightened, but was in its darkest form. She cursed him, begged him, challenged him, and he responded to it all. But even in the midst of such extraordinary circumstances, he took care that she was with him as his climax was imminent. Their eyes met, his so filled with passion, hers so alight with the onslaught of savage feelings that she could not hold back.

'*Rwy'n dy garu di,*' he whispered. 'I love you.'

Amid her confusion and bewilderment, she felt the sweetness of him coming inside her. She was sobbing and gasping at once, clinging to him, offering herself, taking everything he gave in return, and wanting more and more. And more. Her body undulated against his, and tears were wet on her face. Reason seemed to have deserted her. She was caught up by the attack on her mind and senses, and once again it was Henry Tudor who gave her what she needed.

He held her to him, allowing her everything she sought of his body. His eyes were closed as he whispered her name, and he made no attempt to stop her, or to end her craving, even when his erection had dwindled. But for her, the mere thought of his most precious member nestling against the sensitive folds of the private places between her legs brought renewed excitement, and when she felt its soft movement, she wept for the joy of it.

Never had she known such a wild, unreasoning craving, such a need to almost destroy him with her insatiable passion. It was a force from before time, violating them both, and it frightened her. She was weeping uncontrollably as she clung to him, and felt as if she had lost all sense of truly being.

At last he stopped her. 'Enough, *cariad.* You do not know what you do.'

Oh, she knew! She KNEW! His words opened floodgates, and she scrambled wildly to kneel beside him on the bed, unwise truths bursting from her unguarded lips. 'You sent her, Henry! *You* sent her! You deliberately set about ending my marriage, and now Jon will have the child *I* could never give him! And you tortured Jack when he was wounded! You pulled him to the floor by his hair and then dislocated his shoulder. For the pleasure of it! Above all, you took Richard from me. *Richard!* You took *him* and I can never forgive you. I hate you! I *hate* you!'

Stricken, he gazed at her, and then left the bed to don his robe. He ran his hands through his ruffled hair as he struggled for composure.

She pulled the coverlet up to hide the nakedness which now made her feel so very vulnerable. The heart that had overruled her head now pounded with fear, but the accusations were out and could not be retracted. Contrary feelings still raced through her, and she was shocked and drained, but even so she stretched a hand to him.

'Henry?' She stretched out a hand, hardly knowing why.

He turned, and she saw his raw distress. 'Jesu, lady, what do you want of me? If I have done so much, why make love to me as you just have? *Why?*'

'I do not know,' she said in a small voice, her hand falling back as he ignored it. She was hollow, and did not understand herself any more than he did. But then insight dazzled her. She wanted him to prove her wrong, to prove that he had *not* done these things. She wanted him to be as he had been on those occasions when her intense feelings for him had slipped over into love. Those times had never lasted, for he had always let her down again, but right now she wanted one of those moments to rescue her. And him.

'I cannot return Richard to you, nor would I if I could. He blights my life, and I will never be free of him.' He watched her. 'Why are you suddenly so *sure* I tortured your blockhead of a cousin, mm?' A savage rancour wove through the words.

Her wits began to creep back. 'Because I saw you pull Annie to the floor by her hair, and *know* you did the same to Jack.' Oh, how weak and unconvincing. 'Henry, I do not *want* you to be guilty, can you not see that? I need reassurance,' she whispered, knowing how lame it continued to sound, but right now she *was* lame.

He laughed. 'Reassurance? Of what, pray? You have already decided that I maimed and left Jack de la Pole for dead, and that I set a bawd to fuck your idiot husband until his dried bean of a brain bounced as much as his balls! You overlook my inhuman treatment of John of Gloucester. Oh, and we must *never* forgot that I personally put an end to Richard himself.'

She remained silent, not because of what he said of Jon, but because of the particular phrase he used concerning Jack. Left for dead. How she wished she could read his strange eyes, but they were more hooded and veiled than she had ever seen before. This time she could not reach the man within.

'Let us deal first with the harlot,' he went on. 'You say I am guilty of that, too. Why?'

Should she mention what she overheard in Margaret's Windsor apartment? No, that might be foolish. 'I recognized her. She is your creature, your spy.'

'And how, pray, do you arrive at that conclusion?'

Once again it was safe to explain about encountering Jack—a free man then—at Three Cranes. 'He made enquiries,' she went on, 'and learned that she was in your pay. Now she has entered the queen's household, playing the lady, but she is still only a whore. Was she your whore too, Henry? Did *you* lie with her before you sent her on your low errands?'

'No.' He rubbed his eyebrow slowly.

'You told me, not so very long ago, that you had done something that could no longer be undone, something you did not wish me to ever know. It was that you had employed Alice Penworthy to seduce Jon, was it not?'

He came to a decision. 'Yes, I admit this particular charge, and despise myself for such petty, childish jealousy. When my uncle brought her south again and I saw how deeply in love with her he was, to say nothing of his joy that he was to be a father at last, I knew I had to try to undo it, for the sake of my own conscience—yes, I *do* have one! My uncle was ever a complete and utter prat! He has the woman I want most of all, and yet wishes to toss you aside for a street-walker. But she has gone, thanks to my mother's intervention, so it is entirely up to him whether or not he returns to you. Or tries to. Maybe you have sufficient wit to spurn him this time. And it is as well for Mistress Penworthy that she has gone, because I was about to issue orders for her elimination.' He gave a thin smile. 'It seemed the only certain way of being rid of the problem.'

'If you were so concerned about me, I am surprised you did not resort to her murder earlier in the matter.'

'So am I.' The very ghost of a smile played around his lips.

'Have you *any* notion at all of the desperate hurt Jon will be feeling?'

'Will you take him back?' he asked, ignoring her question.

'I do not know.'

'So, you hesitate. Let him flounder in his own mess, Cicely, because no one *made* him lie with her. He *chose* to do that, and if there is a price to pay for it, he can fucking well pay it. He intended to betray me at Stoke Field.'

'No.' But he was right.

'Liar.'

They gazed at each other, the air crackling between them. Angry words—reproach, hurt, frustration—were suppressed into silence.

'So, you have my admission of guilt regarding your husband. I valued him once, just as I valued Jack de la Pole.'

Complete wisdom still eluded her. 'But you have still lied about Knole,' she said softly.

Time ticked audibly, and his eyes were clear and sharp. 'I am not a fool, *cariad*, nor do I overlook slips of the tongue. My conduct toward Annie has nothing to do with this. So, *how* do you really know that de la Pole had been pulled to the floor by his hair, mm? Who gave you that convincing little titbit? Who, Cicely?' His voice was very soft and fascinating.

A pang of alarm struck through her. She had blurted something in anger. She knew he was wondering if she had the information from Jack himself. Jack, who had been left for dead but most certainly was not, and for whose unavailable body a mastiff had been substituted. 'You think I would tell you? But it was *not* Jon, so do not think it.'

'I know it could not have been Jon, because I was told by my servants, who were with him, that he pursued the second man and did not enter the room where I was attacked and knocked unconscious. Or am I accused of lying about *that* too?'

She drew back. 'No.'

'I must conclude that your informant is the unidentified companion, whose capture Jon Welles managed to botch, as he botches everything.' He paused, waiting for her to blurt about Jack's survival.

'I will not tell you how I know,' she responded, noticing that he had not even considered anyone he had left in the great hall. He did not believe it was Jack's accomplice either, because he had concluded that she knew from Jack himself. He *knew* Jack had not died at Knole!

'So, Lady Welles, you believe it is indisputable that I did those terrible things?'

'I have been told—'

'I do not give a donkey's fart what you have been *told*, madam! *I*—did—not—do—it!' Fury quivered in Henry's voice.

Everything about him in those seconds was a protest, a proclamation of innocence. His very agitation was that of a man wrongly accused. Could he really be such a consummate performer?

But then, abruptly, he became calm. 'He was still alive when I went in there, but died in front of me. At least, so I thought at the time. I had not touched him when I was knocked out, and by the time I regained my wits, the body—no, more likely the living man—had gone. There were two sets of footprints in the snow, so I know de la Pole is still alive. Unless he died subsequently from the knife wound.'

Such an explanation was the last thing she expected, and her shock was genuine, although she had to dissemble. 'You are saying that Jack escaped?'

'Two sets of footprints told me so.' He smiled coldly. 'Oh, to find out what *you* really know,' he murmured. 'I imagine that if de la Pole *is* alive, he remembers nothing. Am I right?'

'Jack is dead,' she said quietly, for his question was another trap.

He paused, gauging her. 'I will tell what is known to me. De la Pole was there—I saw him myself!—but then he disappeared, alive, dead, or close to it. So I took a chance on his death, and buried a mastiff in his place, praying to the Almighty that the deception would not be discovered. If word of anything at Knole got out, I wanted it to be coloured with the story of de la Pole's final extinction. The addition of a willow stave was intended to add weight to the story. I really believed your cousin was dead or close to it.'

She stared at him. He was telling her the truth, and yet not telling it. How could she know where the real facts lay?

He held her gaze. 'Is he dead, Cicely? Or are *you* all deceit now? Did your cousin survive, and have you lain with him since then? Have you come to me tonight, still warm and sated from *his* dick?'

She gazed at him.

'Do you not dare to answer, my lady? Do you fear my dark self?'

'I always fear your dark self, but no, I have never come to you from Jack's bed.' It was true, for she had always been very careful not to do so. She held his eyes. 'If Jack de la Pole is still alive, I have not seen him. I thought he died at Knole, and I believed you buried him there. Jon believes it too. So what you say now—that he may have survived—is completely new to me.' She had a grip of iron upon herself. Not by anything at all did she give herself away. 'Henry, I think Jack *must* be dead, because if there is one thing his living self would do, it would be to get word to me. There has been no word. If a mastiff was buried at Knole, then Jack's true grave exists somewhere else.'

She knew the huge risk she took now, because if Jack had been recognized in the court when Alice Penworthy departed—or at any other time when she, Cicely, was also present—then Henry would *know* Lady Welles and the Earl of Lincoln were still very much acquainted. But she guessed he did not know. Oh, the punishment that awaited if that guess was wrong.

There was a long silence, and then, to her unutterable relief, his eyes changed and he nodded. 'Forgive my doubt, *cariad,* but I have been tormented by the thought of his survival. I know I cannot triumph with you over him. Even less over Richard.'

She did not know how she maintained her calm mien as she lied again. 'I do not deceive you, Henry.'

'My heart's jealousy is relentless. I rule England, Cicely, but you rule me.'

Oh, how easy it would be to go to him now, to slip her arms around his neck and invite his kiss. To brush all this aside, and simply relinquish herself to more of his lovemaking.

Henry read her, and smiled sadly. 'The quandary in your lovely eyes is a sight to see.' He went to look at the lights that shimmered on the Thames. 'Have I lost you, even though I am innocent of Lincoln's torture and death?' he asked quietly.

The influence he exerted over her in those moments was almost insupportable. He was across the room, not even facing her, and yet she could feel his arms around her and his lips upon hers. She could even smell the cloves, taste his mouth and the salt on his skin.

'You have no answer?' he asked, and came slowly back to her, his robe parting to reveal his pale, elegant body. And the royal yard.

He smiled, in the ascendant again. 'You cannot abjure me, can you? Because there will always be too much between us. Even if I had confessed to ejaculating while driving red hot irons into de la Pole's fundament, you would still not find it easy to say the words that will end everything between us.'

'You are an accomplished liar, Henry,' she whispered, as one liar to another.

'Yes, and I would say anything, *anything* to keep you. It just so happens that I have been telling you the truth. Besides, my darling, do not forget that you have told me some veritable fairy tales too.'

He was winding inexorably around her again, the enchanting Harri Tudur, with his irresistible charm and wry humour. From the beginning he had often seemed to confirm every bad thing she expected, but then a glance, a word, a gesture, would force her to view him differently.

'*Cariad*?' He halted by the bed. 'Please, my darling, think whatever you will of me, but do not cast me off. Please.' His voice was loving. 'I will die without you, Cicely, because death will be all I seek if you are gone from me.'

The sweet temptation that was Harri Tudur crept so close she felt its breath on her hair. To be in his arms again now would not only rescue him, but her as well. Dear God, would he have to commit bloody murder in front of her before the scales finally fell from her eyes?

He took her hands to pull her from the bed to her feet, and stretched their arms down so that her body was pressed against his. Then he swayed slowly, gently. Erotically. 'I command that you dance with me at the Hallowe'en disguising.'

She managed to spar a little. 'Like *this*?'

'With a little more decorum, methinks. Suddenly Hallowtide seems far longer than a week away.'

His lips moved against her forehead as she moved with him. Here she was, still in Henry Tudor's fascination; still fearful for those she loved. No one knew what this powerful, unpredictable royal lover might yet do, so she had to stay with him. While he had her in his arms, he could be soothed. So her lunacy of today must never be repeated. Never.

But as he rested his cheek gently against her hair, he was bitter and cold. Not toward her, whom he dreaded to lose, but toward all those who sought to destroy him in her eyes.

Chapter Twenty-Four

CICELY AND MARY were in the parlour at Pasmer's Place, stitching silk and velvet autumn leaves and other decorations to the gown Cicely would wear for the forthcoming Hallowe'en disguising at Windsor. They worked in amiable silence.

Diversion was what Cicely needed after those wildly irrational moments of release with Henry. No, not release, for she was still chained. She was confused and upset, because every time it seemed she had finally seen Henry Tudor for what he really was, he slipped through the net, emerging with such a gloss of innocence that she could almost feel guilty for having doubted him in the first place. And then, when he made love to her, he robbed her of willpower. She loathed herself for wanting him to be innocent. The insight had been shaming; the outcome the same as ever. Invisible shackles still bound her to him, even though she loved Jack de la Pole infinitely more.

Regarding Jack, her fears about the security of Flemyng Court had proved well founded, and it was fortunate he had not stayed there, because while Tal was absent, the house was subject to several unwelcome visits from unknown men, intent upon searching every corner and crevice. Jack was no longer on Elizabeth's barge either, but had taken himself to the Southwark inn that had sheltered him after his escape from Knole. There, he was safe among Yorkist sympathizers.

Since that night in Windsor, Cicely had been to him at the inn, and would go again tonight, with Tom to escort her under cover of darkness. How slowly the intervening hours ticked by. She sometimes felt that time was turning backwards. Sometimes she wished it would.

Jon stayed on at the house he had shared with Alice

Penworthy. He attended to his royal duties and was seen at court in Windsor, but his wife heard nothing from him. Everything was exactly as it had been before, just without his mistress. But at least he had not returned the ring, which was something Cicely had feared he might. She hoped they could at least be reconciled as friends. A vain hope? Well, today, 27 October, was the Feast of Saints Simon and Jude, and St Jude *had* become the patron saint of lost causes. She could not help a wry smile.

Tal was also on her mind. First for not mentioning his wife's presence in London, and now for having apparently returned to Kingston l'Isle in some haste, without a word. According to Jack, there had been unsettling news concerning the forthcoming pagan bonfire. The nature of the news was unknown, but it had upset Tal a great deal. Henry's consent to the departure had been immediately forthcoming when Tal, at his most Christian and Templar, promised to crush the profanity and witchcraft that flourished around Kingston. There was nothing more likely to obtain the prompt consent of a man as superstitious and fearful as Henry.

A letter from Elizabeth had arrived that morning. It did not mention Lady Talbot, but Leo's escapades were recounted in great detail. He seemed in excellent spirits, with an ever-increasing command of language, including some words that were *not* for repeating in polite company! Several of the Kenninghall grooms had been sternly lectured on the matter.

Horses clattered in the yard, and Cicely rose hopefully. Jon? But when she went to the window, she was dismayed and astonished to see Sir John Cheney's black-and-white colours. He dismounted from the enormous horse that a man of his size required, and within seconds Cicely heard his loud voice thundering up through the house. 'I wish to see Lady Welles, and bring me a cup of something strong. Not gnat's pee!'

As charming as ever, she thought, turning to nod at Mary. 'My gown is demure enough, so I will receive Sir John here in the parlour, but I wish you and Tom to be present. Tell Tom.

Be quick. Then conduct Sir John up here.'

'Yes, my lady.'

It was a relief when Tom came to the parlour barely a minute later. She smiled. 'You will not be required to say anything, Tom. Just be here. Discreetly.'

He bowed. 'I can be discreet, my lady.'

'Yes, I know.' She turned as she heard heavy steps on the stairs.

From the moment Cheney entered, his gigantic figure commanded the room. She guessed he had either just come from Henry, or was on his way to him, because every jewel from the Cheney vaults appeared to adorn his great frame, including a golden SS collar of interlinked Tudor roses, enamelled and set with rich pearls. From it hung a pendant of his silver bull's-horns badge. Every finger boasted a costly ring, and he no longer stank of horses and sweat, but of costmary. Of all the herbs and fragrances he might have chosen, it had to be that one!

He observed Tom, standing with due discretion at the far end of the room, and then glanced back as he realized Mary was also intending to stay. 'You have no need for guardians, my lady, for this is merely a social call.'

'I prefer my servants to be present, Sir John. To protect your good name as well as mine.'

Something in his eyes suggested she had no good name left to protect, but he did not put it in words.

'Why do you wish to see me, Sir John?'

'Merely to be civil. Neighbour to neighbour, so to speak.'

'I do not understand.'

'I have acquired the house at the other end of the lane.'

'Indeed?' She did not know what to say. 'I trust Lady Cheney is well, and contented with your new residence? She *is* here in London?'

'She is well, and yes, in London.' He was not interested in

his unloved wife, who was not only older than him, but had been married solely for her fortune. 'Dare I enquire after Lord Welles?'

'You would dare even if I said no, Sir John, and it is hardly becoming of you to make such an enquiry when you know full well the situation of my marriage.'

'Well, I rather thought—'

'Yes?'

'You were at Kingston l'Isle.' His tone was suggestive.

She faced him, her cheeks warming. 'Meaning what?'

'You do not need me to tell you, Lady Welles. You and Sir Humphrey are clearly very close.'

Shocked, Cicely drew herself up in all her Plantagenet pride. 'Do you know to whom you speak in such a flagrantly disrespectful manner, sir? If I should tell the king of your words, you would most certainly feel his wrath.'

He recoiled from the sudden flare of Yorkist fire. 'I crave your pardon, my lady.'

After clearing his throat, he went to help himself to the wine that had been brought, and then seized a handful of the accompanying honey cakes. The wine was Jon's best, but was guzzled without respect or any real appreciation. He smacked his lips. 'We seem to be at odds, my lady, and that is not what I wish. Truly. But there are things I wish to discuss with you that should definitely not be uttered in front of servants. I am sure you understand the need for complete discretion.'

When Cicely did not respond, he became more direct. 'Lady Welles, I wish to speak to you about a very private matter, and so I request, respectfully, that you dismiss your servants. By all means station them outside the door, but *not* within hearing.'

'Do I have your assurance that you will not be guilty of any further jibes about Sir Humphrey? Or about anyone else, come to that? Be warned, if you do not so swear, I will have you thrown out.'

His deep-set eyes had become small and almost porcine. 'Of course, my lady.'

She nodded at Mary and Tom, and they withdrew, but she knew they would come immediately should she call out. She did not know exactly what she expected Cheney to do, just that she disliked him more with each passing minute.

When they were alone, he drew a heavy breath and held up an apologetic hand. 'With your leave, I will speak of Sir Humphrey again. No, not in any way you will find offensive. You see, I knew Lady Talbot when she was in her true mind. I saw how she changed and what she became embroiled in. It was very sad, and I know Sir Humphrey was much affected.'

'Sir John, I really do not wish to discuss Sir Humphrey and his lady with you.'

'No, of course. Then let me come to the point. Lady Talbot *did* steal the chalice and the dagger we spoke of at Kingston l'Isle, as Sir Humphrey knows well.'

'What has this to do with me, Sir John?'

'Both the chalice and the dagger belong to my family.'

She looked at him. 'That was not mentioned at Kingston, and I still fail to see why you have come to me.'

'Because I believe that you *are* well enough acquainted with Sir Humphrey to approach him on my behalf.'

She stiffened. 'I think you should leave.'

He raised both hands. 'Please, Lady Welles, I am *not* suggesting impropriety, merely that you and Sir Humphrey are on good terms. The chalice is safely in Kingston church, but the dagger is in Sir Humphrey's possession.'

'It is hardly *my* place to do anything. If you wish to know about the dagger, I suggest you ask him.'

'He is not in London.'

The room felt cold suddenly, and she noticed that the fire in the hearth, so bright with flames a few minutes earlier, was now dull and smoking. 'We have nothing more to say to each other, sir.' She swept a hand to encompass the door.

'Do you understand the enormous value of the missing dagger? And indeed of the chalice?'

'I am surprised by your interest in such pagan abominations. Unless, of course, you are pagan too.'

Sir John was very still. 'No, lady, I am not, and it ill becomes you to suggest such an unholy thing.'

'On the contrary, Sir John, under the circumstances, I think it is a very reasonable question, especially—as you yourself suggested—the pagan leader might be your twin! The prerogative for asking blunt questions is not yours alone.'

'So it would seem. Well, I repeat, I am *not* pagan, nor have I any connection with their leader, but I *am* jealous of my family wealth. The chalice and dagger are priceless Anglo-Saxon treasures, the richest of gold and enamel, and each with a single large sapphire of superb quality. Such *rare* stones. Would you like *your* coffers to be short of such items?'

'I will not act on your behalf by approaching Sir Humphrey. He said that he did not know the dagger's whereabouts, and I am satisfied that he told the truth.'

'You accuse me of lying?' His tightly controlled fury had been evident all along, but now became almost palpable.

'Yes, I do. You are anathema to me, sir, and I am only sorry you did not break your neck when my uncle unhorsed you at Bosworth. Now, leave!'

To her relief he turned on his heel and went swiftly out, passing Mary and Tom, who waited anxiously. He did not seem to even see them as he went to the stairs and down to the great hall. Moments later he spurred his horse angrily from the yard, followed by the men who had accompanied him.

Cicely watched from the window. 'I hope you eat blue cheese and suffer every torture known to the damned,' she murmured.

That night, Cicely was drowsy and complete as she lay in Jack's arms, watching the sky lighten toward dawn. The autumn wind had died away, and the morning quiet was broken by the sound of seagulls as they flew in from the outer estuary. Then the inn began to stir, and travellers congregated in the yard. The main thoroughfare to Canterbury and Dover commenced in Southwark, and from here it was possible to reach every town, village and hamlet in Kent. But for all the noise and activity beyond the bedchamber, it was calm and so very cosy in the bed with Jack.

He still slept, his breathing gentle and relaxed, and they were both naked. It felt so good to be close to him again like this, to feel his living warmth and his heartbeats. How long might it be before they were able to sleep together again?

She wriggled a little, to lean over and kiss the tangle of dark hairs on his chest. Thyme filled her nostrils, and quickened her pulse. Her eyes closed as she trailed kisses down to his abdomen. 'I love you, Cousin,' she whispered, reaching the forest at his groin. Oh, how subtle and delicious the scent was now. Not just thyme, but him. This was as close to paradise as she could ever be, now that Richard had gone.

But the moment was shattered by the vicious yowling and spitting of fighting cats. It was so loud and furious that it set the inn dogs barking, and frightened a nervous horse. Cicely's eyes flew open again. Was Tybalt out there? Did it mean that Sir John Cheney was close by?

She shook Jack, and he awakened just as more caterwauling broke out. He saw her uneasy face and felt her wariness. 'It cannot be that damned tommer.'

'Dare you be sure? If it *is* Tybalt, it may mean Cheney is here!'

Jack went to the window, his body pale and lean in the grey light. He could see the squabbling cats in the light of a lantern, and smiled. 'Well, my darling, unless the amazing Tybalt can change colour to ginger or tabby, he is *not* outside.'

He held out a hand and she went to him. Together they watched as the cats suddenly dashed away in opposite directions and disappeared. The dogs barked a little more, then fell silent. The horse settled too, and the customary sounds of an inn resumed.

A Franciscan nun—a Minoress—waited among a group of travellers who intended to ride together to Canterbury, and reminded Cicely of the one who had followed Tal, and then escaped Tom in Thames Street. 'Jack, do you remember the nun who eluded Tom?'

'Of course. Why?'

'Because she was a Minoress, like the one down there, and Tal's wife always lodges at the Minoresses without Aldgate. She was in London at that time, and has only just returned to Kenninghall.'

Jack turned her slowly to face him. 'You think it could have been her?'

'Why not? She, of *all* women, would have reason to follow him.' She looked anxiously at him. 'Jack, I am fearful of her, and constantly anxious about Leo.' Then she remembered the tender way Tal had greeted her. 'What if she saw how Tal kissed my hand? It meant nothing more than friendship, but could very easily have been misinterpreted.'

Jack thought back, and nodded. 'Yes, I suppose it could. Well, before he left for Kingston, Tal told me she made an abrupt, unexplained decision to go back to Kenninghall earlier than planned—'

'At least he told you she had been in the capital. He said not a word to me.'

'He avoids mentioning her to you because of Leo. Anyway, the Minoresses did not know why she left so suddenly, just that she became very agitated about something.' Seeing the alarm in Cicely's eyes, he cupped her chin gently. 'Do not leap to conclusions. Tal said it was not long after his one and only meeting with her, concerning a house in Calais. The meeting was confrontational and she became overwrought. When she is in such a state, only the duchess can comfort and soothe her. He felt that was the reason for her flight back to Kenninghall.'

Cicely wanted to be reassured. 'Do *you* think so too?'

'I do not know her any more than you do, sweetheart. I do not recall ever seeing her, let alone meeting her.'

'You do not think it has anything to do with Hallowtide?' She could not fend off thoughts of the bonfire, and the small boy who had been changed and marked for life.

Jack shook his head. 'Cicely, Kenninghall is a long way from Kingston.'

'But not an impossibly long way, and you know it.'

He smiled, and tried to allay her fears with a little teasing. 'Jane Champernowne has merely returned to her home. That is all. Seeing Tal again was too much, which I can understand.' His smile became a grin. 'Now then, when it comes to Hallowtide—at least, when it comes to the *disguising*—you will have the chance to dance with me right under Henry's long nose.'

She was startled. 'What do you mean?'

'That I cannot resist the notion of being there without him realizing it.'

'Please do not! It is far too reckless!' She was both anxious and horrified.

'My mind is made up, and I have even acquired a disguise. We will share a measure with His Majesty looking on.'

If Jack's intention was to banish all thought of Jane Champernowne, he succeeded.

Chapter Twenty-Five

THE EXTRAVAGANT TWO-DAY Hallowtide jousts at Windsor were a sight to be seen. The weather was so unexpectedly balmy that few people were enveloped in warm cloaks, resulting in a feast of colour that was worthy of high summer.

Both river meadows and the upper ward were brilliant. Banners streamed, minstrels played, polished armour shone, hooves thudded, weapons clashed, and the crowds cheered. Heralds announced their lords, blacksmiths' hammers clanged, and trumpets blared. There were few spectacles more popular than this, and it seemed the entire populace of Windsor and surrounding towns and villages had flocked to watch, as had most of the nobility. There was an immense crush on the meadows, and spilling outside the castle walls down into the town.

On the second day, Hallowe'en itself, the excitement and thrill of the occasion intensified, and many onlookers already adopted disguises. Henry presided from a crowded stand in the upper ward, but did not participate. He never indulged in anything that would put his life at risk, and when a young knight was mortally wounded, dampening the proceedings, who was to say Henry's was not by far the wisest point of view? He wore crimson and ermine, with a circlet of rich red-gold, and was every inch regal and imposing.

Bess was beside him, in a glittering silver gown that was as jewelled as the coronet around her head. Among her ladies was Annie, in amethyst velvet.

The tournament was the sole preserve of the lords, clad in their costly armour and riding their richly caparisoned coursers. Each one had been preceded on to the field by his squire, riding the courser and carrying his master's crested helm and lance. Then came the lord himself, on foot, led on a golden chain by a lady on a palfrey. She wore her knight's colours, as did the squire, and the courser was similarly garbed. Behind the lord came his minstrels.

The second day, however, was also for younger knights and novices, including Roland and Thomas. Edmund was obliged to watch from the side of the field, and for him the humiliation was compounded by having to attend Thomas Howard, who made his horse prance, dance and toss its head. It was a trick Edmund himself had perfected, so Howard salt was being rubbed in de la Pole wounds. Edmund's consolation came when Roland, resplendent in red and black, unseated the red-and-white-garbed Thomas, who landed ignominiously on his backside. Edmund's joy was blatant, and he cheered loudly when Roland received a prize from Bess's hands.

Cicely was on the dais, although not among Bess's ladies. Instead she sat with Margaret, worrying about Jack coming to St George's Hall right in front of Henry, and also wondering if Jon would attend, for surely an occasion like this would be perfect for healing some of the wounds in their marriage. But he did not come. She learned later that he was once again attending to his seemingly interminable duties at the Tower. Did he really have so many? Or were some invented to avoid awkwardness in his private life?

The Hallowe'en darkness came soon enough, and with it fears of demons and all manner of evil, unearthly entities. Henry's court thronged St George's Hall for the great disguising, filling it with music and laughter, for were they not safe from the supernatural here within the castle walls?

The hall was a huge chamber, adorned with evergreens and autumn leaves, and lanterns that illuminated demonic faces. A splendid wood-beamed ceiling curved overhead like the hull and skeleton of an upturned ship. On one side hung a series of costly tapestries, all depicting scenes from the Arthurian legends, while opposite was the row of large, arched windows seen from the upper ward. At the far end of the hall was a dais, with a canopy beneath which Henry and Bess sat in purple cloth-of-gold majesty. On the wall behind them was displayed a treasure trove of golden plate, jewelled and embossed with more Arthurian scenes and figures.

A great variety of costumes was in evidence, with many of the men dressed as animals, with horns, antlers, fur and skins. There were ghosts, witches and imagined supernatural beings, but this was Henry's Christian court, not a pagan bonfire at Wayland Smith.

The ladies wore masks, some only covering their eyes, others their entire face, and everyone entered into the spirit of the occasion, which had begun with the royal couple being conducted into the hall by torchbearers and musicians. Then they commenced the proceedings by dancing alone in the centre of the floor. Neither of them wore a disguise.

They trod an elegant measure that offered no threat at all to royal dignity, but although Bess's gracious smile was constant, Henry gave no indication of his feelings. He danced so infrequently that, as always, most eyes were upon him. Then, when they left the floor to be seated in grandeur beneath their canopy, the festivities ensued in earnest, with much dancing, gallivanting and applause as acrobats, tumblers, tightrope walkers, mummers, hobbyhorses and morrismen showed off their skills.

Three pageants on wheels had been hauled in by men dressed as lions, bears, harts, ibexes and domesticated beasts, and accompanied by singing children. Pageants were moveable stages, in this case depicting a castle, a ship and a mountain of love guarded by knights errant wishing to free distressed maidens from the castle. "Battle" had been joined, the knights liberated the weeping maidens, after which everyone danced a morisco, which symbolized the victory of Christianity over the Moors during the Crusades.

A fussy controller had charge of the proceedings, and rapped his staff crossly on the floor if anyone took a false step. He was very strict about announcing new arrivals, and took no nonsense from even the highest magnates. Tonight *he* was the master, and *they* did as they were told!

Henry had certainly opened his purse for Hallowtide. He was ever a contradiction, and would have looked entirely majestic, but for the chattering, excited monkey now permitted to perch on his immaculate shoulder. It was impossible for even Henry to appear serene with Crumplin scrambling from one shoulder to the other.

Annie sat at Bess's knee, in a bright tawny gown that was trimmed with white fur. She had a cat-faced mask with pretty little whiskers, and cat's ears protruded from her hair. A long furry tail was looped over her arm, and she looked quite enchanting. She would, Cicely thought, become the loveliest of Edward IV's daughters. Even Crumplin liked her, clambering down from Henry's shoulder when offered a shelled walnut.

Cicely had made certain not to arrive early, intending to slip in unnoticed, and she lingered discreetly by the doorway, for the time being unobserved by the controller. She wore her autumn-leaves gown, her hair was plaited and looped beneath a little leafy headdress, and her upper face was concealed by a golden mask. Her feelings were mixed about the hours ahead, and she prayed that Jack had serious second thoughts about attending. Fate had spared his life many times, but such charity would surely come to an end. Maybe tonight. She glanced around the ocean of people, wondering if he was here already. Would she even know him? He had refused to tell her about his costume.

She looked around again, recognizing some people in spite of their disguises. Lord Stanley and his brother, Sir William were there, as a monk and a Viking respectively. Whether or not Sir William was a suitable Viking was another matter. His wavering at Bosworth had not smacked of a fierce Norseman, because he had left his intervention until it was almost too late for Henry, who would not forgive or forget.

Sir John Cheney, dressed as a sharp-fanged wolf, towered above others around him. Whatever disguise he wore, his height would always identify him. But his presence caught her interest. Surely if he was the pagan leader, he would already have left for his Berkshire lands?

Her name was announced suddenly, and the giant wolf turned toward her. She felt Cheney's eyes shining behind his mask. Henry reacted as well, leaning back as he watched her. His hand was to his mouth to conceal. . .a smile?

But as Cicely moved into the hall, a slender green-clad figure suddenly appeared before her, bowing low and with great gallantry. She did not for a moment think it was Jack, because the long auburn curls gave Edmund away. He made a very dashing and romantic Robin Hood, with a longbow and quiver of golden arrows over his shoulders and was quite the most beautiful being present, she thought. At least, well, she tried not to recall his ears.

'Cousin,' he murmured, accepting and kissing the hand she extended.

'Cousin.'

'Did you enjoy the tilts?' he asked, not a little dryly.

'Indeed.'

He smiled. 'So did I. Eventually. It was worth waiting to see Howard's arse dumped on the ground.' There was an echo of Jack in his eyes,

'I noticed your mirth,' she replied.

'Cousin Cicely, you and I are not natural enemies, I think. I trust you will honour me with a dance?' He indicated the floor, where sets were beginning to form for a slow, solemn measure.

'I have only just this moment arrived, as you know, and must first make obeisance to their majesties.'

'Ah, yes. Of course. Later it is. I will hold you to that promise.' He smiled, again with that hint of Jack.

It had not been a promise at all, she had actually declined his invitation, but somehow he had pinned her into a measure with him.

'Cicely?' He became serious suddenly. 'Maybe you will resent what I am about to say, and rightly so, but I *must* ask you – beg you – to please be so kind as to remember me to Annie.' He glanced toward the dais. Annie was watching.

'You imagine she will be interested?'

'She is, as much as I am in her. It is more than interest. It is love.'

'Is it? You, Cousin Edmund, have done more than enough damage already.' Cicely was reproving.

'Not out of ill intent. Please believe me.' He hesitated. 'I was never happier than I was with her, although I did not know until it was too late.'

'I could almost believe you.'

'Then *do* believe me. Please. She commands me, heart, body and soul, as I believe I command her. We are meant to be one, and for her, I would – '

'Yes?'

'Jack is my older brother, and rightful heir to York. I accept this, and – for her – I will no longer set myself against him.'

She was shocked. 'You suggest a dishonourable bargain, sir. My sister in exchange for your loyalty?'

'Dishonour was not intended. There is nothing I want more than to have Annie as my bride, and I know that Henry would never agree. I also accept that I am not going to garner the Yorkist support that would go to Jack, were his survival to become known. My past actions and intentions were regrettable. They shame me. A lot about me is shameful, as you will no doubt quickly agree, and my purpose now is purely selfish. I want, above all else, to marry Annie, and if Jack were king, he might agree to such a union.'

'Such a match would be as dangerous to Jack as to Henry.'

'Richard was loyal to his senior brother. I would be loyal to mine. Look at me, Cicely. I am in earnest.'

She found herself gazing into his eyes, and – unwillingly – believing him.

He smiled, then bowed to withdraw, but paused. 'My lady, now that I know you believe what I say of my love for Annie, I will tell you something. The Penworthy woman is Nicolas Stalyn's half-sister, and therefore another link to the boy in Lisbon. She is from Penzance, Cornwall, and I gather his Stalyn father, a widowed merchant, traded in and out of Penzance. He was in and out of Alice Penworthy's mother as well. Her Cornish cuckold of a husband was a sailor and often away for long periods, which is how the girl Alice could be born and given to Stalyn without Penworthy ever knowing. Stalyn took her to the Low Countries, and she was brought up with her half-brother Nicolas.' Edmund paused and cleared his throat. 'I know all this because Nicolas Stalyn loves me, and would divulge anything for my favours. *Oh, que dis-je?*' He laughed a little, but then became serious again. 'Please tell Jack what I have said, but no one else.'

'Why have you confided in me?' she asked, startled by what she had learned.

'Because you are Annie's sister and were so kind to her when she was in need. For that I will trust and aid you. You may also trust me.'

With another bow, he left her. The eyes of both sexes followed him, and the folly bells were audible around him, but not on him. Never *on* him.

Annie observed him as well, and was not sophisticated enough to hide her feelings. Her expression was soft with longing, and yes, love. In spite of everything, Ann Plantagenet was still as drawn as ever to Edmund de la Pole, as he was to her. It was indeed a powerful attraction. But doomed, surely.

Bemused, Cicely made her way toward the dais, where a small queue had formed to pay full respect to the king and queen. Henry's covert glance encompassed her, and she knew he would ask her about her conversation with Edmund.

When it was her turn, Henry was gracious, but Bess was not. She looked right through her sister. Annie smiled shyly, being careful that Bess would not see.

Cicely took the first opportunity to withdraw from the dais, and as soon as Bess was obliged to give some attention to the next in the queue, Annie slipped away as well, and caught up with Cicely.

'Cissy?'

'Hello again, Annie.' Cicely manoeuvred them both behind a particularly large group of guests, so that Bess would not observe them. 'How are you now, little puss?'

'I am well. Cissy, did Edmund speak of me?'

Cicely's heart sank. Only trouble could ensue from doing anything to help such lovers, but at the same time she was very loath indeed to lie to Annie. 'Yes, he did.'

'Does he still love me?' Oh, how much hope and heartache there was in the question.

'Yes, sweeting, he does.'

Annie's eyes shone and she clasped her hands. 'Please tell him I love him too.'

'I do not need to, for he knows already. Annie, please be careful. You have escaped once, but if you should find yourself in that same scrape again. . .'

'I will not do anything from which I need to escape, truly. I want him so, Cissy. Really want him.'

'Sweeting, you think *I* do not know the strength of physical temptation? I am fearful for you.'

'Oh, I will marry Thomas Howard, as I am supposed to, but I will love Edmund until the day I die. Knowing that he loves me too is all I need.'

From intense yearning to the act of love was a very small step. Who knew that better than Lady Welles?

Annie caught up her skirts, and twirled her cat's tail playfully, suddenly so bright and happy that she would surely dance her way back to the dais. 'I must return to Bess, or she will scold me. Do not forget now. You must tell Edmund I love him.'

Cicely did not answer as the girl disappeared into the gathering, to reappear within moments at Bess's side. Bess did not seem to have noticed she had been absent.

Later, when the revels were at their height, Henry summoned Cicely to the dais. As she approached, he rose and lifted a rather cross Crumplin from his shoulder to place him on Annie's lap, which pleased both monkey *and* girl in equal measure.

He turned to Bess and bestowed a smile upon her, before taking her hand and raising it gallantly to his lips. It was an attentive gesture that gave the impression of all being well in the royal marriage. Which perhaps was true. But when he then extended his hand to Cicely, his queen's face resembled flint. There was interest all around the hall, for the court was always alert to anything that concerned the king and his sister-in-law.

'Lady Welles, how very charming you look tonight.'

'Thank you, Your Majesty.'

'Will you dance with your king? I am of a mind to dance with *both* my sisters-in-law tonight,' he said, glancing at Annie, whose face drained of colour. It was a moment for him to savour, for he liked to do the unexpected.

'The honour will be ours, Your Majesty,' Cicely said quickly, to give Annie time to recover from the clearly appalling thought of dancing with Henry Tudor.

Henry led Cicely out on to the suddenly empty floor. 'There, that will give the little minx something to think about,' he said.

'You are unkind, Henry Tudor.'

'Unkind? No, I am showing her that she is now accepted at court. Royal approval is being bestowed. Besides, Crumplin likes her.'

'And that is reason enough?'

'Animals have no side, Cicely. He looks at her and likes her. I respect his judgement.'

'Perhaps you ought to seek his opinion of many of those who surround you. Empson, Dudley, Morton, the Stanleys, and Sir John Cheney, to begin with.'

He paused. They had reached the centre of the floor, but he made no attempt to indicate he was ready to dance. The minstrels waited, the court waited. 'Why Cheney?'

'Because I do not like him.'

'I see. Cicely—'

'Yes?'

'Is all well between us again? After our last encounter, I cannot be sure.'

'I stayed with you that night, did I not?' Yes, she had, and the pleasure had been as great as it ever had been. She simply could not resist him. The attraction between them was overwhelming, and obscured all else. It was all fire and lust. Nothing more.

'What did Edmund de la Pole have to say to you?' he asked suddenly.

'He greeted me. That is all.'

'A rather long greeting.'

'Indeed.' She met his gaze.

'Well?'

'Well, what, Your Majesty? It was a long greeting. That *is* all. Truly.'

His left eye wandered. 'Do not play with me, Cicely.'

'He spoke to me of someone for whom he nurses a tendresse.' From the corner of her glance she saw Robin Hood, gazing, not at the scene in the centre of the floor, but at the dais, where Annie was still struggling for composure. Cicely continued. 'Edmund spoke to me in the utmost confidence, and I will not break that confidence. Even to you.'

'Even if I am Harri Tudur?'

'Even then.' She smiled, because she knew he accepted her answer. 'Henry, it is but a matter of young love, and certainly does not warrant the attention of the king himself. And no, *my* heart is most certainly *not* involved.'

He smiled too. 'That is me put back in my place?'

'I fear so.'

He held her hand aloft, signalled to the minstrels to play, and as the dance began his thumb caressed her palm. The wraith of Winchester floated in the air while the king and Lady Welles turned and turned again, clasping hands, bending close as if to kiss, and then turning away once more. The music was sweet, and as Henry moved with grace and sensitivity, Cicely knew—even if the rest of the court did not—that he was claiming her. It was not until she saw him glance at a corner of the hall that she realized he was doing it for Jon's benefit.

Undisguised and wearing dove grey with a sapphire-studded collar, her husband leaned back against a wall tapestry, arms folded. Seeing him sparked something within. She did not quite know what. For a split second her eyes met his sharp blue gaze, and she was whisked to those brief moments in the Windsor house, when he had given her the ring and told her to leave. Did he wear it again now? She wanted to know. It was of such consequence to her. But she could not see his left hand, and then the dance took him from her view anyway.

When the measure brought her back again, he had gone.

Chapter Twenty-Six

HENRY HAD OBSERVED Cicely's expression as she watched Jon. 'Do you know your mind yet, *cariad*?'

'No,' she replied honestly.

'He wears the turquoise.'

She hid her gladness about the ring. 'There is no reunion. When the woman had gone, I sent it back to him. It was not given lightly in the beginning.'

'*Diawl*, lady, how capricious you are. You *know* he will see that as an invitation to resume your marriage.'

She smiled. 'Oh, Harri Tudur, who are *you* to complain of caprice in marriage?'

He threw his head back and laughed, which caused a multitude of exchanged glances.

The dance separated them, and when they came together again, he leaned closer. 'I wish you to come to me tonight.'

'To drive the ghosts away?' she asked lightly.

'To drive something, *cariad*,' he responded. 'In as far as it will go, I trust, and I promise to play the very devil with your body.'

'And I with yours.'

He smiled. 'My God, I am glad I wear a kingly robe, otherwise my excitement would be there for the world to see. A veritable iron rod awaits you.'

'Would that I dared to examine it here and now.'

'A very pleasurable thought, but maybe a little too much for our audience.'

'Would you like me to be on my knees before you now, Henry, with that iron rod between my lips?' she enquired.

The dance took them apart again, and when they joined once more, his fingers were tighter around hers. 'I doubt I can survive until later,' he said lightly, but the tautness in his voice told of his struggle with his intense desire.

'You must.' She enclosed his thumb, and moved her fingers to and fro along it.

He grasped her tightly to stop it. 'This is the first time I been ravished while dancing.'

'I would like to do this properly, Henry, right here, in front of them all. I am quite capable, you now.'

He smiled. 'Yes, I rather think you are.' She caught his thumb and manipulated it again, while making sure he saw how her tongue passed seductively over her lips.

'Jesu Christus, *cariad*, any more of this and I will shame myself unspeakably.'

'Admit it, Henry, you are enjoying every moment.'

'Being violated in front of the world?'

She smiled. 'Yes.'

He returned the smile. 'You are right, of course. I must make a point of dancing with you again, Viscountess Welles. For now, though, I must be content with insisting that you come to me tonight.' He stopped dancing to bring her hand to his lips and kiss the palm, while his court watched.

True to his word, he danced next with Annie, who at first moved like a frightened little kitten. But he was kind to her, and quite suddenly, or so it seemed, she relaxed and enjoyed the measure. She was beautiful and very graceful, and kept her eyes lowered demurely. Annie Plantagenet was growing up.

And throughout the dance, Edmund de la Pole's gaze did not move from her.

It was much later, when the celebrations were lively with wine and other beverages, that Jack made his entrance. Cicely was dancing with an elderly Bacchus when another figure of Death came into the hall. Several Deaths were present already, all robed in black that was painted with a white skeleton. They all held scythes, too, but this one had a white vizard resembling a skull over his face as well,

Jack was aware of precisely what she would be wearing, and so claimed her the moment the dance ended. 'Your hour has come, sweet lady, and the hereafter awaits.'

His voice was a little muffled, but she would have known it anywhere. She wanted to say his name out loud, hug and kiss him, but had to be content with a fitting response to his greeting. 'I am sure you are mistaken, Lord Death, for many more years are still allotted to me.'

Jack spoke quietly. 'Sweetheart, Henry watches your every move, so pay attention to me now. I am going to ask you to dance, but I want you to pretend to be feeling the heat a little, and we will stroll toward that corner, where there is a bench and fewer people. Then, do not react in any way to what I say. Your face can be partly seen, mine cannot.'

Something was wrong, she thought, alarmed, but she nodded. Her pulse had begun to race, and her heart pounded. Was it Leo? She felt weak as all manner of dread possibilities flooded through her mind.

He offered his arm as if for the dance, and when they had only gone a few steps, she drew her hand across her forehead. 'I—I feel a little unwell with the heat and would prefer not to dance after all,' she said, knowing that those nearby would hear. Besides, she spoke the truth, she *did* feel unwell now.

'Allow me to attend you.' Jack ushered her toward the bench and addressed a page. 'Some wine for the lady. She is a little indisposed.'

The boy hurried away, and Jack assisted Cicely safely to the bench. She continued to feign the onset of malaise, and accepted the goblet the page brought. Her hands shook and she was frightened of what she was about to hear. 'What is wrong, Jack? Is it Leo?'

He nodded reluctantly. 'Sweetheart, the Duchess of Norfolk has sent an urgent message to Tal, whom she believed to be at Flemyng Court. I happened to be there, briefly. There is no soft way to say this. Tal's wife has abducted your boy.'

Cicely was so numb that the hall and everyone in it might as well have been carved of ice.

'Sip the wine, my love, it will distract you a little.' Jack was aware of Henry summoning a squire who was dressed as a bear, and indicating that enquiries should be made after her. 'Henry is sending a messenger over to us, sweetheart. Just maintain that you are feeling the heat and will soon be well again.'

The bear was Roland. '*Madame*, the king is concerned about you. Do you require the services of his physician?'

She contrived a wan smile. 'It is only a matter of resting a while, *Écuyer* de Vielleville. I have danced a little too much and this lord is kindly attending to me, for which I am very grateful. I am also grateful to His Majesty for his gracious enquiry, and am truly privileged that he should bestow such an honour upon me.'

Roland bowed and returned to the dais, holding on to his bear's head, which was in danger of falling off. Henry listened to what he had to say, and seemed satisfied, for he sat back again and allowed his attention to wander elsewhere in the hall.

Jack immediately spoke to her again. 'Forgive me, my love. I would not have brought such news for all the world. I had to tell you right here in the hall, because removing you on some context would only draw Henry's attention more.'

'Tell me what you know.'

'The duchess believes Jane Champernowne has taken your boy to Kingston l'Isle. Apparently the woman made overt arrangements to go alone to Calais—something to do with the properties she and Tal have there—but it was only to cover what she really intended. She was observed handing a sealed note to a messenger and instructing him to ride to Kingston, but *not* to Tal. The intended recipient is not known. The eavesdropper thought nothing of it and did not report anything until Tal's wife disappeared a few days later, taking Leo with her. She is firmly believed to have gone to Kingston.'

'Where the rites will take place at Wayland Smith at sunset tomorrow.' From ice, Cicely lurched to feeling so hot and sick she almost retched. 'I must go there, Jack. I must rescue Leo!'

'There is no need for you to go anywhere, because I can ride for Kingston directly, with Perry and others. Tal and his men are there as well, do not forget. Unfortunately, he has sent Tom away on some business or other, or so I have learned. But between us we can rescue Leo and put an end to the disgusting things that go on there. And you will not have fallen fatally foul of Henry Tudor.'

She had noticed Tom's absence. Where had he gone for Tal? And why? But for the moment, her thoughts centred on Leo. 'If you do not take me with you, Jack, I will follow anyway. There is no question but that I go to my boy. Richard's boy. Surely you understand?'

He smiled a little wryly. 'Oh, I understand, which is why Perry already waits beyond the castle walls, with horses and some of Tal's men from Flemyng Court. Mary is in attendance too. But remember, it is forty miles as the crow flies, more by road, and must be accomplished in the cold and dark.'

'I would rather risk Henry's wrath than fail my child.' It was no small risk, for she had promised to share Henry's bed tonight! Now she would not only fail to so do, she would also have left Windsor.

Something occurred to Jack, and he glanced around carefully. 'Where is Cheney?'

'He is here somewhere, dressed as a wolf.'

'Well, there is no wolf of his height here now. If Tal's suspicions about him are correct, maybe he is already on his way to the rites. I daresay he *had* to show himself here tonight, for some reason, but has now slipped off.' Hidden by the folds of her gown, he rested his hand briefly over hers. 'Now then, you must make an excuse to Henry for leaving, but reassure him too. We will quit Windsor immediately, and then stop for you to don more suitable clothes, which Mary has waiting. I will stay here for a while, and then slip away to join you.'

She nodded, and summoned a page. 'Please tell His Majesty that I am still a little unwell and will retire to the apartments of his Lady Mother. But assure him that I will keep the arrangements for later.'

The boy bowed low and then hurried away to Henry, who was engaged in conversation with Margaret's husband, Thomas Stanley. Henry leaned back for the page to speak, and then nodded, his glance moving to Cicely, who stood awkwardly, requiring Death's assistance. She inclined her head low toward her royal lover, openly refused Death's clear offer to escort her, and then made her way alone from the hall.

Jack remained where he was, and then selected a young lady dressed as Diana. He flirted with her, danced with her, and then with a more mature lady. Minutes passed, but eventually he decided it would be safe to leave. As he did so, however, he was almost brought down by a particularly agile and adventurous acrobat who misjudged a leap. Jack's vizard was jolted aside, and for a second his face was revealed. He hid it again hastily, and hurried on out. But he had been seen from the dais.

Henry was frozen. He could not move, could not think. His heart thundered within him, and seemed to be all he could hear. Jack de la Pole *was* still alive, and had the temerity to come *here!* What was more, Cicely knew it! She had been with her Yorkist lover in front of the entire court, sitting with him in conversation while the Hallowe'en merriment went on all around. And she had done it after having danced with her gullible fool of a king, to whom she had virtually made carnal love as they danced! She was a whore after all. '*Putain*!' he breathed, almost choking on the word.

Bess was startled. 'Henry?'

He did not respond as he struggled to recover from the emotional snare that had tightened around his throat. Cicely had been laughing at him all along! *Laughing*! Bitterness welled slowly through his consciousness, eating into his flesh. And then a craving for revenge crippled his heart. His mouth was dry and his pulse raced so much that he felt his whole body shaking from it. He rose slowly to his feet, and in a snatch of utter, uncontrollable rage, dashed the unfortunate page aside. The boy rolled like a ball, and then lay there curled up, too wise to attempt to get up. The disguising came to a confused halt, and there was a loud stir of gasps and whispers as everyone stared at the king.

Henry was both stiff and trembling, but at the same time certain that the guilty pair could not know they were discovered. He would see them captured and punished! He beckoned Thomas Stanley, who had drawn away, but now hastened back promptly.

'Your Majesty?'

'That bastard Lincoln is here, in the castle!' Henry's teeth were so clenched he could barely speak.

Stanley's jaw dropped in disbelief. 'But. . .Lincoln is dead!'

His voice was clear enough and the hall fell into absolute silence, including the minstrels, who had played on bravely after the incident with the page.

'He is here, I tell you!' Henry cried, finding his full voice. 'I saw him a moment since. Garbed as Death!' His knuckles were white as he gripped the arm of the throne.

Bess was shocked. Then her shock turned to outrage as she saw by Annie's face that Jack de la Pole's survival was not news to her. More had gone on during Annie's "illness" at Pasmer's Place than had ever been revealed to her eldest sister!

'Find him!' Henry cried. 'This time I will sever his fucking head with my own hands!' He paused, then added with cruel humour. 'And Lady Welles will watch Death's death.'

Stanley moved into action swiftly, summoning guards and others, including his brother William, to apprehend Jack de la Pole. The Stanleys led the search party, but as they ran from the hall, shouting to their supporters to follow, a tall figure in grey velvet strolled across their path, and they all fell like ninepins.

The man in grey got to his feet again, brushing his sleeves a little crossly, and Lord Stanley scrambled up as well. 'Get out of the way, Welles!' he cried.

There was stifled amusement in the hall, and Henry's face might have been a freshly honed axe as Jon stood aside and swept a bow. 'By all means, Lord Derby, but do look where you are going. If you are seeking Death, which I imagine you are, by the speed of his departure, you had best go *that* way.' He pointed.

The Stanleys scowled at him, but then dashed on in the direction he indicated. Their search party streamed after them. Jon advanced toward the dais, still brushing imaginary dust from his sleeve.

'Damn you, Jon Welles!' Henry breathed, his face pale and pinched, his nostrils flaring.

Cicely's image hovered between the two men as Jon bowed low. 'I crave your indulgence, Your Majesty, and vow that my unfortunate presence at that moment was entirely accidental.'

He could not have appeared more innocent had he acquired a halo and white wings, but if Henry thought the collision with the Stanleys was deliberate, he would have been right! Henry had not been the only one to glimpse Jack's face, Jon Welles had too, and had very knowingly aided Cicely's cousin and lover to escape, even to hiding his disguise and supplying his own hooded cloak. But there Lord Welles stood, the very personification of honesty and truth. He was repaying the debt he knew he owed to Cicely.

Henry was suddenly aware of the silence in the hall, and that everyone was watching. He whirled about to order the disguising to be at an end, and then almost screamed a dismissal at the entire gathering.

Virtually incapacitated by his bitter passion, Henry had to

steady himself with a hand on his throne. He was enraged, humiliated, embittered and aroused, all at the same time. It was a fusion of white-hot emotion with which he could barely cope. His dark side was in command now, and if Cicely had been within reach, he would have murdered her with grim satisfaction. But she was not, she was with Jack de la Pole!

Seeing his tumult, Bess became alarmed. She stood to place a gentle hand upon his sleeve. 'I am so sorry, Henry. I had no idea. If I had, I would have told you.'

Her voice, cool and calm, penetrated the red haze that almost blinded him. He looked at her, and hesitated, knowing she would indeed betray her sister for him. His damaged vanity was soothed. Taking a long breath, he closed his eyes for a moment then found a calmer voice. 'I will come to you tonight.'

Her eyes, limpid and welcoming, revealed nothing of the gratifying sense of triumph she felt within. 'I will await you with joy. If you do not know it already, Henry, I love and want you. It is no trick. I have no ulterior motive and bear you no ill will. When you come to me tonight, you will not wish to leave me again.' With that she turned and, followed by her ladies, made her way from the hall to her apartment, to await her lord and king.

The Stanleys' search of the castle came to nothing. No one had seen the figure of Death, let alone Jack de la Pole himself, and there was no sign of anyone answering the Earl of Lincoln's description. Then came a report from the town that an unknown party of riders, including two women, had been witnessed galloping west out of Windsor as if the Wild Hunt itself was in pursuit. All trace of them had been lost in the Hallowe'en night, and no one knew which road they had ultimately taken.

Henry's mind raced. Where might Cicely and Lincoln go that lay to the west? Then he remembered the visit to St Margaret's Well, and his Silver Hound, who had gone home to

Kingston l'Isle so suddenly. Was it possible that Talbot was involved in some way?

Henry whirled about to a waiting esquire. 'Find Sir John Cheney and bring him. Immediately!'

As the esquire ran off, Henry stood with his head bowed, struggling to swallow his fury and pride. He had loved Cicely; now he despised her. And wanted revenge. If she thought he would stay his hand regarding her son, she was wrong! Except— He closed his eyes. She knew the truth about Roland. And now it was an obvious step to guess that Jack de la Pole and other Yorkists knew as well, and were waiting for their perfect moment to destroy the hated Tudor king!

Perspiration stood out on his forehead, and he felt his face draining of colour. Dear God above, what a fool he had been to confide in her. So much for solemn vows, sealed with incomparable lovemaking. Every word she said to him had been false, and every caress had been empty. He would never, *never* surrender his heart again.

A chill calm replaced the hot emotions. He would not be fool enough to wait for the calamity to strike, but would apprehend those she wished to protect. Their lives would dangle upon what her Yorkist friends did. And he, Henry, would commence with the man who was instantly to hand. Her husband.

Turning, Henry beckoned a sergeant-at-arms, who knelt before him. 'Arrest Lord Welles and imprison him at the Tower. You know those I trust to attend to my most private and important commands. The royal apartments are *not* an option. Uncle or not, Lord Welles has failed me. Gravely.'

The man was shaken. 'Yes, Your Majesty.'

'And then send trusted men to Friskney in Lincolnshire. There may be a boy there, two to three years old. His name is supposedly Leo Kymbe. I want him, is that clear? I want *anyone* by the name of Kymbe brought here!' A belated thought struck him suddenly, and his lips parted. Of course! If Talbot was involved, then so might be his sister, the Duchess of Norfolk. Who had been there when Cicely visited Kingston! 'And send a large party to Kenninghall in Norfolk, to look for the same boy. And to apprehend the Duchess of Norfolk. She is to be kept close until further orders.'

'Yes, Your Majesty.'

'Get on with it then!'

The man scrambled up and ran off. Henry closed his eyes again. There was clearly a Talbot link. Woe betide the Marshal of Calais if he was caught up in this. And his damned sister. Well, Cheney had better soon find out!

That night, Bess tried to kiss away her king's agony, but it was still Cicely to whom he really made such passionate, tortured, heartbroken love. Bess writhed beneath him in a welter of exquisite fulfilment. This was what she wanted, what she needed. And for the moment, here in this bed, Henry Tudor was hers.

Chapter Twenty-Seven

THE CLEAR SKY overnight had led to plummeting temperatures, frost and fog, and the tired riders from Windsor huddled in winter cloaks as they rode into the lantern-lit market square at Wantage. It was before cockcrow on the first day of November, and Hallowe'en had given way to All Hallows itself.

The hospitality of the White Hart awaited, and the landlord, Bassington, roused from his bed, immediately recognized Perry and the two women. As he ushered them inside he was shocked to also recognize the Earl of Lincoln. His round face lit up with delight, and he so far forgot himself as to clap Jack on the back. 'My lord, my lord! I am so happy the rumours of your demise were untrue!'

Jack, always amiable, grinned. 'I share your happiness, I assure you. But pray keep your voice down.'

Mary and Perry stayed in the tap room, which was almost empty at this early hour in autumn, but had been crowded on the summer day that Romulus had met his untimely end up on the Downs. The rest of the party was accommodated in a barn, where the hay provided comfort when food and drink was taken to them.

Cicely and Jack were shown into Bassington's private parlour, where they were able to remove their outer clothes and enjoy the warmth of the fire. There, seated together on the settle by the hearth, they relaxed with cups of warm, spiced wine. Jack's arm was around her, and she rested her head against his shoulder.

She was beset by fears for Leo. Where was he? What was happening to him? If she ever laid hands upon Jane Champernowne, blood would surely be shed. And then there was Henry, to whose bed she had not gone as promised. Weighed by so much of great concern, she did not think she would be able to sleep at all, but she was exhausted from the ride and soon drifted off.

Jack had to rescue her cup. He too feared for Leo, but until they reached Kingston there was nothing to be done. Cicely did not yet know of Jon's timely assistance at the disguising, or that Henry was aware of their deception. Jon had managed to warn him as he offered his own all-concealing cloak. Time enough to add to her worries. But what would Henry do? Certainly he would not sit back and play with himself. Would he think of Kingston, though? Jack could only hope not.

The sun was up later when, rested and with fresh horses waiting in the yard, the party prepared to ride the final miles to Kingston l'Isle. A layer of mist still lay over the landscape, so that the sun was little more than a vibrant glow to the east.

Departure was delayed by Bassington seeking a private word with Jack. 'I pray you will forgive this unwarranted boldness on my part, my lord, but will you please convey some information to Sir Humphrey?'

'Of course. What is it?'

'Please tell him that the white stallion has been installed where he wishes, ready for tonight's happenings at the bonfire, and that I have had everything else taken there too. All with the utmost secrecy, and two of my men now keep guard. Only the donkey remains to be brought from Sparsholt.'

'Donkey?' Jack was bemused. 'Why in God's own name does Sir Humphrey require a donkey?'

'Why, for his plan, my lord.'

'He has a stratagem prepared for tonight?'

'Oh, indeed so, my lord, a bold one, and the good folk of Wantage are eager to assist. It will be a fine thing. A very fine thing.' Bassington grinned, and then continued. 'Please tell him that I will come tonight as agreed, with as many men as I can raise. There will be thirty or more. We will arm and clothe ourselves at the hut, and take ourselves to the copse in time for sunset. We will then await him.'

'I will tell him.'

Bassington scraped a very respectful bow, and withdrew.

Jack smiled at Cicely. 'I await this great plan with immense interest.' He brushed his lips to hers, paused, and then kissed her again. This time it was much warmer and more lingering, and for a few wonderful seconds nothing else mattered but their love.

Then they raised their hoods and emerged into the cold, clammy autumn morning, but as Jack passed through the doorway, he ripped his leather glove on a jagged splinter of wood and cursed beneath his breath. He thought no more of it as he lifted Cicely on to her pony.

But the incident greatly alarmed Mary, who rushed to seize his hand. 'Have you drawn blood, my lord? I *must* see!'

Puzzled, he pulled his hand away, but humoured her by removing the glove.

There was a scratch, but no blood.

Mary relaxed. 'All is well, my lord.'

He drew the glove on again. 'What did you fear, Mistress Perrings?'

She blushed. 'Oh, a superstition, my lord. It is said that no man can live whose blood has been let on this day.'

'Indeed?' He smiled, and gave her a chuck under the chin.

'But take care anyway, my lord.'

'Well, I have no time for such witchy things, and *always* endeavour to take care of my handsome hide.'

They left Wantage, and the horses' hooves clattered loudly as they rode west. The mist swirled around them, but was gradually thinning, and there was a luminous glow over the countryside as the sun rose in the east. Red, gold and orange leaves were strewn on the way, and the scent of wood smoke drifted through the haze, but Cicely's thoughts were only for Leo. When he had been rescued, she would definitely send him away with Jack, whom she had yet to tell of her decision. She knew Jack would urge her to go with them, but if she did, it was *certain* that Henry would punish others. Her conscience would not permit that.

Jack looked at her and smiled. 'Deep in thought?'

The time was right. 'When Leo is safe again, I want you to take him to Bruges.'

'And you as well.' It was a statement, not a question.

'No.'

'Cicely—'

'No, Jack. Please do not press me.'

Words fought on his lips, but he held them back, not because he had accepted her answer, unpalatable as it was to him, but because he would take the matter up with her again as soon as an opportunity presented itself. Instead, he told her that Henry had seen him at the disguising and knew she had deceived him.

She did not reply. What was there to say? Jack's escapade in Windsor had led to exposure, just as she feared, but she did not blame him. Jack de la Pole was too precious for her to blame him of anything. She loved him, and accepted his nature in all its facets.

The sun chose that moment to finally burst through in a dazzling orb behind them. It had begun to warm the autumn air by the time they approached the crossroad at Blowing Stone Hill. On the advice of one of Tal's men, they left the road to follow the woodland path about which Cicely was so curious. It was only possible to ride single file down toward the valley where she knew the fish ponds to be, and they had almost reached the southern perimeter of the trees when two horsemen—Tal and Friedrich—rode toward them. Tal was not expecting to see his men from Flemyng Court, but then grinned as Jack and Cicely turned back their hoods.

'Good God! What are you two doing here?' Tal cried, alighting and handing his reins to Friedrich, who was as impressive as ever in his blue-and-yellow striped leather. The Landsknecht knew Cicely, of course, but also knew Jack, under whom he had fought at Stoke Field, and for whom he had a great deal of respect. To him, Jack de la Pole was a fine commander, and a good lord, of whose survival he had learned from Tal. His broad grin and waved greeting was ample evidence of his regard.

Jack alighted as well, and then lifted Cicely down.

Tal came to them, caught her hand and raised it to his lips warmly. 'Welcome, welcome, Cicely. I did not expect you to return to Kingston l'Isle.' But then he saw the anxiety in her eyes. 'What is it, *cariad*?' His glance moved urgently to Jack, who nodded warningly at the rest of the party, waiting nearby. Leo should not be mentioned in their hearing.

Tal turned. 'Dismount and rest your horses. Friedrich is in charge. You are to obey him.' Then he ushered Cicely and Jack from the path and into the trees, where fallen leaves were a cushion underfoot. 'Now then, what is all this about?'

'Have you seen your wife?' Jack asked flatly.

Tal was taken aback. 'No, not since a very brief and rancourous parting in London. Why do you ask?'

Cicely's heart sank. She had fixed all hope on Jane having come here, maybe even that she had fallen into Tal's hands, so that Leo would be safe again. Instead, Tal knew nothing, and the trail led nowhere.

Jack explained the situation, and Tal was shocked. 'My sister is *sure* Jane was coming to Kingston?'

'As sure as she can be.' Jack sought in his purse for the letter that had been delivered to Flemyng Court, and handed it over. 'You are certain she is not here?'

'Be fair, Jack, it is not possible to be certain beyond *all* doubt. We are in the countryside, where there are a thousand

and one places to hide. One thing I *can* say, if Jane realized I was here, she would keep well away from the manor house. It was as much as she could do to be in the room with me when those Calais documents were drawn up and sealed.' Tal read Elizabeth's hastily written words.

Cicely looked at him. 'Do you think she knows Leo was here before?'

He shrugged. 'God knows how Elizabeth explained him away.'

Jack looked at him. 'What was so urgent that you sought Henry's leave to come here?'

'Gwen Woodall sent me word I could not ignore.'

'Go on,' Jack pressed.

Tal was reluctant to answer. He glanced unhappily at Cicely. 'The significance is now only too clear. I am sorry, *cariad,* but Gwen was specific that a boy of royal blood, intended for this year's rites, would soon be here, in this area. I need say no more, I fear.'

Cicely closed her eyes and held her breath, striving to remain calm. Leo was to be involved in tonight's bonfire rites!

Jack pulled her close. 'We will save him, sweetheart. I promise.'

Tal gave a grim little smile. 'I merely told Henry that terrible things were planned at the Smith. His Lady Mother was present, and swore to entreat the aid of no less a being than the Archangel Michael, whose first duty is to fight Satan—and thus Woden too, it seems. So we will have the greatest of God's angels at our side, for not even Michael would *dare* to ignore the King's Lady Mother.'

Jack's arms tightened around Cicely as he replied. 'Tal, can you think of anywhere your wife *might* go?'

'Well, I would have suspected Cheney, but he is in Windsor. I thought maybe he would be here by now, for why else would he have attempted to find out about the dagger from Cicely, if not to use it at the bonfire? Certainly he had no

Christian reason for the way he behaved at Pasmer's Place.' Tal paused. Jack had told him about Cheney's visit to Cicely, and now the evidence seemed to be mounting for a terrible climax at the bonfire.

She closed her eyes, for the bonfire was tonight. *Tonight!*

Tal continued. 'I have had men watching Compton Beauchamp since I returned, and so far only Cheney's usual household and estate workers have been in evidence. If Jane is on his land, it will be some unlikely cottage or other.'

Jack pursed his lips. 'We think Cheney left the disguising before we did, so he might be coming by a different route. Or, unlike us, he knows he has time enough to take it steadily. If he is involved, he will certainly be here before nightfall today.'

'I will be told when he looms on our horizon,' Tal replied.

'Are you *sure* you have the dagger hidden securely enough?' Jack asked.

Tal was a little irritated. 'Yes, Jack, I am. It is in the house, in a place known only to me. Jane is certainly not aware of it. The damned thing was still there this morning.'

Jack remembered Bassington's message, and relayed it. 'What is it all about?' he asked then. 'And why the donkey?'

'Ah. Come with me now and I will show you. I have been preparing carefully for the destruction of Woden, and petrify his followers in the process. Tonight I pray it will all come to fruition. Your participation will be invaluable, Jack.'

He led them further into the trees, and after about fifty yards a clearing opened. There, almost completely hidden by undergrowth, a low, moss-covered hut had been cut into the slope of the land, and outside it waited two men—Bassington's guards, Cicely thought.

Tal ushered Cicely and Jack inside, where the hut proved to be much larger than appeared on the outside. Among many other things, it was cluttered with piles of lanterns, torches, and disguising masks of every animal, devil, witch or monster that could be thought of. There too, blanketed, fed and comfortable, was Bassington's great white horse.

Tal looked around approvingly. 'My old friend has certainly found everything I asked of him.' He indicated the horse. 'And behold, Woden's Sleipnir!'

'I see only four legs,' Jack observed pragmatically.

'How disagreeably logical you can be at times,' Tal replied, pointing to a wall, where hung a strange white leather contraption fashioned into four hollow legs that were attached to it with straps. 'He will have eight when it matters, and will certainly be Sleipnir by the light of a bonfire, torches and lanterns. It is all set, to the last detail.' He smiled at Cicely. 'Courage, *cariad*. Bassington and his friends, with a number of my most trusted men, will wait at a copse of trees on the track to Lambourn, within sight of the Smith. The men are to be the Wild Hunt. Pray forgive my language, but I intend to terrify the very shit out of Cheney and his disgusting acolytes.'

'But it may not be Cheney,' she reminded him.

'Possibly, but I will need a lot of convincing, especially after his unwelcome visit to you. In the meantime, the chalice has disappeared from the church, and the bonfire was built overnight at the Smith. I decided not to do anything about it, because I mean to catch them out and then decimate them once and for all.'

'Can they proceed without the dagger?' Jack asked.

Tal pursed his lips. 'I can only hope they will try. They are certainly not getting their claws on it.' He breathed out slowly. 'I also need to apprehend Jane. She is bound to be there tonight, and so too will—' He broke off, thinking better of saying what was in his mind.

Cicely responded quietly. 'And so too will Leo? Yes. Tal, it must have been her that day by Gough's Alley, and she misinterpreted the way you kissed my hand. Perhaps she believes Leo is our son. It is what Cheney appears to believe, and would surely be cause enough for her to act as she has.'

He nodded regretfully. 'I should not have been quite so

warm, but in truth, I was glad to see you again.'

'So, what is to happen tonight, Tal?' Jack prompted.

'I have to wait until the light is fading, because the terrain up there is exposed. We will strike at the final moment, when the sun touches the horizon and shadows are long. Every undulation will be a pool of darkness. The copse is downhill from the Smith, and will offer secrecy until then. Any pagan lookouts will already have been eliminated and replaced with my men.' Tal paused, smiling. 'And my own Wild Hunt will await my signal. Oh, I intend to produce the loudest, most terrifying and dazzling attack imaginable. Believe me, they will think Woden and his hordes have been summoned.'

He turned to a long cloak hanging on the wall next to Sleipnir's extra legs. 'There you see Woden, and here is his famous hat.' He picked up a wide-brimmed hat, with an attached mask of a grim old one-eyed man, whiskered and bearded. Then he donned it and faced her. 'Will I do?'

She gazed at him, thinking of bonfire light and the multi-legged white horse, and one-eyed Woden in his fluttering cloak. 'Oh, yes. You will do.'

'The men of Wantage will be equipped with all these lanterns and torches, and also drums, rattles, whistles and anything else they can think of, including Irish pipers and drummers who could silence a riot!. Men will bring their dogs and hounds, and the donkey, which I am assured will bray on command. One of the local men has lungs enough for the Blowing Stone, as he proved three years ago at the last bonfire. As for Friedrich—' Then Tal chuckled. '*He* will make a very strange sound from his homeland.'

'Sound?'

'A fast, very loud whooping and warbling racket. It can be almost tuneful, but can also be a cacophony of jarring notes. He tells me it is how goatherds communicate across mountain valleys in the Alps, to the south of his home at Augsburg. He sometimes entertained us at Calais. Berkshire will never have heard the like before.'

Tal became serious. 'I consider myself a good lord, and take full care of my tenants and workers, but I will not suffer ungodliness. My faith demands the eradication of the evil that has come to this part of England. It grieves me that hitherto I have not made a concerted move against them, but this will rectify my failure. Everyone with me tonight will be loyal to God and to me. But I do not intend to let *anyone else* know about all this, do you both understand? You are not to speak of it once you reach the house, because someone there does not keep faith with me.'

'Who?' Jack asked.

'I do not know. Yet. To be truthful, I trust only Friedrich and Gwen in the house. My gut tells me my sister is right about my steward Deakin, although I have never caught him out. One other thing, Cicely. Gregory Melton is sadly changed from the hale young fellow you met in the summer. Now he is thin and haggard, and seems in dread of every shadow. He no longer removes ungodly things from the well, has stopped educating the local boys, and takes no care of the church. He believes he has been overlooked. Bewitched. That the "eye" has been put upon him.' He glanced at Jack. 'I speak of the local priest,' he explained.

Jack was confounded. 'The *eye*? Oh, for Heaven's sake, Tal, surely *you* do not believe in all this?'

'Whether I believe in it or not is irrelevant, because many in these parts *do* believe! You do not appreciate the forces that are at work here, Jack. Believe me, Christianity has a very real, fierce and dangerous foe in this part of Berkshire. Gregory Melton has been cursed, and as a result is petrified for his life. I have tried to reason with him, to offer protection and even to see that he is moved to a parish far from here, but he is oblivious. Whether the Archangel Michael will be fighting with us tonight, I cannot say, but locally, Holy Church's representative will not.'

'Sweet Jesu,' Jack murmured.

Cicely thought of something. 'Tal, where is Tom?"

'Somewhere important, *cariad,* and that is all I intend to say. He will return as soon as possible.'

She had to accept the answer. 'When are we to prepare for tonight?'

'I will set out from the house two hours before sundown. Cicely, I do not want you there.'

Jack gave him a look. 'Save your breath, friend.'

Tal was frustrated. 'Very well, but Cicely, you must give me your word you will not interfere. Everyone has an allotted task to do, and hopefully all possibilities have been taken into account. Get in the way and you may well ruin everything. Leo's rescue could depend upon it, so *please* tell me you understand to the full and will obey.'

'Yes, unless something happens and I know my help will be of benefit.'

Tal sighed. 'There are no conditions, lady. You will do as I say, or be forcibly confined at the house.'

'You would not dare!' She was shocked.

'Test me and you will soon find out,' he retorted. 'I mean it, Cicely. Plantagenet princess or not, I will do whatever I consider to be necessary for the satisfactory completion of tonight's little exercise.'

She treated him to one of her haughtiest glares, but nodded. 'I will do as you say.'

He smiled, and removed all tension by taking her hand and kissing the palm. 'Thank you.'

Jack had been thinking. 'Tal, if Leo *is* there, how do you mean to rescue him?'

'I had already anticipated a boy being there tonight, as happened last time, so I have delegated someone to snatch him away as soon as the distraction of the Wild Hunt commences.'

'*I* will do it,' Jack said quietly. 'No argument, Tal. This is to be *my* task, no one else's. Cicely, I will bring your boy safely to you. Be strong now, sweetheart. We will prevail.' He embraced and kissed her.

Then he looked at Tal again. 'I need to tell you what happened in Windsor. At the Hallowe'en disguising. Henry saw me, I fear, and knew I had been with Cicely right there in front of him. But I cannot think he will make the link to you.'

Tal drew a heavy breath. 'I pray you are right, my friend. In the meantime, I do not intend to identify you to anyone here. Please remember that. I cannot disguise Cicely, because she has been here before, but there is no need to broadcast *your* name. The fewer who know who you are, the better. Friedrich can be trusted to the full, and Perry, but the others in your party will have to be strictly warned. Or they will incur *my* wrath. Not a light threat, eh, Cicely?' He grinned at her.

Chapter Twenty-Eight

SHORTLY AFTERWARD, THEY all rode out of the woods beside the fish ponds. The house was clearly visible atop the opposite slope, with the church behind it. Everything looked so peaceful that it did not seem possible there could be such evil close by. Cicely glanced up at the Downs, from where the distant past was seeping relentlessly into the modern realm of England, and for once she was able to share to the full Henry's fear of the supernatural.

There were men by the ponds, talking in a huddle, but they moved hastily apart on seeing Tal at the head of the riders. One of them sprinted away up toward the house, while his fellows waited politely, removing their bonnets as the horses crossed a sturdy wooden bridge that spanned a narrow neck between two of the ponds.

When the riders reached the courtyard, they found an uneasy atmosphere. As at the ponds, men stood around in whispering groups, together with some women, and they all turned quickly as Tal's party clattered beneath the gatehouse.

Jack felt uncomfortable. What was going on? Only one man continued his work, standing on a stool to fix some wild garlic bulbs, known as ramsons, over a doorway to fend off evil. It was more superstition, of course, but *Christian* superstition this time.

Then Gwen emerged from a doorway to run to Tal. 'Sir Humphrey! Sir Humphrey! I must speak with you!'

He reined in and leaned down to her. She was animated, gesturing toward the house as she spoke, and then indicated a lady's palfrey that was being led toward the stable entrance. It was very richly saddled, and had not been ridden far, for it was not sweating. Its rider must have come alone, for there was no sign of mounts for the ladies who should serve the owner of such a palfrey.

Tal's face had changed, becoming taut with anger. He nodded at Gwen, who ran on toward the porch, where she came face to face with Deakin.

The steward blocked her way for a moment, his manner nothing short of threatening, but then he allowed her to pass, before coming down the steps. After a curious glance at Jack, he bowed low to greet Tal and his companions.

'Sir Humphrey! I thought you would be away for some hours yet.'

Cicely could feel the man's underlying tension. Indeed, she could feel tension and foreboding all around. It was very different indeed from the last time she had been here. Tal's swift return was not at all welcome to some. Had an underhanded plan been foiled? That was how it felt. Friedrich and the men with him were on the side of right, she thought with relief, but it was frightening to realize that even Tal's residence was not as entirely Christian as it should be. Just how many people here were the worshippers of Woden?

'Then you thought wrong,' was Tal's rather terse, dangerously controlled response to Deakin. He dismounted and fixed the steward with a bitterly dark gaze. 'A close word, sir, *if* you please.'

As Jack helped Cicely down from her pony, they both watched Tal upbraid the steward, who could only stand there, head hung. The attitude of the rest of the courtyard indicated aknowledge of the reason for Tal's fury.

Friedrich came to stand next to Cicely and Jack, also observing the scene. His expression was as hooded as Henry's or Margaret's, and Cicely was curious.

'You do not like Master Deakin?'

'Er ist ein Dämon!'

The German word for demon could not be mistaken, and Jack was curious too. 'Why do you say that?'

'My lord, I am Sir Humphrey's *Schutzengel,* his guardian angel. And now I am yours too, and my lady's. An *Engel* is needed ven such as Deakin is near. He is *teuflisch*. Evil.'

Cicely and Jack gained the firm impression that at the very least Friedrich believed Tal's steward was pagan. Maybe even high-ranking among them.

Tal was still incensed as he beckoned the Landsknecht. 'Get your Augsberg hide over here, Friedrich. Take Deakin to his room and stay with him. He is not to be let out of your sight!'

'He vill not move a step, Sir Humphrey,' Friedrich replied with relish, grabbing the steward's shoulder and shoving him toward the house. *'Komm schon, du unheiliger Bastard!'*

Deakin cried out desperately. 'Please, Sir Humphrey! I have done nothing wrong!'

'You disobeyed my strict instruction, and I give no quarter to my enemies.'

The alarmed steward was jostled away, and there was shocked silence from all around the courtyard. Tal's jaw was set as he came over to Cicely and Jack. 'We need to be private inside.' He glanced at Perry. 'You and your wife come too.' Then he preceded them all beneath the porch, where some of the white roses were still in bloom. And where more ramsons had been fixed above the door.

The warm smell of fresh-baked soul cakes filled the screens passage from the direction of the kitchens, and two maids were counting the candles that would be placed in every window as darkness approached.

Once divested of their travelling clothes, Jack and Cicely joined Tal in the firelit parlour, while Mary and Perry remained in the solar, to be sure no one could come in and eavesdrop. Mary had brought her casket, having tied it to her saddle, and now she placed it carefully on a table. Like Mistress Kymbe, she possessed the sight, but although she knew the casket and her skills would soon be needed, the recipient was as yet without a name.

In the parlour, servants hastened to set out warm spiced wine, soul cakes and fresh-picked apples, and then left. A new log crackled on the fire, and smoke wound up the chimney to the perfect autumn day outside. Tal closed the door and ushered Cicely and Jack to the window.

'I am so sorry, Cicely. Jane has just arrived here, but completely alone, without Leo.'

Cicely was stricken. Without Leo? Where was he?

'She must have been waiting for me to leave this morning, because she arrived the very moment Friedrich and I disappeared down toward the ponds. Deakin has always known that she is to be refused entry here. My instructions in that respect were issued long before all this. He chose to not only disobey me, but went so far as to *invite* her in. She came straight here to the private apartments, and then the shout went up that I was returning with others, one of whom was you, Cicely. A maid saw Jane hurry up to her former accommodation on the next floor the moment she heard your name. The rooms are now generally Elizabeth's. She has bolted herself in and a manservant heard furniture being dragged against the door. She does not respond to enquiries.'

Cicely's stomach churned. 'Is it known what she wants?'

'Deakin may know, in which case he will soon be "persuaded" to divulge. But my wife seldom has a logical reason for anything,' Tal replied.

'How does Deakin explain himself?' Jack enquired.

'He claims to have been afraid not to let her in because she is still Lady Talbot. And this in spite of my strict instructions! Well, he will be dealt with, you may be sure of that.'

Jack knew Cicely was thinking of her son. 'Sweetheart, I think we can at least be sure that for the moment Leo is safe and well.'

'How can we be sure?' she demanded.

'Because he will not be harmed. They need him tonight, if indeed that is why he was taken from Kenninghall.'

Tal nodded. 'By midnight tonight you will have your boy back, *cariad,* I swear it. Do not forget either that Gwen's grandson was returned safely a day or two later.'

'Yes, marked indelibly with an image of the White Horse, and his character apparently changed forever!' Cicely's voice was level, but really she wanted to scream with frustration, dread and anger.

Tal left the window to lean his hands on the back of a chair. 'Who is to say Luke Woodall would not have been a difficult brat anyway?'

'You do not believe that,' she said.

He gave her a rueful look, and then turned the conversation. 'Friedrich warned me that Deakin could be one of the pagans, but I did not believe it. Now I know I was wrong. Deakin will have to go, permanently, but first you and I will question him, Jack. Agreed?'

'Agreed.'

Tal drew a heavy breath. 'Why has Jane taken the risk of coming here, alone, when I might, as has happened, return earlier than expected? Now she is trapped. She must know I will not leave that door in place indefinitely.'

Jack was pragmatic. 'The only thing I can think of that might be worth such a risk is the dagger.'

Tal's face changed. He stepped swiftly to the fireplace and used his knife to ease out one of the stones in the surround. Then he felt in the space behind it. Cursing, he shoved the stone back and turned to face them. 'It is not there now, yet it was this morning! I have always been infinitely careful not to be seen when I look, and would have sworn on my family's honour that I alone knew. Jane has to be the thief.'

Jack pursed his lips and nodded. 'Well, I doubt Deakin can be the one, for I am sure he would have purloined it before now. Jane is the obvious suspect. Perhaps she remembered the hiding place from some time ago. It would explain why she came up here to these apartments.'

Tal drew a sad breath, for there had been many good times in his marriage, when he and Jane had been carefree and in love. Now, those times might never have happened. He took the two wedding rings from his purse, where he had kept them since the last bonfire. As he placed them on the table, the others saw that one—his—was clean and shone brightly, but the other was still muddy. He explained why.

Jack felt for him. 'I am so sorry, Tal, truly. The bitter ending of a marriage is enough on its own, and does not need the added pain of evil and idolatry. The strength of your Christian beliefs must make it even worse to endure.'

'I cannot hate her, Jack, because even now, I remember those early days.' Tal breathed out slowly, and drew himself up. 'But that is of no consequence now, for we must be practical. I think we can be certain she has the dagger. We have to get it from her, even if we need to break the door down to get to her. But she is safe where she is for the time being. First I must deal with Deakin. Come with me, Jack.'

Jack nodded and turned to Cicely. 'You stay here with Mary. When Tal and I are satisfied one way or the other about Deakin, we will confront Jane.' He kissed her cheek again, and then he and Tal went through into the solar. There they took Perry, too.

As the sound of the men's footsteps faded down the staircase, Mary came to Cicely. 'As far as Lady Talbot is concerned, everything is your punishment for being, as she believes, Sir Humphrey's lover. We dare not wait until tonight to rescue Master Leo. Sir Humphrey's plan may fail. My lady, do you remember what we did to Judith Talby?'

'Of course.' Together, they had turned Jon's witch mistress's own spell upon her, and thus put an end to her once and for all. 'But we had some of Judith's hair, which gave us power. This time we have nothing.'

'Hair is not the only thing to give power, my lady.' Mary went to the table, where Tal had left the two wedding rings. She selected the one with mud on and held it up. 'Sir

Humphrey said this is her wedding ring, and so is as potent against her as her hair or nail clippings. Hers was the last finger it adorned.'

Mary opened her casket, and began to gather what she needed. It was a strange mixture, dried plants, a black ribbon, and what appeared to be a dried toad cut in half. She wrapped them deftly with the ribbon, muttering strange words as she threaded the ribbon through the ring and tied the whole together. Then she gave it to Cicely. 'Just as before, *you* must do it, because you are Leo's mother. Keep it hidden, but you must be able to produce it quickly.'

'What will happen to her? We cannot *kill* her, especially when we do not know where Leo is!'

'I have used very special herbs in the spell, so that when she sees it burning, she will be unable to withhold the truth. She will tell us what we need to know. Believe me.'

'And if there is no fire this time?'

'I will take a lighted candle, to be certain. You only need to be sure the ring is in a flame, while I say the true words.'

'She may not even open the door.'

'She will. She wishes to confront you, face to face. I will stay out of sight, to act when I know for certain the moment is right.'

Cicely nodded. The maid held a candle to the fire, and then they left through the solar to ascend to the next floor.

Gwen was keeping watch on the door, and remained silent after Mary gave her a meaningful glance. The two wisewomen were in harmony, and the housekeeper seemed to know Mary's intentions without a word being uttered. Gwen wanted revenge for the abduction and harming of her grandson, and would do all she could to help.

She and Mary stayed out of sight as Cicely knocked at the door, concealing the charm in the folds of her gown. 'Lady Talbot?' she enquired.

'Who speaks?' came the muffled response.

'Lady Welles.'

There was a long silence, and for a moment it seemed Jane would not do anything, but then came the sound of furniture being dragged from the door, and the bolt was shot back. Silence returned.

Cicely waited, but the door remained closed. Her hand shook as she opened it herself. The room beyond was shadowy, being on the side of the house away from the sun. There was no fire, but a thick lighted candle stood on a table in the centre of the room. The furnishings were luxurious, as befitted the lady of the house, but the pristine neatness Elizabeth insisted upon was no more. The bedclothes had been hauled away and bundled into a corner, and the pillows were slashed so that feathers were scattered everywhere. Elizabeth's prayer stool had been overturned, and the cross that Cicely knew should have been on the wall, had been removed and placed upside down against the blackened hearth. A great chest was close to the door, and had been used to wedge it.

Cicely was not surprised that Tybalt was seated on the table beside the candle, which had been scratched to grade it in inches. Perhaps indicating hours? A pin had been inserted at a point low down, and would fall when the candle burned down to it. What did it signify? The time until the bonfire? But what caught her attention most of all was the third thing on the table, the jewelled white dagger! There it was, almost as if deliberately displayed to tantalize.

Jane was waiting by a window at the far side of the room, facing the door. And her hands were thrust into the front folds of her habit. Her taut face still bore remnants of the pretty woman Tal had married, but was now hard and bitter, and her large, wide-set brown eyes were bright with fanaticism. She was younger than Tal, although it was hard to tell by how much, and she exuded such an air of loathing and ungodliness that Cicely lingered in the doorway.

The table was halfway between the two women, and Cicely wondered if she could reach it before Jane. But then any thought of snatching the dagger was lost as Jane pre-empted her by approaching the table. The motion revealed her to have an enviable figure for a woman of her age. Halting, she calmly held the palm of her hand just above the candle. It must have been searingly hot, but she did not seem to notice. There was a triumphant smile on her lips.

'So, here you are, Lady Welles, as I knew you would be. Step closer, that I may see you properly.'

Cicely obeyed, for it took her nearer the dagger.

Jane studied her. 'You are a disappointment to me. I have been told of your beauty, yet you are plain.'

'I claim no beauty.'

'Then what does my husband see in you? Oh, I have made you pay for rutting with him, have I not?' Jane's hands tightened into fists.

Cicely answered as levelly as she could. 'Lady Talbot, if you think I am Sir Humphrey's lover, you are wrong. He has no lover.'

'Liar! You have borne him a bastard son!'

'No. I did not even know Sir Humphrey when Leo was born, so it would have been a miracle if he had been the father. Leo's father is dead, and I loved him very much. More than you will ever understand.'

'You would have me believe *that*?'

'Yes, because it is true.'

Something else seemed to occur to Jane. 'But the child *is* yours? Not a foundling, or a changeling?'

Cicely was startled. 'He is most certainly mine!' Her pulse, already fast, now began to race, but she strove not to show it. 'How did you learn that he is my son?'

'A letter the duchess wrote to you. So I went to London and followed my husband. Sure enough, there you were, sharing a fond moment in broad daylight. It was all I needed to know. I returned to Kenninghall and laid my plans for tonight. The boy had already been marked, of course.'

'Marked?' Cicely's hands crept to her throat.

'Noted and singled out to serve Woden.' Jane stepped closer to Tybalt, and stroked his soft black fur. She had only to reach out to the dagger. 'My personal interest in you is simply a satisfactory coincidence. I serve only Woden! The All-Father! The Grim One!' Barely controlled fervour entered her voice.

Cicely edged forward, hoping it would not be noticed. She needed to be as close to the dagger as Jane, preferably even closer.

Jane's eyes flashed and her face became twisted and ugly. 'You foul, adulterous whore! You are a stain upon your House. The White Rose devoured by worms!' she cried, her voice rising so alarmingly that she upset Tybalt.

The tomcat hissed and lashed at her, but his unsheathed claws caught the candle instead. Splashed by molten wax, he yowled and leapt from the table. As he fled, he was in too much pain to care about seeing Mary and Gwen.

Jane struggled to control herself again. 'My revenge is complete, and from now on all that is needed is the royal blood. It will please the Grim One. Our leader has said so.'

'You mean Sir John Cheney has said so,' Cicely replied, watching the other's face closely.

Jane smiled. 'You think to outwit me, my dear? Our leader has no earthly identity. He is just the leader. Woden's lieutenant in this world.'

'Master Deakin has been apprehended.'

Jane's face was impassive.

Cicely persevered. 'You should not have come here today, Lady Talbot, for not only are you trapped in this present fix, but your actions have embroiled the steward as well. Two birds with one stone.'

When there was still no reaction, Cicely tried to call upon all her charm. 'If you return my son to me, I will see that you are taken safely to Kenninghall. To Elizabeth.' The offer was uttered soothingly, as if Norfolk were the only peaceful refuge.

Such wiles were lost upon Jane, who reacted as if prodded with a burning stick. 'You think I care about *Kenninghall?*' she cried. 'My destiny is *here!* With the All-Father, who will soon reign again! Your pathetic God will be crushed and banished, and there will be no more Christianity. Only Great Woden!'

Cicely recoiled, and then threw caution to the winds. 'You can blaspheme with such ease? You, who stand there in the habit of the good Minoresses, can turn your back on the true God and prate to me of a foul and profane deity who offers nothing but pain, hatred and horror?'

With a cry that was half screech, half cackle, Jane snatched the dagger and leapt around the table at Cicely, who tried to move aside but stumbled against a corner of the fallen prayer stool and fell. The charm was jolted from her hand and she did not know where it went.

Jane was upon her like a devil, seeming to have the strength of several men. The fingers of her left hand twisted viciously in the hair at the nape of Cicely's neck, tugging and tearing as her right hand flailed around with the dagger.

Mary and Gwen rushed to help, trying to haul Jane away, but in the confusion, they were knocked aside. In those chaotic seconds, Jane escaped.

Cicely was dazed, but still the first to clamber to her feet to give chase. She hurried down the steep stone stairs, but on reaching the landing below she ran into someone so forcefully that she almost knocked him down the next flight to the ground floor.

The man was Deakin, and of Jane there was no sign at all.

Chapter Twenty-Nine

THE STEWARD REGAINED his balance swiftly, and made much of trying to prevent Cicely from losing hers. He was all kindness and concern, as if nothing whatsoever had happened earlier in the courtyard.

She wrenched free of him. 'Do not touch me!' she cried.

He seemed genuinely surprised and turned to someone behind him.

Then she saw Jack and Tal at the top of the next flight of stairs, and it was clear they were not pursuing the steward, but were *with* him! Bewildered, she scanned their faces.

Jack came quickly to hold her for a moment. 'All is well, sweetheart. We misjudged Deakin.'

Misjudged? Catching the steward's eye, she felt that on the contrary, they had judged him with complete accuracy.

As Jack ushered her to a chair in the solar, her thoughts were muddled. Where was Jane? They *must* have apprehended her on the staircase. How could they *not* have?

Now Mary and Gwen came running, and halted in the doorway in astonishment on seeing the scene in the solar. Mary had retrieved the charm, but held it out of sight swiftly.

Deakin hastened to pour some wine, but Cicely would not take it from him. Jack handed it to her instead. 'All *is* well, truly, sweetheart,' he repeated. 'Why were you rushing down like that? What has happened?'

She stared at him. 'You *know* why!'

'Sweetheart, if I knew why, I would not ask.'

'You did not see her?'

'See who?' His eyes changed. 'Tal's wife?'

'Yes. She escaped and I was chasing her. If you were coming up the staircase, you cannot help but have seen her. Surely you have apprehended her?'

'We have not seen her, sweetheart.' He straightened to look at Tal.

'She had the dagger with her,' Cicely said then, glancing at the steward. Was that a smothered smile?

Jack searched the parlour, which seemed the only other possibility for hiding, but there was no one there. Tal examined the tower door on the landing, but it was still firmly locked, so without further ado he ran down toward the ground floor to raise the alarm.

Crouching by Cicely, Jack took her hand. 'She will be caught, sweeting.'

Her fingers coiled in his. 'Why do you suddenly trust Deakin? Does he know who you are?'

'No to your second question.' He beckoned the steward, who had retreated discreetly. 'Explain yourself to Lady Welles.'

'You have nothing to fear from me, my lady,' Deakin assured her, 'nor should you mistrust me, for I am a good Christian and serve Sir Humphrey faithfully.' He glanced at the windows as Tal's shouts echoed from the courtyard.

'You are a pagan, sir,' Cicely replied coldly. 'I know it, even if you have somehow bewitched Sir Humphrey.'

'Tell her, Deakin,' Jack instructed.

The steward looked awkwardly at Gwen, who was still by the door with Mary.

'Only the truth will do,' Jack prompted.

The steward cleared his throat. 'My lady, I have as much reason as you to despise those who worship Woden, and I also want revenge. You see—' He glanced at Gwen again. 'You see, Luke Woodall is my son.'

Gwen erupted into instant fury. 'No! You lie!'

Deakin was distressed. 'Please, Mistress Woodall, it is the truth. Agnes and I were lovers, but she would not marry me. I offered, God knows I did, but she washed her hands of me. At least, she did until her deathbed, when she told Luke.'

Gwen was distraught. 'You vile abomination!'

'Then tell me, mistress, who *is* Luke's father?' the steward challenged. 'You cannot, because Agnes refused to tell you. But when she told Luke, she proved me to be truthful now. I *swear*, upon all that is holy, that I am his father.'

'Luke has never said a word, nor has he shown any interest in you,' Gwen answered, refusing to believe a word of the steward's testimony.

'I have always met him when he wished it. Secretly, of course.'

'I *will* ask him!' she cried.

Jack looked at her. 'Mistress Goodall, Sir Humphrey and I have already spoken to the boy. He confirms it all. Deakin *is* his father.'

Gwen hid her face in her hands, because of all the men who might have been her grandson's father, Deakin was the one she detested the most.

Mary tried to comfort her, but to no avail.

Deakin was anxious. 'My purpose has always been to destroy the pagans who did such things to my son! Protecting one's child is always uppermost in any parent's mind.'

He looked at Cicely, but she met his gaze coolly. She was not convinced by everything he said. Yes, he was probably Luke's father, but as to the rest—well, as far as she was concerned, he was a repulsive pagan!

Jane was not found. One of Friedrich's men had seen her take a white rose from the main entrance, and then dash for the gatehouse. That was all anyone knew.

Before riding off to search for her with Tal, Friedrich, Perry and half a dozen others, Jack urged Cicely to rest if she could. It was a vain hope, but he felt he had to say it. Deakin was left in charge of the house, as trusted a steward as he had ever been.

But Cicely could not rest. She was agitated and frightened, her neck was sore and her head aching because Jane had tugged her hair so furiously. Fresh air seemed to offer the best cure, so she and Mary went for a walk before the afternoon sun began to lose what warmth it had. As they crossed the courtyard in their hoods and cloaks, the maid told her that she had destroyed the graduated candle that Jane had lit.

'It was a wicked curse, my lady. When the candle burned down and the pin fell, an intended victim would perish. Not Master Leo, for he must live, as Luke Woodall lives.'

Cicely imagined the victim would be herself, or Tal. Or both. After all, they were the two people Jane abhorred the most. But something else was puzzling. 'Mary, how did Lady Talbot manage to avoid the men on the stairs when I was following her? I was not at all far behind, with surely the staircase's spiral all that prevented me from seeing her. Where can she possibly have gone?' She thought for a moment. 'I really wondered about the old tower, but the door *is* locked and by the cobwebs does not seem to have been opened in many a year. Yet she definitely left the stairs at some point. It can only be the tower.'

Mary nodded. 'I also examined the door, my lady, and agree with you. It really could not have been opened, least of all in such a short time. Wherever Lady Talbot went, it was not through that door.'

'Well, no matter what we *think,* there is not another possibility,' Cicely replied. 'I can just *feel* it. Oh, it is an impossible puzzle.' She glanced at the church. 'Come, I must pray for Leo.'

They went around to the porch, which faced onto the road to the village, away from the manor house. The door opened easily, and once inside they gazed around at what was a surprisingly sumptuous country parish church. It was silent and smelled of incense, but there was also a strange air of neglect. Some withered honeysuckle lay on the floor, dropped weeks ago. How long had it been since the church had last been cleaned? Cicely recalled what Tal had said of the sad change in Gregory Melton. What could have happened? The Gregory of before would *never* have allowed this deterioration.

Sunlight shone through small windows in the nave, and slanted in brilliant beams from the arched stained-glass window behind the altar. There was a little vestry, its entrance closed by a rather old, grey velvet curtain. Fine wall paintings were everywhere, depicting Peter, Paul, Herod and Salome, as well as the Baptist's head on a platter. Their style was of the previous century, as were the carved wooden benches. The frontal cloth of the altar was intricately and brightly embroidered, and the display of plate included a cross of great beauty. The chalice, of course, had already been taken away.

Mary waited by the font as Cicely walked slowly down the aisle to the rood screen that guarded the chancel. She intended to kneel at the altar to pray, but as she drew close, she saw something on the floor, half hidden by the frontal cloth. It was not meant to be seen at all, she thought. On retrieval, it proved to be a fresh apple wrapped in a strip of rich woven wool that was identical to one of Leo's tunics.

She raised it for Mary to see, and the maid came running, only just managing to prevent Cicely from untying the cloth. 'No, my lady, do not do anything! I have seen these things before. It is a spell, like the candle, and when burned will give the ill-wisher a great hold over someone. Over Leo, because the cloth is his. Remember what has been said of Luke Woodall? He was one child before the bonfire, but entirely another afterward. He fell into their power, as will Leo unless we interfere.' She eased part of the cloth binding aside. 'There, do you see? The apple has been cut into two halves, and will have been hollowed out. There will be something inside.'

With infinite care, twisting and unlooping very precisely, Mary gradually removed the cloth and placed the apple on the altar, where it promptly fell apart. Its core had been gouged out, and in the resultant hole were numerous little nail clippings.

'Leo's?' Cicely whispered.

'Yes, for they will not belong to any other. Quickly now, as his mother, and therefore stronger than me in this, you must take one of the clippings, any one, and then put it safely in your purse. It must not fall out, or be lost.'

Cicely obeyed without question, and Mary carefully retied the apple, reversing the exact looping and weaving until it was exactly as before, and then replacing it under the frontal cloth. She smiled. 'When the clippings have been in a holy Christian place for a certain time, they take on a great power, in this case it will be for whoever acts for Woden. There will be twenty of them in all, one from each of Leo's fingers, thumbs and toes, and twenty must be there when the charm is burned. If one is removed, the spell is destroyed. You have just broken it, but they will not know unless they count the clippings, which they will not, for they will not even realize the apple has been tampered with. When they use it tonight, which is what I believe, it will fail them.' She replaced the apple where Cicely had found it.

At that moment they heard voices in the porch, a man and woman arguing in low but heated tones. There was barely time to think as Mary caught Cicely's hand and pulled her into the vestry behind the heavy curtain. They peeped out as three people entered the church, a man, a woman and a boy. All were hooded and cloaked, but tossed their hoods back as the door closed. They were Deakin, Jane and Luke Woodall.

Jane was scornful. 'That fool of a priest thought he could resist us!'

'Well, he is spellbound now and cannot do anything,' Deakin replied. 'When our leader uses his powers, he *never* fails!'

Cicely and Mary looked at each other. So the steward *was* a pagan after all. Jack and Tal had been completely gulled.

'I am aware of all the leader can do,' Jane replied coldly.

'And so you are also aware that *I* am his deputy,' the steward answered acidly. He turned to the boy. 'Keep watch, Luke. No one must come in.'

The boy nodded. 'Yes, Father.

'Tonight will be your night too, remember,' Deakin continued. 'You are to assist for the first time, to commence your path to becoming the next leader.' Parental pride shone in the words.

Jane was mocking. 'You surely do not believe the boy really is yours?'

'And what does *that* mean?' Deakin demanded.

'That he is my husband's.'

Deakin guffawed. 'Oh, *please*, lady! If Sir Humphrey Talbot fucked all the women you seem to think, he would be walking bow-legged by now! If he could walk at all.'

'How *dare* you speak to me like that!' she cried.

'I dare because you have been even more unutterably stupid than usual. Right from the beginning, all you had to do was tell me where the dagger was concealed, but no, *you* had to do everything yourself, and thus jeopardize everything. You must have been within a second of being seen on that landing, and could have escaped that way the moment you knew Sir Humphrey was returning unexpectedly. But no, when you learned Lady Welles was with him, you had to engineer a confrontation with her! Now you come *here,* to the church, at the very time they are searching for you! I was supposed to get the apple and give it to Luke, who would then take it to you. That would have been perfectly safe. You, madam, are a threat to us all!'

Jane flushed. 'I escaped, did I not? With the dagger. If I had told you, you would have taken the accolade. I know your stamp, Martin Deakin.'

'You never mention losing the dagger in the first place.'

'My husband *took* it from me!'

'Because you did not have the wit to hide it! I said then that you should be disposed of, and I think it even more now. Having to rely on you for anything makes me very uneasy! And if you imagine the leader is going to praise you, think again, for he is tired of you and your selfish games.'

'I am important to him. And *I* have brought the child.'

Deakin did not trust himself to respond, but strode down the aisle to retrieve the apple. He hardly glanced at it, because his attention was drawn to the shining golden cross. Muttering something, he dashed it over and spat on it before returning to Jane, who held out a large key. 'You had best take this back, for I will not need it again. Where is the boy now? Where did you take him?'

'Never you mind. He is safe and kept quiet with dwale.' Deakin took the key.

Cicely bit her lip, for dwale was a mixture of many poisonous plants with sedative properties. Too much, and a man would die, let alone a small boy.

Jane was thinking the same. 'Is that not a risk?'

'Not when administered by someone who understands it.' Deakin pressed the apple safely into her hand. 'Take care. It must stay as it is, without a single scratch or dent.'

'I know what to do.' She pushed the apple into her purse.

'Who is the man who arrived with Lady Welles?' Deakin asked. 'Have you seen him?'

'No. Why the concern?''

'Sir Humphrey calls him Jack, but has been very careful not to identify him further. He is clearly very highborn, and I have just been told by a fellow on estate business from Compton that he recognized the Earl of Lincoln, the Yorkist nephew who was going to be King Richard's heir. Some called Lincoln the White Rose, but he is supposed to be dead. I believe this informant, who is known to always be reliable.'

Jane smiled coldly. 'I care not a fig about him, because *my* White Rose is the royal whore, so-sweet Viscountess Welles.'

She took the plucked rose from her purse, and ran to place it on the altar. After uttering an evil curse that fed on true holiness, she returned with it.

Deakin awaited her, his fury such that he trembled visibly. 'Damn you, woman, have you no vestige of sense? If the boy is hers, then he, too, is a White Rose! As is Lincoln. How will you select just her? If whatever you have in mind ruins our plans, I will kill you.'

'It will not harm anyone else, for I have her hair.'

Cicely's lips parted. So *that* had been the creature's purpose in their struggle! The significance was not lost upon her. Judith Talby's fate had been brought about by seeing her hair alight.

Jane glanced up at the sunlight penetrating the altar window. 'I must leave. It is no small walk to the Smith.'

'I am not happy about your personal plans, nor will the leader be. It distracts from our main purpose. Give the rose to me, *and* the hair.' Deakin held out his hand authoritatively, and took a step toward her.

'No!' She moved away from him and dug into her purse to pull out the apple, which she held out to one side, as if about to drop it. 'The rose is mine, steward, and I will do with it as I please! Take not one step more, or I will drop this apple. It cannot help but be bruised on these stone flags. And you had best know that I do *not* have the dagger with me now, for I am *not* the fool you choose to think. So laying violent hands upon me will achieve nothing. And if you send that bastard boy after me, I will destroy or throw away all the things that you think to take from me. I wait upon the Grim One, *not* upon arrogant, self-serving men! Not even the leader if he should prove himself to be no better than you.'

A nerve twitched in Deakin's temple, but he stepped back again. 'Very well. Get out now. Then Luke. I will be last.'

Luke opened the door, and after glancing outside beckoned to her. Hood raised, she slipped out. Deakin and the boy waited a while, and then left one after the other.

A minute or more passed before Cicely and Mary emerged. Cicely strove to put Jane's plans for the rose from her mind as they hurried toward the gatehouse, beneath which Deakin was walking, with Tybalt at his heels. Jane and Luke were nowhere to be seen. The sun was a little lower in the clear heavens, but there were still hours of daylight left.

Cicely drew a heavy breath. 'I wish Jack had not been recognized.'

'It cannot be helped, my lady,' Mary replied practically.

Just then came the sound of hooves as Tal's search party returned from the direction of Blowing Stone Hill. The two women saw there were many more riders than before.

Tal's men wore no colours, but the black-and-white of Sir John Cheney was much in evidence. Cheney himself, looking grey nigh to death itself, slumped in his saddle with Friedrich riding double behind him to prevent him from falling.

Cicely and Mary pulled their hoods forward as the riders passed. Jack was nowhere to be seen, for fear of being recognized by Cheney, Cicely guessed, although it was probably pointless, because Deakin would soon see that the odious Sir John was apprised of the Earl of Lincoln's presence.

Perry smiled rather grimly at both women. They all knew that Cheney's presence presented a great complication.

Reaching the porch, Friedrich and one of Cheney's burliest men jumped down to pull the sick man from the saddle. They supported him under each arm, and virtually hauled him up the steps of the porch, just as Deakin emerged as if having been inside all along.

Cheney promptly vomited all over the steward's boots.

Chapter Thirty

CICELY AND MARY would soon learn that while returning to Compton Beauchamp from Windsor, Cheney had been taken unwell suddenly as he reached the Blowing Stone Hill crossroad. It was one of his incapacitating headaches—his migraines—and was so bad that he was forced to dismount. He collapsed at the roadside, retching and holding his head as if it might split. His men had been on the point of sending to Compton for a litter, when Tal's search party had descended the hill.

Kingston was much closer than Compton, and Tal felt constrained to offer its more immediate refuge. So Cheney was lifted back on to his horse and supported by Friedrich's strength for the short ride to the house.

By the porch, Cicely saw Tal lean closer to Friedrich, who nodded and rode off immediately, out beneath the gatehouse and then toward the valley and the lakes.

Cheney was taken to a bedchamber on the second floor. Mary refused to attend him because of his conduct at Pasmer's Place, and also for fear of him realizing who she was. Her presence at Kingston would surely alert him to Cicely being there too. Instead, the maid prepared a highly soporific potion and poured it into a jug of wine that she gave to Gwen, who smiled and nodded, before taking it up to him.

Cheney had been propped carefully on a mound of pillows, a large bowl beside him in readiness. It was needed almost immediately as his stomach began to heave again, and by the sounds in his abdomen, the great evacuation was not over—from both ends of his large anatomy. He did not seem aware of anything around him, even thinking he was still in Windsor. He was sensitive to light, so the shutter was put up at the window. There were flashes and rainbows in his head, he cried, pressing his hands to his temples and groaning in great distress.

Gwen soothed his burning forehead with a wet linen cloth, and then applied rosewater to his nostrils, temples and veins, before binding his head gently with a red cloth. Then she administered the wine and sent for furs and blankets, so that he could be kept as warm as possible. And also to encourage drowsiness and then sleep. The fire was kindled in the hearth, and fed until it roared, so the room soon became almost unbearably hot.

When all had been done, and Cheney at last drifted into sleep, Gwen left two maidservants watching over him, and took the wine jug down to the parlour, where Cicely, Tal and Jack waited in silence. Mead and soul cakes had been served, but were untouched.

'He sleeps,' she said, 'but I do not know how deeply.' She placed the wine prominently on a table. 'He is to have as much of this as is needed to be sure he stays asleep. I do not want those silly maidservants to drink it, so, with your permission, Sir Humphrey, I will leave it here and come back soon to take it up to him again.'

'Again?' Tal frowned. 'You think he feigns it?'

'Maybe, sir. I cannot tell, but he closes his thoughts, even when ill, which makes me suspicious.'

'Very well. Do as you see fit.'

Gwen curtsied and hurried away again.

As silence returned, Cicely at last felt able to relate what she and Mary had witnessed in the church. Not least that Jack had been recognized.

Tal's face changed. 'I will wring Deakin's fucking neck!'

Jack urged caution. 'Give no hint of anything just yet, Tal. It is better that the fellow does not know he has been unveiled after all. And best he thinks I am still unaware of being known.'

'You are right.' Tal held his gaze. 'Cheney may not learn about you. He cannot know yet, because Deakin himself has only just learned.'

Nothing more was said, because Gwen rushed back. 'Sir Humphrey! An urgent message has been brought from Friedrich.'

He beckoned and she whispered to him. His response was irritable. 'Cannot it wait?'

'Friedrich thinks attention is needed now. He believes Mistress Perry's skills are particular in this instance, and he is probably right. She has more knowledge than me.'

'Oh, very well. Is Friedrich attending to a pony for her?'

'Yes, Sir Humphrey. And your horse."

Tal's lips twitched at the foresight. 'Find Mistress Perry.'

As she hurried out again, Tal turned to the others. 'Something has happened, and Mary is needed. I will go there too. We must *all* leave soon anyway, and I will tell Friedrich to bring you when required.'

Alone with Jack, Cicely looked at him. 'Is there something I have not been told?'

'Yes. Cheney was not the only one we happened upon during our search. Earlier we found Gregory Melton hiding in a ditch. He was in a bad way, his wits almost lost, mumbling about pagans and Woden, so Tal had him taken to the hut, to be away from what terrified him so. I imagine he must have worsened.'

He came close enough to embrace her. 'Cheney notwithstanding, everything will go well tonight, we *will* defeat the pagans and Leo will be safe again. Then you and I will sleep together here until dawn, make love and share a thousand kisses. After that, we will take Leo with us to Burgundy, where we will be together as we are meant to be.'

'No, Jack. Do not try to persuade me. You will only take Leo with you. I want to try to allay Henry's suspicions.'

'Please, sweetheart—'

'I cannot. I love you with all my heart, Jack, but my conscience insists that I stay here and face Henry.'

'Now that he knows you were at the disguising with me? That is madness. He will punish you, my darling. We both know his capabilities in that respect, and your womanhood will be no obstacle. He is no Plantagenet, but a new and far lesser breed.'

'I know,' she answered.

'Tal would *never* agree to this, and you know it.'

'You are *not* to tell him, Jack! Or Jon, whom I include in this. Do you hear?'

He was loath. 'Very well, I swear. I will not say anything to anyone, but you are making a mistake, Cicely.'

'I consider myself to have been amply warned and advised,' she replied, linking her arms around his neck.

His lips toyed lovingly with hers, and then dwelt fully upon a tender kiss. 'I love you, Cicely, but God alone knows how difficult a creature you can be. And yes, before you say it, it *is* part of your charm.'

Then they pulled apart sharply on hearing the sound of heavy, stumbling footsteps descending the staircase. Cheney's grunting breaths were unmistakable, and he was almost at the landing! Cicely decided to confront him, but pushed Jack toward the parlour, determined to keep Cheney in ignorance about him if possible.

There was no time to argue, and Jack withdrew just as Cheney's huge figure lurched into the solar. He appeared so feverish and in pain that Cicely found it astonishing he had managed to negotiate the steep stairs.

He paused and frowned, seeming to find it hard to focus on her. 'L-Lady W-Welles?'

She came forward reluctantly. 'You should not have left your bed, Sir John.'

'I m-must sit. If you pl-please?' He stretched out a wavering hand for help.

She almost fell herself as he leaned on her. Edging carefully, she manoeuvred him around the nearest chair and somehow managed to stay on her feet as he almost collapsed into it. He winded himself and struggled to recover, but showed no sign of relinquishing her hand.

She was uneasy about his great size and strength, and the strong possibility that he might be the pagan leader. Everything about him was threatening, and her heart thundered as she tried to wrest her hand free, without success. The thought of Jack being close by was a source of comfort, because she would have no chance at all should Cheney turn upon her.

Suddenly he relaxed his grip and gestured toward the jug of wine. 'A drink, if you please, my lady,' he said.

The words were quite forceful and clear, she thought as she poured the wine gladly. May it send him into oblivion! The sudden clarity of his speech made her share Gwen's doubts. Was he *pretending* to be suffering from a migraine? Had he taken something to induce his symptoms? She managed to glance into the parlour, and saw Jack. He gave an encouraging little smile.

'So, here you are again, Lady Welles. This corner of Berkshire is honoured. Especially at the feast of Hallowtide.' He drank the wine in two gulps, and held the cup out again.

'How remarkable a recovery you have made, sir,' she responded, replenishing his drink. Her conviction had increased that he was not as ill as he had appeared. What could he be up to? Especially *now,* only hours from the Hallowtide bonfire. 'Sir John, is not All Hallows under Woden's rule? Or so his worshippers imagine.'

'Do they? I would not know.' His voice was smooth, and as he placed the cup on the floor beside his chair, she almost expected the flicker of a forked tongue. 'My lady, I was extremely disagreeable and lacking all chivalry when last we spoke, and must belatedly crave your pardon. But I will understand if you do not forgive me at all.'

Forgive him? If she had the white dagger, she would cut his throat!

He continued. 'I have concluded that it is wiser not to be associated with such devilish trinkets. Better to be more concerned about the persistent rumour that I am the pagan leader. So perhaps it is a boon that I have been taken ill here again, because if I am indisposed beneath Sir Humphrey's so-Christian roof, I cannot also be up at the Smith overseeing the obscenities.'

Only then did Cicely remember that this same thing had happened three years ago. Sir John Cheney had been ill here at Kingston at the very time of the bonfire. And who had borne witness for him then? Why, *Deakin!*

Cheney might almost have heard her thoughts. 'Well, everyone here will be able to vouch for my whereabouts. One way or another I will be exonerated from being the leader of these filthy pagans.'

She did not answer, and after a moment he changed the subject. 'Who is the gentleman who accompanied you here, my lady?'

The question caught her off guard, and she could not hide her start. 'Gentleman?'

'Yes. From the description I was given, I could almost imagine it was your cousin Lincoln. But that cannot be so, of course.'

'Clearly it cannot, Sir John, for he is dead.' How could he know anyone else had come here with her? Not from Deakin, who had yet to see him. And how could it be the man who had identified Jack to the steward? Unwanted images began to flood her mind, of Tybalt, the crows, and nameless, invisible beings sent at Woden's behest. No! She would *not* succumb to such primitive alarm! She clenched her fists, digging her nails into her palms to halt the savage charge of superstitious panic.

'But Lincoln *did* come back from the dead, did he not?' Cheney said then.

'Did he? I cannot believe so.' She could feel the intensity of his scrutiny, as if he possessed an abnormal intelligence that could penetrate her resistance. But in the past she had successfully fooled Henry Tudor, who was a far more formidable adversary than this despicable traitor to Richard. She brought the dish of soul cakes and almost pushed it under his nose. 'I must not forget hospitality, Sir John.'

He diverted the subject again. 'I trust Sir Humphrey's baseborn son is well away from here?'

'Why do you say that?'

'Well, I would have thought my reason was obvious, Lady Welles. Tonight there is to be a pagan bonfire, and a boy will be required for the ceremonies.'

'You seem to know a great deal about such things, Sir John.' Was that a yawn he struggled to stifle? She prayed it was a sign that the wine was beginning to work.

'How many bonfires and stolen boys do you think it requires before I become vaguely aware of some details?' he enquired sarcastically.

'And how many wicked chalices and daggers that belong to your family before I wonder about your religious truths?' She was pleased with her response, and gained more confidence from it.

The frozen stare to which he subjected her was intended to intimidate, and only moments before might have succeeded, but she was in command of herself now, and could *feel* Jack's silent support.

'Do not tell me you actually believe in this pagan nonsense, my lady?'

Cicely flushed. 'Is that not why you are here now?'

Time paused, and a shadow of anger passed through his eyes before he smiled blandly. 'Hardly. That implies premeditation, and you may take my word for it that my indisposition is entirely beyond my control. But tell me, why are *you* here again, my lady? I saw you at the Hallowe'en disguising in Windsor only last night, and suddenly you are here.'

'You were also at the disguising, Sir John. And suddenly you are also here.'

'Ah. There you have me.'

His smile was cadaverous, but then, to her immeasurable relief, he yawned. Yes, he was submitting to the drugged wine. Five minutes later she knew it for certain, because his loud, shuddering snores resounded through the chamber.

Jack ushered her out immediately, and then down to the ground floor, where he paused in the screens passage to hold her tightly. 'My admiration for you knows no bounds, sweetheart. You were splendid. And I do not think Cheney knows Henry saw us at Windsor.' He tilted her lips to his.

As they kissed, and Cheney's rattling snores continued unabated on the floor above, she prayed he was right.

Deakin was not alerted that his duplicity had been exposed, and Cicely and Jack did not behave as if they were about to leave for the woods. They finally departed secretly by a postern, outside which Friedrich waited among bushes with horses. The late afternoon was bathed in gold as they rode quickly into the nearest woodland, and then around the head of the valley to avoid crossing the ponds, where vigilant pagan workers might observe and report their activities. Across the wider vale to the north, the first candles had begun to twinkle in windows.

When they reached the hut in the woods, the final group of Bassington's men was just departing for the Smith, with the great white horse, which sported a large blanket to conceal its extra legs.

Other men, from both Wantage and Kingston, led by Perry, had already left in twos and threes, crossing the Icknield Way to use a small path that led up past the agricultural strips on the northern slope of the escarpment.

They would go over the summit and then approach the copse from the south, unobserved by anyone at the Smith.

Cicely and Jack followed Friedrich into the hut, where a shock awaited, because the first person they saw in the gloom was Edmund de la Pole.

Chapter Thirty-One

JACK'S BROTHER WAS bound to a post with his hands behind him. He was blindfolded and, by his taut attitude, more than a little frightened. His clothing was unremarkable brown leather, and his hair was tied back, although still arranged to cover his ears.

Friedrich went to press a knife to the prisoner's throat, and proceeded to make it loud and clear that he would happily nail *der hübsche Junge*, to the post, scion of the royal House of York or not. Edmund would not have appreciated being referred to, rather contemptuously, as "a pretty boy".

Gregory Melton lay on a pallet, well covered with furs, and Mary knelt beside him. He looked dreadful, was feverish and restless, and mumbled the Lord's Prayer. Or parts of it, for he seemed unable to remember it all.

Tal waited nearby, arms folded as he slouched against the wall where his Woden disguise had hung, but all disguises had already been taken up to the copse near the Smith. He straightened with relief as Jack entered with Cicely, and put a warning finger to his lips. Not a word, that finger said.

Then he led them back outside, and whispered what had happened. 'Melton has taken a turn for the worse, which is why I came here with Mary, but I found that Edmund had been apprehended on the road from Wantage. He encountered men in my livery, identified himself and requested to be taken to me. Not knowing him, or whether he was friend or foe, they blindfolded and tied him, then brought him here. He seems to believe you are here. Something to do with witnessing events at the disguising. He only referred to you by your first name, so probably guesses your full identity would not be announced to all and sundry. Anyway, now he is all yours to question.' Tal paused. 'What goes with Cheney and Deakin?'

Jack explained in a few words, and then they went back into the hut. Tal ordered everyone else outside, except Friedrich and Perry. Taking off his gloves, Jack went close to Edmund and put his fingers to the bound man's chin. 'Can thyme tell the time, little brother?' he whispered.

'Jack?' Edmund's head jerked gladly toward the voice. 'Jack? I *knew* you would both be here! Tell them to free me, for I have something vital to tell you!'

'You do not need to be free for that.'

'The king suspects this is where you have come, and has sent Sir John Cheney here to deal with you both, Sir Humphrey included, and to apprehend the boy, Leo.'

The words dropped into a horrified silence.

Jack glanced around at Cicely and Tal. So Cheney *did* know who was here, which cast even more doubt upon his "indisposition". Friedrich was instructed to put his dagger away and untie Edmund's blindfold, but not his hands. When it had been done, Jack addressed his brother again. 'Why should I believe *you,* Edmund? How could you even *know* such a thing?'

'I was present at the Windsor disguising.' Edmund saw Cicely. 'You know that, Cousin.'

She nodded. 'Yes, I know it.'

'Jack, when Henry saw your face, I made it my business to observe everything that happened next.' Edmund described it all. 'He sent someone for Cheney, who had returned to his residence in Windsor town prior to leaving for here anyway.'

'How do you know Cheney has been sent here on such an errand? Henry sending for him is one thing, overhearing every word is quite another.' Jack was suspicious.

Edmund cleared his throat. 'I knew where Cheney lodged, and that I would be able to find out all I needed to know.'

'Go on.'

'Alice Penworthy has not only been gracing Jon Welles' bed, she warms Cheney's as well. The child she carries is his.'

Cicely's lips parted. Alice and *Cheney?*

Edmund continued. 'Cheney is protecting her, *and* her half-brother, Nicolas Stalyn. Of whom you may know?'

'We do,' Jack replied. 'And of his. . .um, regard for you.'

Edmund smiled. 'Indeed. Well, I spoke to him when Cheney had departed in haste, with a party of his men. Stalyn told me everything I wanted to know. His sister, of course, is elated by developments. She has not forgiven Jon Welles for turning from her. Now, not only has he been thrown in the Tower, but Lady Welles is about to be apprehended for treasonous activities.'

Cicely stared at him. 'Jon is in the Tower?'

'Henry does not believe that his interference at Windsor was accidental. Cicely, Henry is vicious about you. And you Jack. I witnessed that moment when he recognized you. I have never seen more hatred, almost madness, on a man's face before.'

Jack caught Cicely's hand and drew her closer. 'We will elude him, sweetheart. Cheney has yet to act, and I imagine he does not intend to until after tonight's activities at the Smith.'

Tal's voice was a growl. 'And by then I will have him in my hands for the pagan bastard he is. Oh, he carried his pretended illness off well, even to throwing up his guts. God alone knows what he imbibed to bring about such symptoms. And all in order to plant himself beneath my roof, just as he did before. He will be able to ape innocence of any connection with Woden worship.'

Mary looked anxiously at Cicely. 'You are sure he is asleep now, my lady? It is not more playacting?'

'He sleeps, I am certain, because he drank a *lot* more of the wine. He had to have been dissembling before. No one could recover as swiftly. One moment his voice was drowsy and slurred, the next it was sharp and clear.'

Tal smiled grimly. 'If he imagines he can simply arrest us and trot us back to Henry, he has another thought coming. Not only am I now aware of his consorting with Alice Penworthy and Nicolas Stalyn, but I already knew something that will stop him in his enormous tracks.'

Jack was intrigued. 'What have you found out?'

'All in good time. We have more immediate things to deal with now.'

Jack turned to Edmund again. 'Do you know more?'

'Stalyn has now learned that the boy in Lisbon is—or is supposed to be—Cicely's younger brother, Richard Plantagenet, Duke of York. Our first cousin, Jack.'

The silence was so complete that when one of the guards outside coughed, Cicely gasped.

'Stalyn is from Tournai,' Edmund continued, 'where the Lisbon boy was living as a native of the town. Therefore the boy *should* have spoken fluent French, which is the language of Tournai, but his French was not perfect, and his accent was English.' He looked at Jack. 'Surely you already know this?'

'I will hear what *you* know,' Jack replied noncommittally.

'His name is supposedly Pierrequin Werbecque, or some such, and he was produced one day by Stalyn's wealthy uncle, who owns a barge fleet on the River Scheldt. The uncle claimed the boy was a bastard son from Bruges, whom he intended to treat as legitimate. Stalyn does not believe it. He is sure the boy is English, and from a very wealthy background, judging by his air and manners. Then, equally as suddenly, this Pierrequin was taken in hand by our aunt the duchess. Stalyn knew nothing more until he was selected to be Pierrequin's companion. Our aunt is financing everything to do with the boy. Both he and Stalyn were given into the care of Sir Edward and Lady Brampton and sent to Lisbon to learn the ways of a foreign court. But if you hope I will produce proof of all this, I cannot. I only have Stalyn's word.'

'But Nicolas loves you, does he not?' Cicely said.

Edmund nodded. 'Indeed he does. He would lie *with* me, but not *to* me.'

Tal drew a long, heavy breath. 'If this boy *is* Richard, Duke of York, and Alice Penworthy knows of it, we can probably take it that Cheney also knows. . .and therefore Henry does as well.'

Edmund spread his hands.

Tal laughed. 'Poor, dear Henry now finds himself burdened with an inconvenient firstborn son *and* a surviving brother-in-law whose blood claim to the throne is far and away superior to his own. Tudor committed bigamy, and in order to do so, he made Edward IV's marriage to Elizabeth Woodville lawful. Henry has only himself to blame. Oh, sweet, sweet justice.'

Cicely looked at them all. 'There will be one certain way to prove if this boy is my brother, and that is the crescent-shaped scar on his elbow, the result of a fall from his horse. Henry will know that, because I am sure Bess will have told him.'

Jack pursed his lips. 'We are not likely to learn. At least, not for a while, anyway.'

Tal smiled. 'Oh, we will, and sooner than you think. I have sent Tom Kymbe to Lisbon to find out. I knew of that scar and realized it would confirm if the boy there was the Duke of York. Its absence will not prove who the boy actually is, of course, just who he is not.'

'One last thing, Jack. Henry ordered that Kenninghall and Friskney are to be searched for Leo. I sent a swift rider to warn the duchess to remove all trace of him. I have also sent a warning to Friskney, with instructions to take Mistress Kymbe to a safe place.'

Mary pressed her hands to her mouth, and Cicely's heart tightened. But, thanks to Edmund, the old lady was secure, and, thanks to Tal, Tom was far away in Lisbon. But Jon was in Henry's clutches.

'Thank you, Edmund,' Cicely said earnestly. 'Mary and I are very grateful.'

'I am sorry about Jon Welles,' he responded.

Jack untied his hands, and then put an arm briefly but warmly around his shoulder. 'Ned de la Pole, you redeem yourself more by the minute. I am glad to be on good terms again, if only so that I can keep an eye on you!'

'And I on you,' was the swift rejoinder as Edmund rubbed his wrists.

'Is this transformation due to Annie? Oh, yes, I know what you told Cicely at the Windsor disguising.'

Edmund nodded. 'We love each other, Jack. I want her so much, but she is destined for that perverted bastard Howard. I may give the deliberate impression of indulgence in vice, but I do not actually *do* anything. It is a façade.'

Jack grinned. 'What a consummate actor you are. And here I am, *convinced* of your debauchery.'

'Thank you, brother. It is good to know you have such faith in me.' But Edmund gave a small smile. 'Tomorrow is Annie's birthday. She will be thirteen. In a year's time she will be old enough to be fully married to him. I cannot bear the thought.' He paused for composure. 'I am your true supporter now, Jack, and if you become the next Yorkist King of England, I will beg for her hand.'

'Oh, Edmund, you were ever a scheming little sod.'

'Maybe, but I would support you now anyway. I am ashamed of my previous conduct, and pray you will find it in your heart to forgive me.'

'After what you have done for me now, you know I will.'

'And while I am here, please make use of me. I gather you have something important afoot. Whatever it is, I will be with you. Allow me a part in it, Jack. Let me prove I am your brother again, not your enemy.'

Jack smiled. 'Of course.'

But as he turned back to Cicely, his hand struck a rusty nail on the post to which Edmund had been tied. It was the same hand as before but, this time, blood *had* been drawn. He glanced down at it, and then at Mary, whose eyes had widened with fresh dismay. Cicely saw too, but no one spoke as he pulled his gloves on.

Tal went to the entrance of the hut. The sun was sinking, and the woodland shadows now touched one another. It was getting colder, and he turned to the others. 'We must get on with it. All this blathering, fascinating as it is, has cost us time.'

Jack's face was grim as he looked at Cicely. 'We do not forget Leo, my love. He will soon be in your arms again, I vow it. And *I* will place him there.'

Melton was now very deeply asleep, so Mary left with them. She saw Jack, caught in an angled shaft of fading sunlight as he gathered the reins of his horse and mounted with grace and ease. How she wanted to plead with him not to go, but the coolness of his eyes told her not to say a word.

As they climbed the escarpment, the cloudless western sky was aflame with shades of crimson and yellow. The blinding orb of the sun descended relentlessly toward the moment of touching the horizon, and in the ensuing hours of darkness, the ancient god would hold sway. No one knew what extra powers Wayland and his followers would gain because of Leo's royal blood, they only knew that it must all be stopped. Forever.

Cicely looked back at the vale. Lanterns had now been placed at crossroads, to guide the souls of the faithful dead to their eternity in Heaven. More and more candles twinkled in homesteads, and curls of smoke rose straight into the stillness of the cold night.

The riders made their way to the summit, and were briefly outlined against the skyline before they crossed the Ridgeway and then negotiated the long, slow southern decline on the far side. They had not seen anyone, nor could they hear anything from the direction of the Smith. It might have been any other autumn night, but what took place in the hours to come could be of vital importance to the realm of King Henry VII. No one involved in Tal's plan cared about Henry himself, but the realm and its people were of infinite importance.

If Tal's careful planning and preparation failed, the dark forces of Woden would receive an ecstatic welcome at the Smith, and be offered a royal boy. If that were to happen, not only might Woden become supreme, but the real Leo might be lost, changed forever from the happy child he was now.

As they eventually reached the copse, there was sudden activity at the Smith, which was just visible up the slope from the perimeter of the trees. Torches were lit, revealing a large gathering of men, women and children, as well as the great bonfire that awaited kindling.

It was silent in the copse, where men, horses, hounds and other animals were concealed among the trees and bushes. A night traveller on the ancient track to Lambourn, which descended from the summit crossroad right past the hidden gathering, would not have known anyone or anything was there. The donkey that would bray on command was silent, head low, resting one hoof as it dozed, unconcerned by the atmosphere of intense anticipation all around.

Bassington's men were also wearing their animal heads and other disguises, or just plain black cloaks and hoods. One dimmed lantern had been placed low in a grassy cranny, ready to light other lanterns and torches for Tal's Wild Hunt.

Mary and Perry—who was now a boar, complete with fearsome tusks—waited together a little apart from everyone. Cicely was at the trees' edge, watching the Smith, and when Jack joined her, he wore black leather and carried a black horse's-head mask under his arm. He put the head down and then pulled her into his arms. 'It will soon be over, sweetheart.'

'Please do not take part tonight, Jack. I trust what Mary says about your blood having been drawn.'

'I am a man full-grown, and will not cry craven because of a damned scratch. No, hear me, Cicely, I will *not* withdraw from this, and I do *not* believe in this particular superstition.' Then he smiled, his eyes alight in the brilliance of the sunset. 'I will survive this, and will bring Leo to you myself. You already have my word.'

Edmund, now wearing splendid antlers and a fully gathered wine-red cloak, came to take Jack to Tal for a last minute talk. Jack donned the horse's head, and turned to her a last time. 'We will carry the night, I vow it.' His voice was muffled. Distant. As if he were far away.

Tal, resplendent in his Woden robes and wide-brimmed hat, but not yet his grim face mask, was waiting with Perry and Friedrich. The latter was now a bull. He was speaking to Tal as the brothers approached. 'Ze lookouts have been attended to, Sir Humphrey. Our men have replaced them all.'

'Excellent. Is everything else under control?'

'Oh, *ja*, nothing is left to chance.

Cicely heard, and closed her eyes. Nothing? What if the *real* Woden were to be raised here tonight? What then? What chance would they have of rescuing Leo if the great pagan god set the true Wild Hunt upon them?

Tal addressed Jack. 'You are still to be responsible for saving Leo. And that is *all*, Jack. There must be no deviation. The moment you hear Friedrich's Bavarian cacophony you are to get to the boy and remove him as quickly as possible. In, out. No hesitation, no change. The boy is all-important. Then get him back here to Cicely. You must not allow yourself to be diverted by *anything*, even if hellish imps materialize and jab at your royal balls with hot, stinking garderobe shovels.'

Jack nodded.

Tal turned to Edmund, who had brought Perry. 'Your task, gentlemen is solely to keep a watch on Lord Lincoln, to shield him, and send word to me of *any* problem. Is that clear too? Once the child is safely with his mother again, you are all free to join battle as you please, but *not* until then.'

Jack rode off first, with Perry close behind him, but Edmund delayed a moment, leaning down from the saddle beside Cicely. 'I will take care of him for you, Cousin.'

'I know you will.'

As they disappeared up the track toward the crossroad, Tal moved closer to her. 'I presume you now trust Edmund de la Pole?'

She was surprised. 'Why, yes. Do you not? Annie makes the difference to him, Tal. They have both changed so much.'

'Let us hope it is for the better.'

'Do – do you think he is false?' He unsettled her.

'No, not really, but a man does not reach my age without becoming a little too jaded to always take things at face value.' He smiled. 'All you have to remember tonight is that Jack is a born survivor. He has defied death twice now, and will survive it again.'

Or will Death prevail if there is a third time? She did not put the fear into words.

'God will be with us, *cariad,*' Tal said, reaching inside his robe to touch his Christian pendants. Then he had gone to join Friedrich, who waited with Sleipnir.

A minute or so later, the sun was so low that it was virtually brushing the horizon. The western sky was like a great furnace, but darkness now pressed toward it from all sides, as if intent upon dousing the glorious display. Mary now stood with Cicely, and they held hands. Neither of them mentioned Jack, but he was in both their minds. Mary was confident Perry would come to no harm, but knew no such certainty for the Earl of Lincoln.

Chapter Thirty-Two

The sun finally alighted upon the land, or so it appeared. Within seconds the bonfire flickered into life, and the sounds of chanting carried to the watchers in the copse. Strange music jarred the night, and figures circled the flames. Most of them wore costumes—antlers, animal heads and beribboned clothes—but some were naked, seeming not to feel the cold. It was a sinful abomination, and very far indeed from the almost elegant proceedings at St George's Hall.

It was impossible to identify anyone. There were children, but not one as young as Leo. Luke Woodall could have been there, though, for there were a number of boys of his size. One person was as yet notably absent. The leader. Or anyone tall enough to be Sir John Cheney.

The sun was sliding beyond the western horizon in an ever-darkening palette of colour. The circling of the bonfire continued, but was louder and more licentious. Fresh wood was tossed on the flames, and a million sparks whirled up toward the heavens, illuminating the Smith still more. It was an unholy scene.

Perry suddenly rode back urgently and sought Tal. 'The leader has arrived, Sir Humphrey, but has not yet appeared to them all. He has a "nun" with him, and a very small boy! I think it is Master Leo, but he is hooded.'

'Do you recognize the leader?' Tal demanded.

'Only that I would hazard him to be Sir John Cheney, but he is covered from head to toe, and wears a great golden goat's-head mask that has curling horns. From where we were, the fellow seems to be waiting for a candle to burn down.'

'How is the boy?'

'Quiet. I do not think he knows what is happening. He is in the care of the nun, who I think must be Lady Talbot. Certainly she is garbed in white.'

'Almost certainly. Thank you for bringing word, now get back to the other two.'

Perry turned his horse, kicked his heels and rode off.

Tal gestured for Friedrich. 'Just one last reminder that you are to pick off the leader the moment you have a clear view. Disable him, do not kill him. I want him alive.'

'My crossbow never fails me, Sir Humphrey.'

Tal nodded. 'It had better not. A flawless aim is what is needed tonight.' He glanced at the western sky. 'Right, I intend to move everyone up to the Ridgeway, to await the signal. But no one is to act until the lantern shows, is that clear? I want every last man and animal on the alert. The moment I ride on to the track, everyone is to follow. But slowly, and above all *quietly*. There is not to be any chance of forewarning our friends at the bonfire.'

Friedrich grinned and nodded toward the scene around the bonfire. 'Vith the noise zey make, you think zey vill hear *anything*, Sir Humphrey? *Einer von Thors Donnerkeil wird erforderlich sein*. Vun of Thor's thunderbolts vill be needed!'

The word was spread, and the Landsknecht collected the lantern from the dip. There were darkened panels all around it, but one was hinged, and when opened would reveal a signal beam that would be clearly visible to those toward whom it was directed. Not to anyone else.

Tal addressed Cicely and Mary one last time. 'Ladies, once we have left, you stay *here*. Jack must be able to find you quickly when he brings Leo. Remember that.'

Then he left, and his Wild Hunt moved slowly and silently out of the copse behind him.

Those at the bonfire sensed nothing as they gave themselves to their wantonness. There was no restraint, and Cicely even saw one couple copulating on the ground. Another man, enveloped in a pale sheet of rough cloth, carried a bull's skull aloft. It had glittering eyes and its jaw snapped with fearsome power as he tormented those leaping and dancing around the bonfire. Their contortions were ever wilder, sometimes turning cartwheels, sometimes heads-over-heels, sometimes merely whirling like flotsam caught in a maelstrom. There was no grace, no self-discipline, just hysteria that would surely lead to a trance. They were drunk, yes, but it was more than drunkenness. Cicely wondered what herbs they might have taken. Did they think they flew on invisible besoms, like witches?

A shallow cauldron had been pushed into the blaze at the foot of the fire, and somehow its contents already bubbled and splashed, spitting with steam. Whatever was in it was ladled out by different people, and flung on to the bonfire as propitiation. It was a thick white liquid that burned with a purple light. The music, if such it could be called, was now dominated by two drummers, who delivered a constant, compelling beat that Cicely was sure was gradually stupefying the senses. Even she could feel its effect.

The light had almost gone, and there was only the thin rim of the sun above the horizon. Then it too slipped from sight, leaving a sky the colour of dried blood, and at last the masked leader appeared atop the Smith, holding the chalice aloft. Everything about him spoke of Sir John Cheney.

There was immediate silence, and everyone around the bonfire fell to their knees, moaning as the leader offered the chalice skyward, before descending to stand in the centre of the gathering. As he placed the chalice on the ground, Jane emerged from the mouth of the Smith in her white habit, cradling Leo in her arms.

The little boy's hood had been turned back, and he did not move at all as he was handed to the leader. His head lolled, and his limbs were loose and relaxed as the leader pulled his tunic up and then swung him high to reveal his back. There, exactly as three years before, was the outline of the White Horse, and it was greeted with cries of joy.

Cicely was so overcome that she had to grip Mary's arm, while not daring to look away from her child, for fear of missing a movement that would reassure her he was still alive.

The maid tried to comfort her. 'Do not fear, my lady, for they need him to live. He has only been given dwale. And remember, their magic cannot work now that we have the nail clipping and the spell-candle has been destroyed.'

Of course! In her anguish and dread, Cicely had forgotten. But did she dare to be sure? She watched as Leo was placed gently on the ground beside the chalice. Jane took off her habit until she was wearing only a thin shift. The heat of the bonfire must have mingled alternately with the chill of the night as she circled once around Leo and the chalice, before commencing a repulsively voluptuous and erotic dance. Cicely was sickened, and could only guess how Tal must feel to see the wife he had once loved sinking to such depravity.

Mary put a hand urgently over hers. 'There is Lord Lincoln, my lady! On top of the Smith, just beyond the light from the bonfire. See?'

Sure enough, Jack was there, a blacker shadow than the night around him, only recognizable by the horse's head he wore. As they watched, he dropped to his belly and squirmed toward the front of the Smith, directly above the entrance. The last sheaf of the harvest was fixed there, to seek Woden's grace for the next year, and it offered some concealment as Jack lay flat to await his moment.

Jane continued her salacious dancing, rubbing her body against some of the naked men and fondling their aroused genitals. Around and around the bonfire she went, until finally coming before the Smith again. There she took the white dagger from among the folds of her discarded habit, and waited as a billy goat was brought forward by the boy Luke, who wore a white robe. Cicely looked away quickly as Jane cut the goat's throat with the dagger.

There were rapturous cries from the onlookers as the blood was collected in a bowl, which was presented to the leader. Jane fell to her knees, arms outstretched to the fire as he dipped his fingers in it, drew a symbol on Luke's forehead and shouted out.

'Behold, the next leader, who will be your lord when I am gone! He will prepare our new king, the boy of royal blood who will reign over England in the name of Woden.' His muffled voice was loud and booming, and could have been Cheney's. And yet, might not.

The words were greeted with wild cheering, and Luke walked slowly around the circle, showing himself to them all. His manner was grand and superior, announcing to all that he was one of Woden's chosen ones.

He had now been fully initiated, Cicely thought, and faced his great future in the Grim One's service. This was what was intended for Leo. Tears wended down her cheeks, while nausea and dread vied within as she watched the leader approach the bonfire with the bowl, which he hurled into the flames. To her amazement, the great fire seemed to recoil and die, leaving only thick smoke rising toward the lurid red sky. There was absolute silence, and a tangible air of expectation.

Crying out a dreadful incantation, the leader produced the apple taken from the church. 'Come, All-Father, accept these boys!'

He tossed the apple into the smoking heart of the fire. The flames immediately leapt high again, but were now ghastly green. There were shrieks and moans from the gathering, until the green suddenly settled back to the customary red and gold. Consternation spread, and the leader's complete immobility revealed him to be as shocked as everyone else. Something vital had failed!

Mary's eyes shone as she nudged Cicely. 'The missing nail clipping has destroyed the spell. Woden will *not* be pleased.'

A terrible sound blared through the night, from the direction of Blowing Stone Hill. The noise reverberated over the countryside, resounding until it seemed to come from all directions at once. For a moment Cicely feared it heralded Woden and the real Wild Hunt, but then remembered what Tal had said about the Blowing Stone.

Jane screamed out at the sound, and scrambled to her feet, still gripping the dagger as she cast around for the source. The leader, as at the previous bonfire, had no doubt and turned toward the hill above Kingston.

Cicely's gaze swung to the crossroad, watching for the blink of the lantern. There it was! Then a proliferation of lights flickered as torches and lanterns were kindled. Friedrich commenced his terrible singing sound. It was louder than seemed possible for a single man to make, and it warbled and soared so effectively that it must surely have hurt the Landsknecht's throat. It vied quite horribly with the Blowing Stone, but then a devastating new commotion erupted over the Downs as Tal's Wild Hunt charged along the Ridgeway toward the Smith.

Those at the bonfire were petrified as the dread horde swept into view. Lanterns bobbed, torches waved, and there were yells and screams, pipes, drums, horns, dogs and hounds giving voice. Friedrich's hellish racket rose above everything, and the Blowing Stone continued its booming. Horses whinnied and the donkey brayed, and at the head of them all was Woden on eight-legged Sleipnir.

Tal's hunt descended upon the Smith, where there was utter havoc among the terrified worshippers, only some of whom put up resistance. Jane was too confused to do anything, but the leader was not taken in by the nature of the hunt. He knew it was human enough, and ran toward Leo. Cicely cried out in dismay as she realized he was going to take her boy.

But Jack jumped down to snatch Leo from the ground before the leader reached him. The black-clad giant was confounded. He and Jack stared at each other behind their masks, before Jack sprinted away into the darkness with Leo in his arms. Perry and Edmund stepped in to confront the leader, brandishing their swords until he backed away. Then they too disappeared after Jack.

The leader knew the night was lost, and shouted to his closest cohorts, before making off in the confusion. Cicely and others present were convinced he was Sir John Cheney, but still there was no true evidence, only his height and voice. And now he had vanished into the night.

Jane was rooted, apparently unable to think clearly. There was a melée all around her, people on foot, men on horseback, animals of all kinds, and she did not know what to do. Then a man garbed as a bear grabbed her arm. At first Cicely thought he was trying to rescue her, but he was only interested in getting the dagger. Jane realized the same and wrenched free, managing to knock his bear mask, revealing Deakin!

The steward abandoned all thought of the dagger to pull his mask back into place and then ran off in the wake of the leader. Within moments Cicely glimpsed horsemen riding off at a gallop from behind a clump of shrubs. Toward Kingston, not Compton Beauchamp, she noted.

There was utter turmoil around the bonfire as the Wild Hunt laid waste to the remaining pagans and the bonfire itself. The attack was ferocious and unforgiving, and could only end in Tal's victory.

Jane still remained, the dagger held among the folds of her shift. Tal directed Sleipnir toward her, but she found the wit to move at the last moment, ready to stab his horse.

Thinking he had not seen the weapon, Cicely could not help screaming a warning at the top of her lungs. 'She has the dagger, Tal!'

Incredible as it seemed, her cry carried above all the noise. It was almost as unearthly a moment as the green flames, and Tal tugged his mount safely aside just beyond his wife's deadly reach. The dagger flashed, but did not find its target.

Cicely closed her eyes with relief, and her attention was then diverted by the thudding hooves that announced Jack's return with Leo. Thus neither she nor Mary saw that Jane had turned toward the warning cry. Tal's murderously disturbed wife grabbed a discarded cloak from the ground nearby, and wrapped it around herself to blend into the shadows of the incline as she began to lope steadily toward the copse, dagger in hand.

Jack reined in and bent down to relinquish Leo to his mother. Then he removed his horse mask and tossed it away. 'As I vowed, sweeting, I have given your boy back into your arms,' he said, smiling.

'Thank you, Jack! Oh, thank you,' she sobbed, dropping kisses all over Leo's little face. The boy remained motionless, but she could feel his warmth. And the beating of his heart.

Jack alighted and put his arms around them both. 'Keep him safe now, sweetheart, and soon we—'

He did not finish, for the words died in his throat and his arms relaxed.

'Jack?' Her heart tightened as she sensed something terrible was happening.

Mary cried out fearfully 'Take care, my lady! *She* is here!'

Jane had seemed to come out of nowhere beside Jack. She was easily within reach of Leo, but as Cicely pulled safely away, the woman knelt to place the white rose on the ground. Cicely did not need to be told the bloom was twined with her hair. Two-handedly, Jane plunged the blood-stained dagger into the rose, before Mary wrenched the weapon away.

Jane spat out her madness and hatred. 'Oh Woden, I have given you the royal blood of the Earl of Lincoln, and now I give you the whore's as well! Praise to the All-Father, the Grim One, the Master of Winter! England is *your* realm again and—!'

She said no more, because Mary hit her hard on the head with a stone and then trampled the rose, scraping it underfoot until it was barely recognizable. She too uttered an incantation, but the words could not be understood by anyone present.

Cicely realized that Jack had not said or done anything.

She turned to him. He was leaning weakly back against his horse, a hand pressed to his left breast. The side where Jane had been. His face was clearly pale and strained in the distant light from the bonfire, and when he took his hand away, it was covered with blood.

'Oh, Jack!' Cicely was stricken.

'I am done for this time, sweetheart,' he breathed. Then his knees sagged and he sank to the ground.

'No!' She gave Leo into Mary's arms before kneeling to hold Jack, but the blood was flowing fast from his left breast. She kissed his hair and whispered his name, embracing him as tightly as she could, as if she could give of her own life.

Mary watched, her own tears hot and bright, for Jack had always meant so much to her, even though he only teased her about it.

More hoofbeats sounded, and Tal arrived with Edmund and Perry. 'Sweet God,' he cried on seeing Jack. 'What happened?' They all three slid down from their horses and discarded their disguises.

Cicely was intent upon Jack. 'Do not leave me, my darling. Please.' Her voice was broken, and her heart was too.

'I love you, Cicely,' he whispered weakly. 'I always have and I always will.'

'Please, Jack, you are strong and will survive.'

'No, sweetheart.'

Edmund flung himself on his knees beside them. 'Jack?' His voice was choked and his eyes shone with tears.

Jack's dimming gaze moved slowly to him. 'Be a worthy head of the House of York, Edmund. Our father offers no leadership, so you must take my place. No matter who may or may not be in Lisbon, King Edward was married to Tal's sister, and so his children by Elizabeth Woodville can *never* be legitimate. Do you understand? Carry the White Rose proudly.' His weak voice rattled ominously, and a trickle of blood appeared from the corner of his mouth.

Cicely could not see for hot tears. Her lips dragged lovingly over his, and her arms could not have been more tender and caring. She could feel him slipping away, and wanted to slip with him.

'I have come for him, my love.'

Richard's voice. She gasped and looked around. He was there, her shining king, uncle and lover, as clear as if he stood in daylight. He had not changed at all. Still the same slender masculine beauty, the long chestnut hair and arresting grey eyes. Still the ultimate master of her heart.

He smiled at her. *'I will take care of him, sweeting. Do not fear for his soul.'*

'Richard?'

Edmund glanced at her and then in the direction she looked, but he saw nothing.

She knew the moment Jack's life finally ebbed away. His eyes were closed and his body was limp, but she felt the end. She had lost another great love. Glancing up again, she saw him standing with Richard. As she watched, they faded until there was only the night.

Chapter Thirty-Three

JACK DE LA POLE'S body was in Cicely's arms, but his soul had gone with Richard. She was dazed with grief. That Jack should have survived so much, only to die at the hand of a madwoman was almost insupportable. She could not accept it! She *would* not! 'Bring him back, Mary! I cannot lose him! Please!'

Tears ran down Mary's face as she held Leo close. 'I cannot, my lady.'

'Yes, you can! Do it!'

'I do not have the power, my lady. Only my aunt can bring the dead back. And then not always.'

'Please!' Cicely implored, her voice a broken whisper. 'Save him, bring him back so that I may care for him.'

Tal, in tears himself, drew her gently to her feet. 'There is nothing to be done *cariad*, he has gone.'

Such was the violence of her emotions that she wanted a death for a death. Jane must die for murdering Jack! She almost hurled herself to reach the dagger that Mary still held, but Edmund helped Tal to restrain her.

Tal took the dagger from Mary, and pushed it safely into his belt, and then embraced Cicely lovingly. His own grief was great. He had lost the man he always regarded as a son. Edmund was no less devastated, having been robbed of the brother with whom he had only just been reconciled. The success of the night's hard-planned venture had been a Pyrrhic victory, triumph destroyed by the murder of Jack de la Pole.

Cicely gazed down at him, still finding it hard to accept that he was not merely sleeping. A strange calm descended over her. 'He must be laid to rest with Richard,' she said quietly. 'Please Tal, Edmund, see that he is taken to the Greyfriars in Leicester, to be with his uncle and king.'

Tal retrieved the cloak he had worn as Woden, and laid it gently over Jack before beckoning to Friedrich and Perry, who waited nearby. They crouched to wrap the dead man carefully, and then lifted him up over his horse. Tal instructed Friedrich to take him to the hut in the woods, and to stay there until he, Tal, could see to a safe, secret removal to Leicester.

The Landsknecht, also distressed, agreed to only part of Tal's instructions. '*Bitte, vergib mir,* Sir Humphrey. Please, I beg you. Not to ze hut, for it is no place for such a man as zis. I vill take him secretly to my lodgings at ze house, and lay him out as should be done. I served under him. He vas young, but a good and great lord.'

'As you think fit, my friend.'

Friedrich was tearfully grateful. '*Danke. Danke sehr.*'

Jane was also to be taken to the hut, until Tal made other arrangements for her. She was bound and gagged, and when she regained consciousness no longer seemed to know anything of her surroundings. Her open eyes were unseeing as she was bundled up on a pony that would be led from the Downs by one of Tal's men-at-arms.

Still holding Leo, Mary went to Tal, and took the charm with the ring from under her cloak. 'You can be rid of your wife forever if you wish, Sir Humphrey. Throw this into the remains of the bonfire when she is looking. She *must* see it being done.'

He stared at her and then at the charm. For a moment it seemed he would accept it, but then his Christian scruples gained the upper hand, and he shook his head. 'No, I cannot do such a thing. She is still my wife, and that does not change because her mind has gone. Besides, her eyes are open but she does not see. Such an act would meaning nothing to her. It is my Christian duty to do right by her, and so she must go back to Kenninghall. My sister will be instructed to guard her much more vigilantly from now on.'

Mary still extended the charm. 'Please reconsider, Sir Humphrey. This woman worships the Grim One, and is responsible for killing Lord Lincoln *and* for abducting and marking Master Leo. I believe I have destroyed her curse with the white rose, but must still take many steps to be sure of it. The one way to be truly certain is to bring about her death.'

He was adamant. 'I cannot. I made vows to her.'

Mary could barely hide her anger and frustration. To her, Jane Champernowne's demise at the hands of her husband was an obvious course. But the maid decided that there was still Cicely, whose desire for revenge had to be strongest of all.

It was some time before everything was gathered together and Bassington and his men were able to leave for Wantage with their animals and weapons. There was no sense of victory or joy. Jack's death had destroyed everyone's spirits.

Leo had still not stirred in Mary's arms as she rode her pony, led by Perry on his horse. Cicely had wanted to carry him, but Tal decided – rightly – that she was in no state to do so. And so she rode next to him, clutching the charm that Mary had pressed upon her so purposefully. He rescued the chalice as they passed the bonfire, and tied it to his horse, pushing the lid inside his tunic. He said nothing as Cicely threw the charm into the remains of the bonfire, where it burned very brightly for a moment.

Mary watched Jane's face as the spell disintegrated, and had the satisfaction of seeing some reaction. It was as the maid suspected; Jane Champernowne was not quite as unaware and senseless as she pretended. Both the maid and her mistress prayed the burning of the spell marked the beginning of a long torment and painful death for the woman who had stolen Leo and robbed the world of Jack de la Pole.

Cicely glanced behind and saw Friedrich's shadowy figure leading a pair of horses, one his own mount, the other bearing Jack. He had waited until everyone else had gone, and would walk slowly beside the Earl of Lincoln all the way to Kingston. He was serving Jack for the last time.

Cicely remembered looking back like this once before, when she had departed from Nottingham in 1485, leaving Richard to defend his life and realm against Henry Tudor. Now Richard spoke again, softly, in the distant reaches of her mind. *'Take my love with you, and always keep it close, for it can never belong to another.'*

The night seemed to be shrinking around her. It was not Richard she was leaving behind now, but Jack, who had taken her up before him that other time, high on his great white stallion Héraut, away from Nottingham toward Yorkshire, and the castle at Sheriff Hutton. She was vaguely aware of everything beginning to revolve slowly around her here on the Downs, gathering speed until her head was spinning with it. She no longer cared. Let her leave this world and join those two men who were so beloved.

Tal was not close enough to catch her as she fell from the saddle, briefly losing consciousness so that she landed particularly awkwardly, and lay bruised and winded. As her wits returned, she knew the fall was worse than the incident at Windsor. This time she had done something to herself inside.

Tal jumped down to crouch beside her. 'Can you move, *cariad*?'

'Yes. I think so.'

'What happened?' he asked, as Edmund alighted as well.

Memory returned, and she avoided his eyes. 'My grief became too much,' she managed to say.

Edmund helped her to her feet. 'Can you stand, Cousin?' he asked.

'Yes. I am a little shaken, that is all. And bruised' Bruised? She was in pain, deep inside, and it was not grief. In fact, it made her breath catch and she wrapped her arms instinctively around her belly.

Tal was concerned. 'Would you rather ride up with one of us, *cariad*, or are you able to manage your horse again?'

The echoes. Oh, the echoes. Jack had asked her the same

thing after leaving Nottingham. 'I will ride,' she replied quietly, but the pain stabbed anew as Tal helped her to mount again. What had she done to herself in the fall? Oh, what did it matter? All that was of consequence now was that Jack was dead. She would never touch him again, see him again, or hear his voice.

The physical pain subsided, and she was able to ride on. They left the Ridgeway to descend Blowing Stone Hill. Whoever had sounded the Blowing Stone had gone, for it was deserted, and the night was now silent. When they reached the crossroad Tal suddenly reined in with a curse.

'Sweet God above, I must have lost my wits! With Cheney at Kingston – which he will be by now, I am sure of it, as will that bastard Deakin – Leo cannot possibly be taken there, nor should you return, Cicely. Not now we know Cheney is here legitimately, fortified by Henry's orders.

She was trying to assemble her thoughts, but one thing was clear, and she turned to Edmund. 'I used to think you were a posturing little maggot, but I now know differently. You have grown up, Edmund, and you made your peace with Jack. His future has become yours. Which is why I wish you to ride back to Windsor now. Henry may not even know you have been away. So behave as if you never left the capital, and thus cannot possibly know anything that happened here.

'Cicely – '

'Go, Edmund.'

Tal agreed with her on this, and slapped the rump of Edmund's horse, which tossed up its head, leapt forward, and set off toward Wantage, almost unseating Edmund.

As the hoofbeats dwindled into the darkness, she turned next to look at her son, sleeping so deeply in Mary's arms, and reached across to run loving fingertips through his hair. 'Mary, you and Perry must take him to Bruges. But without me.'

Mary was horrified. 'Oh, my lady – '

'I must stay. No, do not argue, for my mind is made up.

Jack knew of my decision and would have taken him alone. Leo must be safe, and can no longer be in this country.'

Tal did not agree with her decision to stay behind, but was not going to argue. He tossed a purse to Perry. 'I will send my men with you as far as Wantage. Go to the White Hart and seek Bassington's help. He sends a waggon to London regularly, and can also help you to acquire whatever you need for Leo. There is no one he does not know in the town. The purse contains more than enough money to make certain of a comfortable journey. Go to Three Cranes, where my vessel *Elizabeth* has been unloading a cargo of wine from Calais. She will sail again soon, and John Pasmer will be aboard four days from now. He will take care of you, and if you ask him, he will give you more than adequate funds for the future. He will also see you safely to the duchess. The password to his trust is "chantress".'

'Chantress. Yes, Sir Humphrey.' Perry shoved the purse inside his coat.

Cicely searched in her purse for Richard's ruby ring to give to Mary. She did not want to part with it, but knew her aunt would recognize it and accept that Leo was being presented to her under honest colours. She pressed it into the maid's hand. 'My aunt will know this ring. Tell her it is Leo's father's, and if I am not present when Leo is of age, tell her I wish her to give it to him. Stay there with my boy.'

Mary was in fresh tears. 'I do not want to leave you.'

'And I do not want to let you go, but Leo needs you more than me. If there is anything of yours at Pasmer's Place, I will see that it is sent to Bruges. Sir Humphrey and I will continue to protect Tom and Mistress Kymbe.'

Tal dismounted suddenly, took Leo from Mary's embrace and placed him in Cicely's arms a last time. She held Richard's son close and dropped kisses on his little face. Yet again she was parting with him for his own safety.

Tal allowed her a few moments, and then returned the child to Mary. Cicely bit her lip to quell sobs.

When the little boy was firm and comfortable in the maid's care, she and her new husband rode away in Edmund's wake, but at only half the pace, accompanied by all but three of Tal's men. The three who remained were those he trusted most.

Tal looked up at Cicely. 'I am so sorry, *cariad.*'

'I have to do it this way.' Her voice quivered a little as she struggled with tears. 'If I am here in England, I can help Edmund. Maybe only provide a friendly ear for him, but it *will* help him. And if I can make my peace with Henry, maybe I can continue to protect those who matter.'

'Henry will probably hear you out, and then have you dismembered,' Tal said harshly. 'Do not do this, Cicely. There is still time to ride after Leo and go with him.'

She smiled. Maybe he was right, but she knew the power of Henry's obsession with her. And if she fled now, she would be exposing Jon, Tom, Tal and Mistress Kymbe to the Tudor king's dark self.

He pressed his lips together regretfully. 'As if this day has not ended badly enough, it began badly as well. There has been another blow from Brittany. The priest who officiated at Henry's wedding to Tiphaine de Rieux has passed away without having signed another document to replace the one that perished in the church fire. And copies of other papers that were lost at the same time have proved impossible to acquire. I begin to see our chances of destroying Henry through Roland fading beyond recovery.'

A new agony suddenly cramped Cicely's belly. She gasped, bending forward in an effort to ease it.

He was alert. 'Cicely?'

She had to wait until the pain relented. 'I must have twisted something when I fell. Nothing more.' She knew he thought she must be with child, and was in danger of losing it, but she also knew he was wrong. 'No, Tal. How many times must I repeat that Leo will be my only child? Whatever is hurting within me now was caused when I fell, that is all.'

'I trust you are right.' He remounted.

'The pagans *were* destroyed tonight, Tal?' she asked.

He nodded. 'Yes. Those who think they have escaped will by now know they have not, for I have stationed men all over the area to apprehend anyone who is obviously returning from the Smith. Kingston will be wiped clean and the filth wrung from it.

'And Cheney and Deakin?' she asked.

'When we get back to the house, just follow my lead. I know things about friend Cheney that he really would prefer Henry did not find out. And not simply his association with Alice Penworthy and her brother. Suffice it that I believe I hold all four aces. As for Deakin, he will soon be of no consequence. Come, let us get to it. But, Cicely—'

'Yes?'

'Trust me now, as never before. Whatever happens, trust me.'

She gazed at him. 'I do, Tal.'

'I am about to test your forbearance, as I did at the White Hart,' he warned, and then caught her hand to kiss it tenderly. 'You are an extraordinary woman, Cicely Plantagenet.'

'Or a very tiresome one.'

'That, too.' He moved his horse onward.

Chapter Thirty-Four

ON REACHING THE deserted courtyard, where a single lantern was suspended beneath the porch, Tal calmly murdered Martin Deakin. It happened so suddenly, and was over so swiftly, that Cicely could hardly believe it.

Deakin had hurried out as Tal dismounted at the porch. The steward was all false smiles and welcomes as he assisted Cicely to alight, but then he saw the chalice tied to Tal's saddle, and savage hatred flooded his eyes.

Tal could brook no more. Jack was still too fresh in his mind, as was what had been done to Leo. He reached for the white dagger from his belt and advanced to the steward. 'Do you recognize this bauble as well, pagan?' he asked quietly. 'See? Here it is.' Darting forward without warning, he clamped a hand over the man's mouth and stabbed him in the heart. The steward struggled momentarily, before collapsing.

The crows, strangely alert at such an hour, started up an agitated noise and flapped in the fruit trees, scattering autumn leaves, and Tybalt came from nowhere, yowling and spitting, dancing toward Tal, back arched, tail like a brush. Tal's response was not very Christian. 'Oh, fuck off, you mangy malkin,' he muttered and kicked out. Tybalt jumped back, just avoiding a well-aimed boot. Still spitting and swearing, the tomcat bounded away toward the gatehouse. The crows continued their alarm.

Tal hauled the steward's body the few yards around to the side of the porch and dumped him like a sack in the shadows beneath the white rose. It was done in seconds, then he wiped the dagger and concealed it in his tunic.

He glanced all around, and when he was satisfied that no one else had witnessed anything, he nodded at two of his men, who had observed everything without emotion. They were fiercely loyal to Tal, and no one liked Deakin. 'Bury him somewhere down by the ponds,' Tal instructed. 'Make sure you are not seen, and keep your tongues still, do you understand? Not a single word is to pass your lips about anything that has happened tonight. Do not fail me in this, because what has befallen Deakin can as easily befall you. Please me now, and you will be rewarded.'

They hastened to fling the steward's body over a horse, which they led across the courtyard, before making their way toward the valley.

Tal rescued the chalice from his saddle, and then ordered the remaining man to take the horses to the stables. After kicking earth and leaves over the bloodstains beneath the rose, he turned to Cicely, whose face was almost white in the light from the porch lantern. '*Cariad*, you did not honestly imagine I would let Deakin live after what he has done? We saw him. Knew his face. There is no doubt at all about his treachery, or that he participated in what went on at the Smith. You know by now that I am a lethal enemy.'

'Do you mean to dispose of Cheney the same way?'

He smiled. 'That might be a little risky, especially as I am confident of silencing him by other means. Come.' He held out his hand and she went to him hesitantly.

His fingers closed reassuringly over hers. 'I have no further brutal intentions, and from now will be the perfect knight. When we confront Cheney, you must not deny anything I say. Will you agree?'

'Yes.' She glanced back at the gatehouse. 'It is impossible to accept that Jack has gone. I feel that he will ride beneath the gatehouse at any moment, and call out to us.'

He drew her cold hand over his sleeve. 'Sweetheart, I wish it could be, but he *has* gone this time. There is no mistake.'

But even so, she glanced back. This time a figure stood there beneath the gatehouse. A boy. Luke Woodall. And Tybalt was with him. 'Look, Tal!' she breathed.

He was in time to see the boy dash away, with the tomcat at his heels.

'Do you think he saw what you did to Deakin?' she asked.

'I hope not, but something will have to be done about him. I will have him found, and then Gwen must remove him from all contact with this place. Now, *cariad,* be strong for what happens next.'

'I saw Richard when Jack died,' Cicely said suddenly. 'I had my arms around Jack's body, and Richard spoke. He said he would care for Jack. Then Jack was standing with him, and they disappeared.' Fresh tears filled her eyes.

'Oh, *sweetheart*.' Tal pulled her close and kissed her forehead.

'I know Jack is safe now,' she said softly, 'and that one day I will be with them both again.'

'You will indeed, sweetheart. But not quite yet, mm?'

The first thing he did inside was enter the side passage to the kitchens, and then go into a small storeroom that contained nothing but a large chest, very strong and heavy, with iron bands and several quite new padlocks. Placing the chalice and dagger inside, he then secured every padlock, before making sure the storeroom itself could not be opened by anyone but himself. He returned to Cicely, who waited in the screens passage. 'That will do for now,' he said, 'before I dispose of them for good and all.'

As they reached the staircase, Gwen descended toward them. She carried her shoes in order to make no sound, and spoke to Tal in a whisper. 'Oh, I am glad you have returned, Sir Humphrey. I think you should know that although I did not see Sir John and Deakin leave the house while you were away, I am sure they did.'

Tal responded in a similar whisper. 'Deakin certainly left, because we *saw* him at the bonfire. I am equally sure our unwelcome guest from Compton Beauchamp was there as well, although I could not identify him for certain.'

Gwen nodded. 'Sir John is in the solar now, as if he had never left, but Deakin had earlier warned me not to let *anyone* go up there. There is something I have discovered, about how Lady Talbot escaped earlier.' She produced a heavy old key from her purse. 'I found this. Deakin had left it openly in his parlour.'

Cicely recognized it as the one Jane had surrendered to the steward in the church.

'I had not seen it before,' Gwen went on, 'and as it resembles the one to the solar, I wondered about the tower door. I have just been to investigate, and did not make a sound, because I could hear Sir John snoring. Anyway, it *is* the key to the tower. The door opens very easily, although you would never expect it, and the cobwebs just fall back into place, undamaged. The staircase inside is crumbling in places, but I risked going down it. At the bottom there is a way out into the garden behind the house. The tower's outer wall is thickly covered with ivy, and there are broken leaves and mud on the lowest steps *inside*, showing that someone has very recently entered that way. I believe it to have been Sir John and Deakin. I came back up, locked the landing door again and was coming down now when I came upon you and Lady Welles. Sir John is not aware of anything.'

Tal accepted the key. 'Oh, Gwen Woodall, you are surely Kingston's greatest treasure.' He gave her a kiss on the cheek, and she blushed.

He became serious. 'Gwen, I know you do not like Deakin, for various reasons, but he will not be here from now on. He certainly will never again have influence or even contact with Luke.' He paused. 'I will be seeking another steward, and think I should also seek someone for your position.'

'I am dismissed?' she was shocked.

'No, not at all.' He put a kind hand on her sleeve and told her about Luke. 'For Luke's sake, I think you should consider going elsewhere. This place is poisonous to him. Things went very wrong for the pagans tonight, and I think you have a chance to retrieve the boy he once was. If you decide you wish to do as I suggest, be assured I will provide generously for you, so do not fear penury. I value you, Gwen Woodall, even if your grandson has not endeared himself to me.' He smiled, and then told her what had happened at the bonfire. And that they had just seen the boy beneath the gatehouse with Tybalt.

Cicely watched him. The gentle, considerate man he was now was a universe away from the one who had just murdered Martin Deakin in cold blood.

Gwen was a little dazed and tearful to learn the whole truth about Luke. 'I do not know what to say, except that I thank you, Sir Humphrey. With all my heart.'

'I think you should also know that the lord who accompanied Lady Cicely from Windsor has left. He parted company with us and will not return.'

'Yes, Sir Humphrey.'

'Be sure to let all the servants know, especially Sir John's men. And tell them that the lord in question, whose name you do not know, was under arrest here, but has now escaped.'

She stared at him. 'Arrest, sir?' She glanced at Cicely, noticing for the first time the marks of tears and wretchedness on her face.

'That is what I said. Do not question anything, Gwen, just let it be known that he has gone. That is *all* you know.'

'Yes, Sir Humphrey.'

He nodded. 'Go then.'

She hurried on down the staircase, and he turned to Cicely. 'How are you, *cariad?* Can you face Cheney?'

'Yes.'

'Just be strong for the coming minutes, and afterward—Well, then you may weep your full for Jack.'

They went up to the parlour, where Cheney sprawled in the same chair by the fire, his long legs stretched toward the heat. He looked tired, as well he might do, and had made himself very much at home by helping himself to Tal's wine.

But not to more of the drugged wine, Cicely noticed. To look at him, one could be forgiven for thinking he had been there all evening. He did not seem to hear them enter.

Tal could not hide his feelings. 'Trying Kingston out for size, Cheney?' he asked loudly.

The other sat forward with a jerk, and took a moment to collect his thoughts. 'Why so sour, Talbot? Have you eaten something that disagrees with you? Perhaps Lady Cicely's wondrous maid should attend you.'

'The wondrous maid, and her equally wondrous husband have gone away for a while, to enjoy their married life. But as it happens, I have not eaten anything that disagrees with me, but perhaps you did in order to prompt a migraine? Blue cheese, perchance? You probably know exactly how much to eat to achieve the required result, and how long it will last.'

Cheney smiled. 'What an imagination you have, to be sure. You think I would *choose* such suffering?'

'My sourness, as you term it, is all to do with your monstrous duplicity. There you sit, as if your arse is permanently fixed, yet we know better, do we not? Your great bonfire did not turn out well. Someone interfered, and everything went awry.'

'What in God's own name are you talking about?' Cheney demanded.

'You *are* the pagans' leader.'

Tybalt strolled in, and jumped up to Cheney's lap. The giant smiled as he stroked the pleased tomcat. 'You could not be more wrong, Talbot. I am not the leader, and defy you to prove that I am. I have not left this house tonight, and until moments ago was asleep where you find me now. Deakin will confirm what I say.'

'As he did at the previous bonfire, mm?' Tal smiled.

'Did he? Yes, I suppose he did.'

'Do not make me laugh, Cheney, but I fear I cannot ask him anything. He has gone.'

Cheney's face changed. 'What do you mean?'

'I have dismissed him, rather permanently. Oh, and my wife is on her way back to Kenninghall, no doubt with fewer wits than she had before. I now have the dagger *and* the chalice, and intend to have both melted down.'

A nerve twitched at Cheney's temple. He did not care about Deakin or Jane, but the dagger and chalice were important. 'You would not *dare!*'

'You think not? I follow the True Faith, Cheney, and it is my opinion that neither item has a place in this Christian realm. Oh, and I know how you managed to leave here tonight. Through the tower, as my wife did earlier.'

Cheney ignored him and turned his attention to Cicely. 'What has happened to you? You look unwell.'

'I had a fall,' she replied.

'May I offer you my chair?' He rose, tumbling Tybalt.

'I would prefer to stand,' she answered. Sit in the warmth left by his great backside? Never!

'Oh, I tire of this foolishness.' The giant reached inside his coat and took out a small, rolled document from which dangled Henry's seal. 'Having taken advantage of your hospitality, I fear this little scribble makes things rather embarrassing for me.'

'Ah, so you are the king's little messenger boy?' Edmund's warning rang loud for both Tal and Cicely.

'I am indeed. This is a royal warrant to arrest Viscountess Welles and the Earl of Lincoln. And you as well, should you be caught up in anything involving them. Which I fear you must be, seeing that the lady is here and is known to have left Windsor in Lincoln's company. The king no longer fully trusts you, Talbot, and it seems he is justified.' Cheney's deep-set eyes moved unpleasantly from Tal to Cicely, and back again. 'Feel free to examine it all you wish.'

Tal took it and read. 'Well, I already knew you were here on Henry's business,' he said then.

'How could you know that?' Cheney demanded instantly.

'You think you are the only one with informants?' Tal flung the warrant back at him.

Cheney managed to catch it. 'I have no choice in this, Talbot, and you only have yourself to blame. I have been set to watch you for some time now. What on earth possessed you to risk everything for a lost Yorkist cause?'

'I am as much an innocent as you are a Christian.' Tal's smile was almost honeyed. 'Henry has long suspected you too, Cheney, and has set *me* on *your* tail.'

Cheney thought he was merely saying it. 'Enough, Talbot, you cannot avoid a royal warrant by—'

'Listen to me, you oversized Lancastrian ape,' Tal interrupted trenchantly. 'I *have* been watching you, and consequently have become aware of certain awkward little misdemeanours on your part, Misdemeanours of which you definitely do *not* want His Majesty to hear.'

The other stiffened. 'What do you mean?'

'Your mistress, Alice Penworthy, is involved—through her half-brother—in the matter of a certain boy in Lisbon. He is apparently reckoned to be Lady Cicely's youngest brother, Richard, Duke of York, and is being groomed to one day return to England at the head of an army. Not only that, but you have been having secret meetings with Étienne Fryon, who has now fled the country. Cheney, I rather think that when Henry learns of all this, he will think you want to despatch your king into the hereafter.'

Chapter Thirty-Five

THE GIANT'S FACE drained of colour, but his deep eyes narrowed with malice. 'You think to intimidate me with such falsehoods?'

'Not falsehoods. You have been lured into treasonous waters by Fryon, the king's secretary of the French language. He is a Yorkist agent for the Duchess Margaret of Burgundy, and is part of a wide Yorkist network. He has been whispering in your increasingly receptive ear for some while now, but you have not reported him to Henry. Why?'

'That is simple to answer. Because I do *not* have anything to do with Fryon. If you are so convinced of this, Talbot, why have you not done anything about it?'

'I had been hoping to get to the bottom of it all, but your unwanted presence here and disagreeable threats and manner, have changed the situation somewhat. I am prepared to tell Henry that I have *seen* you and Fryon deep in cosy conversation, and that the Frenchman recorded your every traitorous word. Which he did, of course, his aim being to neatly ensnare you. Hard as it is for you to believe, many do not forgive you for turning on Richard. Fryon is among them.'

Cheney gazed at him, his face a mask.

'And now your mistress not only expects your child, but is also part of this Yorkist scheme in Lisbon. It does not look good for you, Cheney. You are dissatisfied with Henry, but then, we all are,' Tal went on, 'and now you wish to return to your original loyalty, Edward IV, whose Woodville marriage you *refuse* to accept as bigamous. *That* is why you refused to support Richard, even though he was undoubtedly the true king. It had nothing to do with thinking *Henry* was the rightful king.'

'Balderdash!'

Tal smiled sleekly. 'My, my, how you do like your ancient gods. Balder, now.'

Cicely could not help interrupting. 'My parents' marriage *was* bigamous, Sir John, and I have it on excellent authority. My mother. Even you must concede that she, of all women, would hardly say such a thing if it were not true. She told me, and my sister the queen, that all the children she bore to my father were baseborn. Why else do you imagine she went to such lengths to plot against Richard? She needed her firstborn son crowned before Richard could even assume his role as Lord Protector. Richard was an inconvenience, and would have to be disposed of.'

Cheney looked at her. 'I do not believe you. You would say *anything* to exonerate Richard, in whom, it would seem, you had an unnatural interest.'

She smiled. 'Yes, I loved him. With all my heart. And I still love him. But you and your kind destroyed him in order to put Henry on the throne. Well, I hope you are all well pleased with your achievement.' Anger stirred her blood. 'You *know* that England would be a much happier place if Richard were still on the throne! Admit it.'

Tal put out a hand to her. 'Do not distress yourself, *cariad*.' Then he smiled affably at Cheney. 'Listen now, and listen well. If you arrest me or implicate me in anything at all, you will sign your own death warrant. I will tell of your dealings with the Penworthy woman, of whose secret Yorkist activities I am sure Henry has no inkling. *And* I will tell him of your cosiness with Fryon, who has wisely quit these shores. For France, I understand, on some or other devious escapade for the duchess. Or maybe simply to defect. Who knows? But he *has* provided written evidence of your treachery. You will find it very hard to convince Henry that you are a good little giant.'

The other's eyes were mere slits. 'And how, pray, will you explain Lincoln away? He must be here.' He glanced at Cicely.

Tal laughed. 'I know nothing of Lincoln's whereabouts.

Lady Welles has sought sanctuary with me, prior to begging the king's forgiveness for failing him. She thought my sister, the duchess, was here again,' he added.

Tal saw Tybalt nearby, watching and seeming to understand every word. With one swift foot, he shovelled the startled cat sideways from the room and closed the door on it. 'We do not want Woden's little lap-cat listening to us, do we? Now then, Cheney, I have not finished with you yet. Henry Tudor is a very superstitious man. If he were to learn one *eighth* of what you have been up to here in Berkshire, he would have you hanged, drawn and quartered, and the remains burned to a crisp.'

Cheney's mouth worked as if he chewed upon something disgusting, but he was not a fool, and knew the threats were very real.

Tal smiled and took a safe jug of wine to pour some for himself and Cicely. 'You want Woden on the throne, not Henry. Oh, I will thoroughly enjoy regaling our Tudor king with a yarn of your participation in ancient magic, ill-wishing and intended regicide. Henry will certainly believe the latter charge, because he knows you attempted just that at Bosworth. It was rather fitting that Richard unhorsed you and you cracked your backside on the good earth of England. Henry is *very* sensitive about those who change their allegiance.'

'You are smugly pleased with yourself, Talbot.' Cheney drained his cup and snatched the jug from Tal to pour himself some more. 'Clearly you have a solution, so, pray elucidate.'

'Ah, I perceive the first buds of common sense. Well, the Lady Cicely is anxious to see the king, to explain herself. She was swept along by family feeling and loyalty, but now realizes that she should not have done it. Lincoln has disappeared, there is nothing I can do about that, but I can still help her. We both can.'

'We? *Me*?'

'Indeed. We can both escort her to the king, and thus we will have discharged our duty as his loyal nobles. I will back you, and you will back me. The lady will support us both, provided we make it clear that she is anxious to be at peace with the king. We will tell him of Lincoln's flight. He will believe us, for why should he not? Then you and I can remain the very best of friends, as we always have been.'

Cheney's eyebrows arched. 'We have?'

'Well, in a manner of speaking. We tolerate each other.'

'That is closer to the mark.'

Tal smiled thinly. 'Of course, it will all hang on your vow to destroy the paganism that blots this part of the land.'

'Talbot, I have told you before that I have nothing—'

'Spare us both! You *are* their leader and you *will* put a stop to it. Do you hear? I will be keeping Fryon's little notebook as surety. Well?'

'Let this be clear, Talbot. I do *not* admit to any paganism, but I realize that in many ways you can make my existence very awkward. Do I have your vow that you will not attempt to implicate me in anything unholy?'

'That is the price?'

The giant smiled. 'Oh, yes. Otherwise I will take my chance with the king regarding treachery, Lisbon and whatever else it is with which you are seeing fit to link me.'

Tal did not answer for a moment, but then nodded. 'You have my vow, but only if *you* abide by *your* side of the bargain. If I detect anything underhanded, my word will no longer hold. Do you understand?'

'We both understand, I think.'

'Let us drink on it, as the saying goes. We do not want any unpleasantness, Cheney, we simply want things to trot along the way they always have.' He smiled and raised his cup. 'To honour.'

All three cups chinked together. The matter was settled.

But then Cicely's cup clattered to the floor as she doubled up in pain, feeling as if she were splitting in two. It was too much. As she lost consciousness, all she could see was Jane stabbing the white rose and uttering her vile curse upon Lady Welles.

Master Lassiter, Tal's physician from Shrivenham, was the mirror image of Master Rogers, with the same black clothes, bonnet and long white beard, but mercifully, not quite the same obsession with the stars and whether a day of the week was auspicious or not. He did ask her some questions about her birthdate and such things, but was in general much more fixed to the earth, believing in making a diagnosis from a careful examination. And so Cicely was subjected to such an intimate inspection that it was as well that Gwen was present.

Cicely was perplexed. 'I simply had a fall, sir, is it really necessary to examine me like this—?'

'It is. My lady, forgive the observation, but I can tell that you have had a child, but several years ago. Forgive me again, but is there any reason why you and your husband have not had more?'

'You are impertinent,' she said, sitting up and fluffing her skirts over her naked legs.

'No, my lady, it is not impertinence that prompts the question. You see, you have commenced a bleeding within the last hour, and—'

Alarm touched her. 'I had my bleeding two weeks ago. There cannot be another yet. And I only have one child because I am barren now. But, there *is* something. Master Lassiter, could I have been overlooked? Cursed?'

He blinked. 'Not unless whoever it was meant you well.'

Unexplained bleeding might be *well meant*?

'I have been very, very thorough, my lady, and can tell you that this new show of blood is not the usual monthly showing, but a very fortunate sign. I have seen it before, and the lady described a fall and then the same pains that you describe. Something within her had been preventing conception, but was rectified when she fell. She soon conceived twins, and she and her lord were happy and fulfilled. I have every reason to believe that your fall has achieved the same outcome, and from now on you will find yourself fruitful again.'

She stared at him. 'That is nonsense.'

'Indeed not, and although you expressed relief that I do not resort to the zodiac and such things, I fear that to a certain extent I do. You were born under the sign of Pisces, and that, together with the thoroughness of my examination, tells me you will bear your husband two more children, and—' He thought better of continuing.

'Tell me.'

'Well, you will have another husband after Lord Welles, and will bear children to him as well. You are most certainly no longer barren.'

'After Lord Welles? Do you mean I am to be divorced?'

'No, my lady, I fear I mean that Lord Welles will pass on to the Almighty. Not yet, but while you are still a young woman.'

Jon! 'If you have invented this, sir—'

'Never! I would not do such a thing. I have told you what I know.' He was offended.

'How long will he live, Master Lassiter? Please, tell me.'

'My lady, I cannot answer you, but know it cannot be imminent. Not if he is to father two children with you.'

'There is no doubt? I *will* bear him two children?'

'No doubt whatsoever.'

She looked away, because if this was true, Henry was not going to execute Jon, or put an end to her when he had her in his clutches again. More, she was to be reunited with Jon. Oh, how she wished Mary were here. Just to exchange a look that communicated everything. Instead there was Gwen. Cicely stole a glance, and the wisewoman smiled. There was communication after all, warm and true.

For now, though. . . Everything turned to grey as thoughts of Jack returned. Without him there could be no colour. When the physician had gone, she curled up and hid her face in the pillows. Gwen sat at her bedside, a gentle, motherly hand on her shaking shoulder.

Cheney left for Compton Beauchamp the following morning to await word that Cicely was well enough for the journey to London. In preparation to put his case first, he composed a long letter to the king, and sent a swift rider before dawn broke. The letter contained nothing that was not in his agreement with Tal, but was just slightly slanted in his own favour. He did not dare do anything more, because he did not know if Tal had already sent a similar letter.

As soon as Cheney departed Kingston, Cicely went to Friedrich's lodgings. Gregory Melton was kneeling by the bed upon which Jack had been laid out with infinite care. The priest was still ashen and weak, but with the pagan ill-wishing broken, had recovered sufficiently to perform all the Christian rites that Jack's soul would require for entry to Heaven. He withdrew, leaving her alone with her dead lover.

Friedrich had shown his former commander the utmost respect and care, even combing Jack's hair and spreading it on the pillow. The *landsknecht's* own rosary, brought with him from Augsburg and kept close through thick and thin, was now arranged lightly around Jack's cold hands.

Cicely stood at the bedside. If she touched Jack now, he would not respond. She gazed at his face, still so handsome, but drained by death. His long lashes did not flicker, and his eyes would never open again. It was too much. She hardly knew that she had crept up on the bed next to him and buried her face in his hair. The scent of thyme lingered. As if part of him lingered too, waiting for this final farewell.

Her grief was so overwhelming that she seemed to be composed solely of emotion. She felt the fading echo that was the living Jack de la Pole. She had lost him forever this time, and the sense of bereavement seemed to cut into her as surely as the white dagger had cut into him.

She cried herself to sleep, and when Friedrich returned, he lifted her easily into his strong arms and carried her to the house, where she was placed gently on her own bed. Gwen made her warm and comfortable beneath the coverlet, and then sat with her as she continued to sleep.

It was not until evening that Cicely awakened, and by then Jack was being taken secretly by lanes, tracks and paths toward Leicester, and a last resting place with Richard. She wanted to hide away beneath the coverlets, but made herself leave the bed to join Tal in the parlour. His kindly silence and understanding offered great comfort.

Two days later, when the bleeding had ceased and Cicely thought she was well enough to travel, she left Kingston l'Isle at the crack of dawn, in company with Tal and Sir John Cheney and a troop of their men. Friedrich stayed behind, in charge of everything until a new steward was found.

Cicely was not without the services of a maid, because Gwen Woodall accompanied her. The woman's face was anxious and drawn, and she was close to tears. Luke had disappeared. He had taken all his belongings and stolen a horse. No one knew where he had gone. Some said he had Tybalt in his arms as he left Kingston l'Isle behind.

Chapter Thirty-Six

THE COURT HAD moved from Windsor to Westminster, and Cicely's arrival at the palace stairs was ignominious. It was high tide and late afternoon, cold, dark and windy. The Thames was choppy and the skiff's oarsmen were disgruntled. Torches had been lit, and the smoke was torn, stinging into her eyes and making her cough.

Neither Tal nor Cheney trusted the other to go into the palace on his own, and maybe gain an advantageous audience with Henry. Nor did Tal want to take Cicely inside, where everyone would recognize her. Events at the disguising were too fresh a memory, so he insisted she remain in the skiff with Gwen. Both women were well wrapped under a robust winter canopy as they watched the two unlikely associates disappear toward the palace entrance.

Cicely was glad of Gwen, for she missed Mary a great deal. The journey had been hard to endure, not only because she had still not recovered fully from the fall, but because of her almost overpowering grief. Gwen had been nearly as much comfort as Mary, and had some of her knowledge. Her attentions had made the journey less onerous than it might otherwise have been, in spite of her own distress over Luke. Mistress and new maid supported each other.

All Cicely wanted was to be in her warm bed in Pasmer's Place, where she could sleep her misery away. Instead, here she was, in a situation that was entirely her own doing. Craven thoughts had begun to encroach, making her wish she had gone with Leo, Mary and Perry.

She had received brief news of their flight, for they had sent a messenger to Kingston. He had followed the travellers on their way to Windsor, and had caught them easily enough, because Cicely was simply not well enough to ride swiftly. Thus she knew they had reached the *Elizabeth*, and that John Pasmer had not hesitated to help them. Now she needed to hear they had reached Bruges safely, and that her aunt had taken Leo under her protective wing.

It began to rain, and as the wind blustered through the torches she saw a royal squire hurrying toward the stairs. He wore a cloak, but when he came aboard and snatched off his hood to bow, she saw it was Roland.

'*Écuyer* de Vielleville?' she said, inclining her head.

'My lady.' He glanced at Gwen. 'Forgive me, Lady Cicely, but the king instructs me to escort you to his Lady Mother at Coldharbour.'

Cicely did not know what to think. Coldharbour was Margaret's fine, recently refurbished riverside mansion in the city. Richard had once given it to the College of Heralds, but Henry had ejected them in order to present it to his mother.

'She is to have charge of you until His Majesty decides what to—' Roland did not finish.

'What to do about me? Very well, *écuyer*, carry out your instructions.'

Gwen's hand crept to take her hand and squeeze it reassuringly. 'I am sure all will be well, my lady.'

'I hope so, Gwen.'

'I feel that it will be. Truly.'

Cicely prayed she could take as much comfort as if it had been Mary speaking.

The oarsmen manoeuvred the vessel away from the steps into the flow of the river. The prow swung and swayed, and Roland soon looked ill as he clung to the canopy support. Barely a minute had passed before he was hanging over the rail to retch into the Thames. When the spasm was over, he was such a picture of misery that Cicely invited him to sit under the canopy. She and Gwen moved along the bench, and he joined them thankfully.

His face was sickly in the light of the prow lantern, and Cicely could feel him trembling. 'You are not a sailor, sir,' she said kindly.

'Forgive me, I wished to be gallant to you, and—'

'Do not fret, for I understand.' *I could almost be sick over the rail myself!*

'His Majesty is in a very bad mood,' he said then.

'Oh?' Because of her? Surely not.

'His secretary, *Maître* Fryon, has gone off without leave. It is said he has returned to France. The king is very displeased.'

I will warrant he is, she thought.

'Lady Cicely, do you know of Lord Welles?' Roland asked then.

'Know?' Anxiety seized her.

'He is safe and has been released from the Tower. There was no charge. I believe his sister, the King's Lady Mother, pleaded for him.'

She breathed out with relief. 'Thank you for telling me.'

Nothing more was said as the skiff slid downstream on the outgoing tide. The oarsmen had little to do except keep the vessel clear of other traffic, of which there was a great deal. It was almost dark, lights twinkled on the water, and the wet streets of London were illuminated on the shore. Coldharbour was ablaze with torches, lanterns and candles in windows, as if some grand occasion were taking place, but there were no vessels at the stairs, and no sound of music from within.

The skiff nudged the moorings, and Roland assisted Cicely and Gwen ashore, but did not accompany them further. 'I must return now, my lady.'

'I wish you well, *écuyer*,' she said, holding out her hand.

He kissed it and then smiled. 'And I wish you well, my lady. I will pray that everything will be safely resolved for you.'

'I pray the same for us both, you may be sure.'

The entrance to the house was through a tall archway at the top of the steps, and the double doors were already open for Margaret's menservants to come down to escort her. Evidently she was expected, for they imagined Gwen was Mary, and took "Mistress Perrings" to be accommodated in the servants' hall until sent for.

Cicely glanced back at the skiff as it shoved off again, and Roland raised a hand to her, his perfect blond under-curl ruffled by the wind before he remembered to tug his hood into place again. There he went, she thought, the rightful Prince of Wales.

'Lady Welles?'

She turned to the man who had spoken. 'Take me where you will,' she said. The coming minutes would be a true test of Margaret's claim of friendship. Torches and lanterns lit the way, but at last the lavish doors of Margaret's private rooms were ahead. Cicely steeled herself as she entered, for she had no idea what the coming minutes held.

Henry's Lady Mother was seated by the fire, gazing at the glowing coals. Richard's stolen book of hours was in her lap. Her white wimple seemed to move as the firelight danced, but the rest of her was as black-clad as ever. She did not rise or even look up.

An ominous silence descended as the servants withdrew, and Cicely found herself gazing out of the window at the lights on the Thames. She could feel her pulse racing.

'How are you?' Margaret asked suddenly. 'I understand you have had a hard fall.' She gestured to Cicely to be seated.

As Cicely complied, she wondered to which Margaret was referring. The riding accident? Or the undoubted downfall of Lady Welles? 'I am recovering now, Lady Margaret. Bruises, that is all.'

'You do not look well. Something is clearly still wrong.' Margaret rubbed an eyebrow, and an invisible Henry seemed to join them. 'Well, my Lady Traitor, what have you to say for yourself?'

'That I was overcome with foolish emotion, to which I surrendered completely. I now regret my actions, but imagine it is too late. His Majesty will never forgive me.'

Margaret's nostrils flared a little. 'Foolish emotion? Is *that* what you call it? My lady, you were with Lincoln, a *traitor,* at Windsor, in front of the entire court. A traitor, moreover, who was believed to be dead!

'He is my cousin and I still love him.' Cicely was careful to use the present tense. 'I did not know he would be there at the disguising. It was as much a surprise to me as it was to the king and everyone else there. I did not set out to do it. I was going to go to the king that night, as agreed, but—' Cicely summoned the tears that had been so close ever since the night of the bonfire. 'I do not know what came over me, Lady Margaret, but I acted upon it. Now I wish I had not.'

'Where is Lincoln?'

'I believe he must now be in Burgundy.'

'Without you. Why, exactly?'

'I changed my mind and wished to make my peace with the king. Sir Humphrey and Sir John Cheney promised to escort me as soon as they had attended to the business of the bonfire.'

'Bonfire?' Margaret stiffened as she recalled the reason Tal gave Henry for needing to return to Kingston l'Isle so urgently.

'The pagan rites.'

Margaret grasped Richard's precious book tightly to her chest. 'Explain everything. From the beginning,' she ordered, as if inviting Beelzebub to materialize.

Cicely explained all about the Smith, although without mentioning Leo, Jack, Sir John Cheney's suspected involvement or Jane's part in it.

Margaret heard her in silence, until mention was made of the green flames. This, in her eyes, was proof of Woden's tangible presence, and with a low cry of anguish, she almost fell from her chair to kneel in prayer.

'Archangel Michael, Archangel of the King of Kings, please hear my voice. By the grace of Christ Jesu, defend our cause, and commend us unto the Lord who governeth all. Protect us now from pagan evil.'

She crossed herself again and again, and was genuinely terrified. Finally she rose shakily to her feet again to face Cicely. 'Is the mark of evil upon you? Speak, child!'

'No, Lady Margaret.' But Cicely's mind's eye saw again the dagger piercing the white rose.

'And the wickedness has now been eradicated?'

'I believe so. It was certainly the intention of Sir Humphrey and Sir John. They have destroyed everything, and the pagans were unable to complete their evil rites, but—'

'But?' The word was almost barked.

'Well, evildoers may have escaped in the darkness. It is not known how many there were.'

Margaret resumed her seat. 'So, your dashing Yorkist hero deserted you. Is that correct?'

'No. *I* deserted him.'

'In favour of *Henry?'*

Cicely hesitated. 'May I speak in the fullest confidence?'

Margaret nodded.

'I feared for my husband. And there is my son, of course. If I fled to Burgundy, I would be leaving them both behind. I could not contemplate that. But yes, I also thought of Henry. My place is clearly here in England.'

'But does England *want* you? That is the question.' Margaret slammed Richard's book on a table by her chair.

Cicely gazed at the book Richard had treasured. It should be Leo's now. Margaret's voice interrupted.

'Cicely, have you *any* idea how much trouble you are in?'

'Yes, but I still hope the king will receive me, to at least let me explain. I begged Sir Humphrey and Sir John Cheney to bring me to him, so that he at least knows I come willingly.'

'Nevertheless, you betrayed him, which is something he cannot endure. Your willingness now is neither here nor there.'

'He will prevail, my lady. He always does. And when I am gone, he will not think of me for long, I am sure.'

'Gone? Where do you imagine you are going?' Margaret's eyes were cool and steady. Uncannily like her son's, but without the cast.

'Well, Henry is bound to punish me. Maybe he deems my sin worthy of execution.'

Margaret's jaw dropped. '*Execution*? Henry would *never* do such a thing to a woman! How can you even *think* he would?'

'Because of the darkness within him, a darkness that stirs when I anger him. I have seen him change. You know it to be so, Lady Margaret. And as I can provoke it, so too can I calm it again, but only if I am there with him. Which I will not be, because at the very least he will imprison me. I imagine I am to be your prisoner now.'

Margaret shook her head. 'You are to be my guest, Cicely, as honoured as you ever have been. I would not agree to *imprison* you, and darkness or not, Henry would not order it. Oh, he might have in those first few minutes of blind rage, but not now. However, if he *were* to throw you in a Tower dungeon, it would be no more than you deserve.'

'He incarcerated Jon there,' Cicely observed.

'And has released him. *I* saw to that!' Margaret picked up the book of hours again, and turned the pages to the one where Richard had recorded his birthday. 'Your uncle was a man of culture and taste, to say nothing of being highly educated and intelligent. Does Lincoln come up to such a standard?'

'In his way.'

Margaret's high eyebrows were raised still more. 'A qualified answer?'

'Would you ever compare anyone with Henry's father?'

'You know I would not.' Margaret smiled at last, and softened her manner. 'Foolish, foolish girl. You were everything to my son, and would have remained so. He will never again love anyone as he did you. Oh, he sleeps with the queen now, and they are reconciled, but it is nothing compared with what he shared with you.'

'Does he intend to see me?'

'I do not know.' Margaret looked at her. 'We have spoken of my son, but what of yours? Is he well?'

'Yes.'

Margaret's gaze seemed to see right through her. 'And still in England, you say?'

Cicely met her eyes with innocent surprise. 'Of course. Why would you think he was not?'

'For the same reason Henry went into exile after Tewkesbury. Safety. I am still your friend, Cicely, and I know that Jon would be reconciled with you if it were possible. Would you consider it?'

Cicely smiled. 'Yes.'

'No condition or qualification?'

'None at all. I may have been angry and bitter these past months, but I have never lost my love for him.'

Margaret's gaze went toward the door, which someone closed softly.

Cicely rose on seeing Jon standing there. He was clean-shaven again, and it made him more youthful. He wore rich blue velvet with golden embroidery, tight-fitting and elegant, and a topaz brooch shone on his hat as he removed it and bowed to her. The turquoise graced his finger.

'Cicely.'

She curtseyed. 'My lord.'

He looked at Margaret. 'Will you be so good as to leave us, please?'

'You know that I will.' Margaret smiled at him, because he was very close to her heart. Then she swept out like a little black-sailed galleon before a good wind.

Jon looked at Cicely again. 'I know now about Cheney and Alice, although not at the time, of course. She knew him before she was set loose upon me. I think Henry was of a mind to have Cheney watched as well.' He came closer, bringing with him the evocative fragrance of rosemary, fresh, sharp and fondly remembered. 'I am told you have suffered an accident.'

'I fell from a horse, but it is nothing now.'

'Are you sure?'

'Tal's physician examined me and said I would recover. But aches and bruises fade slowly.'

Jon drew a long breath. 'I trust he is right. Sweetheart, I eavesdropped quite disgracefully upon you and Margaret, and know you too well. You have been lying today, Cicely Plantagenet.'

'Lying? I do not understand.'

'Jack *is* dead this time, is he not?'

She went to the window to hide her pain. 'Yes.'

'What happened?'

'I cannot talk about it yet.'

'I *am* sorry, sweetheart.'

She managed to look at him. 'He was grateful for the help you gave him at Windsor. Grateful, and surprised.'

'Were you surprised?'

'Not really. You are not a vindictive man.' She returned to him. 'He never took away my love for you. Please know that.'

He nodded. 'I do know. I always did. It just became unbearable.'

She gave a little smile. 'I asked too much of you, Jon. It was not your fault. Nothing was your fault.'

'So, now we have Edmund de la Pole in his stead. A very poor exchange.'

'Do not think badly of Edmund.'

'Oh?'

'He has changed. I would protect him now.'

'You *trust* him?' Jon enquired curiously.

'I do now. Yes. And with good reason.'

'I will bear that in mind.' Jon did not probe more on the matter of Edmund. 'Where is Jack buried?'

Hesitation overtook her.

'You surely do not fear I will tell Henry?'

'He has been taken to Leicester. To Richard.'

He smiled. 'That is fitting. The secret is safe with me. I would never have betrayed anything, even when we were most alienated. Exchanging insults and being on our highest horses did not make any difference. We are man and wife, and neither of us has changed *that* much.'

'Highest horses?' She smiled.

'A suitable figure of speech.' He smiled too.

'I am glad we can at least speak like this again, Jon.'

'What *am* I going to do with you, Lady Welles? You have an unerring talent for getting yourself into dangerous scrapes.'

'I will never change,' she said ruefully.

'Well, I will stand by you now.'

She became serious. 'No, if you do that, Henry will—'

'Henry can play with himself until he loses the other eye as well. You are my wife and I choose to stand by you. I do not care if we have given the gossips fine fodder these past months, only that I support you now. One thing, Cicely, I would *never* have given Alice this ring. Shame on you for believing I would.' He held up his hand.

'She was wearing it. What else was I to think?'

'That she might have purloined it when I was not looking. Anger with you might make me choose not to wear it, but that is all. Know better next time.'

'I do not want there to be a next time.' She suddenly wanted to tell him what Master Lassiter had said. 'Jon, the physician at Kingston l'Isle told me that I am no longer barren. The fall has righted something inside me. He said that you and I will have two children.' She pushed aside what else she had been told.

Jon smiled. 'We cannot do that if we are apart.'

Their eyes met, and he took her hand to kiss it gently.

Chapter Thirty-Seven

TWO WEEKS PASSED, and she and Jon drew close again, although they had yet to share a bed. They did not leave Coldharbour for Pasmer's Place because of Henry's instructions. From him there was only a stony silence.

A letter came from Mary in Bruges. Apart from telling of the duchess's distress to have lost Jack, it conveyed that Leo was perfectly ensconced in her household. Mary had been formally requested to stay to take care of him, and Perry had been offered a position of far greater importance than any he had under Tal or even Henry. Mary begged Cicely to understand, and to ask Tal for Perry's release.

Of course Cicely understood. Who better than Mary and Perry to watch over Leo all the time? And she herself had Gwen now, which made the pain of losing Mary easier to bear than it might otherwise have been. She would also do all she could to protect Mistress Kymbe. Her only request to Mary was that regular letters—which would be destroyed immediately—were to be sent to her, telling of Leo's progress.

And so Gwen Woodall took Mary's place as personal maid to Viscountess Welles, and the dark events at the Smith seemed to drift further away each day. If Henry would only send for his sister-in-law, she would know what the future held.

Of Tom Kymbe there was still no sign, and then Henry sent Tal to Calais. She did not know it, but Tal had brought the dagger and the chalice with him from Kingston, and carried out his threat to have them melted down. The gold had now been fashioned into a handsome dish that was presented to the church of St Andrew by the Wardrobe, and the jewels had been sent to Abbot Sante to swell Yorkist coffers.

Cheney knew nothing of this, having already departed for Barnard's Castle in the north. He did not take Alice Penworthy with him, and she had now disappeared.

Edmund was safe. His absence had not been discovered, and he resumed his existence as before, even to taking Alice's brother, Nicolas Stalyn, back into his household. If Nicolas thought it was out of affection, he was wrong. Edmund's only purpose was to keep abreast of events in Lisbon.

One thing that pleased Cicely very much was a rather indiscreet and unwise little note from Annie, who signed it for Edmund as well. Should it have been intercepted, the brief but friendly message was filled with their love, and repeated her gratitude for what had been done to help her when she most needed it. That her predicament had been Edmund's fault was now so completely overlooked, it might never have happened.

Cicely was careful to burn the note as soon as it had been read. Never would she leave written evidence to be found by an ill-wisher.

Bess, of course, did not send any word to her at all.

Tom Kymbe returned on 21 November, and on finding Tal was in Calais, went to Pasmer's Place, hoping to find Cicely. She was not there, of course, nor was Mary, and so he came to Coldharbour in the hope of speaking to them both. As luck would have it, Henry had gone to Castle Hedingham in Essex, and Margaret accompanied him, so no one prevented Cicely from receiving the gentleman from Lincolnshire.

His return was so pleasing to her that she held out both hands on greeting him. 'Oh, Tom, I am delighted to see you are safe and sound.'

He bowed over her fingers. 'You honour me, my lady.'

'You have lost weight, sir.'

'Portuguese food was not to my liking.'

'And how very brown you are. The Lisbon sun?'

He smiled. 'Indeed. A little warmer than Lincolnshire.' He

became serious. 'The boy in Lisbon *is* your brother, my lady. He has the scar on his elbow. And I believe it is safe to say that King Henry knows this too.'

'I thought this would be the case. Poor Dickon, I wonder if he really understands the nature of the great future being mapped for him.'

Tom searched her face. 'You are not well, my lady.'

'A fall from my horse, but I am better now. Tom, I am reconciled with Lord Welles.'

For a moment something nameless entered his eyes, but then was gone. 'I am glad, my lady. He is a good man.'

'Yes.' She described Alice Penworthy's exposure.

'It is no more than she deserves,' he replied shortly. 'What else has been happening here?' he asked then. 'Where is Mary?'

'Oh, Tom, there is a *lot* to tell. Please be seated.' She poured them both some wine.

When she told of Jack's death, Tom leapt to his feet again. 'That is bad news, my lady! Very bad news.'

'Yes.'

'Is that why you look unwell? Oh, you have had a fall, I do not deny it, but I can tell something else has stricken you.'

'I miss him, Tom, as I once missed Richard. They have both left me.'

'I will never—' He stopped swiftly, having been on the point of a confession they would both regret.

Their eyes met, and she saw his love. 'Tom—' She rose uncomfortably.

'Say nothing, my lady, for there is no need. Just know that I care more than I should, and will defend you to my last breath.'

She hesitated and then went to kiss his cheek. 'I know, and I am more honoured and grateful than you know.'

He took her hand in both of his and kissed her fingertips,

then moved away. 'With your leave, I will go now. You will find me at Pasmer's Place.'

'You do not wish to return to Friskney? If only to see if your aunt will come here to me?'

'I will go there only when I know you are happy and safe again. And my aunt will *never* leave Friskney for long. Visits are one thing, but a permanent move would not be countenanced, no matter how well-meant the offer.' He bowed, his nut-brown hair falling forward.

It was a foggy day in December when Henry at last decided to summon his former lover to Westminster. He sent a small royal barge for her, and there were shouts and horns on the river as vessels nudged their way through the murk. Torches were lit, but only made it worse by adding their smoke to the already thick vapour.

The barge was recognized at the steps, and she was assisted ashore by waiting royal servants, and then conducted into the palace.

Her stomach was knotted with fear as she followed the servants toward the royal apartments. Beneath her cloak she wore a simple gown, dark-green velvet with pendulous sleeves that were lined with silver brocade, and her hair was completely concealed. She did not want to give any impression at all of hoping to seduce Henry, just that she was his subject and was obeying his command. The purse at her waist was empty of all mementos, except Henry's emerald ring and the silver dragon pendant, and otherwise contained only the usual items a woman would need; scissors, ivory comb, small mirror and a little silk kerchief.

She was relieved of her cloak at the doors of the royal apartments, and heard her arrival being announced within. For what seemed an age, nothing happened, but then she was summoned inside. She had not expected to be received in Henry's private rooms, but that was where she was taken. To the room from which the bedchamber was accessed, except that the connecting doors were firmly closed.

The room was deserted, and everything was as she remembered it. Nothing had been moved or changed. There was even a jumble of documents on the table where she had once detected the poison in Henry's wine.

Suddenly she realized she was not quite alone, for Crumplin was asleep on a cushion before the fire. He was curled up tightly, holding his tail around himself with his little hands, and when she touched him, he awoke with a startled squeak. Recognizing her, he expressed his pleasure with delighted noises and clambered up into her arms. Sitting on a chair near the fire, she cuddled and stroked him, and he enjoyed every moment.

When Henry entered she did not know. She was so absorbed in the welcome diversion Crumplin offered that she was unaware of anything else. It was the faint drift of cloves that alerted her, and she looked up to see him standing by the table, upon which his long fingers rested elegantly. He wore purple and cloth of gold, and a beringed thumb was hooked over the jewelled girdle low on his hips. There was not a hint of warmth in the thin, straight line of his lips. His russet hair—topped by a gold circlet—fell about his shoulders, his face was pale and expressionless, and his seascape eyes were at their most hooded. They were uneven, not steady, which told her he was struggling to appear in command of himself.

Setting Crumplin aside, she rose swiftly from the chair and dropped to her knees before the King of England. Her head was bowed, and now that she was actually in his presence again, she felt true guilt for what she had done to him.

'What have you to say to me?' he asked at last. His voice was controlled, but she heard a tremor.

'That I am truly sorry and beg your grace and forgiveness,' she said softly, her head still bowed.

'You think you deserve clemency?'

'No. I know what I did.' She looked up.

He still did not move. 'You were supposed to come to me. I requested it specifically, but you left Windsor, without so much as a by your leave. With *Lincoln* no less. Still that bastard lives, and you said nothing to me.'

At this moment, seeing the suppressed hurt in Henry's eyes, it almost hurt her to be so perfidious to him. But she had to be perfidious. There was no other way.

'You said *nothing* to me!' Henry repeated.

'He is my close cousin, and—'

'How close, exactly?'

Her eyes crept up to his for a moment and were then lowered again swiftly. 'You know how close, Your Majesty.'

'I wish to hear you say it,' he replied coldly.

'Lord Lincoln and I are—were—lovers. We are no longer, because I have finally realized my error.'

His eyes were chill. 'You were going into exile with him.'

'It was only a fleeting thought, soon regretted.'

He turned away, his robes dragging on the floor. 'You have made an arrant fool of me, madam. I cannot forgive it.'

'May I stand?'

'No.'

She remained on her knees.

'Was it really necessary to flaunt him at the disguising? Just how much of an idiot did you wish me to appear?'

How she wanted to tell him all the truth. 'I did not intend to make a fool of you. Please, never think it. I truly did not know he would be there.'

His eyes swung to her. 'Then why was he? I know what you told my mother, but. . .' His voice die away.

'Everything I said to her was the truth, including that I changed my mind and wished to return here. To you.'

'That we may kiss and be friends again?'

'Do not say it like that. *Please*, may I stand?'

He gestured his consent. 'So you, Lincoln, Cheney and my Marshal of Calais have been battling with demons on the Berkshire Downs?' He coughed. A hollow sound.

Tears came to her eyes as she gazed at him. 'I am sorry for failing you, and I deserve to be punished. I cannot offer any excuse, nor can I expect your forgiveness. But I *pray* you will at least believe that I regret it all. Given the time again, I would not have left the disguising with my cousin.' *Oh, false tongue, false tongue.*

He put his fingertips together and tapped his lips. 'You still despise me for Richard, am I right?'

'Richard?' she was surprised by the new direction. 'I *resent* you, but do not despise you. How could I do that after all we have been to each other.'

'At the disguising I would willingly have torn your head off, lady, and it has taken me until today to find the willpower to confront you.'

She went closer. 'I do not wish to forfeit your friendship, Henry. I know all the things I have done, but beneath it all I still hold you in the highest regard.'

A hand bell rang somewhere in the palace, and at the same time a ship's bell was heard on the Thames. Henry glanced toward the river. 'Two bells together. The sign of a parting.'

She did not know what to say.

He looked at her again 'And it is Friday. How many more signs do I need? I have been persuaded by my mother, and by my cursed half-uncle, that you should return to Lincolnshire with him. Is that your wish too?'

'Yes. You should want me gone.'

He nodded regretfully. 'At the beginning, you would never have come to me of your own volition, would you? No, do not answer.' He drew a heavy breath. 'Well, you are now at liberty to return to Jon Welles.'

She hid her incredulity and relief. No revenge, just an acceptance that things between them were at an end.

'Rage can evaporate as quickly as it arrives,' he said then. 'Trying to cling to you now will serve me nothing, and punishing you would, in the end, break my heart anew. I cannot do it.'

Oh, Harri Tudur, Harri Tudur. She wanted to hold him again. Just hold him. To share again that strange fascination they cast over each other. But she made no move. And, this time, nor did he.

'Henry, Jon is my husband and I have deep feelings for him. I have had other loves, including you, but I am Jon's wife, and wish to be so again. I am tired of trying to deal evenly with you and with my blood loyalties, and I want to simply be Lady Welles.'

'With your Yorkist son?'

'Henry, my boy will never amount to the same threat posed by the boy in Lisbon.'

'That is true, but he is still a threat. Royal Yorkist males give me the shits. Only their disappearance from the face of the earth will settle my bowels.' He gave her one of his charming little smiles. 'Do you *really* include me among your loves? I cannot believe that you do.'

'You are part of me, Henry.'

'And we will never again lie naked together,' he said softly.

She lowered her eyes.

He made light of it. ''My dick will be bereft.'

She smiled.

'I will love you forever, Cicely, *but* – '

'But?' Her heart sank.

'My secrets must remain secret, and I realize that by now you will not have honoured your vow to me. Oh, do not look so outraged. If Lincoln is still alive, you are certain to have told him. And others too, no doubt. Well, you had best make sure they "forget", because. . .' he paused. 'Because I am told you are very fond of Roland.'

She recoiled. 'You would hurt your own son?'

'He is inconvenient too, and is the price of Yorkist silence.'

'Oh, *Henry!* Just when I really like you again, you spoil it all! Can you not help yourself?'

'I fear not.' His eyes were not without warmth, but she knew he had meant the veiled threat to Roland.

'I heed your warning,' she answered ambivalently.

'See that you do, or the consequences will be very disagreeable.'

'Stop threatening me, Henry, for it is becoming a sport with you.'

'A *sport?'* He laughed, but then his eyes saddened. 'Believe me, *cariad,* this time it is anything but sport. I wish I did not have to say anything, but under the circumstances, I believe you will see why I do. Shared pillows lead to indiscretions.'

'Nothing will happen because of Roland.' It was true, because the Yorkists had no proof, nor would they acquire it now. 'I should return these.' She took the emerald ring and the silver dragon from her purse and held them out to him.

He shook his head. 'They are yours, Cicely. Would you offend me again?'

They looked at each other, and for a moment were too close again. She returned the jewels to her purse.

'You may go now,' he said, 'but I have one last request.'

'Request?'

'A final kiss.'

She gazed at him. 'It is better we do not.'

'Bugger what is better, lady! I will have one last kiss from you, and when I go to my queen tonight, I will fuck *you* until *her* teeth rattle.'

She took his extended hand reluctantly, and he drew her into his enchantment. His lips were pliant and adoring, his body was hard and ready, and his embrace so tender and loving that her heart broke for him.

But he knew she was not his and never really had been. He cupped her face in his. 'I must feed off this moment for all time, Cicely Plantagenet, and curse Almighty God for binding me to the wrong sister.'

His lips brushed against hers again and then he released her. 'Go. I relinquish you.' He turned away, dismissing her.

She went to the door and then looked back. His shoulders were shaking, and she knew he wept. Crumplin knew too, and climbed up to make comforting little noises in his ear.

Tears blurred her eyes. How easy it would be to go back to him now. But she left, and the doors were closed behind her.

Snow had fallen that Christmas, and the marshes around Wyberton in Lincolnshire were white, but in the great hall there was merriment and happiness. Musicians played and there were all the entertainments expected of the season.

Lord and Lady Welles danced a measure. Alone on the floor, they moved together as if they had never been parted. They were beneath the mistletoe when the music ended, and they kissed and held each other close.

A cheer went around the hall, and echoed out into the cold Yuletide night, where the silver moon was suspended amid a million diamonds.

Author Note

I WILL NOT repeat too much from my previous Notes, except to say again that the affairs *my* Cicely has enjoyed are fictional. There is no basis for Richard III, Henry VII or the Earl of Lincoln being her lovers. These books have been stories woven around historical fact, with never a single claim to be accurate when it comes to physical relationships or paganism in darkest Berkshire. They are fiction, and should never be viewed as anything else. However, there *is* good reason to believe Tom Kymbe was in love with her, although I will not explain it here. That is something to be saved for a sixth and final book in the series.

It should be noted that in the medieval period, girls were regarded as being mature at a much younger age than we accept now. Intercourse was allowable when a girl was only twelve, although in reality it was frowned upon and mostly took place when girls were around fifteen. Even kings bedded very young wives, Henry IV's first wife, Mary de Bohun, was pregnant at fourteen. More notoriously, Margaret Beaufort was pregnant and a widow at around thirteen.

In this present book I have used Sir John Cheney's reputation quite abominably, and do not for a moment believe he was involved in the worship of Woden, who may well have been a benevolent god. Nor do I imagine the area around Kingston l'Isle was once overrun by such pagan goings-on. Sir John is buried in Salisbury Cathedral, which I take to mean he was most certainly a Christian.

The same must be said of Jane Champernowne, who was buried at the Minoresses without Aldgate, where Sir Humphrey Talbot's (Tal's) sister, the Duchess of Norfolk, also chose to be interred. That Tal's other sister, Eleanor Talbot, survived as I have depicted is my fabrication, but there are theories that she did live on for longer than seemed to be the case. Tal himself was to pass away some time in 1492, at St Catherine's Monastery, Mount Sinai, to which he had finally made his long-promised pilgrimage. The cause of his death is not known.

Roland did exist, but was never acknowledged by Henry. To this day there is no proof that he was even Henry's son, let alone that he was legitimate too. There were rumours, of course, and so I have made him trueborn for the purposes of my story.

I have also been high-handed with Edmund de la Pole and Cicely's younger sister, Ann, who may have loathed the sight of each other for all I know. Not so high-handed with Thomas Howard, however. The stories of laundry maids are true. Chivalrous he was not, and he became poor Ann's husband.

Most of the other characters, I confess are my invention. Mary, Perry, Deakin, Friedrich, Gwen Woodall and Luke, Bassington and so on are fictional.

One thing; the name Wayland's Smithy is fairly recent, and was preceded by Wayland Smith, which is why I have called it that throughout.

This book has ended on a hopeful note. Cicely and Jon, having been reunited, dance the Christmas night away at Wyberton. A very new future awaits them now.

Sandra Heath Wilson

Gloucester, England,

Hallowtide 2018

Printed in Great Britain
by Amazon